A Greater Victory

A Greater Victory

The Collins Family Saga
Book 2

William R. DeHay

Blythe
&Sons

To those who have overcome.

Chapter 1

The Palace

Friday, 30 May 1919—Letterman Army General Hospital, the Presidio of San Francisco.

It was Decoration Day, a time for Americans to place flowers on the graves of those killed in battle—and the day Major Jamie Collins was to be discharged from the hospital.

Most soldiers are happy to be released from the hospital. Jamie was scared. He could walk again, thanks to the excellent care he'd received. The problem was, he'd convinced his doctors he'd fully recovered from shell shock. He hadn't. A sight, a sound, a taste, a touch, a smell—little things most people wouldn't even notice–and in his mind, Jamie was right back in the trenches reliving the mud, the stench, the screams of the wounded and dying, the terror. Jamie could cope while in the company of other patients who'd lost a limb or been paralyzed. They'd been to hell and back. They understood. Beyond his hospital ward, the world would be a dangerous place.

That wasn't going to hold Jamie back. He had a promise to keep.

* * *

More than a dozen of Letterman's staff, including Doctors Thornburgh, Crandall, and Regenstein, Nurses Eliot and Hobbes, and Corpsman Hendricks, had gathered in the hospital's foyer to give Jamie an informal sendoff. They had been instrumental in giving Jamie back the use of his legs.

"You've all done so much for me," Jamie said. "If there's ever anything I can do in return, you can find me in front of a classroom full of physics students just 30 miles south of here. Please don't hesitate to reach out to me."

The staff lined up to shake Jamie's hand and wish him well. To avoid workplace gossip, he and Nurse Eliot—Andi—agreed it would be best not to let on that they had anything more than the usual patient/nurse relationship. Nevertheless, when Andi reached the head of the line, Jamie felt he should get down on one knee and kiss her hand rather than shake it. Without her support and encouragement, he might never have walked again.

He thought back to three months earlier when Corpsman Hendricks wheeled him onto Andi's orthopedic ward. Before seeing her for the first time, Jamie hadn't believed in love at first sight. Now he did.

After Andi shook Jamie's hand and moved on, Hendricks stepped up to Jamie. "Sir, you've been an inspiration to us all." He stood at attention and saluted. Jamie returned his salute with a smile.

As Jamie looked around the foyer at the people who had literally lifted him to his feet again, he struggled not to break down in tears. Early on, he'd confided in Andi that he wasn't the man he was before being wounded. He cried for no reason, laughed at inappropriate times, jumped at sudden sounds, had an explosive temper, and couldn't bear the thought of being left alone in the dark. Andi assured him those were lingering symptoms of shell shock, and they'd lessen over time.

But shell shock presents itself in many ways. Lately, a more disturbing symptom began to raise its ugly head: a growing distrust of everyone around him—even those he'd grown to care about so much. In his darkest moments, he even doubted Andi, the woman he loved.

Jamie realized everyone was staring at him. He forced a smile. After all their efforts to restore his health, he'd hate for his emotions to overcome him and reveal to the staff how far he really was from full recovery.

Jamie's taxi was waiting at the foot of the walkway that led to Letterman's main entrance. When his ambulance deposited him there three months earlier, Corpsman Hendricks had picked Jamie up like a toy soldier, placed him in a wheelchair, and pushed him up the walkway. Now that he was able, Jamie felt like running to his taxi and putting Letterman Army General Hospital behind him forever. Only the decorum required of a uniformed field-grade officer stopped him.

Soon, not even decorum would be a deterrent. Despite only a residual limp and manageable intermittent pains throughout his body, Jamie would be medically retired from the Army on 01 July. In the meantime, he'd be using up his accrued leave and never have to serve another day on active duty. "Terminal leave," the Army called it. Not an expression one liked to hear around a hospital.

Nurse Eliot's time at Letterman was also coming to an end. All Andi had left to do was complete the paperwork associated with a permanent change of station. She'd then be on ordinary leave until she had to report for duty at Walter Reed Army General Hospital, Washington, DC, also on 01 July.

She and Jamie could spend a solid month together before Andi had to take up her new post as Assistant Dean of the Army School of Nursing.

Jamie approached his taxi in a jubilant mood. That changed when he saw the taxi company's name painted on its door. Pacific Taxi Service was one of Kavanaugh Enterprises' companies. Unlike Jamie's lingering symptoms of shell shock, which were all in his mind, he had a concrete reason to be fearful where Kavanaugh Enterprises was concerned.

Despite rumors that Matt Kavanaugh was the West Coast's most consummate racketeer, Jamie had agreed to work with him to establish a charity to help educate disabled veterans. The cause was noble, but Jamie's involvement threatened to entangle him in a web of intrigue. Worse, unless Jamie were very clever, he'd be drawn deeper and deeper into that web and inevitably come into conflict with Sonny Kavanaugh, Matt's psychopathic nephew.

Jamie put his head down and pressed on. He'd worry about the Kavanaughs later.

"The Palace Hotel," Jamie told his cabbie. He handed the man his duffle bag. His driver tossed it into the taxi's trunk as though dealing with it was an imposition.

Jamie immediately became suspicious. In addition to this blatant display of disrespect, the man looked far too athletic to be someone who sat in the driver's seat of a taxicab hour after hour, day after day. The man wore the cab company's leather jacket and captain's hat, but they were old, the jacket was too small, and the hat too big. In Jamie's state of mind, these were warning signs that the man might not be a cabbie but an impostor working for Sonny Kavanaugh. If Jamie got into that cab, he was afraid he might disappear without a trace.

Jamie got in the back seat anyway. He wasn't going to be controlled by the paranoia he knew was a product of his shell shock. Nevertheless, he would be prepared to bail out and run if the cab took a wrong turn.

The way his driver mercilessly ground the gears as they set off toward the Presidio's main gate, one would suspect he'd never driven a cab before. Jamie's suspicions ramped up another notch. "New at the job?" Jamie said.

He caught sight of the man's angry eyes in the review mirror. "Jobs are hard to come by these days," his cabbie said. "A man's got to take what he can get."

True. The newspapers were full of stories about the brutal recession the country was suffering through. A more reasonable explanation for his cabbie's behavior was that the man had been laid off from more suitable employment, his jacket and hat were secondhand, and he was working a job he hated.

"Sorry," Jamie said. "I hope the job works out for you."

His cabbie only grunted. Jamie sat back and tried to relax.

Beyond the Presidio's gate was a world Jamie could only imagine while in France. Overseas, every building he saw was scarred by the war. In San Fransisco, one would never know there'd been a war—a war that, as far as Jamie could tell, accomplished precisely nothing.

The last time Jamie rode in a taxi was back in April 1917 when he visited San Francisco for the first time. He had hoped a day trip would put worries about the impending deployment of his infantry unit out of his mind for at least a few hours. Jamie planned to ride the cable cars, see some sights, have dinner in a nice restaurant, and then catch the last evening train back to campus. He certainly hadn't planned on meeting anyone as captivating as Rachel.

The cabbie stopped at a red light. A cable car crossed in front of them. Jamie imagined Rachel sitting in the front of the car with her blonde hair blowing in the breeze. Thoughts of her sustained him throughout the war. Thoughts of her since meeting Andi always turned to how difficult it would be to tell Rachel he'd met someone else.

Rachel. What a remarkable woman. She said that since she practically forced him into their relationship, she'd understand if he found someone else while he was away fighting an unnecessary war, and his survival was so uncertain. Could she be that understanding?

She promised to wait for him. What if she'd turned down an opportunity that would never come again because of her promise? No matter how much he loved Andi, it would be cruel just to walk away from Rachel.

When the stoplight turned green, Jamie's driver tortured the gears again as they set off toward The Palace Hotel.

* * *

Jamie was so grateful to reach the Palace Hotel without any high drama that he gave his cabbie a nice tip. The man accepted it as though touching Jamie's money would contaminate him.

The Palace Hotel's bellhop took Jamie's duffle bag and followed him up several steps to the hotel's lobby. As Jamie crossed an expanse of marble the size of a football field, he asked himself for the hundredth time whether he was doing the right thing.

It was common for front-line army nurses to suffer recurring nightmares. Andi's were particularly intense. At times, she was afraid they might drive her mad. That she turned to Jamie for help was one of the greatest honors of his life.

Societal norms had changed during the Great War—eroded, many would say. If he read Andi correctly, hers hadn't. Nevertheless, she trampled all over convention by asking him to spend the next several nights with her and hold her when her nightmares scared her awake.

Her request was outrageous even by post-war standards. Jamie understood. She wasn't suggesting anything sexual. Andi was desperate, and she believed he was the only one who could help her. Jamie was known throughout the Army as "the hero who was raised from the dead." Andi was convinced the ghosts of the soldiers she couldn't save would stop tormenting her if they found her in the protective arms of one of their own.

Of course, Jamie would do as she'd asked. He loved her, more than he thought possible. So he promised to chase away her nightmares—forever.

But how? Jamie was a physics professor. He hadn't been trained to deal with nightmares.

He'd gone to Letterman's medical library and learned

how psychiatrists treat patients who suffer from recurring nightmares. He developed a plan. They would indeed be spending the next several nights in bed together. But his plan was not without risk. In his ignorance, he could do more harm than good by meddling with Andi's psyche.

And was it credible that they could spend time in bed together and not yield to their carnal desires? He didn't doubt that Andi was strong enough. But was he?

His plan posed a further risk. They'd met and got to know each other on their orthopedic ward. They'd never been truly alone together. The intimacy Jamie's plan entailed would strip their true selves bare. Such a sudden and deep dive into their relationship could end their hope for a future together.

Enough, Jamie said to himself. He stepped up to the Palace's reception desk.

The clerk greeted him with a welcoming smile. Miss Helpling, her nametag said—an appropriate name for someone in the hospitality business. "May I assist you, sir?"

"Yes. I'd like to check in. My name's Jamie Collins."

Miss Helpling's smile broadened. "Ah, Mister Ashburn is expecting you, sir. He'd like to check you in himself if you don't mind waiting a minute."

"I don't mind." Howard Ashburn was the Palace's acting general manager and Andi's cousin's husband, the man who had agreed to provide them with a room "free of charge." But few things in life are free. Jamie expected at least a stern lecture from Mister Ashburn about the bounds of the agreement.

Miss Helpling entered the office behind the counter and returned with a tall man who wore a finely tailored suit and walked with a purpose.

"Major Collins?" the man said without smiling. "I'm Howard Ashburn. I've been expecting—" He stopped mid-sentence and stared at the ribbons above Jamie's left breast pocket. Howard came to attention and held a salute.

Jamie was uncomfortable when soldiers saluted his Medal of Honor, which Army regulations required him to wear while in uniform. He hardly knew what to do when a civilian saluted. The simplest thing was to return the salute, which Jamie did smartly.

"My wife told me you were a decorated veteran," Howard said. "Leslie didn't say you'd been awarded the Medal of Honor." He went silent for a moment. "Jamie Collins . . . Now I remember. You're the one they call 'the hero who was raised from the dead.'"

Jamie lowered his eyes. "Some people call me that. I prefer 'Jamie.'"

"I served as an intelligence officer in France. I know what a man had to do to be awarded the Medal of Honor." Howard rubbed the side of his neck. "Please step into my office for a moment."

Jamie didn't like the sound of that, yet he'd survived greater peril.

Howard shut the door behind them. He indicated a chair in front of his desk. Jamie sat. Howard walked to the other side of his desk and remained standing. He stared at Jamie like a hanging judge about to hand down a sentence. "My wife and Andi are cousins, but they're as close as sisters. Leslie knows about Andi's nightmares. And since Leslie and I share everything, so do I. We're desperate to help her." His eyes bore into Jamie's. "We just want to be sure that help comes in the proper form. I was initially strongly opposed to the idea when Leslie asked me to provide you two with a room. I was afraid you'd use the opportunity to have your way with Andi and then leave her broken-hearted."

Jamie sat upright. "I give you my word of honor. I'd never hurt Andi."

Howard studied Jamie's face. "I'm inclined to believe you. And I understand about nightmares. I have a recurring one in which . . .." He stopped and cleared his throat. "The point is, Leslie convinced me you two are in love, and Andi believes you're the only one who can help her—so I agreed to give you two a room."

Jamie relaxed a bit.

"But despite your Medal of Honor, I warn you," Howard puffed out his chest and stood tall, "if you hurt Andi, you'll have to answer to me."

Jamie grasped the arms of his chair and leaned forward. "A battery of German machine guns couldn't intimidate me." He slowly leaned back and smiled. "A man standing up for his family does."

Howard's entire demeanor softened. He walked around his desk. "I'm glad we understand each other." He extended his hand. Jamie stood, and they shook. "Please, follow me," Howard said.

They returned to the reception desk. "Miss Helpling," Howard said, "now that the Carnegies have checked out, how long will the Presidential Suite be available?"

"The Presidential Suite!" Miss Helpling checked the reservation book. "Until Tuesday, sir, the third of June."

"Then please book Major Collins into it until the morning of the third, free of charge."

Miss Helpling's eyes opened wide. "Yes, sir. Four nights, sir."

If Howard's generous offer was his way of repaying a

Medal of Honor recipient for his service, Jamie felt he'd be cheapening his medal if he accepted. That he spared his men from being slaughtered by a battery of machine guns was benefit enough. "Thank you, Mister Ashburn—"

"Howard."

"Thank you, Howard. I appreciate the gesture, but . . ."

Howard held up his hand. "Consider it a gift to Andi. You want the best for her, don't you?"

Jamie smiled. "You've twisted my arm. We accept."

Howard gestured toward the Palace's grand entrance. "And speaking of Andi."

When Jamie turned toward the promenade that led to reception, he had to steady himself against the desk. He and Andi had only seen each other in military clothing, which weren't exactly flattering. The angelic vision gliding toward him took his breath away. Andi's pastel blouse and simple black skirt revealed a figure few women could equal. Her flowing copper hair sparkled in the light of the dozen chandeliers in the Palace's lobby. And her walk. Only an angel could move with such grace. It was her smile, however, that practically stopped Jamie's heart. It was a smile that said she'd endured trauma and heartbreak and was now looking forward to unsurpassed joy.

Could a smile say all that? Jamie's answer was an emphatic yes!

"I'm blessed beyond reason," Jamie said to the world in general, but especially to himself.

"I'm the one who's blessed," Andi said. They embraced openly for the first time. Jamie was inordinately proud that this angel of mercy was willing to show the world he was her man.

Howard smiled broadly. "It appears to me you're both

blessed. Now, please allow me to show you to the Presidential Suite."

"The Presidential Suite?" Andi looked at Jamie.

He hardly knew what to say. "A most generous gift from Howard."

"My wife's cousin deserves nothing less."

Andi gave Howard an affectionate kiss on the cheek. "We're very grateful."

As Howard led them to the elevator, Jamie noticed a man who looked vaguely familiar, furtively watching from a distance. Jamie didn't mention it to Andi. He didn't want to worry her.

A bellhop picked up Jamie's duffle bag and Andi's suitcase and brought up the rear of their little procession. The elevator operator bowed slightly and held the door for them.

Jamie had never been in an elevator before. The operator shut the door, and they began to rise. Jamie would have marveled at the engineering behind the conveyance under normal circumstances. In this case, he could only marvel at Andi.

In Jamie's imagination, they were moving through the clouds as the elevator took them higher than he'd ever been before. He could hear Howard enthusing about the luxuries of the Presidential Suite. Hardly a word registered. Jamie was mesmerized by Andi.

They exited the elevator and faced the suite's grand entrance. Howard ushered them through.

The Presidential Suite's living room itself was large enough to accommodate an entire infantry platoon.

The bellhop tipped his cap. "I'll take your bags to your bedroom, sir."

Jamie walked to an arched window and peered down at Market Street. There wasn't even a hint of war damage.

He turned back to Andi, Howard, and the Presidential Suite. The corner of the living room provided a perfect setting for a baby grand piano. An impressive fireplace took up most of the opposite wall. Everywhere Jamie looked, stunning area rugs complimented wall-to-wall inlaid hardwood floors.

"Howard, this suite is *spectacular.*" Andi rose onto her tiptoes and again kissed him on his cheek.

Jamie was overwhelmed. "I never imagined I'd get to stay in a place this fine."

Howard stood tall. "I'm glad you like it." He looked at his watch. "I have a meeting in a few minutes. Sometime soon, I'd love to hear how these humble accommodations suit you."

Jamie intercepted the bellhop and handed him a silver dollar. Howard closed the door behind them, leaving Jamie and Andi truly alone together for the first time. Doctors, nurses, corpsmen, and even the occasional patient were constantly passing Jamie's hospital room door.

Jamie wanted this moment to last. He reached out to Andi. She stepped into his arms. For Jamie, the world stopped rotating on its axis and revolving around the sun as they shared their first uninterrupted, prolonged embrace.

Jamie had never been so happy—until his suspicions crept up on him again.

How does one suppress unwanted thoughts when trying to do so only brings them to the surface? The question that haunted Jamie was whether Andi really loved him, or was she merely trying to snare a rich husband.

Jamie hated having such thoughts. All indications were that he'd never met a more honest person than Andi.

Shell shock, Jamie told himself. Who wouldn't be struggling psychologically after being grievously wounded, mistaken for dead, abandoned, and paralyzed for five months? In his more rational moments, Jamie knew his suspicions were unfounded. After all, they were based on nothing more than a look that passed between Andi and Matt Kavanaugh when the two almost collided in the doorway of Jamie's room a week earlier.

Kavanaugh had seen how Jamie looked at Andi. "Maybe she'd be interested in you if you were rich," Kavanaugh said. "I could talk to her for you."

Jamie had bristled. He didn't want Kavanaugh anywhere near Andi. "You do," Jamie snapped, "and I'll never work with you."

A devilish grin spread across Kavanaugh's face. "How do you know I haven't already?"

Upon seeing the devastating effect his question had on Jamie, Kavanaugh said he was only teasing. But in Jamie's fragile state of mind, the damage was done.

As Jamie fought to suppress his suspicions, another thought invaded his mind, uninvited, unwanted: better keep your options open with Rachel.

With the greatest effort, Jamie quelled the silent battle that was tearing him apart. He smoothed back Andi's hair and kissed her delicate neck. "And to think, I was afraid to tell you I love you."

She arched her neck to give him better access. "Am I that intimidating?"

"You've seen me at my worst. I never dared to think you might love me despite myself. I guess I'm not as brave as people say I am."

"I know how brave you are. I watched as you left your

private room and moved out onto the general ward next to Corporal Wilkins when no other patient would go near a colored man. I heard about how you performed surgery on yourself to inspire the men on our ward to endure their rehabilitation. I saw you nurse Sergeant Binney back to health, knowing how contagious he was."

Jamie was about to speak. Andi pressed her fingers to his lips to stop him. "And bravest of all, I saw you walk away with dignity when those in the brotherhood you created said you were no longer one of them."

Jamie looked into her eyes. "You may be the only person who can appreciate that creating that brotherhood was one of the greatest victories of my life."

Andi took both his hands—he always marveled at how strong her soft, skillful hands were. "You gave the men a sense of belonging and a purpose, which is no less a gift than saving a man's life."

"You *do* understand." He hugged her tight. "No wonder I love you."

"And I love you," she whispered. She stood up straight. "Why am I whispering? I'm not on duty. We can be as open as we please." She leaned back and shouted, "I love Jamie Collins, and he loves me."

"Those," Jamie said, "are the most beautiful words I've ever heard."

"And here we are, alone together for the first time." She glanced at her wristwatch. "It's early. What shall we do next?"

Jamie's baser self had a suggestion, but he kept it to himself. He caught sight of his reflection in a mirror. Corpsman Hendricks had done a fine job pressing Jamie's uniform. Still, Jamie couldn't wait to change into civilian clothes. "I'm tired of seeing myself in uniform. Do you like to shop?"

"I'm a woman, aren't I?"

Jamie smiled. "I'm far more aware of that than is good for me at the moment."

Jamie saw a flash of anxiety in Andi's eyes.

"Don't worry," he said, "for a good soldier, the mission always comes first. We're here to chase away your nightmares, not to fulfill my fantasies." Jamie could feel the tension leave Andi's body. "Let's go out and buy some civilian clothes that won't make me look like a scarecrow."

Andi glanced around their suite. "I'm almost afraid to leave for fear we'll return and find this was only a dream."

"Don't worry about that. Thanks to Howard, this suite's ours for the next four nights."

"*Four nights?*" Andi lifted her arms heavenward and did a pirouette that landed her right back in Jamie's arms. "Thank you, Howard!"

Jamie placed his hands on her tiny waist. "I've been confined to a hospital for the past seven months. Let's step out into the world. I want to see if it's anything like I remember." Jamie patted his right hip. "I have seven months of backpay in my wallet, and I'd like to spend every penny on us before you leave for DC."

Worry lines creased Andi's forehead. "Oh, you mustn't. What will you do when it's all gone?"

"Spoken like a true preacher's daughter." He stood with his hands clasped behind his back. "If I were in a certain Midwest city standing before a preacher who shall remain nameless, asking for his daughter's hand in marriage, and he asked if I could provide for a wife, I'd tell him about my army retirement pay, which will be augmented by a Medal of

Honor bonus, and my associate professor's salary that the university's been banking for me since the day I was wounded—and will continue to pay until I'm well enough to return to teaching. And I'd let that unnamed preacher know about the consulting fees I earn on the side." Jamie looked into Andi's eyes. "I'd also tell him I'd inherited a small fortune." Jamie was comforted by Andi's apparent surprise at hearing this. "In other words," he said, "should I ever be fortunate enough to marry, my wife will have all the comforts money can buy."

Andi canted her head. "You've never mentioned an inheritance before. Still, it wouldn't have mattered—to me or my dad." She took his hand. "I'd be just as happy if you were penniless."

Jamie hadn't been bragging. He wanted to see whether there was any indication Andi knew he was rich. The sincerity in her voice and the look in her sparkling green eyes said she was being truthful.

He looked her up and down. "Considering how many envious looks I'm sure to get, it will boost my self-esteem to be seen in public with such a beautiful woman."

Andi shook her head. "You are an incorrigible flatterer—which I appreciate."

"I only speak the truth when complimenting you, Andi Eliot." He closed his eyes. "Andi—your name's music to my ears after knowing you only as Nurse Eliot for so long."

"And I much prefer Jamie to Major Collins." She angled her head. "Which I've wanted to ask you about. I saw in your medical records that your first name really is Jamie and not James. What's the story behind that?"

Jamie grinned. "My mother was a big believer that we shouldn't take ourselves too seriously. She hoped naming me

Jamie would help me stay grounded. Which sounds more approachable, 'Professor James Collins,' " he said in an exaggerated New England accent, "or plain old 'Jamie?' "

Andi smiled. "Your mother had a point. Now, if you'll excuse me, I'd like to freshen up before we go out."

Jamie took the opportunity to explore their suite. To the left of the living room was a formal dining room with seating for six and a butler's pantry with kitchenette. To the right was an extensive private library. Several pamphlets on a large desk in the library outlined amenities their concierge recommended.

Beyond the library, an airy bedroom led to the master bath.

"As a guest of management," Jamie said loud enough for Andi to hear, "I'll be in the guest bathroom."

Chapter 2

Stepping Out

Jamie and Andi exited the elevator and entered the Palace's sumptuous lobby. Having been conditioned on the battlefield to be wary of his surroundings, Jamie quickly scanned the area for any threats. The man he suspected had been watching them earlier was nowhere in sight. Paranoia, Jamie said to himself.

After speaking with the hotel's concierge he and Andi left the Palace, took New Montgomery Street a few paces, and then turned southwest onto Market. Among the gaggle of people walking the floor of the "canyon" formed by the surrounding eight- and ten-story buildings, Jamie didn't see a single military uniform, except for the reflection of his own in storefront windows.

He and Andi veered right onto Geary Street and quickly found Dibowski's Men's Fine Clothing, the haberdashery the hotel's concierge recommended.

The way Andi looked around the shop, you'd think she'd never been in a men's clothing store. And maybe she hadn't.

"I'm afraid I'm not very adventurous when it comes to fashion," she said.

"One thing I liked about the army was I never had to decide what to wear." Jamie took a brightly colored plaid shirt off a rack and held it up to a pair of gray pants. Andi raised an eyebrow.

"As you'll discover," he said, "I'm hopeless regarding style. Which is why I wore gray from head to toe day after day before being called up."

Andi glanced down at her pale blue blouse and black skirt. "We might be in trouble. This outfit is about as wild as anything I own." She walked over to a mannequin dressed in attire suitable for a casual evening on the town: tweed jacket, knitted wool sweater, cotton shirt, and necktie. She held out the jacket's sleeve. "I like this."

"What? The jacket?"

"No. The entire outfit."

The haberdasher's expression when he saw Jamie was more appropriate for a mortician than a dealer in men's fine clothing. He quickly put on a happier face. "Frederick Dibowski, at your service." He bowed slightly. Though he'd probably delivered that line a thousand times, he still sounded enthusiastic.

Andi placed her hand on Jamie's forearm. "My man here needs some civilian clothes."

Jamie was warmed to the core at hearing Andi call him her man.

"We're both used to wearing uniforms," she said, "so we're out of our depth in a shop like this." She ran her fingers up and down the lapel of the mannequin's jacket. "How do you think my man would look in this?"

Frederick pointed to the ribbons above Jamie's left jacket pocket. "Are all those combat awards?"

Jamie couldn't get out of his uniform fast enough. Even civilians were reminding him of the war—a war he wanted to forget. "Some are campaign ribbons," he said.

Frederick pressed his hand to the side of his chest. "I wasn't at the front long enough to do much fighting. A sniper sent me to the hospital my first week in the field."

Jamie's eyes opened wide. "As deadly as German snipers were, it's amazing you're still alive."

Frederick squinted. "The man the sniper was aiming at wasn't so lucky. A bullet passed through our point man's neck before ending up in my left lung." Frederick rubbed the side of his nose. "My 'buddies' left me where I fell. If a stretcher-bearer hadn't braved the sniper's field of fire, I'd be dead."

"We have a friend who was a stretcher-bearer," Andi said. "Nothing would have stopped him from coming for you."

"I spent a month in a hospital in France," Frederick said. "The nurses there took great care of me." His eyebrows pinched together. "Is it a nurse's uniform you wear?"

"Yes. Army Nurse Corps."

Fredrick closed his eyes for a moment. 'Did you serve overseas during the war?"

"Yes, sir. AEF Base Hospital 21, Rouen."

Andi turned crimson as Frederick bowed, took her hand, and kissed it.

Frederick stood up straight. "Being an army nurse and having a friend who was a stretcher-bearer, you've come to the right shop. When you leave here, your man will outshine that swashbuckling movie star, Douglas Fairbanks."

Jamie tugged on his uniform here and there. "I lost a lot of weight in the hospital. My old sizes would make me look like a little boy dressed in his father's clothes."

"Don't worry." Without his leave, Frederick held Jamie's arms out to his sides. As in their hotel suite, Jamie imagined himself a scarecrow. "This is a multi-generational family business," Fredrick said. "I was born with the ability to size men up." He let Jamie's arms drop.

"You seemed a bit hesitant when you first saw me."

Frederick's smile disappeared.

Jamie lowered his head. "I'm sorry. I don't mean to sound critical."

"No, no. I apologize to you. It was the uniform. It reminded me of the war, that's all."

"I understand," Jamie said. "I'd prefer to forget the war myself." He smiled. "You have ready-made clothes that will fit me, don't you?"

"Yes, sir," Frederick said with a convincing smile. "Now that Grandfather Dibowski has passed away, we carry a wide selection of ready-made fashions. Or, if you're not in a hurry, our tailors can make anything you desire. And speaking of Grandfather Dibowski, if he knew I didn't make every customer feel welcome in 'his' shop, he'd roll over in his grave."

"Don't be hard on yourself," Andi said. "We all need a tap on the shoulder now and then." She looked at Jamie. "When Jamie came onto my ward, he thought I was stiff and unapproachable. That's the last thing I want a patient to think."

"I never said you were unapproachable."

"You didn't have to. I could tell."

Jamie combed back his hair with his fingers. "It wasn't that at all. I was in awe of you."

Frederick looked at Andi. "Understandable."

Andi blushed again, which, with her light complexion and sensibilities, Jamie had come to expect. He put his arm around her waist and drew her near.

The way Frederick smiled, one would be excused for thinking he was responsible for drawing them together. "Let's get started turning you into a 'gentleman about town' your lady will be proud to be seen with."

Andi assumed her Nurse Eliot bearing. Frederick cleared his throat. "That your lady will be *even more* proud to be seen with."

* * *

Frederick couldn't convince Jamie to forgo a vest for a knitted sweater. "I wouldn't have a place for a pocket watch," Jamie said.

Frederick pointed to a display of wristwatches. "Gentlemen are beginning to wear one of these rather than carry a pocket watch."

"I had to wear a wristwatch while on active duty. I much prefer a pocket watch. No matter the modern trend, I'm not ready to start wearing a bracelet when I don't have to." Fredrick was happy to sell Jamie an expensive pocket watch.

Arrangements were made to send the purchases Jamie wasn't wearing and his uniform to the Palace's Presidential Suite.

Jamie and Andi left Frederick's shop with Jamie in brand-new civvies. After walking a few paces, Jamie stopped to admire his reflection in a window of the stationery store next to Dibowski's.

Was he imagining things? Could that be the reflection of the man who had been watching them as they entered the Palace's elevator? And damned if Jamie didn't also see his disrespectful taxi driver. Gone was the cabbie uniform, replaced by clothes that actually fit.

This is getting ridiculous. Next, I'll be seeing reflections of all the soldiers I killed.

He didn't mention his concern to Andi. She had ghosts of her own to deal with.

Jamie forced himself to concentrate on his and Andi's reflections.

Fredrick had done a fine job outfitting Jamie. "I look like a true gentleman—or a professor," he said, admiring his tweed jacket, lighter-colored tweed pants, vest, cotton shirt, and tie.

Andi took his arm. "Don't we make a handsome couple?"

"Only because you overshadow all of my deficiencies."

Andi shook her head. She plucked a tiny thread from Jamie's sleeve. "It was strange that Frederick didn't mention your Medal of Honor."

They began to walk. "I liked that he acknowledged the work you nurses did."

"And intrepid stretcher-bearers like Hendricks."

Andi was always one to deflect attention from herself. Jamie stopped in the middle of the sidewalk and stretched out his arms. "No uniform, no medals. It feels great to be plain old Jamie again."

"I'm sure it does, Professor Collins."

"Very funny, Dean Eliot." He took both her hands. "As

far as I know, I'll only have to wear my uniform one more time."

"Really? What for?"

"I've been asked to speak at a fundraising reception for the charity I told you about a few weeks back."

"The one that's going to help educate disabled veterans?"

Jamie nodded. "The reception's scheduled for Monday evening at an art gallery here in town. I promised I'd be there, in uniform." Jamie took a step back. "Will you do me the honor of accompanying me?"

Andi's reply was immediate. "Of course. I'd be happy to."

"Great. Then, instead of dreading the event, I can look forward to spending the evening with you." And he'd get to see whether there was any indication Andi and Matt Kavanaugh knew each other. "Now, let's forget the whole blasted army and just enjoy our time together."

"Let's." Andi turned toward the west. "Union Square's only a block or two from here. Do you feel like walking that far?"

Union Square? That would bring back memories. "Sure, now that I'm able to walk. We can go even further if you'd like."

Andi took Jamie's arm. They sauntered on. As they approached Union Square, sights and sounds brought back memories of Jamie's friend Ainsley, God rest his soul—and Rachel. Men looked at Andi as they might a Vermeer painting. Sadly for them, they couldn't also see the beauty within her.

After a few hundred yards, Jamie whispered, "I see envy in the eyes of every man we pass." And it was true.

"I think you're only seeing what you want to see."

"I am when I look at you," Jamie said.

When they reached the corner of Geary and Stockton Streets, the statue of the Goddess of Victory atop the monument in the center of the Square came into view. Jamie had found it so captivating two years earlier his neck hurt from looking up at it. He pointed. "There's an example of man putting woman on a pedestal."

"From which she has nowhere to go but down," Andi said.

Jamie came to a stop. "I do look up to you. You know that, don't you?"

Andi smiled. "I hope we'll always see eye-to-eye."

They strolled arm-in-arm as they aimlessly wandered through the square. The smell was mouthwatering as they passed a vendor selling pretzels. They heard a cable car bell over the din of voices and traffic.

"The last time I was here," Jamie said, "America had just declared war on Germany. In my wildest dreams, I couldn't have imagined all that's taken place in my life since—some good, some bad. But if the bad were necessary to bring me here with you, I wouldn't change a thing."

Andi rested her head on his shoulder. "Nor would I."

They ended up back on the corner of Stockton and Geary. Andi indicated the six-story Beaux-Arts building facing them. "That's the City of Paris Department Store."

Jamie turned to her. "That's a strange name for a department store."

"It's named after the ship that brought the founder to America. My cousin Leslie loves the place, especially their reasonably-price reproduction designer dresses."

Jamie had no idea what a designer dress was. It didn't

matter. If such a thing excited Andi, he was happy to play along. "Do you want to go in and look around?"

"Maybe later. Now, I'd just like to stroll with you."

With Andi setting their course, they crossed Geary and continued toward the west. Jamie wondered whether Andi would stop in front of Hutchins Fine Art.

She did. Jamie didn't know what he'd say if one of Rachel's paintings were on display and Andi commented on it. The small painting of a cable car Rachel had given him was the only tangible proof he had of her existence, and he hadn't seen it since stashing it in the Physics Department's storeroom before heading off to war. He'd visit the storeroom the first time he returned to campus to confirm that Rachel wasn't just a dream.

"I love art," Andi said. "Painting, music, literature, poetry—you name it." She sighed. "I wish I were talented."

Jamie gently turned her to face him. "Andi Eliot, you are an extraordinary nurse. You give patients back their health—and their lives. That's a talent far more significant than pressing an ivory key at the right moment or smearing a certain color of paint here or there."

"Maybe."

"Come on, Andi. I've been watching you for months. I've seen the way you treat your patients. Even Sergeant Binney." He drew her nearer. "I know you hated that Binney discouraged other patients, yet you put that aside and treated him like any other patient. That's a talent to be proud of."

Andi smiled. "We had some German POWs pass through our ward in France. I made sure I treated the swine the same way I treated our boys."

Jamie laughed. "Andi Eliot, I'm shocked and dismayed by your language. Swine indeed."

Andi blushed. "You can't spend as much time as I have around soldiers without picking up some of their bad habits. I'm just glad you haven't heard me when I get angry. I could make a muleskinner blush."

"I'm sure even then, your voice would sound like music to my ears."

She gave him an affectionate kiss on the cheek.

Jamie stood taller than the Goddess Victory. They began to walk again.

"I'm happy to see you walking so well."

Jamie picked up his pace. "Someday soon, I hope to start running. I used to love to run, and I was fast."

"How about now? Let's see if we can catch that cable car." She took off in a sprint. Jamie wasn't about to be left in the dust. He caught up with her, and they jumped onto the platform on the side of the moving cable car in perfect unison. A choreographer couldn't have staged their arrival more perfectly.

"If I'm not mistaken," Andi said, "that's the first time you've run since being wounded."

Jamie smiled. "You baited me, didn't you?"

Andi tossed her hair back and laughed. "Yes, and aren't you glad?" She sat down on the lateral bench in the front of the car.

After a glance to see whether Leonard was their gripman —he wasn't—Jamie sat next to Andi and put his arm around her shoulders.

As their car picked up speed, Jamie was sure he saw the two men who seemed to be following them. Their persistent appearance made it unlikely they were hallucinations, although the paranoia that often accompanies shell shock can be even more persistent.

Jamie's cabbie—*Angry Man*, Jamie named him—wasn't very good at concealing himself. The other man was doing a much better job of staying hidden. *Sly*, Jamie named him. Angry Man looked like he could handle himself in a fight. Sly looked like someone who'd resort to something underhanded if he wanted to make trouble. Andi must have noticed them, but she hadn't said anything. Oddly, Angry Man and Sly seemed unaware of each other.

Jamie suspected Angry Man was working for Sonny Kavanaugh, Matt Kavanaugh's psychopathic nephew. If that were the case, he presented less of a threat than Sly. Sonny had too much to lose if he or one of his henchmen laid a hand on Jamie or Andi.

Jamie had no idea what Sly was up to. One thing was certain: if either got anywhere near Andi, they'd find out how well Jamie had mastered his army hand-to-hand combat training.

But these mortals weren't Jamie's primary concern. He could deal with a psychopath or his henchmen. A greater concern was Andi's belief that she was cursed regarding marriage. Before the war, she'd been engaged to an army doctor. He died of malaria shortly before their wedding was to take place. Several years later, she became engaged to an army pilot. He died in a flying accident the week before they were to wed. Behind her back, Andi's more insensitive colleagues "joked" that "Putting a ring on Nurse Eliot's finger was like putting a noose around your neck."

Andi's mind was in such a state after dealing with so much trauma during the war that she believed in "The Hangman's Curse." For Jamie and Andi to have a future together, he'd have to overcome her fear that if he proposed to her and she accepted, it would be the death of him.

The curse didn't scare Jamie. He was a scientist. He didn't believe in such things. But Andi did.

There was yet another problem. Everyone believed the doctor who declared Jamie dead made a mistake—everyone but Jamie. As crazy as it seemed to others, he believed he really was dead and that he was raised for a purpose.

What purpose? Jamie was still searching for an answer to that question. All he knew was that it wasn't anything as dramatic as Jason and the Argonauts' quest for the Golden Fleece. Nevertheless, fulfilling his purpose was just as important to Jamie as his relationship with Andi.

He could only hope he'd never have to decide between one or the other.

He was brought back to the present when their cable car stopped at a crossroad.

"Where would you like to go?" he asked Andi.

She looked out over the cityscape with a faraway, contented smile. "How about Land's End? It will be sunset soon. We can watch the sun disappear into the ocean."

He was glad they had to change cars twice before reaching Land's End. Doing so made it difficult, if not almost impossible, for anyone to follow them.

Their journey was well worth it as they watched a giant red ball sink deeper and deeper into the white-capped ocean. It was cold near the shore even late in May, with the wind blowing straight off the open sea. They huddled together to keep their teeth from chattering. Little was said as they stood mesmerized by nature's beauty. The sun's rim inevitably dipped below the waves, engulfing them in velvet darkness.

Andi's eyes sparkled even in the fading light. "Shall we go back to the Palace for dinner?" she said.

And after dinner? Lurid images of what once occurred in

Rachel's little artist's studio quickened Jamie's pulse. He forced himself to focus. "Dinner at the Palace would be nice, and then we're going to address your nightmares."

Andi signed. "I'm sorry, Jamie. I know I'm asking an awful lot of you."

"No, you're not. I'd do anything for you." He caressed her cheek. "People say it's a miracle I'm still alive. If so, I can't think of a better way to show my gratitude than to be of service to someone who's dedicated her life to caring for others."

Andi rested her forehead against Jamie's and quietly wept. After a moment, he gently lifted her chin and looked into her eyes. "Have I said something wrong?"

"No. You've said just the right thing." She smiled through her tears. "I'm so very, very thankful we've found each other."

Chapter 3

***

Dream Shaping

Jamie and Andi took a different route back to the
Palace Hotel. "We'll see different sights," he said, not
mentioning that doing so would also make it harder
for anyone to follow them.

Before going to dinner, Andi changed into a sleeveless
evening dress with a V-neckline. Jamie's pulse quickened the
instant he saw her. "Andi Eliot, you are the most beautiful
woman I've ever seen."

Andi lowered her head modestly. "I doubt that. I do
know I'm the happiest." She reached up, centered Jamie's tie,
then held onto the knot and drew his lips to hers.

Jamie imagined himself floating halfway to Mars.

"I'm starving." She took Jamie by the arm. "Let's see if
the Palace's Garden Court Restaurant is as fabulous as
people say."

Their maître d' was happy to seat them at a table in a
quiet corner of the restaurant.

"This is lovely," Andi said.

Jamie sat next to her. A busboy removed two unneeded place settings.

Andi scooted her chair a little closer to Jamie's. "We can people-watch from here without being too conspicuous."

And Jamie could watch for the two men who seemed to be trailing them.

At that moment Angry Man walked into the restaurant as though he had a right to be there. As the maître d' headed toward the middle of the restaurant, Angry Man redirected him to a table where his back would be against a wall—and he'd be facing Jamie.

If Sly was around, he was doing a much better job of concealing himself.

Their waiter, an immaculately dressed young man, stepped up to their table. His nametag identified him as Robert. "Good evening." His tone was pleasant and welcoming. "May I take your drink orders?"

Jamie folded his hands on top of their table. "Andi?"

She looked up at Robert. "Water, please, with a slice of lemon."

"Lemon?" Jamie said.

"It's something restaurants in Paris offer. It's very refreshing."

"No alcohol?" he said.

Her adamant "No, thank you" was reinforced by her sour expression. "I never touch the stuff."

Jamie's smile was so broad he was afraid it might tear his face apart. "That's great. Neither do I."

Jamie looked up at Robert. "I'll have the same as the *lady*." Respectful emphasis was placed on "lady."

Robert strode off.

Jamie picked up his menu. "After eating only hospital food for the past seven months, I could eat a horse."

"As your personal nurse, I recommend you not eat anything too rich. You wouldn't want to overload your system."

"Seriously?"

"You said yourself you haven't had anything but hospital food for seven months."

Jamie set his menu aside. "Why don't you order for us both?"

"That sounds like a challenge." After studying the menu for a minute or two, she set it aside and waved Robert over. "We'd each like your house salad without dressing, the roasted chicken, and steamed broccoli."

When Robert left them alone, Andi sat back, looking rather pleased with herself. "Have you heard of *The St. Francis Cookbook?*"

Jamie smiled. "That's not one of the texts we use in the physics department at Stanford."

Andi ignored his wise answer. "It came out just before the war. It was written by the head chef at the Saint Francis Hotel here in San Francisco. It emphasizes a light 'California' cuisine made possible by the locale's easy access to poultry, fish, fresh fruits, and vegetables. It substitutes salads, natural herbs, vegetables, fish, and poultry for the heavy meats, breads, and animal fats found in most American diets."

"Is that the way you eat?"

"It is."

"Then maybe everyone should." He appraised her like a fine work of art. "Nurse Hobbes told me you seemed to enjoy torturing the student nurses with calisthenics, self-defense drills, and daily runs."

"Of all the bluebirds, Nurse Hobbes is the last one I'd have thought would complain."

"I'm sorry. I was trying to be funny. She didn't complain. She's thankful you prepared your bluebirds for any situation the Army might place them in. She particularly appreciated the self-defense training you gave them."

"I'm rather proud of that myself," Andi said. "I'm sure you're aware that Army nurses operate in a man's world. I want the bluebirds to be able to protect themselves—both from the enemy and overly friendly patients and staff. Especially the staff."

Corpsman Hendricks told Jamie there was a doctor at Andi's hospital in France who wouldn't leave her alone. Winters was his name. After about the hundredth time Andi declined Winters' insistence that she go out with him, he pinned her against a wall and, with his face only inches from hers, accused her of thinking she was too good for him—which obviously she was.

Hendricks had been nearby. Before Andi could put Winters in his place, Hendricks picked him up and dumped him headfirst into a half-full fifty-five-gallon drum of freshly washed bed linen waiting to be hung out to dry. Instead of the linen, it was Winters who was hung out to dry. Everyone knew what kind of man Winters was, so Hendricks escaped punishment.

Just before Jamie was discharged from Letterman, Hendricks told him Doctor Winters was scheduled to report for duty there in late May. God forbid that Sly was Doctor Winters.

Jamie wasn't going to mention Winters to Andi, but he'd

keep an especially sharp eye out for Sly, or Winters, or whoever the man was.

"Where'd you learn self-defense?" Jamie said.

"From the most respected instructor wherever the Army posted me. It always took considerable cajoling to convince him—it was always a 'him'—to teach a woman, but I was able to.

Jamie could imagine. One smile and any man would be putty in her hands.

"And I learned more than self-defense. Over the years, I've been trained in every hand-to-hand combat technique front-line soldiers are taught."

Jamie let that sink in for a moment. He smiled. "I'm comforted knowing you'll be able to defend me if you ever need to."

Andi gave him a cold stare. "You may think that's amusing, but believe me, if the need arises, you'll see how serious I am."

The look on her face said it would be a mistake to doubt her. "All kidding aside," Jamie said, "I pity anyone who incurs your wrath."

She lowered her eyes. "As crazy as it may sound, sometimes I wish I could test my skills on someone who needs to be taught that women aren't easy targets." She looked up and smiled. "Now, let's talk about something more pleasant."

"First," Jamie said, "I want you to know that every year I was part of the Student Officer Training Corp at Stanford, I volunteered to extend my summer training an extra month to receive extensive hand-to-hand combat training. I became so proficient that the instructors used me to demonstrate that with the proper training, a smaller man can easily destroy someone much larger. And unlike you, my skills were tested on the battlefield. That I'm alive should tell you how that turned out." Jamie leaned toward her. "My point is, no matter the situation, I will protect you with all my skill and every ounce of my strength." He gave her a cold stare. "And I will prevail."

Jamie leaned back in his chair. "*Now*, let's talk about something more pleasant. Nurse Hobbes said you led your bluebirds in a run every day. That's more than I asked of the men in my infantry company."

"I gave my bluebirds Sundays off—although I invited them to join me in a nice leisurely run before Sabbath services."

"Did any of them ever join you?"

"Sarah Hobbes did a few times." Andi tilted her head. "I hope she'll forgive me for whisking you away from her like I did.

Jamie felt himself blush. "I'm sure she will. She thinks you can just about walk on water."

Andi laughed. "Sarah Hobbes is going to be a great nurse."

"I'm sure of it."

"If I get my way," Andi said, "physical training will be part of the Army School of Nursing's standard curriculum—along with self-defense."

Jamie smiled. "Who would dare oppose the new Assistant Dean?"

"Perhaps the Dean?"

"I believe you said you know her."

"Yes, fairly well." Andi smiled. "Julia Stimson and I worked together in France. We get along great. She'll also be reporting for duty on o1 July."

"What? The school's going to have a new dean and

assistant dean starting on the same day? What about continuity?"

"The school's part of the Army Nurse Corps. They'll provide the continuity." Andi frowned. "Perhaps more than we'll want."

"Do you anticipate a problem there?"

"Perhaps." Andi massaged her triceps. "In my first assignment with the ANC, I contradicted my supervising nurse in front of a patient and an attending physician. Worse still, I was right. That nurse has never forgiven me, and now she's the Assistant Superintendent of Nurses, which makes her Dean Stimson's immediate superior."

Jamie rested his elbow on the arm of his chair. "She'd have to be awfully petty to hold that against you."

"She questioned my appointment as Assistant Dean. She claims that a competent head nurse would have detected Nurse Wolenski's conspiracy to ignore Private Lightner's call button and put a stop to it immediately."

"She knows about Wolenski?"

"Of course. The ANC is a close community. Every member would know about something that consequential."

"And Julia Stimson's boss blames you for not reading Wolenski's mind? I don't think I like the ANC's Assistant Superintendent of Nurses."

Andi smiled. "I put a lot of trust in my staff, which I believe is the right way to treat people if you want them to grow. Unfortunately, that exposes me to the small minority who betray my trust. I also believe in giving people a second chance, which again exposes me. I don't mind. I'd rather take the risk than stifle the initiative of my people."

Jamie crossed his arms. "Andi Eliot, you give me reason after reason to love you." He would have taken her in his arms and kissed her in any other setting. In the middle of a restaurant, he had to settle for giving her hand a worshipful squeeze. "What are you going to do about your boss's boss?"

Andi thought for a moment. "I'm going to give her the benefit of the doubt and hope for the best."

Robert brought their meals to the table. Andi ate deliberately, pausing between each bite. In the trenches, Jamie had developed the habit of wolfing down his food since he never knew how long he'd have before an inconsiderate enemy might interrupt him. Andi's table manners were as refined as she was. Jamie felt like a pig by comparison.

When Jamie looked up from his plate, Angry Man was gone. Jamie could have kicked himself for losing sight of such an obvious threat. But it gave him a chance to call their waiter over and ask for something without worrying about Angry Man overhearing which room they were staying in. "Will you please pass along a request to have a fire lit in the living room of our Presidential Suite?

"The Presidential Suite?" Robert stood straighter than Jamie's soldiers on the parade grounds. "Yes, sir."

Andi sighed contentedly. "It will be nice to have a well-established fire going when we return."

There was a sudden crash behind them. Jamie instantly pushed Andi down to tabletop level and shielded her with his body.

"Jamie—someone dropped a plate, that's all."

Jamie settled back in his chair. Set his napkin back on his lap. He could feel his cheeks burning. "Sorry about that. I'm still a bit jumpy."

She touched his hand. "A month ago, you would have hit the floor. You're making terrific progress."

"Thanks to you."

"It's my mission to help you recover completely."

If anyone could restore his health completely, it would be Andi. "I'm forever indebted to Doctor Lawrence for placing me on your ward."

Andi smiled. "Me too." She took a sip of water, leaving her lips glistening deep red in the light of their candle. The sight filled Jamie's mind with erotic thoughts. He searched for something to say, anything that would divert his mind from those tantalizing lips. "Please, tell me about your sisters."

Andi stared off into the distance as though seeing them in her mind. "Cyndi, the middle of us three girls, married young. She already has three kids."

Jamie regained some composure. "And the youngest?"

"Debbi—"

"Debbi? You all go by shortened names that end in 'i?' That's rather modern."

"My father believes Andrea, Cynthia, and Debra are too old-fashioned and formal for women like us."

"Please, go on. You were going to tell me about Debbi," Jamie said.

"I'm worried about Debbi."

"Why?"

She set her fork down. "Debbi's a gifted mathematician about to receive her Ph.D. from the University of Chicago—"

"And you're worried she won't be able to find work in her field?"

"How'd you know?"

"It's an old story. My sister had the same problem when she was starting out."

"You have a sister?"

"Alice Collins, MD," Jamie said with undisguised pride.

"Impressive. How'd she handle the situation?"

"She's a strong woman. She just put her head down and pressed on."

"Sounds like you have every right to be proud of her. Is she your only sibling?"

"Yep."

"Older or younger?"

"A couple of years older. Though not quite over the hill . . . yet."

"I'm a bit older than you myself."

"But mighty young to be a head nurse."

Andi's smile disappeared. "War always brings rapid advancement in the military."

"You're right. I'd never have made major so soon during peacetime." He leaned toward Andi. "When exactly is your birthday?"

"The ninth of March. Which, if you've forgotten, was the day you arrived on my ward. My twenty-seventh birthday, to be exact. And you were by far the best birthday present I've ever received."

"That means you're a little over two months older than me." He appraised her critically. "You're remarkably well preserved for a crusty *old* head nurse."

* * *

As Jamie and Andi left the Garden Court Restaurant, they heard music coming from the closed doors of the Palace's ballroom. They paused to listen.

A man walked up to them. "That's our 50-piece dance orchestra rehearsing for tomorrow evening's Spring Ball. You're welcome to come in and watch. They won't mind."

Jamie gave him a questioning look.

The man pointed to his nametag. "I'm the Palace's director of entertainment." Mister Timmons opened the door wide for them.

"Thank you," Andi said. She took Jamie's hand and led the way.

The orchestra began a waltz. The conductor stopped them after a few bars. He turned to Jamie and Andi. "You two aren't professional dancers, are you?" he said in a friendly tone.

"Far from it," Jamie said.

"That's great. You'd be doing us a huge favor if you'd waltz to this piece. I need to get the tempo right for the hotel's guests."

Jamie looked at Andi. "I dance almost as well as I play the piano."

She canted her head. "I didn't know you play the piano."

"I don't."

Andi shook her head. "Let's give it a try anyway."

They did their best, which, if Jamie was any judge, wasn't bad at all. When the piece ended, Andi was beaming with excitement. "That was beautifully played," she said to the conductor. "And just the right tempo. Was it a Strauss waltz?"

"Yes, ma'am. Johann Strauss II's *Voices of Spring Waltz.*"

"I could dance to it all night."

"Then please humor us as we go through it one more time."

Jamie welcomed the chance to hold Andi again.

"Wonderful," the conductor said when the piece ended. "Thank you very much. We'll dedicate this piece to you tomorrow evening if you'll give Mister Timmons your names." He then cued up the orchestra for another waltz.

"Are you staying in the hotel?" Mister Timmons said.

"Yes," Jamie said. "We have the Presidential Suite for the next several nights."

"The Presidential Suite? Then you must be Major Jamie Collins. Mister Ashburn asked me to extend his invitation for you two to be his guests at tomorrow's ball."

"We'd gladly accept," Andi said before Jamie could decline the offer. "But we didn't bring any formal attire."

"You needn't worry. The Palace has a contract with a rental company that will outfit you like royalty. I can have one of their representatives come to your suite within the hour and take your measurements."

Jamie couldn't stop himself from thinking of what he'd rather be doing in their room within the hour. But they were there to chase away Andi's nightmares. And he'd promised Howard Ashburn he wouldn't take advantage of the situation.

Andi was so excited about the Spring Ball there was no way Jamie was going to disappoint her. "That's perfect," Jamie said to Mister Timmons.

There was a cheerful blaze in their fireplace when Jamie and Andi returned to their suite.

The evening attire rental company's representative came and took Andi and Jamie's measurements and was soon gone.

The next several hours were spent cuddling against each other on their leather couch, watching the flames dance about while Jamie and Andi got to know each other better. Inevitably, only glowing embers remained. Andi yawned. "It's been a big day. Why don't we turn in?"

She took him by the hand and led him to their bedroom. She stopped at the foot of their four-poster bed and turned her back to him. "Would asking you to help with my buttons be too provocative?"

Jamie bowed. "Not at all. I'm always happy to assist a lady." With trembling hands, he started at her top button but soon gasped.

A wicked-looking, three-inch-long welt zigzagged down the back of her right shoulder. "Oh, Andi, my brave soldier." He kissed her battle scar as though that would remove this insult to her otherwise flawless skin. "Hendricks told me how stoic you were when he sutured your shrapnel wound—and how he nearly fainted."

"My scar's nothing compared to those of some of my patients."

"You were a noncombatant." He tenderly ran his fingertip over the scar's rough edges. "This should never have happened to you."

"It's my red badge of courage." She glanced over her shoulder. "It gives me the right to look an injured man in the face and tell him I know something about what he's going through." She turned and faced Jamie. "And it brings me closer to you." She kissed him, which he was sure he would never tire of. "If you'll excuse me, I'll run into the bathroom and change into my night clothes."

Jamie bowed. "Certainly, my lady." He retreated to the guest bathroom, where he washed up quickly and put on a fresh set of pajamas he'd stolen from the hospital. On his way back to their bedroom, he turned off all the lights in their suite except for a small lamp in their library and one bedside. The thought of being in total darkness still terrified him.

When Andi stepped out of the master bathroom, Jamie had to hold onto one of the posts of their four-poster bed. With the bathroom light on behind her, it was immediately apparent that she wasn't wearing anything beneath her nightshirt. The hint of what was barely concealed was more erotic than if she had been naked. It would be a challenge merely to hold her throughout the night.

"Did you steal those pajamas from my ward, soldier?" She flipped off the bathroom light, giving Jamie a chance to come back to earth.

"Yes, ma'am. I hope you can find it in your heart to forgive me. I've never owned a pair of pajamas. I was required to wear them in the hospital. In the trenches, I slept in my uniform. Before the army, I slept naked." He immediately regretted that disclosure as being far too suggestive.

Andi smiled shyly. "I believe that's healthier. I bought this cotton nightshirt for this occasion, thinking it would be a good compromise between being bound up head to foot and wearing nothing at all." She stepped closer. "If you're like me, you'll be more comfortable without your top. Feel free to remove it."

Jamie's mouth had gone so dry he was unable to speak. His hands shook as he struggled with the buttons.

Andi helped. As an experienced nurse, she showed no reaction to his hideous shrapnel scars.

She took Jamie by the hand and led him to their bed. She pulled back the covers and held them up for Jamie to slip between the sheets. Andi followed and snuggled up against him.

"Do you think you'll be able to sleep with a stranger in your bed?" Jamie said.

"You're not a stranger." She sounded slightly hurt. "We've been together every day since early March."

"I was beginning to think you never took a day off."

"I wondered if you'd notice."

"You mean it's true?"

"Yes." She put her hand on his cheek. "Initially, I came in every day because I was curious about you. Then, it was because I was fascinated. Then it was because I couldn't stay away." She placed her hand over his heart. "Lastly, it was because I'd fallen in love with you."

He drew her even closer, pressing himself against her from head to toe. "I'll rephrase my earlier question. Do you think you'll be able to sleep with my arms around you?"

"I was able to sleep through air raids in France."

Jamie couldn't resist the urge to trace the curve of her hourglass waist. "Please understand that I'm no more immune to temptation than any other man. If we get carried away during the night, I'd like your assurance that we won't compromise your future with the ANC."

She raised her head from their shared pillow. "Compromise? In what way?"

"If the Army Nurse Corps won't allow their RNs to be married, I doubt they'd look favorably upon their new Assistant Dean of the School of Nursing being great with child."

Her demure smile was almost more than Jamie could resist.

"It's gentlemanly of you to be concerned., but you needn't worry. In case you've forgotten, I am a registered nurse. And before the war, I did a stint in an obstetrics and gynecology clinic."

"What? Why'd the army need an obstetrics and gynecology clinic?"

Andi rolled her eyes. "Soldiers have been known to marry."

Jamie laughed at himself. "Wives and daughters—I've been cooped up with single men so long I'd forgotten."

"I was also lead nurse on a year-long fertility study."

"Then I assume you know where babies come from."

"I have a pretty good idea." Her Nurse Eliot façade replaced her smile. "For our fertility study, we collected data from patients and nurse volunteers. Every woman is different. My reproductive cycle is remarkably stable at 28 days. My core temperature and urinalyses show that I ovulate almost exactly 14 days after the start of my menstrual period. That means I'm *infertile* for the twelve days that begin two days after ovulation." She turned her face toward him. "Those twelve days started this morning."

He sighed. "My dearest Andi," he put his hand on her hip, "thank you for the clinically precise, yet far from romantic, assurance." He pursed his lips. "Unfortunately, in this instance, your state of fertility may be of no consequence. Having overseen my recovery and knowing how conscientious you are, I'm sure you noticed in my medical records that I suffered serious shrapnel wounds to my groin."

"From which you have recovered."

"Perhaps. Perhaps not. Since you were blunt with me, I'll be equally blunt with you. While I was paralyzed, the doctors said they had no way of knowing the state of the ducts and tubes that are critical to reproductive competence. Once I regained feeling below my waist, I was afraid to bring up the subject again for fear of what I might learn." He took a deep breath. "You say you'll be infertile for the next twelve days? I may be for life."

"And you're worried that would make you less of a man?" She shook her head. "To me, you're perfect."

He half-sat up and leaned on his elbow. "You mean . . .?. . . Are you saying . . .?" He swallowed hard. "Knowing I may be unable to father children, you'd still consider a future with me?"

Andi sat up all the way. "After my second fiancé died, I reconciled myself to dying a childless old maid." She smiled. "Then you came into my life. You're more than I could ever ask for."

Jamie could barely speak. "I . . . I've been afraid you'd leave me if we were to marry, and I was unable to give you children."

She tenderly placed her hand on his cheek. "You have a far greater legacy than biological children. You can be credited with bringing generations of children into this world."

"What children?"

"Those born to the men in your infantry company—the men you saved. Your men's bloodlines would have ended with them if not for you. And think of the men on our ward to whom you gave new life. You are the patriarch of an ever-expanding tribe. And if you were to honor me by making me your wife, I would be their matriarch. What you can or can't give me biologically pales by comparison."

Jamie was so relieved he could hardly breathe. He pushed her onto her back and practically climbed on top of her. "I do love you, Andi Eliot."

He realized she was holding her breath. "I'm sorry," he

said. "I should be more sensitive. I'm merely reaching for the lamp. It's time we chase away your nightmares."

She laughed—a shallow laugh of relief. "I was sure you had something else in mind."

He turned off their bedside lamp and rolled onto his side, facing her. "I haven't forgotten why we're here. We're going to chase your nightmares, and we're going to do it using something called 'dream shaping.'"

"Dream shaping?"

"I read about it in Letterman's medical library."

"I'll try anything," Andi said. "Tell me what to do."

"Think of a new ending for your recurring nightmare, a way you'd like it to end. Then concentrate on that ending as you fall asleep. When your dream comes again, it will have the new ending."

Andi clutched their blanket and adamantly shook her head. "I never want that nightmare to come again, no matter the ending."

"I'll be here to protect you."

She trustingly let go of their blanket. "All right. You've obviously given this some thought. What new ending do you suggest?"

"I've given it a lot of thought." He'd been anguishing over it for days. "Here's what I want you to do. Picture me standing between you and the ghosts of the men you couldn't save. They'll recognize me as one of their own who is alive again. That will give me authority over them. I'll order them to retreat—and they will obey."

Andi was silent for several seconds as though she was waiting for more. "That's it?" She sounded more than dubious. "Can anything so simple really make a difference?"

"Scientists always look for the simplest solution to any

problem. Give dream shaping a try. You'll discover that you have control over your dreams. Then we'll take the next step toward banishing your nightmare forever."

"Are . . . are you sure about this?"

He had to sound confident to give her courage. "The Navajo have been using dream shaping successfully for centuries. And I'll be right by your side. I'll keep you safe. Now let's get started. You've said that in your nightmare, you see yourself standing on a hillside overlooking a graveyard somewhere in France. The dead rise from their graves and approach you. Picture me there standing between you and them."

"The scene is so terrible, I don't want you to see what I see every night."

"The dead don't frighten me. I was one of them. I know all they want is peace."

She let go of their blanket. "Okay. I'll try this dream shaping—so long as you promise to hold me."

"A team of Belgian draft horses couldn't drag me away."

Andi rehearsed the new ending with Jamie until she was ready. She then trustingly rolled onto her side with her back to him. He wrapped his arms around her and held her tight.

To his amazement, she was soon asleep.

Her faith in him made him feel like he could conquer the world. He was supposedly there to protect her. Yet, with her so close, he felt safer than he had since his infantry company was sent overseas.

"Darkness, darkness," he whispered to the night, "you have no hold on me. This good woman has set me free."

Jamie's fears were put to bed, and he drifted off to sleep.

Chapter 4

Sweet Dreams

Before sunrise, Saturday, 31 May 1919

Jamie was awakened by Andi violently thrashing about and shouting incoherently. He was afraid she might hurt herself. He tried to restrain her. She was much stronger than he expected.

"Wake up, Andi. Wake up. You're safe. The war's over. The world's at peace."

She woke with a start. He could feel her heart racing. "Oh, Jamie, I dreamt I was back on that hillside overlooking the graveyard. The dead rose from their graves. They were closing in on me."

Jamie was desperate. "But I was there in your dream, wasn't I?"

"Yes. And I was so frightened for you. But you didn't waver at the sight of their wounds. Missing arms. Missing legs. Gaping holes in their chests."

"Did I order them to retreat?"

Andi's heart was still racing. "You did. And they obeyed!"

"Then take courage. We've demonstrated that you have control over your dreams."

He reached out and turned on his bedside lamp. "Now, let's take the next step toward freeing you of this nightmare."

He laid her on her back and tucked their blanket around her shoulders. "I've been asking myself why the soldiers you couldn't save appear in your dreams. Could it be that you haven't fully come to terms with the cold, hard fact that you couldn't save them all?"

Her chin began to tremble. Tears ran down her cheeks. "I did everything humanly possible, and still, they died by the dozen. There were just so many of them. If only we'd had more nurses. If only I could have been in two places at once."

"If only you could have done the impossible." He wiped her cheek. "As you said, you did everything humanly possible. Beyond that, life and death weren't in your hands. You must accept that. Then we can give your dream a final ending, and it will never invade your sleep again."

"I'll do whatever you say. Just hold me."

"I intend to." For the rest of their lives if his dream came true. "Now picture all your patients who didn't survive rising from their graves fully restored. Watch as they walk away and disappear forever through a distant field of golden poppies. Will you do that? For me?"

"For you, anything." Andi closed her eyes.

"Do you see them? Fully restored?"

"I . . . I do. Walking away. Fully restored. Disappearing one by one beyond a field of poppies."

"Now concentrate on that image to the exclusion of all

else. Let yourself drift off to sleep. When your dream comes again, it will have the new ending, and those soldiers you saw disappear will never bother you again."

Andi rolled onto her side with her back pressed against Jamie. Her body relaxed. Amazingly, she was soon asleep.

"I love you, Andi Eliot," he whispered in her ear.

The soothing sound of her untroubled breathing was like a lullaby to his ears.

* * *

Saturday morning, 31 May 1919

Jamie woke to find Andi staring at him with the most angelic smile. "My dream did come again—with the new ending. And it didn't wake me. I slept soundly for the first time in as long as I can remember."

This was fantastic progress, but only the first stage in what could be a lengthy process. Yet Jamie was greatly relieved. If dream shaping didn't work, he had no idea what to try next. But try, he would. Jamie knew the torment of nightmares. He hated to think Andi was suffering as he had.

"Even now," Andi said, "as I think of the patients I lost, I picture them fully restored, walking through a beautiful field of poppies where before I saw only graves."

"Your patients are at peace, and now you can be too."

Andi's smile eroded into a look of concern. "Can it really be that simple?"

"There's still work to be done. We'll need you to rehearse seeing your patients fully restored until that image is firmly implanted in your subconscious mind. And luckily for me, that means I'll need to hold you until you're fully confident that dream shaping worked. Once we've reached that stage, the ghosts of the men you couldn't save will never bother you again."

Andi lowered her eyes. "You must think I'm a terrible tease asking you to hold me throughout the night and not—"

Jamie interrupted her. "I do not. I know how terrifying dreams can be. Why do you think I used to sleep with a light on in my room?"

"You, Jamie Collins, are a dear." She kissed him tenderly.

"I hope you'll still think I'm a dear after I tell you what I want to do next."

Andi pressed herself even tighter to him. "I think I can guess."

"I'm sure you can't." He was almost embarrassed to say it. "I want us to go on a picnic."

Andi's eyes narrowed. "A picnic," she repeated tentatively.

"Hard to believe, but true." He didn't dare tell her that if they didn't get out of that room soon, his promise to Howard not to take advantage of the situation—and to himself that he would do everything right with Andi—would fall by the wayside.

"A picnic," Andi said again. "Like a couple of carefree kids." The corners of her mouth slowly turned upward. "What a lovely idea." She stared off into the distance. "I didn't have much chance to be a wide-eyed, carefree little girl growing up. With our mother gone, I took it upon myself to stand in as mother for my younger sisters." Her smile lit up the room. "I'd love to spend a few carefree hours in the fresh air with you. No longer a responsible adult; no pretense of being a sexy woman; just the wide-eyed, carefree little girl I never was."

Andi threw back their covers and sat on the edge of the bed. She twisted at the waist and looked at Jamie over her shoulder. "Jamie Collins, you're better than a dream come true because I've never dreamt of anyone as wonderful as you."

He jumped out of bed, rushed into their library, returned with a pamphlet, and handed it to Andi. "I noticed this pamphlet earlier and have been thinking about it ever since. The Palace suggests a picnic in Golden Gate Park, which is only about five miles from here. Our hotel will provide a picnic basket. Their estate wagon will drop us off and pick us up." He took a deep breath. "What do you say?"

Andi rose. "A picnic in Golden Gate Park with my hero and best friend—what a wonderful idea."

* * *

Being an army nurse, Andi showered and dressed in no time —she claimed that a lukewarm shower was more invigorating and, therefore, more healthful than a hot bath. Jamie had noticed that she didn't use makeup—few "respectable" women did, although, in these modern times, more and more were beginning to. She was, however, very particular about her hair. She put on a narrow-waisted, sleeveless, floral dress that featured a modest round neckline—a dress that was modesty itself.

As Jamie and Andi exited the elevator, he stepped in front of her and rapidly scanned the hotel lobby. He hoped that someday he'd fully adapt to being back in the States and not be so wary of his surroundings. Thankfully, neither Angry Man nor Sly were in sight.

Another couple joined them in the Palace's estate wagon. The couples were friendly enough, but it was clear they would rather go their separate ways.

Their driver stopped beside a grassy area near Golden Gate Park's Japanese Tea Garden. From the wagon's rear compartment, he passed each couple a picnic basket prepared by the Palace's kitchen staff. "I'll be back to pick you up no later than 2:30," he promised.

After exchanging pleasantries with the other couple, Jamie and Andi headed off on their own.

Jamie hadn't felt so free since his infantry unit was activated. Then he saw Angry Man and Sly. Oddly, they arrived in separate taxicabs and seemed to pay no attention to each other. Jamie feared that he might end up in jail for what he'd do to them if they got anywhere near Andi. She seemed oblivious to their existence.

He realized Andi was staring at him. "I'm sorry. It's going to take a while for me to adjust to a world at peace. I keep looking over my shoulder for the enemy when I know the real enemy is in here." He tapped his forehead.

Andi took his hand. "It's my job to help you defeat that enemy. Now relax. I'll keep watch and make sure no one sneaks up on us."

It was Jamie's turn to stare at Andi. Was she aware of the men Jamie believed were following them? He stopped himself from asking. If she hadn't noticed them, he didn't want to worry her. His mission was to help conquer her fears, not add to them.

They shared the load as they carried their picnic basket

along a paved path toward the east. After a hundred yards, they veered north and crossed an expanse of manicured lawn.

Jamie brought their little procession to a halt just short of a thick stand of Cypress trees where no one could approach them without being seen. "This looks like a perfect place for a picnic," he said. They set their basket down.

Jamie arched his back and stretched out his arms. "It's such a treat to be outside in the fresh air and sunshine without someone shooting at me."

"And we're together," Andi said.

They spread out the blanket the Palace had provided. Andi knelt and extracted the food items from their basket.

The Palace's kitchen staff had been thoughtful. Along with sliced chicken breast, Jamie especially appreciated the fruit compote and freshly baked cookies. Letterman Army Hospital wasn't renowned for its cookies.

Andi playfully slapped Jamie's hand away as he reached for a cookie. "Hasn't anyone told you dessert comes last?"

Jamie quickly withdrew his chastened hand. He feigned injury. "You pack a wallop."

"Here, let me kiss it better." She took his hand, turned it over, kissed his open palm, and held it to her cheek.

Jamie basked in her warmth. "I bet you didn't learn this treatment in nursing school."

She smiled. "Perhaps I should add it to the ASN's curriculum."

Andi laid out their lunch items with such geometric precision it was almost a shame to eat anything. Nevertheless, Jamie dug in like the trench rat he was. Andi was much more cultured in her partaking. Nothing went to waste.

After they'd eaten their fill, Andi sat with her legs straight out in front of her. Jamie lay on his back with his head on her lap. She playfully ran her fingers through his hair.

"You look tired," she said. "Close your eyes. I'll keep watch and make sure no one steals our leftovers."

Was that an oblique way of telling him she'd noticed they were being followed?

Regardless, Andi was right. He was tired. He'd been so keyed up during the night he'd only slept intermittently. The Army taught him that soldiers need sleep to remain sharp and effective. In the trenches, Jamie had developed the ability to sleep while surrounded by danger, knowing he'd be fully awake in an instant if the sentry he'd posted woke him. He could trust Andi to keep watch. She'd been keeping watch over her patients her entire career.

Jamie soon dozed off.

* * *

When he woke and realized where he was—more importantly, who he was with—Jamie said a heartfelt prayer of thanks, which was fitting. From his perspective, Andi's head eclipsed the sun. She could have been the model for a Renaissance painting of an angel.

"You make a fabulous pillow," he said.

"I'm glad—except my leg has gone to sleep."

Jamie instantly sat up. "I'm sorry. I'd be happy to massage it for you."

Andi laughed as she rubbed her thigh. "I'll take a rain check." Her smile faded. "Were you dreaming just now? You seemed agitated. I hope you weren't having a nightmare about the war."

"No. The war's over. I was dreaming about something else that's been troubling me."

"Do you want to talk about it?"

He didn't even want to think about it, but Andi had a right to know. "I think we should."

She leaned back. "That sounds a bit ominous."

"I'm worried about my involvement in the charity I agreed to help get off the ground."

"The one that's supposed to help educate disabled veterans?"

He nodded. "It will be called the Disabled Veterans' Education Trust, or DVET.

"Why would you be worried about your involvement in the DVET? It strikes me as a great cause."

"It's not the cause I'm worried about. It's the man who's backing it. He's one of the most generous philanthropists on the West Coast," Jamie sighed, "which would be great, except he's also rumored to be the most consummate racketeer."

Andi stared at Jamie. "Seriously?"

" 'fraid so. I've been having nightmares about agreeing to work with him."

"You're right," Andi said. "We should talk about it."

Now that the horse was out of the corral, Jamie had to ride it. "I met him about two weeks ago when Lieutenant Colonel Hunt, the deputy base commander, escorted him onto our ward for a visit with Butch." Jamie raised his chin. "I don't believe you were present at the time."

"I'm sure I wasn't. I would have remembered the deputy base commander visiting our ward."

Although there wasn't anyone within fifty yards of them, Jamie leaned a little closer and lowered his voice. "The man with Colonel Hunt was Matt Kavanaugh."

Initially, there was no indication Andi knew who Jamie was talking about.

"Wait," Andi said. "I've read about Matt Kavanaugh. And seen his picture in the newspapers." She took a startled breath. "Is he the man I almost collided with as I was leaving your room earlier this week?"

"He was."

"I thought he looked familiar."

"You've never met him?"

Andi looked at Jamie as though he'd asked if she'd ever visited Saturn. "Of course not. Where would I meet such a man?"

"Perhaps you've exchanged a word or two about my condition?"

Andi assumed her Nurse Eliot persona. "I'd never discuss a patient's condition with a stranger."

A stranger. The way she said it, she'd have to be a great actress for that not to be the case.

"This is all rather unsettling," Andi said. She stared at Jamie. "Why do you know such a man?"

"Butch worked for Matt Kavanaugh before the war. The day Mister Kavanaugh came to visit Butch, I happened to be in Butch's room."

"And Colonel Hunt? Where does he come into the picture?"

"Colonel Hunt oversees the fist full of contracts for services and supplies Mister Kavanaugh has with the base."

Andi canted her head. "Why was Kavanaugh entering your room the day I almost collided with him?"

Why indeed. "He'd come to see whether I was still going to help with the DVET."

"Helping how, exactly?" Andi said.

"Mister Kavanaugh just wants me to show up in uniform at fundraising events and say the right things."

"That's all?" Andi shrugged. "Surely, you're not worried about speaking at fundraising events. As a professor, isn't public speaking what you do for a living?"

"Public speaking isn't the problem. And it's for a great cause. But the fundraising reception I asked you to attend with me? Mister Kavanagh will be the host, and his guests will be some of his closest business associates. Their reputations are likely to be as sordid as his." Jamie lowered his head. "I'm crazy to get involved with such people. And even crazier to drag you into such a den of thieves."

Andi gave Jamie a penetrating look. "And yet you call a man like Matt Kavanaugh 'Mister.'"

"I'd call the devil 'Mister' if he'd help educate our disabled veterans."

The way Andi looked at him, Jamie was afraid he was close to scaring her off. And he hadn't even told her the worst of it yet. "There's more," he said.

"I'm not sure I want to hear it."

And he wasn't sure he wanted to tell her. But she deserved to know the truth. "Mister Kavanagh is willing to provide the initial funding for the DVET. But he doesn't want to be the sole benefactor. So he's going to offer his associates 'incentives' to persuade them to be equally generous."

"What kind of incentives?"

"For every dollar one of his associates donates over a

certain amount, he's going to throw in another fifty cents out of his own pocket."

"What's wrong with that?" Andi said. "It's a generous offer."

"The problem is how Mister Kavanagh plans to persuade his less generous associates to donate. To entice them to open their wallets wide, he plans to offer them inflated charitable donation receipts they can use to reduce their personal income tax."

Andi crossed her arms. "When you say 'inflated,' do you mean 'fraudulent?'"

"I do."

"Then you're talking about tax fraud." Andi swallowed hard. "And you're willing to go along with that?"

Her tone was enough to make Jamie wince. "That's what's been keeping me awake at night. I don't want to become an accessory to a crime, but I'm afraid Mister Kavanaugh will abandon the whole idea of the DVET if I don't go along."

"That's extortion," Andi said.

Jamie nodded. "I agree. And it's so unnecessary. There's not much I wouldn't do for our disabled vets, and no one has to twist my arm." He took her hand. "But I don't want to do anything that will jeopardize our relationship—or endanger you in any way."

Andi was silent for a moment. Then she surprised him with a smile. "You needn't worry about jeopardizing our relationship. I understand what you'd be doing and why. Nor am I afraid to enter a den of thieves. Remember, I'm an Army nurse. I'm used to facing danger when it's necessary to get a job done. So go ahead. Do what's needed. I'll be right beside you."

"Really?"

"Really. If one of *Mister* Kavanaugh's associates accepts an inflated receipt and uses it to defraud the government, that will be on his associate, not us."

"That's pretty much the same argument Mister Kavanaugh gave me. I didn't buy it from him, but hearing it from you, it's almost convincing."

"Almost?"

Jamie shrugged.

Andi gave him a penetrating look. "Why do I get the feeling Mister Kavanaugh wants more from you than just help raising money for the DVET?"

Jamie shook his head. "The way you can read my mind, I better keep my thoughts from wandering into the prurient, or I might get slapped."

Andi lowered her gaze and looked up at him. "Not if I'm thinking along similar lines."

A jolt of lust coursed through Jamie. But this was neither the time nor place. "Fortunately, the rest of what he wants from me doesn't involve anything illegal."

"Perhaps you should have told me about that first."

It took a moment for Jamie to figure out where to begin. "A few days after I first met Mister Kavanaugh, I was told he wanted to see me in private. We met in Letterman's chapel. After discussing the particulars of the DVET, he said he wanted to tell me about a plan he's putting in effect that will protect the jobs of hundreds of his hardworking, honest employees and assure the continuance of his charities."

"Why?" Andi said.

"Why what?"

"Why did he want to tell you?"

Jamie had to be honest with Andi if he wanted her to be honest with him. "Mister Kavanaugh's hoping I'll help."

"Really." She canted her head. "I can't imagine his plan requiring the expertise of a theoretical physicist."

"You're right. My history of helping others regardless of the consequences is what interests him."

"Consequences?" Andi said. "It sounds as though this plan of his could be dangerous."

"It could be." Jamie became lost in thought.

"Go on," Andi said.

"Mister Kavanaugh wants to retire, but he doesn't want control of Kavanaugh Enterprises to fall into the hands of his nephew, Sonny. So Mister Kavanaugh's in the process of transferring all his businesses and charities to a trust."

"What's wrong with his nephew?"

"Simply put, Sonny is a psychopath."

Now Andi seemed even more on edge.

"By putting Kavanaugh Enterprises in a business trust," Jamie said, "control will be delegated to a trustee who'll have a fiduciary duty to act in the best interests of the trust's beneficiaries. And you'll like this: Mister Kavanaugh's declaration of trust stipulates that all future Trust transactions must be carried out in strict accordance with the letter and spirit of the law."

"I do like that. So, who are the beneficiaries?"

"Initially, around a thousand honest, hardworking employees of Kavanaugh Enterprises and the numerous charities it supports."

"And ultimately?"

"All Mister Kavanaugh would tell me is it won't be Sonny. And that's a problem. Sonny isn't going to be happy about Mister Kavanaugh's plans."

"Have you ever met Sonny?"

"Here's an amazing twist of fate. Sonny went to the same high school as me and Butch. He was a bully and a thug then. According to all accounts, he's even worse now. Rumor has it that he'll stop at nothing to get what he wants."

Andi put her hand on Jamie's forearm. "I don't like where this is headed. Please tell me Mister Kavanaugh hasn't asked you to be one of the trust's officers."

"Worse than that. He's asked me to be his trustee."

"That's preposterous! You two are practically strangers." Her eyes opened wide. "Aren't you?"

"We are. But there's nothing in the law that says a trustor has to know his trustee. In fact, if the trustee's independence is important, it might be better if they're practically strangers."

"But . . . but you're a physicist, not a businessman."

"Mister Kavanaugh's well aware of that. If I accept the job, he wants me to hire a good general manager to oversee the trusts' daily affairs."

"Then what role would you play?"

Jamie averted his eyes. "He wants me to be the trust's moral compass."

"Moral compass?" Andi couldn't have sounded more incredulous. "You just told me you were going to be an accessory to tax fraud."

"Crazy, isn't it? Being trustee would be a balancing act between doing what's right and what's legal, which aren't necessarily the same thing."

Andi stared at Jamie as though he was crazy. "You're not seriously considering accepting the job, are you?"

"I could do a lot of good for Kavanaugh Enterprises' employees and the charities it supports. And Mister

Kavanaugh believes I have what it takes to stand up to Sonny."

Andi looked scared. "But you could get hurt in the process."

"Mister Kavanaugh has thought of that. As a form of insurance, he's had his lawyers insert a clause in his declaration of trust clearly stating that if anything bad happens to his trustee, his trustee's family or household, or any of the Trust's officers over the next five years and there's even a hint that Sonny is responsible, the Trust will immediately be dissolved, and all its assets will be distributed as Mister Kavanaugh has predetermined—specifically excluding Sonny. Mister Kavanaugh assures me that clause will have Sonny praying that neither the trustee nor anyone associated with him catches so much as a cold for the next five years."

"What's five years got to do with it?"

"Again, Mister Kavanaugh wouldn't tell me, other than to say he's sure I'll like it."

"And you trust him?"

"I'm not sure. Which is one reason I invited you to Mister Kavanaugh's DVET reception. I'd like you to meet him and help me decide what to do."

Andi smiled. "I'm always happy to offer an opinion, even when not asked."

Jamie felt bad that he wasn't being completely open with Andi. Another reason he wanted to bring her and Kavanaugh together was to confirm that they didn't already know each other and crush any lingering doubts he had about them conspiring together.

"What scares me," Jamie said, "is if I can so easily rationalize that reforming Kavanaugh Enterprises will atone for the minor sin of aiding and abetting tax fraud, I might start rationalizing away other sins and eventually find myself so deeply imbedded in Mister Kavanaugh's world that I wouldn't be able to escape."

The color drained from Andi's face. "I don't feel like a carefree little girl any longer." She suddenly sat up straight. "What time is it?"

Jamie extracted his pocket watch from his vest. "Two-twenty."

Andi started packing the last items into their picnic basket. "We mustn't be late for our ride back to the Palace."

* * *

At precisely two-thirty, Jamie and Andi arrived at their pick-up point for their ride back to the Palace Hotel. No one seemed to be following them, which was good. Jamie didn't think he could handle any more stress.

They rode back in silence. Jamie was terrified that he'd stepped over the line with Andi. To make the ride even more stressful, Jamie experienced his first traffic jam. He wouldn't be sorry if it were his last.

When they reached their suite, Jamie finally broke the silence. "I'm sorry I ruined our picnic."

Andi smiled for the first time in half an hour. "You didn't. It was great fun pretending to be a kid."

"But you haven't said a word since we left the park."

She avoided eye contact. "You gave me a lot to think about."

Jamie would have been less concerned if a live grenade were rolling around at his feet. "I hope you're not having second thoughts about our relationship"

"Certainly not." She took his hand. "There was never

any question that I'd help make the DVET a success. My concern is *why* I'm willing to help."

"Isn't educating disabled veterans reason enough?"

"Never forget, I'm an *army* nurse—a soldier, like you. Soldiers are trained for battle. If we don't have an enemy to fight, we become restless. In France, the Kaiser's men intended to destroy us. Instead, they brought us together. Wealth, religion, skin color, even gender aside, we became family."

She sighed. "I miss that camaraderie. And that's a big reason I want to help with the DVET. I hope to recapture some of that feeling. You, me, Matt Kavanaugh, three people who, on the surface, appear to have nothing in common, pitted against those who would discard our disabled veterans." She smiled. "Like it was for your Brotherhood of Loss, we'll be family."

"And the Kavanaugh Trust?"

"Someone has to stand up to the likes of Sonny Kavanaugh," she said. "Why not us?"

"Us?!"

"I'm going to be right by your side, making sure you don't become so deeply embedded in Mister Kavanaugh's world that you can't escape."

Jamie had never felt so honored. "Those who haven't experienced war will never understand us."

"Which is one of the many reasons I believe we were made for each other." Andi clasped her hands. "Now we need to go shopping again."

"Shopping?"

"I'll need to wear the right dress if we're going to impress Mister Kavanaugh's guests."

"You'd impress them even if you didn't wear anything at

all." Jamie's cheeks burned. "That didn't come out quite right."

Andi laughed. "I know what you meant—at least, I think I do."

"Let's go to that department store your cousin likes so much."

"The City of Paris?" Andi nodded. "Let's."

* * *

Late Saturday afternoon, 31 May 1919

Jamie walked proudly with Andi by his side. As they approached Union Square, he spotted Angry Man and Sly. They still seemed to be ignoring each other. So long as they stayed on the other side of the street, Jamie needn't worry about going to jail for what he'd do to them if they got close to Andi.

She led Jamie into the multi-story Beaux Arts City of Paris Department Store. He didn't think Angry Man or Sly would have the audacity to follow them, especially not into the women's clothing department. Jamie would be conspicuous even in Andi's company. Two unaccompanied men might as well wear signs saying they didn't belong.

An attendant descended upon Andi. "Welcome. May I be of assistance?" Her name tag identified her as Sheila.

"Yes, please," Andi said with a smile. "I'm looking for a dress to wear to a semi-formal gathering."

Sheila led Andi around the department with Jamie in tow. Being the only man on the floor, he was seriously outnumbered. He was brave enough to handle that, so long as Andi was there to protect him.

They picked out several dresses for Andi to try on.

"Which would you like to see first?" she asked Jamie.

He didn't answer immediately. He'd become intrigued by one Andi passed over with barely a glance. He handed it to Andi. She examined its plunging neckline. "I don't think so."

"Indulge me."

Sheila led Andi to the changing room. When they returned, Andi looked even more like a goddess than usual. "I can't wear this in public. It's far too revealing. It would send the wrong message to Mister Kavanaugh and his guests."

"I wouldn't want that," Jamie said.

From the dresses they had selected earlier, Andi proposed trying on the most conservative one.

Jamie shook his head. "I don't think that projects the right image either."

"I have an idea," Sheila said. "We recently had a fashion show, and several of the show dresses are still in the stock room. I think I know just the one for you. The show's catalog described it as a short-sleeved, unadorned, narrow-belted, calf-length sheath dress with a bateau neckline—a description that hardly does it justice. Wait until you see it!"

Few of those terms had any meaning to Jamie. He'd judge the dress for himself.

Sheila was gone for only a minute. "This dress is from the Evangeline House of Fashion in Paris."

"It looks like a fine dress to me," Jamie said. "Why were you keeping it in the back room?"

Sheila held the dress up to Andi. "Because only one woman in ten thousand has a figure fine enough to wear it."

Sheila looked Andi up and down. "Not even the most

expensive tailor-made corset could simulate a figure as fine as yours. It would be a shame to hide it."

Sheila ushered Andi back to the changing room. When they returned, Jamie was afraid he might melt. His heart pounded. The dress Sheila had picked out managed to be both revealing and modest.

He took both her hands. "You are absolutely gorgeous."

Sheila beamed. "One would think Evangeline had tailored this dress specifically for you."

As Andi did a pirouette, Sheila gasped.

Andi came to an abrupt standstill. "What's the matter?"

Sheila was clearly embarrassed. "I'm sorry. That was rude of me."

"What?" Andi said as she turned to Jamie.

"The top half of your shrapnel scar shows."

Andi looked at herself in one of the many mirrors around the floor. A smile slowly replaced her initial frown. "That could work to our benefit. Mister Kavanaugh's guests might be interested in the story behind it."

"Sold!" Jamie said to Sheila.

Andi put her hands on her hips. "You didn't ask the price."

"I don't care how much it costs—so long as Sheila isn't planning to retire off her commission from this one item."

Sheila laughed. "No, sir. Although it's an original, we'll soon be selling reproductions. We're only asking what we'll be charging for the copies."

"She'll need shoes and a purse to go with it, won't she?" Jamie said.

"Yes, sir." Sheila rubbed her hands together and laughed. "My commission keeps growing and growing." She got Andi's shoe size and went to collect a few likely candidates.

Jamie looked Andi up and down. "There's a problem with that dress."

Andi looked at herself in a floor-to-ceiling mirror as she turned this way and that. "It looks fine to me."

"That's the problem. Mister Kavanaugh and every potential donor at his reception will assume a young woman as beautiful as you can only be there as an ornament."

Andi gave that a moment's thought. "They'll have seen my shrapnel scar. Tell them the story behind my Distinguished Service Cross. That should change the way they see me."

"Really? You wouldn't mind?"

"Yes, I'd mind," she raised her chin, "but at the risk of sounding terribly conceited, it's about time a good-looking woman is seen as an agent for positive change rather than a mere ornament."

Jamie hugged her tightly. "Andrea Jean Eliot, together we're going to change the world!"

* * *

Saturday evening, 31 May 1919

Jamie's rented tuxedo was a perfect fit. Together, with Andi's evening gown, they made a striking couple.

"As an Army nurse," she said, "I never dreamt I'd wear anything this spectacular."

"And I never dreamt I'd get to escort such a beautiful woman to a ball in a hotel like The Palace."

The ballroom manager seated them at a central table adjacent to the dance floor. The conductor faced the audience and raised his baton. "It's the Palace's tradition to open the spring ball with Johann Strauss II's *Voices of Spring Waltz*. This evening, it's my privilege to invite Professor Jamie Collins and Miss Andrea Eliot to be the first couple on the dance floor."

To Jamie, this moment held great significance. Without Andi's help and encouragement, he might never have walked again. And after hiding their relationship while Jamie was on their ward, the conductor's invitation was a public proclamation that he was her man and she was his woman.

The evening passed all too quickly. Eventually, the orchestra played the *Voices of Spring Waltz* a final time to end the ball.

"Thank you for a perfect evening," Andi said to Jamie as they made their way to their suite.

* * *

Saturday bedtime, 31 May 1919

Andi sat in front of their vanity, brushing her luxuriant copper hair. Jamie was propped up in their bed, studying her reflection in the mirror in fascinated silence. Occasionally, their eyes met, and she would smile. She turned to him. "What would you like to do tomorrow?"

"It's been a long time since I was able to attend a regular worship service. Do you know of a church nearby that would let a wretch like me pass through their door?"

"I've been to the Old First Presbyterian Church a few times, and they didn't stone me."

Jamie threw back the covers and patted the mattress. "Come to bed. It's time we reinforce your confidence in dream shaping."

Andi removed the plush robe that came with the Presidential Suite. Beneath, she still wore her cotton nightshirt. Jamie still wore his pajama bottoms. He'd promised Howard Ashburn he wouldn't take advantage of the situation, and he always kept his promises—at least he tried. They cuddled like a married couple who already had four kids and didn't want any more.

Chapter 5

The Old First

Sunday morning, 01 June 1919

Andi's hand felt warm in Jamie's as they admired the architecture of Old First Presbyterian Church. Jamie felt a tap on his shoulder. In one motion, he spun around and stepped between his assailant and Andi, ready to kill.

A gentleman in his fifties quickly raised his hands in surrender. "I'm sorry. I didn't mean to startle you."

Jamie exhaled loudly. "That's okay. I'm still a little jumpy, that's all."

"Would I be correct in assuming you fought in the war?"

"You would."

"Then welcome home, and thanks for standing up for our country."

Jamie was speechless. It was a pleasant surprise to be thanked by a stranger.

Andi took Jamie's upper arm in both hands and smiled at her man.

"Please come in," their new friend said. "All are welcome." He climbed several steps and held the door of the church open. A gaggle of excited youngsters rushed inside. Andi had to do a quick sidestep to avoid a collision.

"Thank you, Mister Maxwell," the kids said in unison.

"Please excuse them," their unofficial doorman said.

"Certainly. I'm happy to see such enthusiasm." Andi entered the foyer on Jamie's arm.

Mister Maxwell smiled. "My name's Ed, but I also answer to Methuselah since I've been a member here longer than anyone can remember."

Jamie introduced Andi and himself and extended his hand. Ed shifted his Bible to his left hand. They shook.

"It's a pleasure to meet you both," Ed said. "Are you new in town?"

"Newly released," Jamie said.

Ed gave him a questioning look.

Andi rolled her eyes. "Please forgive Jamie. He likes to tease. This is his first time out in polite society after being a patient on my hospital ward for the past several months. I'm afraid he needs a bit of remedial training on how to act."

Ed and Jamie laughed.

"As the head nurse of my ward," Jamie said, "Andi oversaw my care." He put his arm around her waist.

Ed nodded. "Care for body and soul by all appearances."

Andi blushed.

The three of them entered the sanctuary together. Jamie was immediately mesmerized by the ornate brick- and woodwork.

"Old First is California's oldest continuously active protestant congregation," Ed said. "And hopefully the most welcoming."

"My father's a Presbyterian minister in Denver," Andi said. "He would be pleased if members of his congregation extended as warm a welcome as you have."

Ed smiled. "That's nice to hear."

"How old is your congregation?" Jamie said.

"We go way back to the first months of the 1849 gold rush."

Andi glanced around the sanctuary. "This building can't be that old."

"No, ma'am. This is our sixth church building on this site. The 1906 earthquake destroyed number five. The current building was completed in 1911."

Jamie pointed to the front of the sanctuary. "I love the arrangement of the organ pipes." And it was nice to see brass used for something other than shell casings.

"I can hardly wait to hear them," Andi said.

"You're in for a treat," Ed said. "We have a guest organist this morning. A musician of national repute—who happens to be my daughter."

"That's wonderful," Andi said. "It will be a pleasure to hear her play."

Ed smiled broadly. "Now, if you'll excuse me, I have duties to perform. After all these years, the congregation still trusts me to pass the collection plate." He gave them a wink. "I hope to see you after the service. I'd love to hear what you think of our guest organist." Ed greeted everyone he passed as if they were his dearest friends.

A young woman entered the enclosure surrounding the organ's three-keyboard console and sat. She had a serious, focused expression. Jamie and Andi found a pew with an unobstructed view of her.

Without warning, Miss Maxwell launched an ever-increasing volume of majestic sound.

"Look at the way she's practically dancing on the foot pedals," Jamie said.

Andi leaned against him. "What a blessing to have chosen this church on this day."

"We have to meet her," Jamie said.

"Absolutely."

The service followed the standard Presbyterian format Jamie and Andi were used to. After several hymns, The Reverend Doctor Clayton began his sermon by quoting John 15:13, "Greater love hath no man than this: that he lay down his life for his friends."

Reverend Clayton's words hit Jamie hard. He leaned forward and covered the back of his head with both hands, his chest almost touching his knees. His back heaved as he silently wept.

Andi put her arm around his shoulders as though she was trying to shield him, as she had her patients in France when shrapnel came whizzing through her hospital tent.

"I can see the face of every man I lost," Jamie whispered.

"No one did more for their men than you. No one."

"I could have done more. I *should* have done more."

It wasn't until Doctor Clayton finished his sermon and Miss Maxwell made the organ sing again that Jamie wiped his eyes and sat up.

"Your work with the DVET tells me you're still fighting for your men. And I'm going to support you every way I can."

The service ended with another virtuoso performance by Miss Maxwell. When she finished with a flourish, Jamie and

Andi sidled to the end of their pew and approached the console enclosure.

Jamie could hardly contain himself. "That was a stunning performance!"

"Thank you." Miss Maxwell was still flush from her exertions. "I wanted to give it my all on my return to Old First."

Ed burst in on them. "Sylvia!"

"Hi, Daddy." She sounded like a giddy little girl. "How'd I do?"

"You did great!" He looked at Jamie and Andi. "I see you've met my friends."

"Not formally." She extended her hand. "Sylvia Maxwell."

Andi was the first to take her hand.

Jamie hesitated. "I'm almost afraid to touch such gifted hands. I hope you've insured them with Lloyd's of London."

Sylvia smiled. "Daddy saw to that. He's in the insurance business."

"Where did you learn to play like that?" Jamie said. "It was the most remarkable performance I've ever experienced."

Sylvia stood tall. "Julliard School, New York City." She wasn't shy about accepting well-deserved praise, nor should she be.

Ed put his arm around his daughter's shoulders. "Since graduating from Julliard, Sylvia's been touring the US." He gave her a squeeze. "Now she's going to settle in Washington, DC, as the Cathedral Organist and Associate Director of Music at Washington National Cathedral."

"That's great," Andi said. "I just accepted a position at Walter Reed Army Hospital in DC. I've heard that the

National Cathedral has a magnificent organ. I can't wait to hear you play it."

Sylvia's face brightened. "What a relief. I've been worried that I don't know a soul in DC. Now, I needn't be. Any friend of Daddy's is a friend of mine. We must get together once we're both settled."

Jamie wasn't going to tell Sylvia he and Andi hadn't known Ed for much longer than an hour. He hoped Andi wouldn't either.

"It would be nice to get together," Andi said.

Sylvia folded a sheet of music in half and handed it to Andi, along with a pencil. "Please write down your DC address for me while I change out of my organist's shoes." She reached for a box in the corner of the enclosure.

"Nurse A. J. Eliot, Assistant Dean, Army School of Nursing, Walter Reed General Hospital, Washington, DC," Andi wrote and handed the sheet back to Sylvia.

"Organists wear special shoes?" Jamie said.

"Absolutely. To do the instrument justice, one must be able to feel the pedals while still having the proper amount of slide and grip."

Sylvia looked over the address Andi handed her. "Assistant Dean? Impressive for someone so young."

Jamie put his arm around Andi's waist. "Until a few days ago, Andi was the head nurse of the orthopedic ward I was on at Letterman."

Sylvia's eyebrows rose. "That must have been a huge responsibility."

Jamie knew Andi wasn't comfortable being the center of attention, so he wasn't surprised when she directed the conversation away from herself. "Jamie's a professor of physics at Stanford University." The pride in her voice rivaled Ed's when he spoke of Sylvia.

"Such accomplished young people," Ed said. "I hope you ladies do get together in DC."

Sylvia took Ed's arm. "Daddy's rather accomplished himself. He's President of Pacific Maritime Insurance."

Jamie looked at Ed with added respect. "I've heard good things about PMI."

"Grandfather Maxwell founded the company," Sylvia said. "Daddy's built it into the biggest insurer of ships and shipping on the west coast. Mommy was so proud of him."

"Was," Jamie said.

It was as though someone had let all the air out of Ed.

"Mommy passed away almost five years ago," Sylvia put her hands on her hips. "Now Daddy's planning to marry again—a much younger woman."

Jamie could feel the tension between them.

Ed put his hand on his daughter's shoulder. "Honey, I'm lonely."

His words sounded like a plea. Jamie remembered Mister Kavanaugh's hobby: matchmaking—pairing rich older men with his "special young ladies." What were the chances Ed's fiancée was one of Matt Kavanaugh's special young ladies? Jamie dismissed the thought. The odds against it were astronomical.

* * *

Jamie and Andi were standing on the front steps of Old First, trying to decide what to do for lunch, when Jamie spotted Sly lurking in the shadows across the street. Angry Man was a few doors down from him.

This has gone on long enough. "Please excuse me, Andi. I need to visit the men's room."

"Fine. I'll visit the ladies' and meet you back here in a few minutes."

After reentering the church Jamie headed one way, Andi another. As soon as she was out of sight, Jamie rushed outside and mingled with a group of worshippers as they crossed the street.

Sly was stealthily moving from one doorway to the next, creeping ever closer to Angry Man. When he was nearly within arms reach, Sly stopped and pressed his back to a wall as though emboldening himself for his next move. Jamie remained out of sight.

Sly sprang into action. He plowed into Angry Man's back, pinning the bigger man to a brick wall. Jamie was close enough to hear Sly say, "Stop following Nurse Eliot. She's mine."

Jamie suddenly remembered where he'd first seen Sly. It was at Letterman, and Sly was wearing the white coat of a doctor. "Angry Man," Jamie said under his breath, "meet Doctor Winters."

Angry Man violently spun around and delivered a well-aimed fist to the side of Winters' head, stunning him.

Jamie quickly moved in from behind and slammed the side of his foot into the back of Angry Man's knee, causing the big man to collapse backward. In one motion, Jamie caught him and expertly applied a choke hold—a lateral vascular neck restraint the Army called it in Jamie's hand-to-hand combat training.

Within a few seconds Angry Man lost consciousness. On the battlefield, Jamie would then have slit the man's throat.

In this case, he let Angry Man harmlessly slip to the pavement.

Winters stood with his mouth open and eyes bulging. "Th . . . thanks." He stared at Angry Man's inert form. "Is he going to be all right?"

"You tell me, Doctor Winters."

Winters took a step back. "How'd you know my name?"

"Your reputation precedes you." Angry Man began to stir. Jamie moved closer to Winters. Real close. "Stay away from Nurse Eliot, or I'll finish what this thug only started. Now get out of my sight."

Winters' eye was already swollen half shut. His cheek was an intense shade of red. Winters still hadn't moved. Jamie drew back his fist. Winters cringed, then quickly staggered off.

Most people regain consciousness in less than 30 seconds after passing out from a chokehold. Angry Man was no exception. He rose unsteadily. There was fire in his eyes. Jamie took a defensive stance. Angry Man practically ignored him as he watched Winters disappear down the street. "Who was that fool who jumped me?"

Jamie had expected a fight, and a close one at that. What was up with this guy?

"That was a man who won't take no for an answer." Jamie picked up Angry Man's Fedora hat and handed it to him. "After Sonny fires you, I suggest you learn how to drive better, or you'll never be able to make a living as a taxi driver."

"Sonny's got no reason to fire me."

Jamie had guessed right. Angry Man was working for Sonny. "He's got a good reason. I noticed you watching me the first time I left my hotel."

"Sonny wants you to know you're being watched."

"Come on? Why would Sonny waste time keeping an eye on me?"

"He wants to make you nervous, so you'll think twice about who you work with." Angry Man jammed his hat onto his head and dusted himself off. He looked around anxiously. "It could ruin things if we're seen together."

Now Jamie was even more perplexed. "Ruin things? Will you please tell me what you're really up to?"

Angry Man rubbed his neck. "You're lucky. You'd have a fight on your hands if I were one of Sonny's men."

"You mean you're not?"

"Sonny's an animal. He couldn't pay me enough to work for him."

"Then who are you working for?"

Angry Man looked Jamie up and down. "Since your background check came back clear—"

"Background check?" Jamie's patience was gone. "Who's been checking up on me?"

"The Bureau of Investigation. And by any measure, you're an exemplary citizen. So I'll be straight with you. I'm a federal agent working undercover."

"And you expect me to believe that?! Let me see your badge."

"I'd have to be pretty stupid to carry a badge while working undercover. Telephone the Bureau's San Francisco field office. Give them your name and ask to speak with Earl Donaldson, the Agent in Charge. Donaldson will confirm my identity."

"Right. As if someone at the Bureau of Investigation would know my name."

"We try to identify all of Matt Kavanaugh's associates."

Jamie could feel his anger mounting. "Who told you that includes me?"

"Never mind who. And relax. Meeting with Matt Kavanaugh isn't an altogether bad thing. Sometimes, his interests and the Bureau's coincide." Angry Man held up his hand to stop Jamie from asking another question. "That's all I'm going to say about Matt Kavanaugh."

"All right, you said you were going to be straight with me. Now's the time."

"Okay. Sorry if this erodes your self-esteem, but the Bureau isn't interested in you. We're interested in Sonny Kavanaugh. I'm tailing you to win his trust. Donaldson figured if I did a good enough job tailing you, Sonny would start giving me more important jobs. Then maybe we can gather enough evidence to lock him up forever."

"Is Donaldson's scheme working?"

"It is, and now I'm much closer to Sonny's inner circle."

Angry Man shrugged. "It was Sonny's idea for one of his men to have an encounter with you as soon as you left the hospital. That way, you'd remember the man, and when you started seeing him again and again, you'd realize you were being followed." Angry Man actually smiled. "Had I known driving a cab was part of Sonny's plan, I might not have volunteered to be your tail—as you noticed, I can't drive worth a damn."

He looked Jamie in the eyes. "Things are going well between me and Sonny. And you can help."

"Me? How?"

"I'm sure you agree the world would be a better place with Sonny behind bars. So until you can talk with Donaldson and confirm my identity, all I ask is that you don't blow my cover."

Jamie thought about it for a moment. "Okay, I'll cooperate—for now." He canted his head. "Now it makes sense that you were so disrespectful when you picked me up at Letterman if you wanted me to remember you."

"I wasn't just play-acting. At the time, I had no idea who you were. I figured you were just another crook Sonny wanted to put a tail on. When I saw all the ribbons on your uniform, I was disgusted to think a Medal of Honor recipient was mixed up with Sonny.

Jamie understood. Being part of Sonny's world would be disgraceful for any man.

"As soon as I dropped you off at the Palace Hotel, I called the field office and briefed them about what Sonny had put me up to. From my description of you, Earl Donaldson immediately knew who you were—there aren't many living Medal of Honor recipients." Angry Man looked up and down the street. "Now, let's put some distance between us."

"Okay, until I can call the Bureau, I'll play along."

"This isn't a game," Angry Man said. "Sonny will do anything to get what he wants. For now, he just wants to make you nervous. But tomorrow? Who knows? And it won't be me tailing you for much longer. As we had hoped, Sonny gave me a new job, one closer to his inner circle. Soon, another of his men will start tailing you. We can only hope he'll also be under orders not to touch you. But there's no guarantee. So be careful."

Angry Man turned to walk away.

"Wait," Jamie said. "Please tell me your name."

"Sure, why not? It's Dufner. Special Agent Vince Dufner." He rubbed the side of his neck again. "Just so you know, if this had been a regular stakeout, and Sonny hadn't wanted you to see me, I'd have been practically invisible—and there's no way that fool you chased away could have snuck up on me."

Jamie understood. Dufner's pride had been bruised—as was his neck. "I believe you."

"Now, how about you cross the street and return to your lady? I don't want to give Sonny a reason to change his mind about me." Dufner disappeared into the shadows.

Andi stood atop the stairs leading into Old First's foyer. She put her hands on her hips as Jamie approached. "It's odd that Old First's men's room is across the street."

"I got lost," Jamie said.

"Sure. And Doctor Winters just happened to be walking down the street with an eye swollen half shut and a deep bruise on his cheek."

"I didn't touch him."

Although true, Andi clearly didn't believe him. "Nick Hendricks and now you. I don't suppose it occurred to either of you that I might want to teach Winters a lesson myself?"

"It had. But I intend to continue depriving you of that pleasure. I love you far too much to let you risk getting hurt."

Chapter 6

The Reception

Monday, 02 June 1919

Jamie called the Bureau of Investigation's San Francisco field office at his first opportunity and talked with Earl Donaldson, the Agent in Charge. To Jamie's relief, Donaldson confirmed that Vince Dufner was indeed a Special Agent assigned to his office.

The rest of the day flew by. It was evening before Jamie realized it. He and Andi enjoyed a fine dinner at Biaggi's Steakhouse, a restaurant around the corner from the Palace— a restaurant owned by Mister Kavanaugh's Pacific Culinary Arts corporation.

When they left Biaggi's, Jamie hoped to see Special Agent Dufner lurking in the shadows. Otherwise, Sonny might have already replaced Dufner with someone unknown —someone who would be especially dangerous until Jamie identified him.

As for Winters, Jamie didn't see him—and hoped he never would again.

After dinner, Jamie put on his uniform while Andi slipped into her Evangeline House of Fashion dress.

"You look fantastic," Jamie said. "And Sheila was right. Only one woman in ten thousand has a figure fine enough to wear that dress."

Andi lowered her eyes demurely. "And few soldiers are authorized to wear the blue ribbon with five white stars you wear on your uniform."

Jamie looked at their reflection in the mirror. "We should make the proper impression on Mister Kavanaugh's guests." He took her hand. "But to be sure, I'm going to make a point of introducing you to Mister Kavanaugh's guests as *Nurse* Eliot. I don't want anyone mistaking you for one of his "young ladies.'"

"Young ladies?"

"That's what Mister Kavanaugh calls the women who work in his Pacific Businessman's Club. Everyone else calls them his 'girls.'"

Andi's smile disappeared. "When I was a student nurse, I did a rotation in a maternity ward. Some of our patients were women who'd fallen on hard times. Feeling they had no other choice, they'd turned to prostitution." Her look hardened. "I remember one girl who was several years younger than I. Her pimp showed up a day or two after she gave birth, demanding to know when he could put her back on the streets."

"That's terrible. What did you do?"

"After our patient recovered sufficiently, a rescue mission worker snuck her out a back door." There was now fire in Andi's eyes. "It wasn't long before she showed up again, pregnant and wanting to know how she could get rid of her baby."

"Mister Kavanaugh claims that many years ago he was tricked into managing a brothel, but he was soon able to transform it into a legitimate working man's social club. And that ever since none of his businesses have had any involvement with prostitution."

"Oh?" Andi seemed far from convinced. "I'd be surprised if the women who work in his so-called businessman's club are paragons of virtue."

"That was a big concern of mine—until he told me he's in the process of selling his club, and he's offered each employee a good job in one of his more conventional lines of business."

"And you believe him?"

"I do."

Andi crossed her arms.

"I know, I know. But before you render a verdict, meet him. Talk with him. If you still think I'm crazy to work with him on the DVET, I won't. Until then, please give him the benefit of the doubt."

"Oh, I have my doubts, all right. But I look forward to meeting him. Then I'll have a better idea of how hard I'll have to work to keep you out of trouble."

* * *

They took a taxi the half mile to Hutchins Fine Art. Two dozen, maybe more, potential donors, with their ladies, were already there when Jamie and Andi arrived. Jamie immediately scanned the gallery to see whether any of Rachel's paintings were on display. He was glad not to find any.

Kavanaugh was off to one side, holding court with

several couples. They seemed captivated by him. Andi didn't seem to take notice.

Kavanaugh soon approached. "Jamie, who's this lovely young lady you've brought into our midst this evening?"

"Mister Kavanaugh," Jamie said with unbounded pride, "please allow me to introduce Nurse Andrea Jean Eliot of the US Army Nurse Corps."

Kavanaugh's eyes opened wide. "It's a pleasure to meet you." Kavanaugh took Andi's hand and kissed it.

Jamie was so relieved not to detect any sign they'd met before that he felt like kissing them both! He restrained himself. Kavanaugh might not have understood.

"I must say, you're by far the prettiest nurse I've ever met," Kavanaugh said as though merely stating a fact. "Beautiful and brave. I believe you're one of only four women to be awarded the Distinguished Service Cross."

Jamie was startled. "How'd—"

Kavanaugh cut Jamie off. "You should know by now I don't like to leave things to chance." He smiled at Andi. "Having you here with Major Collins will definitely help our cause."

So that's why Kavanaugh sounded so matter-or-fact in commenting on Andi's appearance. He wasn't thinking in terms of aesthetics. As a hardcore businessman, he was considering how she could help fill the DVET's coffers.

Kavanaugh looked Andi up and down. "And what a lovely dress."

Andi turned slightly to expose her shoulder to Kavanaugh. "It does little to hide my shrapnel scar."

Kavanaugh gasped.

Jamie had noticed several people looking at Andi behind her back. He was pleased to see their expressions change when they noticed her scar. "It's Andi's red badge of courage," Jamie said, "and it's sure to impress your associates when they learn the circumstances behind it."

"I certainly was," Kavanaugh said.

Jamie was not happy to discover that Kavanaugh had put his and Andi's lives under a microscope. However, since Kavanaugh was going to help educate disabled veterans, Jamie let it go. "Andi's dress is from the Evangeline House of Fashion," Jamie said, trying to sound authoritative when, in fact, he didn't know the difference between a Paris house of fashion and an outhouse.

Kavanaugh smiled. "The Evangeline House of Fashion suits you."

"It's not Evangeline who makes Andi look great." Jamie smiled. "It's Andi who makes Evangeline look great."

"Enough," Andi said. "It's just a dress."

"Yes, nurse." Jamie turned to Kavanaugh. "Head Nurse Eliot has been overseeing my care these last few months."

"And I thank you, Nurse Eliot. The world's a better place for Jamie's presence."

A scuffle broke out at the doorway as a wiry man wearing a crumpled black raincoat pushed his way into the gallery. He wasn't much bigger than Jamie, but how he carried himself made him seem much larger. He was maybe a year or two older than Jamie. The man headed straight for Kavanaugh, who accepted the intrusion calmly.

"Special Agent Mundy," Kavanaugh said. "Welcome to our fundraiser. How negligent of me not to have invited you, considering your patriotism."

At first, Jamie thought Kavanaugh was being sarcastic. The look on his face said otherwise.

Mundy flashed a badge. "This is my invitation."

"To what do we own the honor of your presence this evening?"

"Cut the crap, Matt. I'm looking for that low-life nephew of yours."

Kavanaugh made a sweeping gesture that took in all his guests. "You won't find him here. As you say, Sonny's a low life. My guests have at least a touch of class." Kavanaugh turned to Jamie and Andi. "And my special guests are exemplary citizens. Please meet Jamie Collins and Andrea Eliot."

Jamie offered his hand. Mundy looked like he'd rather spit on it than shake it until he pointed at Jamie's ribbons. "Medal of Honor?"

Jamie nodded. Mundy still didn't shake Jamie's hand. Instead, he came to attention and saluted. Jamie was always surprised when a civilian saluted his medal. He politely reciprocated.

"I was Secret Service during the war." Mundy sounded almost apologetic.

"A reserved occupation, I assume," Jamie said.

"Reserved occupation?" Kavanaugh said.

"A job so important to the war effort that it exempted a man from the draft," Jamie said.

Mundy immediately became defensive. "That didn't stop me from going down to the recruiter and trying to sign up."

"I'm sorry," Jamie said. "I didn't mean to sound judgmental. Protecting our elected officials is a critical job, especially during wartime."

Mundy's "ruffled feathers" lay down. "The director refused to release any of us agents to the military. Still, I know something about the Medal of Honor and how few living soldiers receive it."

Someone across the room was waving to Kavanaugh. "Excuse me for a moment, please. It appears that I'm wanted." He left Jamie and Andi with Mundy.

"Mister Kavanaugh asked me here," Jamie said, "hoping his associates would be impressed by my uniform and ribbons. And that hearing me speak will entice them to open their wallets wide to help fund the Disabled Veterans' Education Trust."

Mundy smiled for the first time. "Matt could get a turnip to donate to a worthy cause."

Jamie canted his head. "You're the only one I've ever heard call Mister Kavanaugh 'Matt' to his face."

Mundy smiled. "I only do it to irritate him."

"It's concerning," Andi said, "that the Secret Service is looking for Sonny Kavanaugh."

For some reason, Mundy didn't even look at her. "I'm no longer with the Secret Service, *miss*. At the government's request, I've been transferred to the Bureau of Investigation."

"Nurse," Jamie said.

Mundy inclined his head. "What?"

"It's *Nurse* Eliot. Army Nurse Eliot."

Mundy's stern expression dissolved. "Oh, I see." He looked at Andi and smiled. "Sorry, ma'am."

Jamie suddenly got it. As he feared, someone had indeed assumed Andi was one of Kavanaugh's girls, and Mundy wasn't going to engage in dialogue with a prostitute.

"I'm curious," Andi said. "What's a 'special' agent?"

"We're law enforcement officers with federal and state arrest and investigative powers." Mundy patted a bulge beneath his raincoat. "We're also authorized—actually, required—to carry firearms."

Kavanaugh rejoined them.

"Why is the Bureau of Investigation interested in Sonny?" Andi said.

"We suspect he may have violated the Mann Act."

Andi looked at Kavanaugh defiantly. "I'm a strong supporter of the Mann Act."

Kavanaugh squared his shoulders. "As am I."

Jamie could see that Andi had hit a nerve. "Please remind me," Jamie said. "What's the Mann Act?"

"In essence," Kavanaugh said, "it says that no woman should be treated like property or forced to do something she doesn't want to."

"It's also called the White-Slave Traffic Act," Mundy said. "It makes it a felony to transport any female across international or state lines for the purpose of prostitution, debauchery, or any other immoral purpose."

"Where does Sonny Kavanaugh come into the picture?" Andi said.

"Sonny has quite a few out-of-state women working for him," Mundy said. He clenched his fists. "I'm interested in knowing how they got to San Francisco. If Sonny transported them here to work in one of his brothels, he's committed a felony."

Clarence Walker, a middle-aged gentleman Jamie had been introduced to earlier, kept staring at Jamie. Walker moved closer. "No offense, Major Collins. I expected you to be seven feet tall and as imposing as a tank."

Kavanaugh chuckled. "I held the same misconception before I met Major Collins. Then I remembered that Goliath towered over David."

Walker laughed. "Seeing that you're not some mythological giant, I'm even more impressed by your accomplishments."

"Sir," Andi said, "Major Collins *is* a giant in the eyes of his men."

Mundy smiled. He excused himself and moved off to stand alone, watching.

There was another commotion at the front door. "Ah," Kavanaugh said. "If anyone's going to donate to our charity, it will be the happy beneficiary of my latest matchmaking success." The face of the gentleman in question was obscured from Jamie and Andi's view by a large painting mounted on an easel. "Please excuse me," Kavanaugh said and then hurried off.

"God help me," Andi whispered in Jamie's ear, "I find Matt Kavanaugh charming."

"Didn't I tell you he had a presence?"

"I'm curious, though. Why'd you look so relieved after you introduced us? Were you afraid I'd embarrass you in some way?"

Jamie didn't want to insult her by admitting he'd been worried she was conspiring with Kavanaugh. After seeing them together and watching them interact, Jamie was convinced she was as honest as anyone he'd ever met. In the future, he'd treat anything she said as gospel. "You could never embarrass me," he said.

His evasive response clearly didn't satisfy Andi, but at that moment, the new arrivals came into full view. "Well, I'll be," Jamie said.

There stood Ed Maxwell, aka Methuselah, from the Old First Church. Ed was arm-in-arm with a lovely woman no more than half his age. She was extending her left arm, palm down. Those around her were admiring something shiny on her ring finger. "Butch told me Mister Kavanaugh was something of a matchmaker."

"She *is* young," Andi said. "No wonder Sylvia is concerned." Andi smiled. "They do look happy, though. Let's go congratulate them."

Jamie drew Andi nearer. "My dearest Andi, every day, you give me another reason to love you."

"I have no idea what you mean, but whatever it was, I'm thankful."

"You're just so good to people."

They approached Ed from behind. "Hello, Ed," Jamie said.

Ed turned around. Recognition slowly transformed his blank expression into a warm smile. "How nice to see you two again."

"And you," Andi said.

Ed squeezed the arm of his young lady. "Please allow me to introduce Miss Catherine Reams, who I'm proud to say has recently consented to be my wife. Cathy, this is Jamie Collins and Andi . . . ?"

"Eliot," Jamie said. "It's a pleasure to meet you, Miss Reams." Since Jamie was better versed in quantum mechanics than etiquette, he followed Kavanaugh's lead and kissed Miss Reams' hand. She seemed genuinely moved.

Andi smiled at Cathy. "We had the pleasure of meeting Ed at church yesterday."

"And the equally great pleasure of hearing his daughter play the organ."

Ed beamed. "Sylvia left for DC just this morning." His smile faded. "I already miss her."

"I'm sure everyone at the National Cathedral will be thrilled to have such a talented musician on their staff," Andi said.

Cathy picked a tiny piece of lint off Ed's jacket sleeve

like a long-enduring spouse. "I've yet to meet Sylvia. I hoped to meet her at church yesterday and hear her play. Unfortunately, I awoke with an appalling headache and thought it best to stay in. I feel just awful that I missed her."

Jamie wondered whether Cathy was deliberately avoiding Sylvia.

Ed put his arm around his fiancée's shoulder. "You'll meet her soon, my dear, I promise."

Cathy looked concerned, but her manner with Ed made Jamie think that despite their age difference, she really did love him.

Kavanaugh joined the quartet. "Excuse me, ladies. May I borrow your men for a few minutes? I'd like them to meet one of my associates."

"Certainly." Andi took Cathy's arm. "We'll keep each other company."

Chapter 7

A Different World

Andi watched Jamie and Kavanaugh weave their way through the crowd to the other side of the gallery.

"Isn't Mister Kavanaugh amazing?" Cathy said.

Andi angled her head. "I do find him charming."

"Charming? He's more than that. He's a lifesaver."

"Oh?"

"Before Mister Kavanaugh took me in, I considered ending my life."

Andi gasped. "That would have been a tragedy."

"I agree, now. At the time, I felt that God had abandoned me."

What could Andi say to that?

Cathy seemed lost in her memories. "I'd been governess for the children of a man named William Sherman. He's a widower a little older than me that I found handsome, charming, and persuasive. He's also very wealthy." She focused her attention on Andi. "As time went by, William began spending more and more time with me and the children, which I believed was due to his affection for his offspring. Over the months, we became close. He began filling my head with professions of love and promises of marriage."

Cathy cast her eyes downward. "I was terribly naïve. The stereotypical prim and proper governess who had never even been kissed."

Cathy began twisting Ed's engagement ring on her finger. "He pressured me into becoming intimate with him."

Andi was shocked that Cathy would disclose such a personal thing to someone she'd only just met. Nevertheless, if Cathy wanted to talk, compassionate as always, Andi was willing to lend a sympathetic ear.

"Once he got what he wanted, it became clear that everything that man told me was a lie—a lie even a child should have seen through. I can only thank God I didn't become pregnant since I knew nothing about human reproduction."

Andi felt she had to say something. "Few young women do."

"About a month after we became intimate, I came home with the children after a day at the beach to find my belongings piled outside the servant's entrance." Cathy clenched her jaw. "William had replaced me with a younger, prettier governess—presumably intending to add to his score of conquests. And to add insult to injury, he said with my morals, he couldn't possibly give me a reference."

"The hypocrite!"

"Without a reference, I had no chance of finding another governess position. I lost all interest in life and couldn't face the world. The only lodging I could afford was a shared room in a boarding house, where I stayed in my room day after day. It wasn't long before I was broke and hungry." Cathy's tone changed to one of self-pity. "My landlord was an enchanting middle-aged man whom I might have liked had he not turned me into a whore."

Andi was stunned. This had become uncomfortably personal.

"My heart was broken, I'd lost my self-respect, and I was determined to punish myself for my foolishness. I degraded myself further by trading 'services' for another two weeks of room and board." Cathy's back stiffened. "I didn't think I could sink any lower—until those two weeks were over. I was just as desperate as before. As a 'favor' to me, my not-so-enchanting landlord passed me on to one of his friends so I could earn enough money to stay for another two weeks."

Andi became as still as one of Hutchins' sculptures. She had no idea what to say to any of this.

"Not only had I proven to be a poor governess, I proved that I wasn't even a good prostitute. At best, I'd say I was a bumbling part-time amateur. I was so unworldly I didn't even ask his 'friend' for payment, assuming he'd already paid my landlord."

She hugged herself seemingly for support. "That was a bad assumption. Since I was still broke, the next day, I was introduced to another of my landlord's 'friends.' I had learned enough overnight to insist that he pay in advance." Cathy sighed. "This next 'friend' was so inept, I lost my patience."

She gave a little laugh. "I've always talked too much and been too free with my opinions. 'You're not very good at this, are you?' I said to him. He became so flustered he just ran off —after delivering an equally inept fist to my jaw."

"The brute," Andi said.

Cathy smiled. "I had to laugh. It didn't hurt that much, and he had evened my balance sheet. One customer who didn't pay and got what he wanted versus one who did pay and didn't get a thing."

Andi didn't think that was anything to smile about. "How'd you come to the attention of Mister Kavanaugh?"

"My roommate was also destitute. But she was lucky. Her sister, Marleen, was one of Mister Kavanaugh's 'young ladies.' My roommate had given up trying to make it on her own and was leaving our boardinghouse to work in Mister Kavanaugh's Pacific Businessman's Club. Marleen took pity on me. She told me the advantages of working for Mister Kavanaugh—room, board, money, protection, and a choice about what I would or wouldn't do with certain gentlemen. Marleen offered to arrange an interview for me with Mister Kavanaugh himself." Cathy gritted her teeth. "You can imagine what kind of 'interview' I was expecting. To my surprise, it wasn't like that at all. Mister Kavanaugh asked me the kind of general knowledge questions I'd been asked when I applied for governess positions."

Cathy glanced across the room to where Kavanaugh was in conversation with Jamie, Ed, and another gentleman.

"Mister Kavanaugh said he saw something in me he liked. He offered me a choice: I could work in one of his laundries, or he would groom me for marriage to a select member of his businessman's club." Cathy put the back of her hand to her forehead. "I was so relieved I broke down and cried on his shoulder."

"Apparently, you chose not to work in one of his laundries."

"Oh, but I did."

"And yet here you are."

"I didn't last a week in the laundry. It was hot, humid, and the work never stopped. That wasn't the life I wanted. I wanted to be a wife and, someday, a mother. But I'd proven to be a very poor judge of men. Mister Kavanaugh had told me that the man he had in mind for me, although twice my age, was a man of honor and a true gentleman. I trusted Mister Kavanaugh to be a better judge of character than me. I begged him to begin grooming me for marriage, and thankfully, he agreed. But not without a warning." Cathy leaned in close. "He said if he invested time and money in me, and I changed my mind again, it wouldn't go well for me."

Andi gasped. "Weren't you scared?"

"Terrified. Which was obviously his intention. Then he assured me I'd be fine if I followed his rules. I'd get all the benefits his other young ladies enjoyed, but I wouldn't have to work in his club or 'date' any of the members. All he would require of me was that I study hard and learn my lessons well. And he'd make sure no one ever got away with hurting me."

Andi wondered what that meant. Would Kavanaugh unleash a couple of his thugs on anyone who hurt her, men like the ones Mundy pushed his way past at the gallery's entrance? Andi didn't want to think about it.

Cathy patted her tightly wound hair. "The next day, I was welcomed into a class with two other women to begin studying under the guidance of Miss Hargrove."

Andi got the impression Cathy expected her to know who Miss Hargrove was. "Who?"

Cathy gave her a curious look. "How long have you known Major Collins?"

"Almost three months."

Cathy seemed puzzled. "That's surprising." Before Andi could think of anything to say, Cathy shrugged and went on.

"I was already a qualified governess. I thought it would be a breeze to hold my own with the other women. Then I met Miss Hargrove. To say she was demanding would be an understatement. And I had a lot to learn. A gentleman's wife should know how to conduct herself at all times. She should know proper etiquette, how to talk, how to walk, how to stand, how to sit, how to show proper respect for her husband without being obsequious."

"My mother died when I was a little girl," Andi said. "She wasn't around to teach me any of those things."

"I'm sorry," Cathy said. And it sounded as though she meant it.

Cathy went on. "Mister Kavanaugh and Miss Hargrove transformed me. They taught me to comment intelligently on current events, art, theater—and Mister Kavanaugh's favorite subject, classical music. I excelled in our science, math, and geography lessons, which had always been my best subjects. They also improved my already passable English." Cathy gave a little laugh. "What surprised me was how much I enjoyed learning about business."

She whispered, "Mister Kavanaugh also wanted us to be thoroughly familiar with human reproduction, about which, surprisingly, we were shockingly ignorant."

Andi smiled. "That's one of my best subjects."

Cathy raised her eyebrows. "A proper lady like you?"

Cathy's question puzzled Andi.

Cathy didn't wait for an answer. "One day, a month or so into my reeducation, Mister Kavanaugh told me how pleased he was with my progress. We chatted for a while before he offhandedly asked what I'd like to happen to my previous employer, William Sherman, for treating me so badly."

Cathy rubbed her upper arm. "I said I hoped he'd break an arm—and I meant it. Then I did my best to forget all about William Sherman."

"Good for you."

Cathy smiled wistfully. "Here's the most amazing part of my story. Mister Kavanaugh wanted me to become thoroughly familiar with the Bible, particularly the New Testament, because the prospective husband he'd picked out for me was a religious man. I struggled with that. What kind of religious man would buy a wife from someone who managed a stable of 'young ladies?' Nevertheless, I did as Mister Kavanaugh wished. That evening, I began to read the Gospel of John, which had always been my favorite."

Cathy looked like she'd entered a different world. "When I got to the story about the prostitute who anointed Jesus' feet and how He forgave her, I began to weep uncontrollably. There and then, I fell to my knees and accepted Jesus as my Lord and Savior."

Andi placed her hand on Cathy's forearm. "Welcome to the fold, sister."

Cathy took a deep breath. "I told Mister Kavanaugh of my rebirth and that I had to withdraw from our agreement, regardless of the consequences. To my surprise, rather than threaten me, he merely asked me to meet Ed before I made any decisions I might regret."

Andi smiled. "Apparently, you're glad you did."

"I was scared at first that the man might turn out to be as bad as William Sherman. But I trusted Mister Kavanaugh when he said Ed was a true gentleman."

Cathy looked across the room at her fiancé and wiped a

solitary tear from her cheek with the back of her hand. "To my amazement, Ed treated me like a lady—me who had fallen to such depravity. And I saw Ed for who he is. A kind, lonely man who just wanted someone to love." Cathy gently bit her lower lip. "I told Ed all about my past, and my rebirth."

Cathy's chin trembled. "Ed told me that since I'd been reborn, he would always see me as my name implies, for Catherine means 'pure.'"

"I'd say Mister Kavanaugh found you a remarkable gentleman," Andi said.

Cathy smiled. "I've fallen in love with Ed. And I swear by all that's holy, I'll do everything I can to fill his days with happiness as a wife should."

"I'm curious," Andi said. "What does Mister Kavanaugh get out of all this?"

Cathy looked at Andi as though she'd asked what two plus two equals. "When Ed and I marry, Mister Kavanaugh, as my adoptive father, will receive a generous bride price. And if Ed predeceases me, Mister Kavanaugh will receive one-third of the dower he's had Ed place in trust for me. Plus, he'll get one-third of anything I inherit from Ed."

Andi was stunned. "That could be a significant windfall for Mister Kavanaugh."

Cathy rubbed the side of her neck. "Isn't that the same arrangement Mister Kavanaugh has concerning you and Major Collins?"

"Me?" Andi shrugged. "I only met Mister Kavanaugh fifteen minutes ago."

Cathy staggered backward a step. "Mister Kavanaugh didn't place you with Major Collins?"

"No. I'm an army nurse. I met Major Collins on my ward at Letterman Army Hospital."

Cathy placed the back of her hand on her forehead. "I told you I talk too much. I also jump to conclusions. I wouldn't have told you the things I did if I hadn't assumed you were one of Mister Kavanaugh's special young ladies."

"I'm sorry if I misled you," Andi said. "In my mind, I was simply lending you a sympathetic ear."

Cathy took Andi's hand. "I went on and on with my story because I never once got the feeling you were judging me." She tilted her head, "In my mind that makes you a remarkable woman."

Andi lowered her head modestly. "You're not alone in having had your heart broken. I've had mine broken—twice. If I hadn't been able to pour myself into my work, I might be the one telling you a sad story."

"No. I have a feeling you're stronger than me."

Andi shook her head. "After my last heartbreak, I swore I'd never let another man into my heart. Then Major Collins came into my life. And here I am, more head over heels in love than ever."

Ed and Jamie began navigating their way back across the crowded floor toward their ladies.

"There's one more thing you should know about Mister Kavanaugh," Cathy whispered. "Soon after I accepted Ed's proposal, Mister Kavanaugh casually mentioned he'd heard that William Sherman had fallen off his horse and broken *both* arms." Cathy briskly ran her hands up and down her bare forearms. "I know William never owned a horse and wouldn't go near one for love or money."

A shiver ran up Andi's spine. A shadow of fear seemed to settle over her.

Jamie arrived by Andi's side. "You ladies appear to be getting along famously."

Andi forced a smile. "We certainly haven't been bored."

Ed smiled. "I'm glad. I'd love for you two to become friends."

Andi sidled up to Cathy and took her arm. "We *are* friends."

"Indeed," Cathy said.

* * *

Kavanaugh clapped his hands to get everyone's attention. "Ladies and gentlemen, I've invited you here this evening to announce the formation of a new charitable trust. We call it the Disabled Veterans' Education Trust, or DVET. Its goal is to pay for the education of American servicemen disabled by enemy action during the Great War."

Kavanaugh looked around the gallery until his gaze settled on Jamie. "With us tonight is Major Jamie Collins, Ph.D., Professor of Physics at Stanford University, and recipient of the Medal of Honor, our country's highest award for valor." He held out his hand. "Jamie, please join me."

Jamie stepped forward to polite applause.

Kavanaugh described to his guests the situation and actions that led to Jamie being awarded the Medal of Honor. Kanavaugh's delivery, Andi noted, was that of a natural orator, although he occasionally slurred his words.

Everyone stared at Jamie.

Kavanaugh then described Jamie's resulting injuries as so grievous that he was initially pronounced dead. "*Prematurely*, Jamie likes to say."

Uneasy laughter was heard throughout the gallery. Jamie acknowledged it with a wave and a smile.

Kavanaugh went on. "Having been confined to a wheelchair for many months, Major Collins is now in a unique position to advocate for disabled veterans."

There was a buzz in the gallery. Shouts of "amazing," "stout fellow," and the like filled the room.

"I've asked Professor Collins to explain why he is one hundred percent behind the DVET." Kavanaugh put his hand on Jamie's shoulder. "Ladies and gentlemen, please give Major Collins a warm welcome.

The gallery erupted in enthusiastic applause.

"Thank you." The applause went on. "Thank you." Jamie raised his hand like a traffic cop. The applause died out. "For a man to feel he's an important contributor to society," Jamie said, "he must have meaningful employment. Many disabled veterans were still in high school when they volunteered to fight for our country. Their only work experience has been carrying a rifle and digging trenches. That would make it difficult for them to find good jobs once they're discharged from the army. Mister Kavanaugh intends to address that situation by giving our vets unmatched educational opportunities."

Applause rippled throughout the gallery.

"I can tell you from personal experience that the men I was hospitalized with will jump at the opportunity Mister Kavanaugh, and hopefully you, will be offering them. As an educator, I can also tell you that their desire to learn is the most accurate indicator of the likelihood of their success. But as I'm sure you can appreciate, the transition from orthopedic patient to student will be difficult."

He glanced at Andi. "To tell you how Mister Kavanaugh

and the DVET plan to ease that transition, I'm immensely proud to introduce Registered Nurse Andrea Eliot of the Army Nurse Corps. Nurse Eliot was head nurse of the orthopedic ward where I regained my ability to walk." He held his arm out for Andi to join him.

As Andi stepped forward, she saw looks of surprise throughout the gallery. They had to be asking themselves whether she really could be a nurse and not one of Kavanaugh's girls.

"Before Nurse Eliot tells you what the DVET has planned for our vets," Jamie said, "please allow me to tell you a little about Nurse Eliot herself."

Andi was never comfortable being the center of attention. Still, since they were at Mister Kavanaugh's reception for a good reason, she didn't mind Jamie telling the audience about her education, awards, and career progression. And though everything he told them were things to be proud of, Andi could only stare at the floor, her cheeks warm from embarrassment.

When Jamie finished, Andi took the floor to thunderous applause. "Ladies and gentlemen," Andi began, "in treating disabled veterans, the army's objective is to help each patient realize the greatest degree of freedom and self-sufficiency their injuries will allow. Sadly, time and resources limit us to addressing only the physical needs of our patients. Just as important is giving them the tools they'll need to establish themselves as valuable members of society. The most powerful tool anyone can bring to bear on that goal is education."

She looked around the room. "Unfortunately, a disability can place serious obstacles in the way of learning. Even something as simple as holding a book and turning its pages is difficult for a man who's lost an arm. That hasn't stopped my patients from digging into books and trying to educate themselves. One of my patients who lost both legs serves as the page-turner for a fellow patient who lost an arm." Andi looked at Jamie. "In another example of the brotherhood that exists among our disabled veterans, I have two other patients who each lost an arm. They take turns reading aloud to each other as they turn pages together."

There were sympathetic faces throughout the room. "To provide a supportive environment similar to their orthopedic ward, I learned from Mister Kavanaugh just a little while ago that the DVET has purchased a building in Berkeley on fraternity row across from the campus of the University of California. The building is being refurbished to house up to twenty disabled students. When completed, it will feature access ramps, wider door openings, and other modifications to accommodate wheelchairs. There, veterans working toward a degree can live together, study together, support each other, and encourage one another." Andi turned to Kavanaugh.

He thanked her and then stepped up to a large fishbowl sitting on a pedestal in the center of the gallery. He pulled a large wad of hundred-dollar bills from his pocket and dropped them into the bowl. His guests watched as the bills fluttered to the bottom. "I'm making a seed donation of ten thousand dollars to the DVET." There were gasps throughout the gallery. "After hearing from Major Collins and Nurse Eliot, I'm sure you'll each dwarf my donation with your own. And to make yours even more impactful, I pledge to donate an additional fifty cents for every dollar an individual donates over two thousand, five hundred dollars."

Another eruption of applause shattered the stunned silence.

"Now," Kavanaugh said, "please help yourselves to champagne and hors d'oeuvres as you contemplate how much you intend to donate to the DVET." He bowed and stepped aside.

Cathy sheepishly approached Andi. "Nurse Eliot—"

"Please, it's Andi."

"You are the most amazing woman I've ever met." Cathy took a deep breath. "I wish we *could* be friends."

Andi smiled. "Aren't we."

"I wouldn't expect you to demean yourself by associating with the likes of me."

Andi took Cathy's hand. "You opened your heart to me. Rather than be bitter about your past, you're optimistic about your future. You're the kind of friend I want. The kind of friend I need."

"Thank you—my friend," Cathy said.

Jamie joined them. "Please excuse us, Cathy," Jamie said. "Mister Kavanaugh wants Andi and me to circulate and answer any questions his associates might have." He bowed slightly to Cathy.

Jamie and Andi joined a group of couples revisiting the buffet table and imbibing more of Kavanaugh's champagne. The guests had lots of questions. Andi was pleased to be treated as an expert in addressing disabilities rather than an ornament. Eventually, the crowd thinned to the point where it was only Andi, Jamie, the caterers, a few hangers-on, and, ominously, Special Agent Mundy. Kavanaugh was in a private room with one of his associates.

Mundy walked up to Andi and Jamie. "You're a nice couple, and I appreciate what you're doing for our disabled veterans, so it's only right that I warn you, you're playing a dangerous game by getting involved in Matt Kavanaugh's world."

Andi and Jamie looked at each other.

"Thanks for the warning," Jamie said. "The truth is, we'd work with the devil if he'd help our disabled vets."

Mundy thrust his hands into the pockets of his rumpled raincoat. "Matt's world is so far removed from yours you can't possibly know what you're getting into."

Andi canted her head. "If Mister Kavanaugh is so bad, why isn't he in jail?

Mundy took his hands out of his pockets. "Matt's a genius at shaping the way people see him and stretching the boundaries of the law. As deeply as we've looked into his affairs, we've yet to find evidence that he ever actually commits anything worse than a petty crime."

Andi was astonished. "Seriously?"

"When the Bureau assigned me to the San Francisco Field Office, I made it my mission to bring down the Mighty Matt Kavanaugh. To my surprise, as I dug deeper and deeper into his business practices, I was surprised to discover that he's more an illusionist than a criminal. He's been deluding the world for decades."

Mundy shoved his hands back into his pockets. "Matt has people so convinced he's dangerous that he gets what he wants almost exclusively through bluster and posturing."

"*Almost* exclusively?" Jamie said.

"He's no saint, but he's nowhere near as bad as he wants people to think he is."

Andi put her hands on her hips. "What about his so-called Pacific Businessman's Club? There are some nasty rumors about their real purpose."

"We've looked into it. The way Matt runs things, we can't charge him with anything even when members take advantage of the "special benefits" they can request when they take one of his girls out on a 'date.' "

"How can that be?" Andi said.

"He makes it very clear to all involved that those dates don't come with a guaranteed happy ending. Without a guarantee, we can't prosecute him under any federal, state, or local law."

"Would I be right in assuming the Bureau cuts Mister Kavanaugh some slack because of his donations to charity?" Jamie said.

"All I'll say about that is his donations don't go unnoticed."

"What about honest businessmen who'd prefer not to deal with Matt Kavanaugh?" Andi said.

"The Bureau doesn't have the manpower or the resources to police the market. Letting Matt maintain his monopolies is like merchants hiring a private police force to keep hardcore criminals from moving in and charging exorbitant fees."

"In other words," Andi said, "the Bureau prefers the devil you know?"

"Pretty much. Thankfully, Matt's smart. He keeps his greed in check. He adds only a few cents over market price for his goods and services. It's the scale of his operations that makes him rich. With thousands of customers, those few cents add up quick, and the public hardly feels the pinch. Sure, sometimes Matt's men get rough, but only when someone tries to horn in on his territory. The funny thing is if it weren't for Matt, we could see outright war between criminal organizations trying to get control of his markets, and innocent bystanders would get hurt."

Andi found this incredible. "You're saying Mister Kavanaugh benefits society?"

"Strange world, isn't it?" Mundy said.

All Andi could do was shake her head.

"Don't get me wrong," Mundy said. "We're not giving Matt a free pass. If he stops giving to charity or becomes too greedy, the Bureau will come down on him like an avalanche." Mundy looked from one to the other. "I'd hate for you two to be collateral damage."

He glanced around the gallery. "Right now, I'm not all that interested in Matt. I want to have a little chat with Sonny Kavanaugh. Identical twin sisters just started working in one of his brothels. They're from a little town outside St. Louis. We suspect Sonny transported them to San Francisco. If we can prove it, he'll wish he'd never heard of twins."

Jamie exhaled loudly. "You may be surprised to learn that Sonny and I attended the same high school." Mundy did look surprised. "Luckily, I was able to stay out of his way. Some of my friends weren't so lucky. Sonny was the stuff of nightmares for kids like me and my friends. He was a cruel and heartless bully then. I can only imagine he's more dangerous as an adult."

"Sonny's not the one you have to worry about. He's just mean and arrogant. Matt is a much bigger danger. He's smart. Fortunately, he's not out to hurt anybody. He just wants their money—a few pennies at a time. And when he thinks someone will be useful to him, he gets what he wants by manipulating them into working for him without them even realizing it."

Andi looked at Jamie. He avoided eye contact.

Mundy took out his wallet. "Here's my card. If you find you're getting in over your heads, don't hesitate to contact me." He gave Jamie a conspiratorial look. "Or any other agent you might run across." Mundy pulled two one-dollar bills from his wallet and put them in the DVET's fishbowl. Those bills, Andi noticed, were the only ones in Mundy's wallet. Without another word, Mundy headed for the door.

"Special Agent Mundy?" Jamie said.

Mundy stopped and turned around.

"Thank you. For the donation and for watching over us."

"Sure thing." He gave them a half-smile.

Andi was amused to see Mundy shove two of Kavanaugh's 'big men' out of his way as he left the gallery.

"I wouldn't want to be on his bad side," Jamie said.

Andi grasped his arm. "That's exactly where we'll end up if we're not careful."

* * *

After the last sheep had been fleeced, Kavanaugh, Jamie, and Andi were alone except for the caterers, who were busy cleaning up.

"It was a great idea to bring Andi with you this evening," Kavanaugh said to Jamie. "My associates were so thoroughly impressed by you two that they've opened their wallets wide." He looked at Jamie. "What did you have to do to persuade Andi to accompany you tonight?"

"Tell her I love her."

Kavanaugh stood up straight. "I hope you meant it."

"With all my heart."

"Well done, my boy," Kavanaugh gushed like a proud father.

It occurred to Andi that perhaps Kavanaugh saw Jamie as a replacement for his son, who had died in the delivery room along with the boy's mother. Could Jamie see Kavanaugh as a replacement for his father, who had died soon after Jamie graduated from high school?

Kavanaugh turned to Andi. "I'm curious. What did you think of Special Agent Mundy?"

"As Jamie and I were just saying, we wouldn't want to be on his bad side."

"Jeff Mundy is a rare commodity," Kavanaugh said, "and something every American should treasure. An incorruptible law enforcement officer."

Andi furrowed her brow. "You sound mighty sure of that."

"Several of my competitors have tried to bribe him." Kavanaugh smiled his most conniving smile. "I can't imagine who made them think that was a good idea. They're now in prison. Such a shame."

How many DVET donors belonged in prison with them, Andi wondered.

"How'd your sales pitch go?" Jamie said.

"Great. A full baker's dozen of my associates donated $2,500 or more." Kavanaugh was silent for a moment. "I have an idea," he said. "If you don't object, I think we could increase the funding of the DVET if I list the three of us as co-founders."

Jamie shrugged. "That would be all right with me. Andi?"

"Sure. If you think it will help."

"I've got to ask," Jamie said, "how many of our big donors did you persuade by promising them inflated charitable donation receipts?"

"They're not all as civic-minded as Ed Maxwell. He's always willing to donate to a worthy cause without any 'inducement.' About half the others aren't as generous." Kavanaugh smiled. "But they came around."

Andi was both pleased and disappointed by the outcome. Pleased by Ed's honest generosity and that the DVET would have so much funding, and disappointed that there were so many crooks in the world.

"That means our initial funding will be around $60,000," Kavanaugh said. "With only around forty percent coming out of my pocket."

"Forty percent?" Andi said. "You're a generous man."

He raised his chin and smiled.

Andi's stomach churned.

Chapter 8

A Proposition

Late Monday evening, 02 June 1919

Back in the Presidential Suite, Jamie was still jubilant. "Do you realize how many veterans we can educate with $60,000?"

Andi sighed. "Quite a few, I imagine."

Her lack of enthusiasm didn't dampen Jamie's. "I did some research in the base's education office. At the best colleges and universities, room and board average around $400 annually. Textbooks, around $40. And general fees, whatever that means, are around $20. That's $460 a year, exclusive of tuition, which is free at most California universities."

Andi remained distant.

"What's wrong?"

She wrapped her arms around herself.

"Are you cold?"

Andi shook her head. Clearly, she wanted to be held. Jamie was happy to oblige.

Andi burrowed deep into his embrace. "Making an enemy of Sonny is bad enough," she said, "but Cathy told me something about Matt Kavanaugh that scared me." Her tone said she was still scared.

"Care to share it?"

"Yes, but first, let me tell you what led Cathy to disclose information that was shockingly personal."

Jamie indicated the couch. They sat. Andi told Jamie a condensed version of Cathy's story—excluding the part about William Sherman's horse.

"I'm sorry Cathy suffered such heartache," Jamie said, "and thrilled about her rise from the ashes. But what made her tell you such a personal story?"

"She wouldn't have told me any of it if she hadn't assumed I was one of Matt Kavanaugh's girls." Andi shook her head. "Ironic, isn't it? Other than Special Agent Mundy, whose job has conditioned him to expect the worst of people, the only person we know for sure mistook me for one of Matt Kavanaugh's girls . . . was one of Matt Kavanaugh's girls."

"Ironic indeed. Now, what was the part Cathy said that scared you?"

"Kavanaugh had asked Cathy what she wanted to happen to her old employer for treating her so badly. Cathy said she hoped William would break an arm. Soon after Cathy accepted Ed's proposal, Kavanaugh mentioned in passing that he'd heard Sherman had fallen off his horse and broken *both* arms." Andi took a deep breath. "Cathy swears Sherman never owned a horse and wouldn't go near one for love or money. And that tells me our charming 'Mister' Kavanaugh is a dangerous man."

But one who looks after his friends, Jamie thought—for

which he couldn't help but admire the man. For now, Jamie would keep that to himself.

"I hate to think about what Kavanaugh might do to you if you displease him."

Jamie took her hand. "We'll just have to be even more careful than we thought."

She leaned into him. "Please don't let anything happen to you. I couldn't bear to lose another fian—" She stopped herself. "I couldn't bear to lose you."

How Jamie wished he were her fiancé! But he'd made a promise, a silly promise he regretted. He put on a happy face. "Let's forget all about Mister Kavanaugh for now." He looked into her eyes. "I have a proposition for you."

Andi gave him a look that could melt diamonds. "I have a feeling I'm going to like it."

Her response scrambled his mind so completely that he couldn't remember what he had planned to say. "Umm, uh . . .." He cleared his throat. "We have to check out of this suite tomorrow morning. How would you like to take a little train ride?"

"I'd love to. What do you have in mind?"

"We can catch the Del Monte Express for the three-hour trip to Pacific Grove and stay for a few days."

"Pacific Grove?"

"It's the little town where I grew up. It's on the tip of the Monterey Peninsula, about 120 miles down the coast from here."

Andi clasped her hands. "I was dreading having to leave the Palace—and for us to part. Pacific Grove sounds grand. When do we leave?"

"Two-thirty tomorrow afternoon." He could hardly contain his excitement. "To quote someone famous whose name escapes me, 'Pacific Grove is one of the most spectacular meetings of land and sea anywhere in the world.'"

"Then tomorrow afternoon can't come soon enough." Andi tossed her hair off her shoulder and looked Jamie in the eyes. "I hate to bring up Matt Kavanaugh again, but I can't stop wondering why you seemed so relieved after you introduced us?"

"I knew you'd ask. I'll just say your reaction dealt a killing blow to another of my fears."

Andi looked like she was going to ask for more.

"Please, it's not something I'm proud of so let's leave it at that."

She studied him for a long moment. "All right. It's not important." Her face brightened. "Now, tell me about your hometown."

"You're going to love it!" He smoothed back his hair. "I hope you won't mind if I mix a little business with pleasure." He didn't wait for a response. "I promised Colonel Thornburgh I'd meet with someone he knows the next time I'm on the Peninsula."

"I have the greatest respect for Colonel Thornburgh. I wouldn't want you to disappoint him."

"Great. Sam Morse is the husband of Colonel Thornburgh's wife's old college roommate. Mister Morse would like to talk to me about doing some consulting work for him. He's a land developer and conservationist on the Monterey Peninsula."

Andi knitted her brow. "Can one be both?"

"Why don't you ask him?"

Andi turned her head slightly. "Me?"

"Join us. Then you can hear what Sam has to say firsthand."

"You wouldn't mind?"

"Mind? I'd be honored."

"What if *he* minds?"

"Then I won't have anything to do with him." Jamie smiled. "Don't worry, it will be fine. Besides, I'd be surprised if it leads to anything. After all, what use would a theoretical physicist be to a land developer? Or a conservationist?"

Andi looked at Jamie through hooded eyelids, a look that always turned him into Jell-O. "I love that you want to include me."

Jamie sighed. "I wish I could include you in everything I do."

Worry lines creased Andi's forehead. "Do you ever think we've jumped into our relationship too deeply, too soon?"

"Never. As we've said, if the war taught us anything, it's how ephemeral life is." He froze. "You're not worried, are you?"

"Me? Not on your life." Her worry lines changed into smile crinkles around her eyes. "I've loved you since I first saw how you treated the staff and patients on our ward—and me."

"I was just being myself."

"I rest my case."

Jamie took her hand. "There's another reason I'd like you to go to Pacific Grove with me."

"Oh?"

"The estate Butch left me includes a house—or, more precisely, a mansion." He hesitated. He had to find the right words. "I'd like to know whether you think an enterprising woman could turn it into a good home."

Andi squinted at him. "It would be cruel to ask me such a question unless you envision me as that woman."

With all his heart, Jamie wanted Andi to be that woman. If not for his foolish promise to Rachel, a woman he hardly knew . . .. "When I meet with Rachel next April—"

"Assuming she shows up."

"Yes. Assuming she shows up, I promise I'll make it clear right up front that I've fallen in love with you and that you're the one I want to spend the rest of my life with."

"What if she has other plans for you?" Andi raised her chin. "She's bound to see you as quite a catch. And she's obviously a captivating woman."

"She has no hold on me. She—"

"But she does. She has a . . . a *bond* with you that I don't." Andi's voice grew quieter. "When you meet her again, you might be drawn to her as before."

"I'm stronger now. And I have a lot more to lose if I give into temptation again. I won't let myself be drawn to her. I simply won't. I promised her I wouldn't commit to anyone before our reunion. Nothing more."

Andi shook her head. "I know you. You keep your promises. That's who you are. That's the man I love. But what if you discover you and Rachel have a child?"

Rachel had said their timing couldn't be more perfect for a couple wanting to avoid conception. But what if she was wrong? "You and I will simply have to deal with that remote possibility if it arises."

"You and I? What about Rachel?"

"You and I," Jamie repeated.

Andi was silent for what felt like half of eternity.

"Okay," she said, "we'll deal with remote possibilities only if they arise." She smiled. "Now I want to hear about this mansion you've inherited."

Jamie breathed easy again. "You're going to love it. It's

the house Butch lived in with his grandmother after his father died and his mother went away. I've never seen the inside, but I can tell you the outside is stunning. It's what architects call High Victorian style. Two stories, plus a walkout basement and an attic. Its fascinatingly complex roofline features at least seven gables, each decorated with gingerbread overhangs. And it has plenty of big windows that look out directly onto the bay from only a couple hundred yards inland."

"It sounds like a fairytale castle," Andi said.

"Butch's grandparents called it *BayView*. Don't you think a house with a name sounds special?"

"BayView," Andi repeated. "I love it. Is the house furnished?"

"I hired a local attorney to handle everything related to my inheritance, a man appropriately named Paul Handler. I haven't met him yet; we've only talked over the telephone, but I like him. Handler tells me the house is full of beautiful period pieces, although I'm not sure what that means."

Jamie walked to their fireplace. "There's a complication. The house is such a landmark that as soon as Butch's grandmother died, several people made unsolicited offers to buy it. John Thayer's offer was particularly generous."

"Who's John Thayer?"

"He's the son of the man whose scholarship paid for my education. Handler tells me Thayer thinks I owe it to him to accept his offer."

"From your tone, my guess is you don't like John Thayer."

"John grew up in Pacific Grove. He's two years younger than me. I remember seeing him around high school, but I can't remember ever talking with him."

"Then why don't you like him?"

"I asked Handler what kind of a man John is. Handler was reluctant to say at first, probably preferring not to get involved in slander. Eventually, he told me John is a big, loud-mouthed bully who's used to getting his way."

Andi's eyebrows rose. "Just because the scholarship you earned is named after his father shouldn't mean you have to deal with him, does it?"

"No. The Thayer Scholarship came with no strings attached."

"Tell me about that scholarship of yours."

"I'm glad you asked." Jamie picked up a glass figurine from the mantel. "Every year since 1893, Stanford has offered a full scholarship in the name of Thomas Thayer to the top male graduate from Pacific Grove High School."

"Do you know much about Thomas?"

Jamie began absentmindedly examining the glass figurine as he tried to suppress any thoughts that he and Rachel could be parents. "Thomas Thayer was the richest man in Pacific Grove."

"Was?"

Jamie replaced the figurine on the mantel and gave Andi his full attention. "Thomas passed away last year. John is his only heir."

Andi slipped her shoes off. Jamie sat next to her. "Here, put your feet on my lap," he said. Andi pivoted, leaned against the arm of their couch, and happily complied. Jamie began massaging Andi's feet with a gentle touch.

"Oh, Jamie . . . that feels soooooo good."

"John has announced that he no longer wants the scholarship to be awarded, that he won't make up any shortages in the endowment, and once the current recipients complete their degrees, he wants to terminate the scholarship altogether."

Andi curled her toes. "That's rather small of him."

"I agree. Fortunately, John won't get his way. It's the University that awards the scholarship, not Thayer's heir. For however long there's money in the scholarship endowment, the University is contractually obligated to present the award."

"Oh, Jamie. Where did you learn to give such a soothing massage?"

He smiled. "In the Presidential Suite of the Palace Hotel."

Andi burrowed deeper into the folds of their couch. "Why does John want to discontinue the scholarship?"

"Handler says John doesn't have much respect for formal education. He skipped college and went into business with his father right after high school—even though he was the top graduate of Pacific Grove High his senior year."

Andi put her feet on the floor. "You mean John would have received the Thayer Scholarship if he had wanted it?"

"Crazy, isn't it?"

She untied Jamie's shoelaces. "Where did Thomas get all his money?"

"He was a big player in the construction business. He built just about every important building in the Monterey Bay Area. That business now belongs to John, and according to Handler, other than John's ruthless business practices, he's the best contractor for miles around."

Andi slipped Jamie's shoes off. "Lean back and give me your feet."

"Yes, nurse."

"Thomas must have had respect for formal education," Andi said.

"So much so that he gave others opportunities he never had."

"What a thoughtful man." Andi began massaging Jamie's feet.

"Very. I only wish his scholarship had been open to boys and girls—although I don't know where I'd be today if it had been."

"What do you mean?"

Jamie stared into their dormant fireplace. "There was a girl—Elaine Stanton—who got slightly better grades than I did throughout high school." He looked at Andi, then quickly looked away. "I got to go to Stanford and earn a Ph.D. in physics while she was relegated to California State Normal School in San Jose, where she earned an undergraduate degree in math and a teaching credential."

"You've kept track of her?"

"Only because I feel so guilty about taking the scholarship away from her."

"Taking it away from her? If you had turned it down to protest Thomas Thayer shutting girls out of the competition, would the scholarship have gone to Elaine?"

"You're the second person to ask me that." He sighed contentedly. "I didn't realize a foot massage could feel so good."

Andi paused her massage. "You haven't answered my question."

"If I had turned down the scholarship, it would have been offered to the next most qualified boy."

Andi resumed her massage. "Then don't beat yourself up over something you couldn't control."

"I should have done something."

"With what Private Lightner left you in his will, you're now a wealthy man. If John Thayer won't cover shortages in his father's scholarship endowment, why don't you? And if Stanford won't or can't modify the scholarship to include girls, establish a new scholarship that will."

Jamie sat up straight. "What a fabulous idea! Then I wouldn't feel half as bad about stealing Elaine's future."

Andi grabbed his arm. "Who says you stole her future?"

"Elaine."

"The cow! It was Thomas Thayer's money. Who gave her the right to tell him what to do with it? And I'd be shocked if you ever stole anything from anybody."

Jamie laughed. "I pity anyone who finds fault in me in your presence. And you're right. I've never stolen anything from anyone." He became serious. "But I would have done anything to win that scholarship—cheat, steal, you name it. Without the Thayer Scholarship, I'd be nothing today. And I wouldn't have met you."

"Let me see if I've got this straight," Andi said. "You didn't do anything to deprive Elaine of the Thayer Scholarship, yet you feel guilty about something you say you would have done if you had to? You know that's crazy, don't you?" She shook her head. "Instead of feeling guilty, why don't you find her and see what you can do for her now?"

"I'd rather face a battery of machine guns."

Andi tossed her hair off her shoulder. "I'll tell you what, why don't we try to find her together, and I'll make sure she doesn't beat you to a pulp."

"Seriously? You'd face her with me?"

"I'd face a pride of lions with you if it would set your mind at ease."

Jamie couldn't hug her tightly enough.

"Now, where do we start looking for her?"

Jamie grinned sheepishly. "That will be easy. She's teaching math at our old high school."

"You *have* kept track of her. Is she happy?"

He pictured her resenting her job. "I have no idea."

"Let's ask her when we're in Pacific Grove."

"I'll consider it, so long as you're there to protect me."

"Fine. Now, what about John Thayer's offer to buy your house?"

"I need to see the place before I decide. As I said, I'm under no obligation to sell it to him—although I would like to do something for his family."

"Won't covering shortfalls in the Thayer Scholarship be enough?"

"I don't know. Handler says John's adamant about letting it expire. He might think I'm interfering."

"If you owe the Thayer family anything, it's to Thomas, not John. From what you've told me about Thomas, I'm sure he'd be thrilled if you covered shortfalls."

"You, my dear, are wise beyond your years." He leaned back. "Maybe you can help smooth out another wrinkle. Handler tells me Butch retained the full-time, live-in house-keeper who worked for his grandmother. If I keep the house, I need to decide what to do about her."

"What's she like?"

"I've never met her. Neither had Butch. Handler tells me the woman is a very proper forty-eight-year-old war widow who immigrated from Scotland at the end of the war. Handler says he's dropped by the house several times unan-nounced and found everything in tip-top order. If she's that good, and I decide to keep the house, I just might ask her to stay on. But then I'd need to decide how much to pay her. She's currently earning quite a bit less than I think a good housekeeper deserves."

"You say she's a war widow?"

"That's the primary reason I've kept her on."

"Have you told her you're coming?"

"No."

Andi pursed her lips. "A surprise visit could get interesting."

"I don't want to come on as the Grand Inquisitor, but I'd like to see what kind of work she does when she thinks no one will be looking. It will go much better if you're with me."

Andi laughed. "It sounds like you're afraid to be alone with her."

"The big war hero afraid of his housekeeper?" Jamie shrugged. "Don't laugh. It's true."

Andi's tone became more serious. "What if you love the place? Would you want to live there?"

"Not full-time. Although I might want to spend the odd holiday or weekend there, and probably summers. If I do, I'll need a housekeeper. If I like the state of the house, I'll ask her to stay on."

"And if John Thayer resents you for not selling the place to him, what will you do when you run into him?"

Chapter 9

Ferroequine Adventures

Tuesday morning, 03 June 1919

Andi was sitting at their vanity brushing her hair when Jamie began to stir. She turned to him. "Awake already?"

"I'm too excited to sleep any longer."

Andi smiled. "Me too. I can't wait to see your hometown. And I love trains."

"Checking out?" Miss Helpling asked as they approached the front desk.

"All good things must come to an end," Jamie said.

As they walked out of the Palace's opulent main entrance, Jamie turned to Andi. "It's hard to imagine life being much better."

"But there's still . . .." Andi stopped abruptly, as though she didn't want to spoil the moment by mentioning anything worrysome.

Jamie sighed. "Rachel would have found a way by now to tell me if I were a father."

Andi shook her head. "That's not what I was going to say."

"Then what?"

"We still must find a way to defeat the Hangman's Curse."

"Oh, that," Jamie said. "I remind you, I'm not easy to kill."

Andi took Jamie's hand. "While I'm at it, I'd feel better if I got all my worries out in the open."

"You mean there's more?"

"We also need to find a way to fully support the DVET without becoming so deeply entangled in Mister Kavanaugh's world that we can't escape. And Sonny needs to leave us alone. And there's your housekeeper. And John Thayer."

Jamie squeezed Andi's hand. "I didn't know you were such a worrier. I say let's deal with such problems only if they become real."

* * *

Tuesday, midday, 03 June 1919

Jamie and Andi took a long walk and grabbed a light lunch to fill the time before the Del Monte Express was scheduled to depart. All the while, Jamie kept a sharp eye out for anyone who might be following them.

They arrived at the San Francisco train station right on time. "Why don't you wait here while I get our tickets," Jamie said, "He excused himself and walked several feet to the ticket counter. He wasn't going to let Andi out of his sight, not with the possibility that someone unknown might be following them.

"What train leaves closest in time to the Del Monte Express," Jamie asked the agent.

The man checked the schedules. "The Overland Limited leaves for Chicago fifteen minutes after the Del Monte Express departs."

"From which platform?"

"Thirteen, sir. The Del Monte Express will be to the right of the platform, and the Overland Limited will be to the left."

"Perfect," Jamie said. "I'll give you ten dollars here and now if you'll tell anyone who asks that I bought two tickets for the Overland Limited, and another ten the next time I'm passing through here, which will be often."

That got the agent's attention. "Ten dollars is a lot of money, sir.'

Jamie rubbed his upper arms to generate a little heat against another cold San Francisco afternoon. "Enough to buy a warm coat."

* * *

Andi had likewise been keeping an eye on Jamie. "You look rather pleased with yourself," she said.

"I am. Along with two round-trip tickets to Pacific Grove, I paid an extra fifty cents apiece each way for the privilege of riding in the parlor car."

"That will be a treat."

"I don't exactly know what a parlor car is," Jamie said, "but it must be special if it costs that much."

"Definitely," Andi said.

He took her hand. "You deserve the best." He lifted her

hand and kissed it. "We'll be on the Del Monte Express, which will be leaving from platform thirteen in . . ." He looked at his pocket watch. "Ten minutes."

Andi practically dragged Jamie to their platform. She planned to astonish him.

When they came within sight of their engine, she stopped. "This is a 4-8-2 steam locomotive known as the 'Mountain' type." Jamie stared at her. "Under the Whyte notation, 4-8-2 represents four leading wheels, eight powered and coupled driving wheels, and two trailing wheels."

"Who are you, and what did you do with Andi Eliot?"

Andi kept a straight face. "The name 'Mountain' originated with the Chesapeake and Ohio Railroad and refers to the Allegheny Mountains for which their first 4-8-2 locomotives were intended. The American Locomotive Company developed the Mountain type by combining the traction of the eight-coupled 2-8-2 'Mikado' driving wheels with the excellent tracking qualities of the 'Pacific's' four-wheel leading truck."

After a moment, Andi burst into laughter. "My father's been a railfan since he was a boy. As a Presbyterian minister, he has most Mondays off. I loved to accompany him on his train-spotting adventures. I think it's fair to say I've become almost as expert in ferroequinology as he."

"*Ferroequin—*" Jamie laughed. "The study of iron horses. Clever, very clever."

"Had I been a boy, I'm sure Daddy would have wanted me to be an engineer—the kind who drives a train."

"I'm glad you're not."

"An engineer?"

"No, a boy."

Right there on the platform, for all to see, Andi pressed her body against Jamie's and kissed him passionately. "Me too."

As they continued their way toward the parlor car, Andi intertwined her arm with Jamie's. "Today's rolling configuration is, from front to back, a mail car, two—no, three-passenger coaches, a news-agent coach, and our parlor car."

"No caboose?"

"They wouldn't put a caboose on a fine passenger train like the Del Monte Express. Our parlor car occupies the trail position on our train." Andi smiled. "Parlor cars are too pricy for a preacher's daughter. I've never ridden in one."

"Then I did well?"

"Very. Parlor cars offer food and beverages and plush interiors with more comfortable seating than coach."

Jamie smiled. "Sounds like money well spent."

"Actually, a professor from a fine university should ride in the parlor car, while an army nurse belongs in coach. But if you don't tell anyone how common I am, maybe they'll let me ride with you just this once."

"You're funny. You're as far from common as anyone I know."

Andi was puzzled when Jamie guided her to the Overland Express on the other side of their platform. "Humor me," he said.

They boarded the Overland and jostled their way through several passenger cars until they came even with the Del Monte Express's parlor car. Jamie surveyed the platform.

"Now," he said.

They sprang from the Overland and mingled with other passengers as they quickly worked their way to their parlor car. Anyone seeing them might have thought they were running from the law—or perhaps a jealous spouse.

They entered their parlor car just as the Del Monte Express began pulling away from the platform. Jamie stood at a window and looked across the platform at the Overland. A man appeared at a window of the train across from them. When he saw Jamie in the Del Monte, he pounded the side of his fist on his window frame. Jamie smiled. Now he knew who Sonny had chosen as Agent Dufner's replacement—and who to look out for in the future. Jamie waved to the man as the Del Monte Express began to roll.

"Another of Sonny's men?" Andi said.

Jamie's mouth fell open. "How'd you know?"

"I noticed we were being watched the minute we left Dibowski's menswear shop."

"Why didn't you say anything?"

"For the same reason I didn't mention that Doctor Winters was following us: I didn't want to worry you."

"*You* didn't want to worry *me*?" Jamie shook his head. "You, Andi Eliot, are remarkable.

"Keep believing that," she said with a smile.

* * *

As Andi glanced around the plush interior of their parlor car, she half expected to be redirected to coach.

"This is much to my liking," Jamie said. "Certainly compared to the accommodations on a troop train." He pointed to the individual high-backed swivel seats. "The only disadvantage is we won't be able to snuggle during the trip."

Andi pointed to the well-stocked bar. "When prohibition

takes effect, the Del Monte Express might sell a lot more parlor car tickets."

"How so," Jamie said.

"If they've stored up enough reserves to continue stocking their bar, I'm sure some people will ride the Express just for the alcohol."

The parlor car attendant intercepted them in the middle of the car. His eyes were fixed on Andi. "N . . . Nurse Eliot?"

Andi studied his face. "Corporal Miller?"

"Millet, ma'am."

It all came back to her. "Of course. Corporal *Oliver* Millet.

"I'm honored youse remembers, ma'am—only now it's just plain 'Oliver.' "

"How could I forget? You told the most fascinating stories about your great-grandfather and his adventures as one of the first white men to trade with the Indians in Northern California. And how he wouldn't have survived without their help." Andi put her hand on his upper arm. "How's your arm, Oliver?"

He smiled broadly. "Fine, ma'am, thanks to youse."

Oliver tore his eyes away from Andi for a second. "Nurse Eliot is an angel, sir. I was in bad shape when the stretcher-bearers carried me into her aid station. I had a concussion and a compound fracture of my upper arm. As I was struggling to stay conscious, I heard the doctors talking about amputating. That would have been it for me if Nurse Eliot hadn't convinced them to let her try to save it. Thank God they listened."

He turned back to Andi. "Youse was the only nurse who bothered to learn my name. Youse made me feel like I mattered."

Andi remembered all too well. Maybe she wouldn't have suffered from such nightmares if she hadn't learned patient's names. And maybe the Hangman's Curse wouldn't be her punishment for losing so many. "You did matter," Andi said. All of her patients mattered. And yet so many died.

"If my wife and kiddies was on this train, we'd all thank you from the bottom of our hearts."

"I was merely doing my duty, Oliver, but I appreciate your kind words."

Oliver bowed. "Youse's glasses will never be empty on this train."

"That's kind of you, Oliver," Andi said, "but we don't drink alcohol."

He smiled. "Youse is probably better off for that, ma'am." He excused himself and left to assist other passengers.

Jamie took Andi's hand. "I'm so very, very proud of you, my angel."

She squeezed his hand and pointed to adjacent plush swivel chairs. "Shall we?"

They sat. Jamie stretched out. "This is pure luxury."

Oliver appeared before them with three glasses on a tray. "Apple juice," he said with a grin. They each took a glass. "To youse's health and happiness," he said. Oliver returned to his duties with a look of supreme satisfaction.

Their three-hour, fifteen-minute, 130-mile journey to Pacific Grove would be interrupted by short stops in San Jose, Gilroy, Watsonville, and at the Express's primary destination, the Hotel Del Monte's own station in Monterey.

Within five minutes of sitting, Jamie was sound asleep. Andi reached across the gap between their chairs and gently placed her hand on his forearm. He didn't wake. She said a silent prayer of thanks that Jamie had been placed on her ward and that he was her man—for now. The Curse. She couldn't put the Hangman's Curse out of her mind.

As the scenery flew by, Andi tortured herself with such thoughts until Jamie awoke forty-eight miles and an hour later as the Del Monte Express stopped in San Jose's large, covered train shed. It reminded Andi of the elegant sheds she'd seen in Europe.

"Did you have a good rest?" she said when Jamie began to stir.

His face reddened as he sat up and peered out the window. "I'm sorry. Train rides often put me to sleep."

"That's all right. I enjoyed the scenery. And I was particularly intrigued as we passed through Palo Alto. I've heard there's a fine university nearby, and their physics faculty is of particular note."

"Unsubstantiated rumors," Jamie said with a smile.

Once passengers, luggage, mail, and newspapers had been attended to, the Del Monte Express departed for Gilroy. Jamie took Andi's hand. Two minutes later, his arm went limp and fell to his side. This leg of their journey was only thirty-three miles. Again, the cessation of motion woke Jamie. "Where are we?"

"Gilroy. It's surprisingly busy for such a small station. Lots of passengers coming and going."

The train was soon rolling again, headed eighteen miles southwest through the Santa Cruz mountains toward Watsonville. Jamie managed to stay awake for the scenic twenty-two-minute ascent and descent. They were presented with a ghostly scene as they pulled into the Watsonville station. Fog had blown into the valley floor at just the right height for the furrows of the plowed fields to be filled with mist while subdued sunlight lit the ridges.

"I've passed through this station maybe a hundred times going back and forth between home and school," Jamie said. "I've only seen it like this once before—right after my division was activated, and I was on my way to report to my unit commander."

"The scene has an otherworldly feel to it," Andi said.

"I'll tell you what's otherworldly. I'm finally going home, and you're by my side."

As their train began to pull out of the Watsonville station she took his hand. "Thank you for including me in your homecoming—and for loving me."

"I've loved you since the first moment I saw you."

"It would be hard to imagine life getting any better," Andi said. Then she remembered the Curse. The damned Curse! She studied the scenery outside her window in a futile attempt to control her emotions. "From the way the trees are bending over, it looks like we're in for quite a storm."

"With a good amount of rain," Jamie said, "if those dark clouds are any indication."

"I don't mind. I love a good storm—when I don't have to be out in it."

Jamie agreed.

Constant heavy rain fell during the rest of the ride from Watsonville to the Hotel Del Monte. When they came to a stop, Jamie took out his pocket watch. "Right on schedule."

All other parlor car passengers de-trained at the hotel stop. It was only lightly raining, but the wind had increased.

"I've heard that the Hotel Del Monte is one of the most luxurious hotels in America," Andi said.

"It should be. They charge seven to ten dollars a night—a

significant amount compared to what an average working man earns in a month."

"I can't imagine what our Presidential Suite at the Palace would have cost us if not for Howard's generosity." Andi pointed to a gleaming private car resting on a siding. "Probably belongs to some east-coast tycoon," she said.

Jamie nodded. "The rich and famous come from all across the country to stay at the Hotel Del Monte. But if the owner of that private car doesn't have a jewel like you, he's a pauper."

After seeing the hotel guests off, Oliver approached Andi and Jamie. "Not staying at the hotel?"

"Professor Collins has a house not far from the beach in Pacific Grove," Andi said.

"Sounds grand." Oliver looked from one to the other. "I noticed youse two have round-trip tickets. Will youse be staying on the Peninsula long?"

"Not sure," Jamie said. "At least a night or two."

Oliver nodded. "Just a short stay then." The train began to move. "It's only five miles to the Pacific Grove terminal. That's where our locomotive rests overnight."

"I know the yard well," Jamie said. "My friends and I were always being rousted from it when we were kids."

"Youse is lucky to be going to the end of the line," Oliver said. "The ride from here to Pacific Grove is my mostest favorite part of the route. The tracks run right along the shore. Youse'll get an amazing view of the bay. And all them people staying at the Hotel Del Monte never gets to see it."

Oliver retreated to the parlor car's bar and began putting away bottles he'd poured from during the trip.

"Please allow me to be your tour guide," Jamie said to Andi. He pointed out their window toward the north, where dozens of boats were moored in the bay. "Monterey's fishing fleet is still mostly sail-driven. Soon, they'll probably all be converting to diesel. A shame from an esthetic point of view." He pointed to the right of the boats. "Fisherman's Wharf won't be alone much longer. There are plans to build a second commercial wharf east of it."

As they passed a row of sardine canneries, the stench was overpowering.

"Don't worry," Jamie said. "It doesn't smell like this at BayView. The prevailing wind is off the ocean. You don't even get a whiff of the canneries in Pacific Grove."

"That's a relief."

Their view after passing the canneries opened to reveal an unspoiled rocky shoreline that the railroad tracks followed as far as Andi could see.

"Oliver was right," Andi said. "This view of the bay is spectacular."

A few minutes later, Jamie pointed to a large, bright yellow house coming up on their left. "That's it."

Andi gasped. "It *is* a mansion! A half-dozen couples could live there and never run into each other." She tried to keep her imagination in reign as she pictured herself as Lady of such a palace.

"That's not much of an exaggeration," Jamie said. "The paperwork my attorney sent me says there are six bedrooms."

"They don't build houses like this anymore. Do you know when it was built?"

"Eighteen eighty-six. Butch's grandfather had it built. He was a builder himself, so BayView has all the latest luxuries—for that era."

Andi moved to a chair with a better view. "I love all the

roof angles." She didn't leave the window until BayView disappeared behind them. "I can't wait to see the inside."

The train slowed as it entered the Pacific Grove yard, coming to a stop at the passenger platform. Andi looked skyward. "It's stopped raining, but it sure is windy."

"Don't worry," Oliver said. "Along with the wagons from the Carmelo and Centrella Hotels, several taxis always meet the Del Monte Express." He turned to Jamie. "Do youse have luggage, sir?"

"Yes. The Palace Hotel was to have it placed on our train to be sent on to my house."

"I'll see to that myself, sir."

"Thank you, Oliver." Jamie raised his chin and looked down at Andi. "My house is only seven or eight blocks from here. I'd walk if Nurse Eliot weren't with me."

Andi stood up tall. "Jamie Collins, if you think you can out-hike me . . .."

"That sounds like a challenge," Oliver said with a smile.

Andi offered Oliver her hand. "I'm pleased that you've made a full recovery, Oliver."

She was surprised when he kissed her hand rather than shake it. "I look forward to seeing youse on youse's return trip in a few days."

Jamie and Andi stepped onto the platform and were met by a mighty gust of wind. Andi pulled a hair tie from her purse, gathered her hair at the back of her head, and put it up in a ponytail as some avant-garde women were starting to do.

"That's an enchanting look on you," Jamie said.

"On your mark, get set, go," Andi said. She took off at a race-walk pace. Jamie's rehabilitation had come so far that he could almost keep up with her".

Chapter 10

BayView

Jamie and Andi rushed along the appropriately named Ocean View Boulevard. The bay was only a stone's throw to their left. An eclectic assortment of houses lined the street on their right. With a near-gale-force wind pushing them from their left-rear quarter, they were in front of BayView within ten minutes.

"All right, you won," Jamie said.

They stood for a moment, taking in the amazing craftsmanship of the house. "The gables, the gingerbread overhangs, all those windows overlooking the bay. It's perfect," Andi said.

Jamie looked enormously pleased.

"How can you even think of selling it?"

"It's even nicer than I remember." Jamie rubbed the back of his neck. "I wonder if the inside's anywhere near as nice." Jamie stepped aside and bowed. "After you, my lady."

The property was surrounded by a short stone retaining wall topped by a two-foot-tall white wrought iron fence. Andi climbed two steps from the sidewalk to the concrete walkway that led to the front door. The walkway was bordered by flower beds, which in turn were surrounded by a luxurious expanse of lawn. Andi imagined how happy her family and friends would be for her to be the Lady of such a fine house. Then she remembered the Curse. Was her fate sealed? Was there no hope? She fought back tears. Surely, if anyone could defeat the Hangman's Curse, it would be Major Jamie Collins, the hero who was raised from the dead.

"Somebody's doing a great job caring for the yard," Jamie said.

Andi surveyed the view across the bay as wind-swept waves somersaulted over the rocks not more than two hundred yards in front of them. She sighed. "It would be hard to imagine a more beautiful sight."

"I see a more beautiful sight every time I look at you," Jamie said.

Andi rolled her eyes and smiled. "Let's go inside." She left Jamie standing by himself, staring out over the bay as she walked to the dozen wooden steps leading up to his front porch. She called for him to join her. They climbed the steps together.

Jamie knocked on the door. In half a minute, they were greeted by a middle-aged, somewhat plump, smiling woman. "Yes, may I help you?" She spoke with a strong Scottish accent.

Jamie just stood there mute as a statue. Andi realized he had no idea how to introduce himself. That he owned the house made no difference. The woman who answered his knock couldn't have picked him out of a police lineup.

"This is Professor Collins," Andi said.

The Scotswoman's expression rapidly changed from surprise to joy. "Oh, sir, what a pleasure to finally meet you.

Your footlocker arrived a few days ago, and I hoped you'd soon follow." She smoothed her apron and stood up tall. "I'm Noreen Ferguson, your housekeeper. Please, come in, come in."

Jamie introduced Andi. "We'll be staying a few nights if you won't mind."

"Mind, sir?" She smiled. "I'm thrilled you'll be staying."

"We wouldn't want to inconvenience you."

"Sir, if having you two stay inconveniences me, it would be time for you to find a new housekeeper."

They stepped into the front room. Andi looked around wide-eyed. "Everything in here is wonderfully neat and tidy," she said.

"Beyond neat and tidy," Jamie said. "Everything is immaculate."

"What a beautiful room. And I love the decor." Andi had to stop herself from adding, "I won't have to change a thing when this becomes my house." She looked north out of large picture windows. "Jamie, look at this view." The house was tucked into a jog in the shoreline at the corner of Ocean View Boulevard and Fountain Avenue, providing an almost 180-degree unobstructed view of the bay.

Noreen moved to Andi's side. "Sometimes, it's all I can do to tear myself away from these windows, ma'am."

Andi had to shake herself out of a trance. "Please, call me Andi." She was desperate for Noreen to like her in case Jamie decided to keep the place.

"Oh, miss, I couldn't. I'm merely the housekeeper."

Jamie had wandered into the equally spotless adjoining dining room. "I wouldn't say you're merely the housekeeper," he said load enough to he heard from the next room. "Everything in here shines. That says to me you're a housekeeper *extraordinaire*. And before I forget, who's been taking such good care of the garden?"

Noreen lowered her head bashfully. "That would be me, sir."

"Taking care of a house this size and the garden is way too much to ask of one person. This place needs a dedicated gardener." He ran his finger across a windowsill and held it up. "Dust-free," he said. "Very impressive. One can tell a lot about someone by the work they do when they think no one will be looking."

Noreen smiled at the compliment. "It helped that I had two days' notice to get everything ready for the other gentleman's visit yesterday, sir."

Jamie canted his head. "What other gentleman?"

"Why, Mister John Thayer, sir."

Jamie's face reddened.

"Oh, sir, he said you gave him permission to come in and inspect the house, along with his building foreman."

The veins in Jamie's neck stood out. "I did nothing of the kind."

Noreen pressed her arms to her sides. "Sir, where I come from, a gentleman would never lie to gain entry into another man's house."

"Don't worry," Jamie said. "It's good to take others at their word. If they betray your trust, that's a clear statement about their character." It was evident to Andi what the problem was. John Thayer simply wasn't a gentleman. "John Thayer's father funded the scholarship that let me go to a fine university," Jamie said. "And now John wants to buy this house."

Noreen clenched her hands.

"Rest assured," Jamie said. "I haven't given him any

reason to think I'm going to sell it—to him or anyone else." Noreen relaxed. "I wonder why Thayer brought his foreman along with him," Jamie said.

"Mister Thayer and his foreman discussed whether they'd have to make any alterations to the house before Mister Thayer moves in."

Andi took hold of Jamie's arm to keep him from charging out of the house, hunting down "Mister" John Thayer and setting him straight.

"He'll move in over my dead body," Jamie said.

Noreen couldn't have looked more relieved. "I'm so glad to hear that, sir." Noreen stepped a little closer to Jamie and lowered her voice. "Sir, please excuse me for saying so, but I don't like that man or his foreman. They stomped around your house like it was already Mister Thayer's. And they asked all kinds of questions about you. Personal questions I didn't feel were any of their business."

Jamie's jaw tightened. "What did you tell them?"

"I said I was merely the housekeeper and wasn't entitled to an opinion about my employer's personal life."

Andi smiled. "How'd Mister Thayer take that?"

A remarkably deep shade of red crept up Noreen's neck. "He said he wouldn't need a housekeeper when he moved in because that's what wives are for." Noreen ground her teeth. "To which his foreman added, 'Keeping house and having babies.' They both laughed. I didn't."

Andi took a step back. "Why that lowlife—" Jamie put his hand on Andi's arm just in time to stop her from exercising her muleskinner's vocabulary.

Noreen looked at Jamie with pleading eyes. "The first thing I did as soon as Mister Thayer left was haul your footlocker up to the master bedroom and put all your things away as I hoped you'd like them. Then I prayed you'd take up residence."

The house groaned under the force of a mighty gust of wind. Rain began to lash against the windowpanes.

"Quite a storm for this time of year," Jamie said. He turned to Noreen. "Will you please give us the grand tour of this finely maintained palace?"

"I'll be happy to, sir." She led them into the library. Jamie slowly turned in a full circle, taking in the floor-to-ceiling shelves filled with books of all colors, shapes, and sizes. The look on his face said he was in paradise. "I love this library," he said.

"Five hundred and twenty-seven books all told, sir."

Jamie looked at Noreen as though she'd pulled a rabbit out of a hat.

"I did an inventory for the estate lawyer, sir."

"Ah. Mister Handler. He does have my permission to enter this house."

"Sir, I'm glad to say, by all appearances, Mister Handler is a true gentleman."

Jamie walked over to the furthest shelf and extracted three adjacent books. He held them with their spines close to his lips and blew across their tops. "Dust-free again." He reached through the gap the books had left and ran his finger over the surface of the shelf. He held up his spotless finger and smiled. "I've inherited a gem!" It wasn't clear whether he meant the house or Noreen. "What do you think of the place, Andi?"

Andi's gaze fell upon a book on the shelf behind Jamie. "I noticed Nurse Hobbes gave you a copy of Jane Austen's *Pride and Prejudice*."

Jamie laughed. "I thought she was crazy recommending

a book like that to a combat veteran. I gave it a chance only out of respect for her." He smiled. "To my amazement, I loved it."

Andi hugged herself. "This place has the same effect on me as *Pemberley* had on Elizabeth." Jamie's smile broadened. Andi could tell Noreen had no idea what they were talking about. "*Pemberley* melted Elizabeth's heart," Andi said.

"Oh, I see." Noreen pointed. "There happens to be a copy of *Pride and Prejudice* just over your shoulder, sir."

"It's settled," Jamie said. "You, John Thayer, and Andi have convinced me. I'm going to move into this mansion and stay until I start teaching again in the fall. After that, I'll spend holidays and summers here. I can also picture myself taking the train down from Palo Alto and staying for the weekend once or twice a month."

Andi impulsively took his arm, pulled him near, and kissed his cheek. "I'm so glad."

Noreen looked ecstatic. "As am I, sir."

Jamie drifted to the center of the library and drummed his fingers on top of the round table in the middle of the room. "I won't need a housekeeper," he said.

Noreen's shoulders sagged. Her arms hung limp.

"Oh, Jamie . . ." Andi caught herself. This was his house and his decision.

"I'll need a household manager," Jamie said to Noreen, "and I hope you'll accept the position." He didn't wait for an answer. "In addition to keeping house, you'll also be responsible for managing an account and paying all the household bills and expenses—all for twice what I'm currently paying you. Oh, and I'd like you to hire an assistant housekeeper. And a gardener."

Noreen's eyes opened as wide as saucers. "You want *me* to be your household manager, sir? With a rise in pay?"

"Yes, madam. You'll also have to do countless other things I know nothing about that are essential to turning a house into a home." Jamie smiled. "What do you say? Will you accept my offer?"

Noreen stood with her back straight and her shoulders back. "Yes, sir! With the utmost gratitude."

Andi put her hand on Noreen's arm. "I'm afraid you'll have to get used to Professor Collins' eccentric ways. It's like him to say he won't need a housekeeper and then offer you a promotion and a raise." Andi folded her arms. "He's something of a mystery to me, too, at times." She smiled at Jamie. "But I guarantee you his heart's in the right place."

Jamie put his hand over his properly placed heart. "Thank you."

"You're welcome, my dear."

"My dear," Jamie repeated. "This incomparable lady calls me, 'dear.' Isn't it amazing how blessed I am?"

Noreen clasped her hands. "Professor Collins, I'm going to love working for you."

"Anthony Lightner willed this house to me free and clear," Jamie said, "but he did state one desire. He hoped I'd fill it with happiness as his grandparents would have wished. That's my intention, and I hope it will be yours too," he said to Noreen.

"You've certainly made me happy, Professor Collins."

"You needn't be so formal. Call me Jamie."

"Oh, sir, I couldn't. That's far too familiar."

"Then how about Professor Jamie?"

Noreen smiled. "I'd be comfortable with that, Professor Jamie, sir."

"And would you be comfortable calling my lady, '*Nurse Andi?*'"

"Yes, Professor Jamie, if she doesn't mind."

Andi smiled. "I'd like that, Noreen."

"Then that's settled." Jamie strode to a closed door opposite the library's double pocket doors. "Where's this lead?"

"Oh, sir, you'll like this." Noreen opened the door to a flight of stairs that descended three steps to a large, airy room. On either side of the steps were built-in floor-to-ceiling bookshelves, currently empty. An ornate desk occupied the center of the room. A sideboard sat against the wall to the left, centered below a long rectangular window. To the right were wooden file cabinets. The desk, sideboard, file cabinets, and shelves were made of matching dark wood, cherry, Andi suspected. A bay window faced the water.

"This was the original master's office," Noreen said.

"I love it." Jamie walked to an exterior door next to the bay window and opened it slightly to a rush of fresh sea air and the sound of crashing waves. "I noticed this door from the street and wondered where it led." He closed it and touched the oval stained-glass window in the door. "This window would suit a cathedral."

"Mrs. Lightner told me this door allowed the master's business associates to come and go without disturbing the rest of the household."

"It would also have allowed him to sneak in and out without his wife noticing," Andi said.

Jamie inclined his head. "What a devious thought." He gave her an affectionate squeeze. "Thanks for giving me the idea."

Everyone laughed.

"What can you tell me about Mrs. Lightner?" Jamie said.

"She's the one who hired me." Noreen shook her head. "It was such a shame she passed away so suddenly. She was a bit reserved, and I'd only been here three months. Still, I believe we were warming up to each other."

"I'm glad you stayed through the transition to her grandson and then to me."

"So am I, Professor Jamie. So am I."

"It's too bad Butch never got to meet you."

They climbed the steps and re-entered the library. "Please show us the rest of *our* house," Jamie said.

There was more to see on the first floor. In addition to the front room, dining room, library, and office, there was an enclosed veranda/sunroom, a bedroom with bath, and a spacious kitchen. The smell of fresh-baked bread was tantalizing. Andi heard Jamie's stomach growl.

In the back of the house, off the kitchen, were two smallish bedrooms that shared a bath. "These quarters were for the cook and the housekeeper in the original household," Noreen said. "I'm currently occupying the larger of the two. I hope that's all right with you, Professor Jamie, sir."

"Perfectly." Jamie looked at Noreen. "I'm curious. Mister Handler told me BayView has six bedrooms. Are these two of the six, or are they in addition?"

"In addition, sir."

"Good. When you hire your assistant housekeeper, she can occupy the room next to yours."

"That would be lovely, sir." Noreen led them up a grand staircase and showed them three large bedrooms, each with its own bath.

"Butch's grandfather designed this house," Jamie said. "Having made his fortune as a builder, he ensured the house was constructed with the finest materials, and everything was the most modern for the time."

"There's another smallish bedroom under an eave in the attic, sir," Noreen said.

"The thought of climbing another flight of stairs is a bit intimidating for a man with my recent history," Jamie said. "Let's visit the master bedroom and save the other for some other time."

For Andi, the master was the climax of the tour. It took up the entire front of the second story of the house and consisted of a sitting room with a fireplace, a bedroom, and a bathroom. Opposite the door was a large window that overlooked the bay. The sitting room featured windows on three sides of a gable. Below each gable window was a cushioned bench seat. Andi had noticed this feature of Bayview from the street. It was the most prominent—and spectacular—feature of the front of the house.

"I love it," Jamie said. "It's no less impressive than our Presidential Suite at the Palace Hotel."

Andi could feel herself blush.

Chapter 11

The Wind and Rain and Crashing Sea

Andi stood in the middle of BayView's master suite and closed her eyes. She pictured herself sitting on one of the gable-end bench seats, watching the waves below while her children played at her feet.

She opened her eyes, and the image was gone.

The wooden box Charlie Gowan made for Jamie's medals sat on top of a dresser. The walking stick the men from Ward 321 had presented him was next to the door. Jamie picked it up. "Did you read the inscription?" he asked Noreen.

She looked nervously from Jamie to the stick and back. "Yes, Professor Jamie. I apologize for being so nosy."

"No need to apologize. I don't have any secrets—at least none I'm willing to share."

Noreen placed her palms on either side of her face. "That inscription, sir—the one officer we'd gladly follow to hell and back—just about brought me to tears."

"Me too," Jamie said.

He walked to the middle of the sitting room's gable end.

Andi joined him. The sea was crashing on the rocks below. A strong gust threw ocean spray far onto the shore. Jamie spoke with his back to Noreen. "Andi and I love a good storm. Especially when we can enjoy it together."

He faced Noreen. "During the war, Andi and I served at the front. We both suffer from nightmares." He put his arm around her waist. "When our nightmares wake us in the night, they're almost more than we can endure. Would you be scandalized if we shared a bed while we're here—just to comfort each other, you understand?"

Andi's cheeks burned. Noreen was speechless.

Jamie let go of Andi's waist. "Your silence tells me you would object."

Noreen was slow to answer. "No, Professor Jamie. My silence means something altogether different." She wrapped her arms tight around herself. "I was never at the front—both the munitions factories where I worked were far behind the lines—but I still have nightmares." She seemed lost in dark memories. "On the 22nd of September 1914, German submarine *U-9* torpedoed and sank the British armored cruiser *HMS Aboukir*. Two other armored cruisers came to the rescue. Within an hour, that cold-blooded submarine captain sank both of those as well." She took a deep breath. "The casualty list is seared into my mind. From the three ships combined, 1,459 men were lost, 527 from *HMS Aboukir* alone—including my husband."

Noreen reached up and smoothed her graying hair. "My silence meant that I would give the world to have someone comfort me in the night when my nightmares wake me. So I have no objection to you and Nurse Andi comforting each other."

Andi almost cried. "I know I speak for Jamie when I say

we're sorry for the loss of your husband. How long had you been married?"

"We married in 1899. We were both older than most newlyweds. I was 28. He was 30. We had fifteen wonderful years together."

What Andi wouldn't give for fifteen years with Jamie!

Noreen smiled. "Fifteen *glorious* years."

Andi added the numbers in her head. That would make Noreen about the age of Andi's mother—had she lived.

"How long did you work in munitions?" Jamie said.

Noreen rocked heel to toe before answering. "I started in October 1914, right after the Kaiser's men murdered my husband. I never missed a day right up to the Armistice."

Jamie gasped. "Working that long in munitions *and* losing your husband—no wonder you have nightmares!"

"I craved munitions work, sir. It let me *do* something for the war effort. I started in Scotland manufacturing artillery shells. When I heard how devastating machine guns were proving to be, I left my homeland and went to work in a vast purpose-built machine gun factory at Burton-on-Trent. That's in Staffordshire, sir, near Nottingham in the middle of England."

"You wanted to make machine guns?" Jamie said with a tremor in his voice.

Noreen twisted the ring on her left ring finger. "Killing with a machine gun is much more personal than with an artillery shell. A machine gunner points his weapon directly at the enemy and pulls the trigger." A low rumbling, almost a growl, came from deep within Noreen's throat. "I said a blessing over every machine gun we sent to the front, knowing our boys would show no mercy as they mowed down the Kaiser's men."

Jamie's face had turned white.

"I'm sorry, sir. I can see I've upset you. My problem is I've yet to find the Christian charity in my heart to forgive the Kaiser's men for taking my husband."

"It's not your bitterness toward the Kaiser's men Professor Jamie is reacting to," Andi said. "It was the mention of machine guns. Professor Jamie singlehandedly eliminated a battery of enemy machine guns in France to keep them from mowing down his men. In the process, he was gravely wounded and pronounced dead. Yet the Lord still had work for him to do among the living. He raised Jamie and blessed me with the privilege of assisting in his recovery."

Most of the color had returned to Jamie's face. "All three of us suffered at the hands of the Kaiser's men. As one who killed his share of them, I can tell you, life is better if you forgive—yet I would never suggest that you forget."

A mighty gust of wind blew a sheet of rain against the side of the house. The tat, tat, tat against the windowpanes sounded like a distant burst of machine gun fire. Bayview didn't flinch. It seemed to stand even stronger as the elements beat against it. From the look on Jamie's face, Andi suspected the sounds had taken him back to the day he was wounded—and abandoned.

"I imagine it can get pretty spooky here at night all by yourself," Andi said.

"Sometimes." Noreen clasped her hands behind her back. "But if you're a romantic like me, you'll come to love it."

Jamie's stomach growled louder than the storm.

"Forgive me," Noreen said. "You must be starving. Would you and Nurse Andi like a little dinner?"

Jamie patted his stomach. "I sure would. And since you weren't expecting us, we'll be happy with whatever you have on hand."

Noreen crossed her arms. "I always have a soup or stew ready, and today is my baking day. It would be good for my waistline if I didn't have to eat it all myself." She lowered her head and looked up at Jamie. "I take pride in my cooking."

Andi looked at Jamie sheepishly. "May I tell you a secret?"

Jamie held up his hand. "Only if it won't shock Noreen more than I already have."

"It may. Take a deep breath, Noreen." Andi turned slightly and looked at Jamie over her shoulder. "I've never learned to cook."

Jamie put his hands on his hips. "You mean you're not perfect after all?"

Noreen laughed. "Ach, lassie, if you want to learn, I'll teach ye."

Please let that come to pass, Andi silently prayed.

"Now you sound like a real Scotswoman," Jamie said.

"Oh, sir. I'm trying hard not to." Noreen held her head high. "I want to sound like an American."

"I understand," he said. "I'll try not to tease you when you slip into your Scottish dialect."

"I like the sound of your accent," Andi said. "But I remember how hard the parents of some of my childhood friends worked to eliminate theirs, hoping that would help them fit in better."

"My parents used to own a business here in town," Jamie said. "It was called the Scottish Bakery when they bought it. They liked the name and never changed it even though they were English. I always associate Scotland with the delicious things my parents used to bake."

They returned to the kitchen. Noreen began gathering up place settings for two. "I'll set you two up in the dining room, sir."

"Let's eat together in the kitchen," Jaimie said, "and get to know each other better."

"The kitchen, sir?"

"I ate from a mess kit in the trenches and metal trays in various hospitals for what feels like ages. I long to eat in a place as warm and homey as your kitchen." A longing Andi shared. "I especially like the idea of eating with the woman whose hands prepared the meal," Jamie said.

They sat around the kitchen table. After saying grace, Jamie broke a loaf of freshly baked bread and doled out generous portions. Noreen filled three bowls with a fabulous-smelling stew.

She was indeed an excellent cook.

Andi was pleased to see Jamie so at home, sitting around the kitchen table, enjoying Noreen's cooking.

"How long have you been in the United States?" Jamie asked.

"Since the beginning of February, sir. Five months, that would be."

Andi dabbed at the corner of her mouth with her napkin. "What brought you to Pacific Grove?"

"I have a nephew, my brother's son, who's been here since before the war. He has a good job here on the Peninsula. He sponsored my move to the US."

"What does he do?"

"David's a surveyor, ma'am. Mostly for a land developer here on the peninsula."

Jamie set his spoon down. "Wait a minute. Is your nephew David MacAskill?"

Noreen sat back in surprise. "Why, yes, sir."

"We have an appointment to meet a man in David's office tomorrow morning."

Noreen's eyebrows arched.

"The commanding officer of the hospital Andi was attached to, and where I was a patient, asked me to meet with the man. Doctor Thornburgh says Mister Morse would like to talk to me about doing some consulting for him."

"It's a small world, Professor Jamie." Noreen held up the stew pot. "Would either of you care for a second helping?"

Andi wondered if all Scotswomen were as impassive as Noreen.

"It's been a long time since I've had a home-cooked meal," Jamie said. "One more small helping would be very much appreciated." He canted his head. "I'm curious, where in Scotland are you from originally?"

"The Western Isles, sir. The town of Stornoway on the Isle of Lewis."

"Hmm." Jamie ran his fingers through his hair. "Do we have an atlas in our library?"

"Yes, Professor Jamie. A big, beautiful one." Noreen left the room and returned with a book a quarter the size of the table. She opened it to a map of Scotland and pointed to an island in the northwest. "The island's northern part is Lewis; the southern part is Harris. Stornoway is here on the east coast of Lewis."

Andi looked up from the map to see whether Noreen was joking. "You mean the north part of the island has one name and the south another?"

"That's the Scots for you," Noreen said.

"I assume that quirk isn't why you left," Jamie said.

Noreen folded her arms. "No, sir. There were just too many reminders of sad times for me on Lewis. And my nephew painted such an appealing picture of America."

Jamie intertwined his fingers over his full belly. "Then I hope you'll soon consider Pacific Grove home."

"I know Callum would have loved it. And it would have been a wonderful place for our daughter to grow up."

Andi canted her head. "Where's your daughter now?"

"Nora is in heaven with Callum."

The way Noreen said it, one would think Callum and Nora were just down the street.

"Nora preceded Callum by twelve years. She was only eleven months old when we lost her—pneumonia takes a wicked toll on infants in cold, drafty croft houses."

Jamie reached out and patted Noreen's hand.

It almost broke Andi's heart to hear Noreen talk about Callum and Nora as though they might walk hand-in-hand through the kitchen door at any moment. She lowered her head. "I was only three when my mother died," Andi said.

"That goes a long way to explaining why you never learned to cook." Jamie looked at Noreen. "Andi and I . . . our relationship is . . . complicated." Jamie took Andi's hand. "Andi has accepted an appointment as the next Assistant Dean of the Army School of Nursing in Washington, DC. It's a real honor to be selected. The problem is army regulations require nurses to be single."

"And Jamie has a commitment of his own," Andi added. "Even if I turned down the assignment with the School of Nursing, we still couldn't marry before next April."

A mighty gust of wind rattled the kitchen windows. The rain continued its tattoo.

"The storm's strengthening," Noreen said. "I admit, having others in the house on a night like this will be a comfort."

Noreen stood and began clearing the dishes. Andi began to help. "Please don't bother, Nurse Andi."

"It's no bother, Noreen. I want to help." Had she been entirely open, Andi would have revealed that she was going to pretend she was helping her mother wash up.

After the table was cleared, Jamie commandeered the atlas and turned to a map of Colorado. "Please, Andi, tell us about where you grew up."

They spent a pleasant hour or so learning about Colorado and then Minnesota, where Andi went to nursing school, at which point Noreen said, "If you'll excuse me for a minute, I'll run upstairs and start a fire in the master suite's fireplace."

"She's great," Andi said once Noreen was out of earshot.

"I totally agree."

Noreen soon returned. "Please, Professor Jamie, tell us a little about the university where you teach."

Jamie loved Stanford University and might have gone on *ad infinitum* if Andi hadn't begun to yawn.

He smiled at her. "What do you say, Andi? Should we turn in?"

"It's been a busy day. Let's."

Jamie stood and put his hand on Noreen's shoulder. "I hope you have a long and happy reign as BayView's house-hold manager."

* * *

In the master suite, the sounds of the wind and the rain and the crashing waves were intense. And to Andi, intensely romantic.

"Just the kind of night to curl up with the one you love," Andi said. She wrapped her arms around Jamie. This suite, this house, this man filled her heart with joy. Cruelly, some women, even nice women like Noreen, lost their men—men it was Andi's duty to save.

Oh, God, here it comes again. Ever since the war, the greater Andi's happiness, the greater her feelings of guilt for not being able to save all the sick and injured soldiers under her care. Her medical training and clinical experience told her that her emotions were a reaction to the trauma she endured during the war. But understanding didn't make her condition any less real. In her mind, she simply didn't deserve her good fortune. And if the Hangman's Curse prevented her from accepting a marriage proposal, how could it be right to sleep in Jamie's bed in his house with him when someday this bed and this house—and Jamie—might belong to some other woman? Andi couldn't stop her tears from flowing. "I should sleep in another room."

Jamie gently lifted her chin. "Tell me what's troubling you. And let me help."

"I wouldn't feel right sleeping with you in this house if someday it's going to be some other woman's home."

"Some other woman?" Jamie drew her nearer. "There can be no other woman for me."

"You deserve a loving companion you can grow old with." Andi choked back a sob. "There could be no happier moment in my life than to walk down the aisle of my father's church and hear him pronounce us husband and wife. But such happiness would be the ultimate affront to the soldiers I couldn't save. And the Hangman's Curse would be the end of you."

Jamie wiped the tears from her cheeks. "Put such thoughts far from your mind. I told you, I'm not that easy to kill."

"You've never faced the Hangman's Curse."

"I've faced artillery shells and machine gun bullets. They're far more real than any curse, and they couldn't kill me. Besides, for you, I would stare down any danger."

Face to face, Jamie could convince her of anything, especially when it was what she desperately wanted to believe. But what would happen when she was 3,000 miles away in Washington, DC, and her fears were free to run wild? Only time would tell. For now . . ..

"Then hold me, Jamie. Hold me until this storm in my mind subsides. And when the morning comes, help me to stare down the Hangman's Curse with your courage and certainty."

"That's exactly what I intend to do," he whispered in her ear.

Andi slipped from Jamie's embrace, went around the suite, and turned off all the lights. She stood before their glowing fireplace for a moment, then moved to the sitting room's gable end, where she was surrounded by windows on three sides, giving her an unobstructed view of the bay, the street, and the sidewalk below.

With her back to him, she undid her ponytail and shook her hair out across her shoulders. She could see a triptych reflection of herself in the surrounding windows. Her copper hair took on the radiance of a sunset in the fire's glow. She stood with her feet apart and her arms spread wide. "I love this house!" she shouted above the din of the storm. "And I love you." She spun around and faced him. "When I'm with you, nothing frightens me."

They quickly changed into their night clothes. Jamie threw back the bedding on their four-poster bed and, like a gentleman, let Andi slip between the sheets first. She held the bedding up for him to join her. They snuggled together and let the wind and rain and crashing sea serenade them into peaceful sleep.

Chapter 12

Slaying the Dragon

Wednesday, 04 June 1919

Jamie was glad the storm had abated by morning. It allowed Noreen to go out early and buy what she needed to prepare a breakfast fit for royalty.

Soon after breakfast, Jamie was surprised to receive a telegraph. He looked at it as though it were some strange, foreign object. "Who even knows I'm here?" He read silently.

"Jamie?"

"I'm sorry. I was lost in thought." He held up the note. "It's from Mister Kavanaugh. He'd like to see me."

"Did you tell him you'd be here?"

"No." Jamie rubbed the back of his neck. "He must have contacts up and down the coast to know where to have sent this telegram."

"That's a bit disconcerting, don't you think?"

Jamie was thinking the same thing.

"Does he say why he wants to see you?" Andi said.

"No." Jamie looked at the telegram again. "But it sounds urgent."

"Where and when does he want to see you?"

"He says he's unable to travel, so he'd like to see me in his downtown San Francisco office Friday at 2:00 pm."

"That's hardly convenient."

"He says he'd be happy if I brought you along and that he'll make it worth our while." Jamie waved the telegram in the air. "He wants me to telephone his office and confirm our appointment. He's already made parlor car reservations for us for Friday morning's Del Monte Express. And an open-ended reservation for a luxury suite at the Saint Francis Hotel for Friday night onward, for as long as we want to stay!"

"Then he knows we're staying together?"

"So it seems." Jamie tossed the telegram aside. "It doesn't matter that we don't have anything to hide. I don't like being spied on."

"Me either." Andi glanced at the telegraph. "It must have cost him a fortune to send a telegram that long."

"No doubt, but he can afford it." Jamie was silent for a moment. "Despite him invading our privacy, I'd like to hear what he has to say. We don't have any other plans. And I wouldn't mind spending a few more days in the city with you. Why not meet with him?"

"Why not?" Andi put her hands on her hips. "Because he's a dangerous man."

"A dangerous man who's going to help educate disabled veterans."

Andi shook her head. "Someday, my curiosity will get me in real trouble." She let her hands fall to her sides. "Let's do it."

Jamie smiled. "I'm sure the Centrella Hotel will let me use their telephone. It's just a couple of blocks up the street. A little walk in the fresh air would be nice, don't you think?"

* * *

Though they weren't paying guests, the manager of the Centrella Hotel was happy to let Jamie use their telephone—for a reasonable price.

Compared to the field telephones Jamie had used in France, the Centrella's candlestick-style telephone was a work of art. Jamie gave the operator the number Kavanaugh had provided. "Kavanaugh Enterprises," a very proper female voice answered.

Though he'd used the telephone at Letterman several times, it was primitive compared to this one. He was startled by the clarity of the voice on the other end of this line. "You sound so . . . so real," he said.

The woman on the other end of the line giggled. "Yes, sir. That's probably because I am."

Had she been able to see through the telephone line, she would have seen Jamie's face turn red. "This is Jamie Collins. May I speak to Mister Kavanaugh?"

"I'm sorry, Professor Collins . . . .." She couldn't stifle her giggles. "Please excuse me, sir. Your comment just struck my funny bone."

Jamie was surprised she knew who he was. "I'm not used to talking on the telephone. I was startled that the sound is so natural."

"It's an amazing device, sir." She cleared her throat. "Now, I'm afraid Mister Kavanaugh is currently out of the office. May I help you?"

With Andi's concurrence, Jamie confirmed their appointment.

Jamie hung up the telephone. "Afterwards, we can dine at the Saint Francis Hotel and sample their California cuisine."

"That sounds lovely."

"Speaking of sounds, the voice on the other end of the line was so life-like I think I'll have a telephone installed in BayView."

"Good idea," Andi said. "Then you can let Noreen know you're coming before descending on her."

"I don't think I'll need to."

"No, but if you let her know you're coming, she can have a nice homemade meal waiting for you."

"Now you've persuaded me."

* * *

Around 11:00 AM, they took the streetcar to downtown Monterey. The population of Monterey was only around 5,500 people, and David MacAskill was one of only two land surveyors in town, so it wasn't that great a coincidence that they would be meeting a land developer in the office of Noreen's nephew. What surprised Jamie was that John Thayer's office was only a few doors from David's.

As they passed Thayer's office, a man almost as big as Nick Hendricks stepped out onto the sidewalk. Jamie instinctively knew who he was.

"John Thayer?"

The man stopped abruptly. "Who's asking?"

"Jamie Collins."

Thayer smiled, or was it a smirk? "Ah, it's your house I'm looking to buy."

Jamie took a step closer. "You've ruined your chances there."

Thayer's smirk became a snarl. "What's that?"

Jamie could feel the beast within him begin to stir. "I won't deal with a man who lied to gain entry into my house and then stomped around like he already owned the place."

Thayer moved within a yard of Jamie and looked down at him. "Didn't your lawyer—what's his name? Handler. Didn't Handler tell you I wanted to buy the place? I wasn't going to close the deal without first seeing the inside."

"I hope you saw all you wanted to because you'll never set foot in my house again."

Thayer's smirk returned. "I expect you'll change your mind once you see my revised offer."

Jamie ground his teeth. "It's not for sale. And even if it were, I wouldn't sell it to a man like you."

"Why, you little pipsqueak. You'd be nothing if it weren't for my father's scholarship."

Jamie was alarmed when Andi stepped between them. "You're wrong, *Mister* Thayer. A man as brave and caring as Professor Collins would be a man of consequence under any circumstances."

Thayer seemed as surprised as Jamie by Andi's defense of her man. He moved back a step and glared at Jamie. "Does the big war hero need a woman to defend him?"

"I'd be willing to bet no one would come to your defense," Andi said.

She obviously hit a nerve. "I don't need anybody to defend me." He glared at Jamie. "I was here building houses, banks, and churches to benefit this community while you were off somewhere in Europe, killing a bunch of teenage boys."

"Boys?" The beast in Jamie rattled its cage.

"That's right." Thayer raised his chin. "Some halfwit king starts a war and condemns a bunch of kids to fight it. And what choice did they have? Serve in the master's army or face a firing squad. It was those boys the Kaiser cared so little for who you sent to their early graves."

"Those 'boys,' as you call them, were trained soldiers," Andi said with her face a few inches from Thayer's. She took Jamie by the arm. "Let's not waste any more time on the likes of him."

They marched off and didn't stop until they were in front of David MacAskill's office. "What fries me," Jamie said, "is that Thayer was right. Kaiser Billy's living in luxury in the Netherlands while all the young men I killed are rotting in graves somewhere in France."

Andi stepped in front of Jamie so they were eye to eye. "You stopped a madman and his army from killing who knows how many innocent people. Yes, the Kaiser lives—in shame, defeat, and exile. And the soldiers you saved and their children are filling the churches, banks, and houses Thayer built."

Jamie's beast crawled back into its cage. He gave Andi a big hug. "It was brave of you to step between Thayer and me, but please don't scare me like that again. You could have gotten hurt."

"That big bag of wind didn't scare me."

"If he had even looked like he was going to lay a finger on you," Jamie said, "I would have killed him."

Andi stared at Jamie. "You're serious."

"Do you doubt me? It's not like I've never killed anyone before."

"That was during the war."

"It would be a war if someone were to hurt you. And don't think being bigger than me would have spared him. The army taught me a dozen ways to kill a man of any size with my bare hands."

Andi blanched. "And I know a dozen ways to defend myself without leaving a corpse in my wake."

"What would you do if someday you're alone and a man like Thayer lays a hand on you?"

"I'd grab his hand," Andi grabbed Jamie's, "twist it backward," she demonstrated, bringing Jamie almost to a knee, "and if necessary, break his wrist." She let go.

Jamie stood up straight. "Even with a broken wrist, he'd still be a threat." Jamie held up his right hand and slowly curled it into a fist. "Had Thayer touched you, I would have delivered a fist to his Adam's apple and then snapped his neck."

Andi took a step back. "Just for touching me?"

"You are more precious to me than life itself. I would do anything to protect you."

Andi assumed her Nurse Eliot bearing. "And I would fight to the death to protect you."

Jamie shook his head. "I suppose that makes us a rather odd couple."

Andi held her head higher. "No, it doesn't. We're soldiers."

They were a few minutes early for their 11:30 appointment with Mister S. F. B. Morse, who allegedly could pull off the trick of being both a land developer and a conservationist.

As they waited in the reception area, they could hear a deep, friendly, but authoritative voice coming from an inner office. Instructions were being given to someone who answered with a Scottish accent, presumably Noreen's nephew. Jamie was struck by how affable their interchange was, unlike a boss talking down to a hired hand. "That sounds like a man I'd enjoy working with," Jamie whispered to Andi.

After a minute or two, a large man emerged from the inner office. Jamie could picture him captaining an undefeated Yale University football team. Jamie stood. "Mister Morse?"

"Yes, sir," he said with a friendly smile, "and you must be Professor Collins."

Introductions were made all around. Sam was impressed to learn that Andi was an Army nurse who had served at the front.

Titles would be dispensed with. It would be Sam, Jamie, and Andi. They got down to business.

"I want to make sure you realize I'm a theoretical physicist and not an engineer," Jamie said. "I'm not sure I could be of help to you."

"Someone with your scientific training will look at things from a unique perspective, making you a valuable consultant."

Jamie hadn't thought of it that way. "I have a lot of responsibilities at this stage of my life. I couldn't devote much time to your projects, except perhaps during the summers."

"That's good. The demands on your time tell me how much others value your talents—which is a fine recommendation, wouldn't you agree?"

A young man with a ruddy complexion matching his red hair came out of the inner office.

"You must be David MacAskill," Jamie said.

He smiled. "Guilty as charged."

"I'm Jamie Collins, and this is my dearest friend, Andi Eliot. We had the pleasure of meeting your aunt yesterday. She's my household manager."

"Household manager?" David seemed surprised. "I thought she was a housekeeper."

"She so impressed us that I offered her a promotion and a raise, and I'm happy to say she accepted."

David brushed his red mane off his forehead. "That was fast."

"The house was immaculate, and I believe in rewarding good work."

"You sound as decisive as Mister Morse," David said with a smile.

Sam glowed at the compliment. "I'm surprised your aunt didn't telephone and tell you the good news," Sam said to David.

"We don't have a telephone at BayView," Jamie said.

Sam canted his head. "They can come in handy. I suggest you have one installed."

Jamie could tell Sam was used to people promptly acting on his suggestions. "I plan to."

"David and I were going over a survey map. May I show it to you? I'd like your and Andi's opinions."

Including Andi clinched it for Jamie. Sam was indeed a man he'd enjoy working with.

They followed Sam into an inner office, where he leaned over a map table and pointed. "I have first option on this tract of land. I'm just not sure what to do with it. But if

I don't buy it, John Thayer will. He'll cut down all the trees, bulldoze it flat, and put up cheap, high-density housing."

"John Thayer?" Jamie said. "We bumped into him just a few minutes ago."

Sam frowned. "Was he pleasant?"

"Not at all."

"He seldom is."

Jamie drummed his fingers on the map table. "Thayer's family funded the scholarship that let me attend Stanford and earn my Ph.D."

"I know," Sam said. "Thomas Thayer and his wife were good friends of mine. They were great people, friendly and generous. It's a shame John doesn't take after them."

Andi had been studying Sam's map. "How about a golf course?"

Sam squinted at her. "Excuse me?"

"This tract of land—why don't you build a golf course on it? You could wind it through the forest, then break out onto the shore, and give the golfers an unforgettable view of the sea at the end of their round." She looked at Sam. "That way, you'd preserve all the cypress and pine trees Thayer would cut down." She stood up straight. "I'd call it Cypress Point Golf Club."

Sam smiled indulgently. "We already have a course on the grounds of the Hotel Del Monte, and we just opened Pebble Beach Golf Links a few miles south."

Andi smiled. "Can you ever have enough golf courses?"

Sam looked at the map again. "I don't suppose you can."

"Then why not make the Monterey Peninsula the country's premier golfing destination?"

Sam bowed to her. "That, young lady, is a brilliant idea."

Jamie shook his head. "Maybe you should hire Andi as a consultant and forget about me."

"Or better yet," Sam said with a smile, "hire you both to thank you in some small way for your service to our country."

"What do you think, Andi?" Jamie asked.

"I think you'll have fun working with Sam. You should jump at the chance."

Jamie smiled. "You heard the lady. I'm your man."

"Great." Sam stuck out his hand, and they shook. "I can't wait to tell Thayer who my new consultant is."

Andi pointed to a small area on the map. "Imagine the challenge you could present the golfers near the end of their round if they had to hit their ball over this little cove and land it on the other side."

David MacAskill laughed. "I always say nobody can out-imagine Mister Morse. I believe you have."

Sam laughed.

After warm goodbyes, Jamie gave David's secretary his contact information, and he and Andi left the office.

They hadn't taken two steps before Jamie scooped Andi up in his arms and twirled her around in a full circle. "You were fabulous. Cypress Point Golf Club—I love it!"

She laughed like she was on a carnival ride. "Just trying to help. Now, put me down before you hurt yourself."

"I've got to ask. Where did an army nurse learn about golf?"

"Me? I don't know the first thing about it. I only know golf courses, in general, are beautiful places, and the grounds of the Presidio's course are a great place to run early in the morning before the golfers arrive and get in the way."

"You're an amazing woman, Andrea Jean Eliot. No wonder I love you."

"I have another idea I hope you'll love." Andi smiled. "But first, let's find a nice restaurant. You'll need sustenance for our next adventure."

"What do you have in mind?"

"We're going to Pacific Grove High School to slay a dragon."

Once Jamie overcame the initial shock, it didn't seem like a bad idea at all. "You know, it's about time I faced Elaine Stanton. And with you there to protect me, it can't be much worse than what I faced in France."

* * *

Their cabbie dropped Andi and Jamie off in front of Pacific Grove High School's administrative office. Andi took Jamie's sweaty hand and led him up to the secretary's desk as though they had a right to be there. "Would it be possible for us to speak with Miss Stanton?" Andi said.

The secretary smiled. "Certainly." She looked up at the clock on the wall above her desk. "Her last class of the day should end just about . . .." The bell rang. "Now." She laughed. "You two look a little young to have a child in high school."

"Professor Collins went to school here with Miss Stanton. We're visiting in town and want to pay our respects."

"Professor, did you say?"

"Yes," Andi answered. "Of physics at Stanford University."

The secretary stared at Jamie. "Wait. Collins, did you say? Jamie Collins?"

"Yes, ma'am," Jamie said.

"Well, I'll be. You're something of a legend around here, Professor Collins." She pointed to a framed newspaper article on the wall just behind him. "The local newspaper ran several articles about you. It's fair to say you're our most celebrated graduate. I'm sure Miss Stanton will want to see you. She never tires of telling anyone who will listen that she was the school's top graduate the year you received the Thayer Scholarship."

Andi covered her mouth. Had she made a mistake bringing Jamie here? "Miss Stanton, is she a popular teacher?" Andi said.

The secretary nodded vigorously. "One of our *most* popular."

That was a relief. Maybe Elaine wouldn't attack Jamie on sight after all. "Might we find her in her classroom?"

"Yes, ma'am. That would be Room . . ." The secretary looked in a well-worn, legal-sized book on her desk. "Room 212." She looked at Jamie. "Do you remember the way, Professor Collins?"

"How could I forget? Thanks for your help."

Jamie led Andi past a gaggle of students, down a hall, and up a flight of stairs. "If she never gets tired of telling people I stole her future, this could get ugly."

"That's not what the secretary said. She said Elaine likes to tell people she got better grades than you. That's all." Andi took his hand. "Don't worry. I'm here to protect you."

Jamie laughed, a hollow, nervous laugh. "Then you'll forgive me if I duck behind you when the chairs and tables start flying?"

Jamie paused outside Room 212. He looked like he was steeling himself for battle.

A tallish woman with broad shoulders had her back to the door as she erased a blackboard. She was singing to herself. Her voice was sublime. Jamie knocked. The woman turned around. She spread her arms wide and, with a flourish, finished the chorus of her song, clearly having fun with it. Andi saw no sign that she recognized Jamie.

"You could go on stage with a voice like that," Jamie said.

"Thank you, but I only sing for my friends."

Jamie ran his fingers back through his hair. "You just sang for us."

"Then you must be my friends," she said with a captivating smile.

"I'm Jamie Collins."

Recognition struck her like a flying brick. She rushed at Jamie. He took a defensive stance. Elaine threw her arms around him. "What a pleasure to see you again after all these years."

Jamie drew back from her. "A pleasure?"

Elaine appeared puzzled by his reaction.

"The last time we spoke, you accused me of stealing your future."

Elaine was silent for a moment. "I did say that, didn't I?" She smiled. "That was wicked of me. I hope you shrugged it off. I'm perfectly happy with the way my future played out."

Andi could only shake her head. Poor Jamie. All those years of self-loathing. And for what?

"I got the Thayer Scholarship when it should have been yours."

"I received a scholarship to the state teacher's college in San Jose, where I earned a math degree and a teaching credential while enjoying every minute of my time there. Several of my sorority sisters will no doubt be lifelong friends. And I love teaching here at our old school." She put her hand on Jamie's forearm. "I did wonder at times how you were holding up under the pressure of studying engineering at Stanford."

"Physics," Jamie said. "I changed my major early on."

"No matter. Everyone here is so proud of you."

Jamie looked like he'd been run over by a truck. He semi-collapsed against the door jam. "I had to work my tail off to earn my degrees, and all the while, I felt guilty as hell for accepting the Thayer Scholarship, knowing it should have been yours."

"The Thayer Scholarship wasn't open to girls," Elaine said dismissively. "I apologize that my hasty words were hurtful. Please forgive me."

Jamie was dumbfounded.

"He should thank you," Andi said. She turned to Jamie. "Would you have been half as successful if you hadn't been trying to make sure the Thayer Scholarship didn't go to waste?"

Jamie shook his head sheepishly.

"Nonsense," Elaine said. "I'm sure I had nothing to do with your success." She smiled at Andi. "Where are my manners?" She extended her hand. "Lanie Stanton."

"Lanie?" Jamie said.

"Elaine is far too formal for a gal like me."

Andi took her hand. "Andi Eliot." Lanie's grip was firm and friendly.

"Sorry," Lanie said. "I've gotten chalk all over your hand."

Andi looked at Jamie. He seemed to have entered a catatonic trance. He had to be asking himself whether it was even possible that this was the woman who so captivated Charlie Gowan, Letterman's master prosthetics craftsman.

Lanie looked at Andi. "Are you two . . .?"

"We're in love," Andi said with unbounded pride.

"Good for you. I'm still single, although I have my eye on the man buying my late father's furniture business here in town. He's a big, bashful, southern gentleman who doesn't yet realize the peril he's in."

"Charlie Gowan?" Jamie said.

Lanie's mouth fell open. "How could you possibly know that? I haven't told a soul."

"Charlie's a friend of ours," Jamie said. "He's the one who makes prosthetics for the men on Nurse Andi's orthopedic ward."

Lanie's cheeks turned crimson. "I'm so embarrassed. Please don't tell him I'm after him."

Andi patted her arm. "Don't worry. We wouldn't want to spoil anything for either of you. Charlie's a fine man. He deserves his good luck."

"I thought your family owned the hardware store," Jamie said.

"A lot of people make that mistake. The Stantins, with an 'i', own the hardware store. We're the Stantons, with an 'o'."

Jamie couldn't begin to calculate the odds of so many lives and events lining up the way they had. A Bible verse popped into his head: *"For I know the plans I have for you,"* *declares the* L ORD , *"plans to prosper you and not to harm you,* *plans to give you hope and a future.* Could that verse from Jeremiah, so often taken out of context, apply to Jamie and the people in his life? "I'd say you being the one Charlie thinks so highly of is a colossal coincidence," he said. "Except I don't believe in coincidences."

Lanie's face brightened. "He thinks highly of me?"

"That's putting it mildly."

Lanie beamed. "I worked closely with my father before leaving for college in San Jose. With my older brother going off to become a doctor, had I been a boy, Father would have wanted me to take over the business. Of course, had I been a boy, I would have disappointed him and gone to Stanford to study engineering instead."

Jamie smiled. "And then where would I be?"

"Maybe you could have gone to teacher's college and taught math here at our old high school," Lanie said with an even bigger smile.

Jamie laughed. "You're something else. It's easy to see why you made such an impression on Charlie."

"Impression?" Lanie's eyes opened wide. "Tell me more."

"He's interested in you. He's just afraid you're too classy for him."

"Me? Classy? I'm just an unpretentious small-town girl."

"I consider that classy," Andi said.

Lanie smiled, a warm, friendly smile. "If you two aren't in a rush, why don't we visit the Scottish Bakery, have a sweet, a cup of coffee, and catch up on each other's lives."

"The Scottish Bakery?" Jamie said. "That would be a trip down memory lane. My parents used to own the place."

"I remember," Lanie said. She turned to Andi. "It's only a few blocks down Forest Avenue. Would you mind a little walk?"

Andi took Jamie's arm. "Sounds like fun to me."

It seemed to Andi that the weight of the world had been

removed from Jamie's shoulders as he stood up tall. "Let's," he said.

They left the high school and headed down Forest Avenue. Every kid they passed gave "Miss Stanton" a friendly greeting.

"The kids like you," Jamie said.

"And I like them."

No false modesty. Andi admired Lanie's self-assuredness.

The smell of baked goods was tantalizing as they entered the Scottish Bakery. Jamie stopped just inside the doorway and took a deep breath. "Ah, that brings back memories. I can imagine my mother standing behind the counter."

"Good memories, I hope," Lanie said.

"Absolutely. And I wanted to show the place to Andi. It was sold as part of the settlement of my mom's estate. I'm glad whoever owns it continued the business and didn't change the name." He sighed. "The timing of my mother's passing was a blessing. She never knew I'd been wounded."

Andi took his hand. "I remember you mentioned that her memorial service took place while you were in the hospital in France."

"I didn't need to attend a memorial service to remember her." He put his hand over his heart. "She's right here."

"I'm sorry for your loss," Lanie said.

Lanie had a way about her that made Andi believe she really cared about others. Maybe nurses and teachers had that in common.

They sat at a small table. Lanie ordered coffee for herself and Andi and tea for Jamie. "I only have my brother now that Dad's passed away." She turned to Jamie. "Do you remember Scott?"

"I do. He graduated two years ahead of us if I remember correctly?"

"That's right. He's a doctor now with a practice here in town." Lanie's semi-permanent smile disappeared. "He works so hard. Never a day off, always on call. He keeps driving himself and driving himself. I so wish he'd take on a partner so he could relax now and then." She sighed. "I'm afraid he's burying himself in his work to keep from having to face . . . I don't know what. He served in France during the war . . .and it changed him. He used to smile all the time. Now . . ."

"Another 'disabled' veteran," Andi mumbled.

"The war," Jamie said. "It changed everyone." He leaned back in his chair. "Your brother, does he have any fellow veterans he can talk with about his service?"

Lanie thought for a moment. "None that I know of."

"Talking to others who'd been there helped me regain my balance." Jamie ran his fingers through his hair. "I recall that Scott started a chess club back in high school."

"That's right," Lanie said. "He still plays when he can find an opponent."

Andi knew exactly where Jamie was heading—and she couldn't have been prouder of him.

"I'll be living here in town throughout the summer. I'll look him up. Maybe I can use chess as a gateway to help Scott regain his equilibrium."

Andi said a silent prayer of thanks that there were such men as Jamie in the world and that he was her man— for now.

Lanie sat back in her chair. She looked like she might cry. "It would mean the world to me if you could give me back my smiling brother."

They spent another delightful hour sharing tales about their lives, some humorous, some heart-rending. They went their separate ways with promises to stay in touch.

Before leaving, Jamie bought a dozen Scottish shortbread cookies to take home, more for the Scottish Bakery box decorated with the flag of Saint Andrew than for the cookies. "Something to remind Noreen of home," he said to Andi. "Of her *old* home, that is."

"Well?" Andi said after they'd left the bakery.

"Well, what?"

She assumed her Nurse Eliot persona. "Now that you know what Lanie really thinks of you, will you stop beating yourself up over that scholarship?"

He sighed. "I might have gone on forever thinking Elaine Stanton was a monster if you hadn't brought us together. And I've learned a lesson through my years of self-loathing. Women deserve equal opportunities. And I'll do everything I can to see that they're treated fairly in the department where I teach. And as you suggested, if the Thayer Scholarship can't be modified to include girls, I'll establish one that does."

Andi gave him a big hug. "Here's what I took away from our meeting with Lanie. If you give her back her smiling brother, you'll have repaid her tenfold for the debt you only thought you owed her."

Chapter 13

A Contract that Can't Be Broken

Friday, 06 June 1919

Jamie woke as the Del Monte Express pulled into the San Francisco train station. He took out his pocket watch and smiled. "Precisely noon," he said to Andi.

They wished Oliver, the parlor car attendant, well and stepped out into bright sunshine.

A taxi took them to The Saint Francis Hotel, which was directly across Powell Street from Union Square. They checked in and then enjoyed a light lunch.

They agreed that the suite Mister Kavanaugh had reserved for them was excellent.

* * *

Kavanaugh's office was in a three-story building on the corner of Grant Avenue and Geary Street, two blocks from the Saint Francis Hotel. Jamie and Andi walked arm-in-arm. A sign above the main entrance said, "Pacific Businessman's

Club, Private." They took the elevator to the third floor and entered Kavanaugh's outer office five minutes early. The faint sound of classical music could be heard through Kavanaugh's closed inner office door.

A good-looking woman about forty years old looked up from a large desk. A nameplate between her typewriter and telephone said, "Susan Faulkner, Executive Secretary."

She stood. "Professor Collins, I assume."

By her voice, Jamie recognized Miss Faulkner as the woman he had spoken to on the telephone earlier. She had obviously been thoroughly briefed as to who Kavanaugh was expecting.

"Yes, ma'am." Jamie couldn't help wondering whether Susan Faulkner had been one of Kavanaugh's young ladies before reaching middle age.

Susan smiled. "And you must be Nurse Eliot."

Andi smiled back. "Yes, ma'am."

"Mister Kavanagh will be with you shortly. Please make yourselves comfortable." She indicated the couch and chair on the other side of the room.

Jamie and Andi sat close together. "If you think you can stay out of trouble," she whispered, "I'll wait here. But just shout if you need me, and I'll come running."

"Likewise," he said.

"I'll tell Mister Kavanaugh you've arrived." Miss Faulkner reached for the office intercom. "Professor Collins is here to see you, sir."

"Please show him in."

Miss Faulkner moved to a door off to the side of her desk. "This way, please."

Jamie followed her into a corner office. The great man

was at his desk. The many houseplants on his windowsills made it look like he was in the middle of a jungle.

"Professor Collins," Miss Faulkner announced. "Sir, with your permission, I'll take that paperwork to the bank now."

"That will be fine, Susan."

She left, closing the door behind her.

Kavanaugh remained seated. "I hope you'll excuse me for not getting up. Sometimes, a dying man can't be bothered with social conventions."

The matter-of-fact delivery of this bombshell caught Jamie entirely by surprise. "A what?!"

"You've seen the way my hands shake. And heard me slur my words." The paperweight he was holding slipped from his hand. "And noticed I drop things."

"I didn't think it was anything serious."

"Neither did I—at first. My symptoms began about five months ago and have only gotten worse. And they'll keep getting worse."

Jamie slumped down onto a guest chair, feeling totally deflated. When it looked like there wasn't much Jamie could do for the country's disabled veterans, Kavanaugh had appeared out of nowhere. Was he going to disappear as suddenly?

"My doctor tells me I have a thing called amyotrophic lateral sclerosis, or ALS. It's a particularly nasty, rapidly progressing, neurological disease that's invariably fatal."

All Jamie could think to say was, "I'm sorry."

"Thank you."

That was all? Just a disinterested, thank you? "How long have you known?"

"Since a month or so before we met in Butch's hospital

room—which should tell you why I was in such a hurry to find a trustee."

"I'm amazed by how calmly you're taking this."

"Calmly? It might look that way. On the inside, I'm churning like a volcano about to erupt. This ALS would lead to a gruesome death if I let it."

Jamie didn't like the sound of that. "What do you mean, 'If you let it'?"

Kavanaugh placed his palms flat on top of his desk. "Unlike most men, I know exactly where, when, and how I'm going to die."

"That's not possible . . . unless—"

"No, no. I'm Catholic. I'm not going to commit suicide. I'd go straight to hell." Kavanaugh leaned back in his chair. "I've hired someone to kill me."

This was madness! "You haven't!"

"I have." He pushed his chair back. "If I let nature take its course, soon I wouldn't be able to walk, stand, or crawl. I couldn't eat, talk, swallow—or even breathe."

"Who'd be crazy enough to try to kill you?"

"Contract killers are a dime a dozen. And I've hired someone special. He's known as Omega—you know, like the last letter of the Greek alphabet. Presumably, he goes by that name because he's the last thing his victims ever see."

Kavanaugh picked up his paperweight again. "Nobody knows how many men Omega's killed. Dozens perhaps. The only thing anybody knows for sure about him is that he communicates through a Chicago gang called the Southside Boys. You get in touch with a Southside Boy, and he'll get in touch with Omega for you."

"Sounds like some kind of spy melodrama," Jamie said.

"You're right, but that's the way Omega works."

Kavanaugh sighed. "In my case, Omega thinks it was Danny Morelli who hired him. Omega won't care. He's already been paid—one hundred percent upfront. And once he collects, there's no way to call him off, even if I wanted to."

"There must be."

"If Omega fails to fulfill a contract, his reputation will be ruined." Kavanaugh put his paperweight down. "In my case, if he succeeds, he'll pay with his life."

"Wait a minute. You're going to have Omega killed for doing what you're paying him to do?"

"Damn right. I'm not going to let some thug get away with murder."

More madness. Jamie had to do something. "When is all this supposed to happen?"

"A little over a week from now. And that's all I'm going to say. If I were more specific, some 'humanitarian' might interfere."

"Meaning me?" Jamie rubbed his hands on his thighs. "If you don't want me to do anything about it, why have you told me?"

Kavanaugh managed to get up from his chair and walk to a window. He began deadheading one of his many houseplants. "If I had it all to do over again, I'd be a gardener in some quiet little seaside town and spend all my days raising beauties like this. And nobody would be depending on me. It'd just be me and my plants." He turned to Jamie. "I asked you here because I wanted to impress upon you how important it is that before I die, I secure a trustee who I know will treat my employees well and carry on my charities."

"Whoa. I haven't agreed to be your trustee."

"Knowing what's at stake, I'm confident you will. In fact,

the paperwork appointing you is signed, sealed, and delivered."

"Hold on. You're getting way ahead of yourself. What about your Pacific Businessman's Club? I told you I won't have anything to do with a business that involves even a rumor of prostitution."

"PBC is no longer part of Kavanaugh Enterprises. I've sold it, buildings and all."

"To Sonny?"

"Never! Each clubhouse is now a separate 'equity' club. The members themselves own and will operate them. And over half of the young ladies who worked for PBC have accepted a good job in one of my more conventional businesses."

That changed things significantly as far as Jamie was concerned.

"As for this building," Kavanaugh said as he looked around his office, "next week, my entire operation will be moving to an even nicer building I own not far from here."

"These new, independent clubs," Jamie said. "Once they're no longer under your control, I'd hate for them to become the kind of establishments PBC was rumored to be."

"I've put the managers on notice that if they violate the Mann Act in replacing my young ladies, I'll have Mundy shut them down tighter than a clam."

"I'm glad to hear it," Jamie said.

"You needn't worry about Kavanaugh Enterprises' gambling and liquor interests either—those I *have* given to Sonny, free and clear. I'm hoping that will placate him—for a while, anyway. All my other businesses and charities are now in a business trust, for which I'm the trustee." He crossed his arms. "Upon my death, you'll take my place. Then I want you to have your general manager run the businesses in accordance with your ethical standards."

"This is insane. You've only known me for three weeks."

"Three weeks is an eternity for a man with ALS." Kavanaugh took a deep breath and let it out slowly. "The sad truth is, I don't have anyone else." He dropped heavily onto his swivel chair. "I employ over a thousand honest, hard-working men and women. Many of them have families. Working for Sonny would be a disaster for them. If Kavanaugh Enterprises were to fall into his hands, he'd liquidate its holdings overnight, take the money, and run, leaving all my people out in the cold. They and their families would suffer. What you did in France tells me you won't let that happen."

"There must be someone else you can turn to. Someone more qualified than me."

"I'm sure there are scores of men more qualified than you —in business matters. But I doubt I could find anyone better to stand up to Sonny."

God help him, Jamie would love to put Sonny in his place. But . . .. "What if I accept and, despite my best efforts, prove to be incompetent?"

"The extraordinary things you've already accomplished tell me that won't happen."

Jamie wasn't immune to flattery, but he still wasn't persuaded.

Kavanaugh raised his chin. "If you and your general manager show an overall profit from year to year," he said, "you'll be doing society a world of good."

The phonograph record that was playing came to an end. Mister Kavanagh pushed his chair back, reached out, and turned the machine off. He looked back at Jamie. "What do you say? Can I count on you?"

With the well-being of more than a thousand of Kavanaugh's employees hanging in the balance, not to mention those who depended on his charities, Jamie felt he was out of options. "You haven't given me much choice."

"It's not me who's left you with little choice. It's your character." He folded his hands on top of his desk. "Illustrated by the fact that you haven't asked what's in it for you. That would have been Sonny's first question."

"It hadn't occurred to me to ask."

"Precisely. As trustee, you'll receive a salary four times what you make as an associate professor. And if under your oversight, Kavanaugh Enterprises remains profitable over the next five years, you keep all my people employed, and you see that my charities continue to provide for those in need, the trust will be dissolved, and all its assets will be yours, no strings attached. And I'm talking about assets worth more than the entire faculty at your university will earn in a lifetime."

"All that for merely overseeing the work of a general manager?" Jamie stood, walked to a window, and stared at the street below. If he took the job, he'd be profiting from a business empire that got its start by preying on the weak. Could he live with that? "I couldn't accept such a windfall knowing the seed money for your businesses came from prostitution, gambling, and liquor."

"Forget about how Kavanaugh Enterprises began. That's ancient history. What's important now is how the profits are used. Do as I ask, and all of society will benefit. Then, whatever you get out of the trust won't be a windfall. You'll have earned it."

Kavanaugh put on his most charming smile. "Look at it this way. With your earnings, you could fund all kinds of charities. You could do for others what Thomas Thayer did for you. In a sense, you'd be cleansing Kavanaugh Enterprises' earnings.

Jamie could feel his resistance weakening. But . . . .. "If I accepted the job, Sonny wouldn't like it. Despite your assurances, wouldn't a bullet in the back of my head be my most likely reward?"

"The way the Kavanaugh Trust is structured, Sonny knows he'll lose all hope of getting his hands on Kavanaugh Enterprises if he causes you any harm. That will have him praying that you and your family don't catch so much as a cold anytime in the next five years."

Kavanaugh rested his elbows on the arms of his swivel chair. "Making a profit in any business isn't easy, even in the best times. And I guarantee Sonny will do whatever he can within the boundaries I've set to see that you fail." Kavanaugh sat back. "You'll earn every penny you get from serving as trustee."

"I remind you, I don't know the first thing about business."

"Surely you don't think I run all my businesses by myself."

Jamie hadn't thought of that.

"The entire third floor of this building is full of managers who run my individual businesses. Plus, I have a chief executive officer, a chief operations officer, a chief financial officer, a chief legal officer, a chief of security, ... Sometimes, it seems I have more chiefs than workers. I've surrounded myself with capable businessmen—in some cases, men with more business savvy than I ever had. With capable people in management positions, you can concentrate on the strategic goals of the trust."

Kavanaugh leaned back in his chair. "If I were you, I'd want to bring in my own management team. So go ahead. My chiefs have all been with me for quite some time. I imagine they're as ready to retire as I am. But if you replace them, all I ask is that you give each of my chiefs a good retirement package. But by all means, keep the rest of my workers."

There was a commotion in the outer office. "Stop! Stop! You're breaking my wrist!" a man yelled.

Jamie had left Andi alone out there!

He rushed out the door to find a slick-dressed man, who he immediately recognized as Sonny, down on one knee as Andi twisted his hand backward.

The beast in Jamie broke free. He flew at Sonny and knocked him over with a rib-cracking kick to the side of his chest. Andi backed away.

"Hold on, Jamie, hold on," Kavanaugh shouted. He wedged himself between Jamie and Sonny just in time to prevent Jamie from stomping on Sonny's neck and crushing his windpipe.

"This is a family matter. I'll deal with it." Kavanaugh turned to Sonny. "Get up."

Sonny rose to his feet, groaning as he clutched his cracked ribs.

"Did you dare put a hand on my guest?" Kavanaugh shouted in Sonny's face.

Andi answered breathlessly. "He put his arm around my waist and tried to slip his hand inside my blouse."

Kavanaugh slapped Sonny's right cheek, then

backhanded his left. Sonny blocked the next blow and doubled up his fists.

"Go ahead, big man, hit me," Kavanaugh said. "You do, and you'll never see another sunrise."

Sonny let his arms hang.

"Can't you tell a lady when you see one?" Kavanaugh gave Sonny a shove.

"In my experience," Sonny said, "a lady's just a woman who hasn't yet settled on her price."

Jamie lunged at Sonny.

Again, Kavanaugh wedged his way between them. "Get out of my office," he ordered Sonny, "before I let my friend here tear your heart out."

Sonny stopped at the door. He pointed first at Andi and then at Jamie. "I won't forget this," he hissed. "I'll find out who you are, and then you better watch out." He backed into the hallway and slithered away.

Jamie wrapped Andi in his arms. "Did he hurt you? Did he?"

"He never had the chance. One second, he was fondling me. The next, he was on his knees. But you were right about my self-defense techniques. Once I had Sonny in my grasp, I didn't know what to do with him."

"Join the club," Kavanaugh said. "After all these years, I still don't know what to do with him."

Kavanaugh staggered to a chair and practically collapsed onto it as though his encounter with Sonny had drained all his strength. "Maybe I should thank Sonny for showing you what kind of man he is," Kavanaugh said to Jamie. "You can imagine how he'd treat my employees."

"If you set this up," Jamie said, "you're even smarter than

I thought because it worked like a charm. I'll serve as your trustee—and Sonny's the one who better watch out."

Kavanaugh smiled triumphantly. "I knew I could count on you."

* * *

Jamie and Andi left the building and walked east toward the ferry terminal. "I'm sorry," he said.

"For what?"

"For agreeing to serve as Mister Kavanaugh's trustee without first getting your approval."

Jamie told her all about Kavanaugh's business trust.

"Seeing what kind of man Sonny is," Andi said, "I understand your decision. And someone has to stand up to the likes of Sonny Kavanaugh."

Jamie smiled, but his smile soon disappeared. "Sonny won't like it when he realizes the man who broke his ribs is Mister Kavanaugh's trustee."

Andi pulled her jacket tighter around her shoulders. "We knew we'd have to be careful. Now, we have to be even more so."

"I apologize again for getting you involved in all this."

Andi stopped and looked Jamie in the eye. "No need. Now, I'm even more willing to support you. You'll be helping not just disabled veterans but also Mr. Kavanaugh's employees and those who rely on his charities."

Jamie took her hand. "You are an incredible woman."

"Like I keep telling you, I'm a soldier."

Jamie took a deep breath and let it out slowly. "There's more bad news." He briefed her on Kavanaugh's diagnosis. "He sees ALS as a death sentence."

Andi stopped in the middle of a crosswalk. "No, no. That's all wrong."

Jamie steered her out of the intersection.

"There's no definitive test for ALS," Andi said. "It's diagnosed based on the progression of symptoms. In Mister Kavanaugh's case, his symptoms are far too mild to say with certainty that he has ALS."

"You mean he might not be dying?"

"Other conditions have similar onset symptoms that don't progress the way ALS does. Even something as simple as benign fasciculation syndrome."

"What's that?"

"Involuntary muscle twitch."

"You're kidding."

"At the very least, he should get a second opinion."

Jamie felt as though a cold, clammy hand had grabbed his throat.

"There's more to the story, isn't there?" Andi said.

"Mister Kavanaugh's so scared of becoming incapacitated that he's hired someone to kill him."

Andi grabbed Jamie's arm. "We can't stand by and let that happen. Regardless of Mister Kavanaugh's past, making a life and death decision based on an unconfirmed diagnosis would be tragic."

"I tried to get him to tell me when, where, and how his killer will strike. All he'd tell me is that he's got a lot to do to get his house in order before the end of next week."

"We have to stop this madness!" Andi took off like a shot in the direction of Kavanaugh's office. Jamie was right behind her. When they reached the lobby, Andi punched the elevator call button like Jack Dempsey, trying to take away Jess Willard's heavyweight boxing title.

The car's response was too slow for her. She ran up three flights of stairs and burst into Kavanaugh's outer office. Jamie was on her heels, panting so hard he thought he might collapse. Miss Faulkner jumped to her feet.

With all the running Andi did on a regular basis, she quickly caught her breath. "We have to see Mister Kavanaugh."

Miss Faulkner stared at them open-mouthed.

"Please," Andi said. "It's important."

"I'm afraid he's left for the day."

"Do you know where he's gone?"

Miss Faulkner hesitated.

Jamie could finally breathe. He stepped up to her desk. "Mister Kavanaugh's in danger."

Miss Faulkner came to attention and spoke as would a private to his commanding officer. "Mister Kavanaugh has gone to his yacht club, sir. He often takes his sailboat out on Friday afternoons. I don't expect him back until Monday morning."

"What's the name of his club?"

"The San Francisco Yacht Club."

"Good. Maybe we can catch him before he casts off."

"Sir, the San Francisco Yacht Club is across the bay in Sausalito." She looked at her watch. "He will have taken the 3:30 ferry. It will be gone before you can get there. Depending on the weather and sea conditions, he might be out on his sailboat until the wee hours. If you need to see him, your best chance will be to wait until tomorrow morning and catch him while he's having breakfast at his club."

"We should telephone the club and ask them to reach out to him," Andi said.

"I'm afraid Mister Kavanaugh doesn't want to be contacted when he's at his club. He's given the club's management strict orders not to disturb him there."

"What should we do, Jamie?"

He thought for a moment. "As Miss Faulkner suggested, let's catch him at his club first thing tomorrow morning." He turned to Miss Faulkner. "If he gets in touch with you before we talk with him, please ask him to reach out to us at the Saint Francis Hotel."

"Certainly, Professor Collins."

They left the office.

"I'd like to spend some time in the medical library at Letterman reading up on ALS," Andi said. "And maybe have a word with Doctor Crandall. I need to be certain of my facts before we talk to Mister Kavanaugh."

* * *

Andi parked Jamie in a study carrel in the quietest part of the reading room of Letterman's medical library. He would have felt less out of place had he been in uniform, although far more conspicuous because of his ribbons.

Andi returned from the stacks with a weighty tome and sat beside him. After fifteen or twenty minutes of intense reading, she slammed the book shut. "I understand why Mister Kavanaugh hired an assassin. In its most severe form, amyotrophic lateral sclerosis can paralyze a person, making it impossible even to breathe."

Jamie shook his head. "No wonder he's gone to such drastic measures."

"And I was right. There is no definitive diagnostic test for ALS. Diagnosis can only be made based on the progression of symptoms. And to complicate matters, several other conditions can produce early ALS-like symptoms." Andi stood. "Let's see if we can find Doctor Crandall."

They navigated a maze of corridors that, true to army tradition, all looked the same. They were lucky. Doctor Crandall was in his office. His door was open.

"Nurse Eliot," Crandall said when he looked up from his desk and saw her. "I thought you were on leave."

"I am." She drew Jamie to her side. "And I'm spending it with the man I love."

Crandall didn't seem all that surprised. "Well, I'm happy for you both."

Andi wasted no time in telling Crandall about Mister Kavanaugh.

"I'm concerned that his symptoms are too mild to give him a definitive diagnosis," she said. "He's a very spry fifty-year-old with minor tremors, occasional slurred speech, and a tendency to drop things."

"I'm intrigued," Doctor Crandall said. "Do you know how long he's been exhibiting his symptoms?"

"Around five months," Jamie said.

"Has his doctor ruled out all other possibilities?"

"We're not sure," Jamie said."

"I see." Doctor Crandall drummed his fingers on the top of his desk. "Our chaplain has been exhibiting ALS-like symptoms after suffering a severe concussion in an automobile accident. You may be surprised to learn that he was a state Golden Gloves boxing champion in his late teens. This isn't his first concussion. And that's what intrigues me. I've come to suspect there's a correlation between repeated concussions and a false diagnosis of ALS."

"Our friend was a professional boxer in his late teens," Jamie said.

"Is that how his nose was broken?" Andi said.

"No. That happened when he was even younger."

Doctor Crandall placed his elbows on the arms of his chair. "It may still be relevant. Obviously, I can't treat a civilian, but I could examine your friend in support of a paper I'm planning to write laying out my suspicions—if you'd like me to."

"Yes, sir. He's so shaken by the diagnosis that a disaffirming second opinion could literally save his life."

"Then I should examine him as soon as possible." Doctor Crandall leaned back in his chair. "Since I'll be stretching the system by examining a civilian, it would be best to do it undercover, so to speak. I was planning to do a little work here in the office Sunday afternoon. Do you think you could bring him in then, say around 14:00?"

"Yes, sir," Jamie said. "We'll have him here even if we have to hogtie and drag him in."

Jamie and Andi returned to the Saint Francis, where they checked the ferry schedule with the concierge. They'd have to get up mighty early to catch the six-ten. But getting up before the sun rose wouldn't kill them. And it might prevent someone from killing Matt Kavanaugh.

Chapter 14

Adventures on the Bay

Saturday, 07 June 1919

Jamie stayed close to Andi as they boarded the 6:10 AM ferry. "Seeing how badly I suffered from seasickness on the passage to France, some of my men were afraid they were going to be led into battle by a weakling. Luckily, a sympathetic member of the ship's company suggested I move out of the bowels of the troopship and spend as much time as possible on deck. Along with fresh air, he said being able to see the horizon would help." To prevent a recurrence of his misery, Jamie and Andi huddled together in the bow of their ferryboat for the twenty-five-minute bay crossing.

After docking in Sausalito, they had to walk less than 500 yards to the yacht club. The sign above the clubhouse entrance said, "Private."

"What should we do?" Andi asked Jamie.

He smiled. "Bluff our way in." He took her hand and led the way. "We're Professor and Mrs. Collins, Matt

Kavanaugh's guests," Jamie told a man who looked like he was in charge. "Would you happen to know if Matt has arrived yet?"

The man almost melted when Andi smiled at him. "He's having breakfast in the men's grill. Please sit and enjoy the view while I let him know you've arrived."

The man left them comfortably sitting in the foyer.

"Mrs. Collins indeed," Andi whispered. "A bit presumptuous, aren't you?"

Jamie only smiled.

Kavanaugh soon appeared. He had his hand inside his jacket, on the grip of his .45, Jamie assumed. As soon as he saw Jamie and Andi, he relaxed. Jamie stood. Andi remained seated.

"Jamie. Andi. To what do I owe this unexpected pleasure?"

"We have something to tell you, and it can't wait." Jamie looked around to make sure he wouldn't be overheard. "Andi and I don't have any secrets from each other. When I told her about your diagnosis, she became very concerned."

Kavanaugh looked at Andi. "Oh?"

"I believe your diagnosis is premature," Andi said. "Amyotrophic lateral sclerosis is diagnosed based on the progression of symptoms. From what I've observed, your symptoms are too mild for your doctor to say with certainty that you have ALS."

Kavanaugh's knees buckled. He slumped down onto a chair next to Andi. "I don't have ALS?"

Andi put her hand on his arm. "That's just it. It's too early to say."

Kavanaugh held out his hands. "The shaking has been getting worse. I drop things. I slur my words."

"Any number of conditions could cause those symptoms. Those conditions should be ruled out before you make any plans that can't be undone."

"My doctor seemed so sure of himself."

"Did he arrange for you to get a second opinion?" Andi said.

Kavanaugh's features hardened. "No. He just advised me to get my affairs in order—while there was still time."

Andi shook her head. "I hate to be critical, but he should have insisted you get a second opinion."

Kavanaugh's eyes narrowed. "His family owned a trucking business Kavanaugh Enterprises bought out about a year ago. He said he was fine with the transaction. I didn't quite believe him. I'm usually more suspicious, but I wasn't myself after hearing his diagnosis."

Andi sat up straight. "Doctor Crandall, Letterman's head of neurology, is willing to examine you."

Kavanaugh canted his head. "How can he? I'm a civilian."

"He has a way around that."

Kavanaugh held out his hands. A slight tremor was noticeable. "There's something wrong with me. If it's not ALS, what is it?"

"That's what we intend to find out."

"We? Not since my wife died a quarter century ago has anyone cared about my health."

Andi put her hand on his forearm. "Then you're overdue."

Jamie cleared his throat. "I also told Andi how you planned to avoid the worst symptoms of ALS."

Andi folded her hands in her lap. "It would be a tragedy to give up your life because of a false diagnosis. Our Doctor

Crandall is willing to see you tomorrow afternoon and give you a second opinion. In the meantime, you need to call off your assassin."

Kavanaugh stood, walked to a window, and stared out at the bay. "I wish I could." He turned to them. "I paid this guy up front. Once he collects, his victims are as good as dead." Kavanaugh rubbed his chin. "We only have a week to think of something."

Jamie was honored to hear Kavanaugh say *we*.

"I do my best thinking at the helm of my sailboat. Why don't you two join me?"

Andi's face lit up. "I've never been on a sailboat." She looked at Jamie.

"Sailboats are small, and the ocean is immense," he said.

"We'll stay inside the Golden Gate, well within the bay," Kavanaugh said. "So, are you on board—no pun intended?"

It would be worth risking a little seasickness if the three of them could devise some way for Kavanaugh to elude his assassin.

Jamie came to attention. Reversing roles from when they first met, Jamie saluted, "Aye, aye, skipper."

* * *

"Here we are," Kavanaugh said. Before them lay a rather unimpressive sailing dinghy. Jamie wrinkled his nose. "The three of us are going to fit in that?"

Kavanaugh laughed. "No. This dinghy is just my plaything. I take it out solo when I need to get *far from the madding crowd's ignoble strife*." He pointed just astern of the dinghy to a very impressive wooden sailboat moored to the dock. The hull and deck were white. The cockpit was trimmed in gleaming dark wood. With its gracefully raked single mast, even while moored, the bow's proud shape and the stern's overhang made it look like it was cutting through the water at 10 knots. "This is my sailboat," Kavanaugh said.

Andi clasped her hands. "It's beautiful."

Kavanaugh couldn't mask his pride. "It's a 1919 Herreshoff S-Boat, a 27-footer, the first on the west coast."

Andi pointed to the name painted on its side. "And *Nieve?*"

"My dear departed wife." Kavanaugh stepped aboard. He offered Andi his hand and helped her into the cockpit. Jamie had to fend for himself.

Two young men were lounging against the mast. "Meet Bruce and Barry Dauer," Kavanaugh said, "a couple of harbor rats who'll be sailing with us today."

There could be no doubt the grinning boys were identical twins.

"Harbor rats?" Andi said. The term didn't sit well with her.

Barry, the younger of the brothers—by a scant several minutes—spoke up. "Most club boats don't have regular crews. Me and my brother are experienced deckhands. We make ourselves available when a skipper needs to add a few crewmembers."

"Their grandfather was a founding member of this club," Kavanaugh said. "Their father was a past president. They've practically grown up here at the club. And it's been profitable for them. Skippers always slip them a bit of cash at the end of a day's sailing, which adds up to a pretty good living, right boys?"

"Yes, sir," Bruce, the older brother, said. "And there's

nobody we'd rather sail with than Skipper Kavanaugh on the *Nieve*."

Kavanaugh smiled broadly. "How old are you now, boys? Twenty? That would mean we've been sailing together in one or another of my boats for about four years now, right, boys?"

"Yes, sir," they said in unison, befitting identical twins.

Jamie had been surveying the boat. "Does the *Nieve* have an engine?"

Kavanaugh smiled. "This is a racing boat. While under sail, a propeller would add drag and slow us down."

"A racing boat?" Jamie said.

Kavanaugh nodded. "Don't worry. We won't be doing any racing today."

Andi touched Kavanaugh's arm. "We're sorry, Mister Kavanaugh, if we've ruined your fun."

"Please, call me Matt. You too, Jamie."

"I didn't think you let anybody call you Matt," Jamie said.

"You two aren't just anybody. You're my guardian angels. And no, Andi, you haven't ruined anything. When we race, we add two or three experienced deckhands. Today, we'll just take the *Nieve* out for a leisurely sail. Regardless," he raised his voice so the Dauer twins could hear him, "we always have fun in the *Nieve*, don't we, boys?"

"Yes, sir," they again said in unison. "Believe me," Bruce added, "with Skipper Kavanaugh at the helm, there's not a boat in the bay that can keep up with the *Nieve*."

"And if we win a race," Matt said, "which we usually do, we throw a nice crew party—with guests."

By guests, Jamie wondered whether Matt meant his "young ladies." The Dauer boys were only sixteen when they began crewing for Matt. A little young for the guests Jamie assumed Matt was referring to.

"If you don't have an engine," Jamie said, "how do you get in and out of the harbor?"

"We put wind and tide to work—and a paddle or two comes in handy in a pinch." The Dauer boys had untied the boat. They pushed away from the dock. Using terminology that sounded to Jamie like a foreign language, Matt set his crew to work manipulating ropes—sheets, he called them—and raising sails. They were creating a wake in no time. The Dauers settled down in front of the cockpit. Jamie and Andi sat near Matt as he manned the helm. Once out in the open bay, Matt and the Dauer boys put the *Nieve* through her paces, executing tacks and gybes like they were performing a ballet. Any sign of seasickness was scared out of Jamie by the way the boat keeled over. Most of the time, one gunwale or the other was underwater.

By the broad smile on Andi's face, she clearly didn't share Jamie's concern. Every time the boat leaned to her side, she would roll onto her stomach, reach across the deck, and let her hand trail through the surging water.

"I'm still getting used to this boat," Matt said.

"I'm surprised," Jamie said. "You manage it like you were born with its tiller in your hand."

"You wouldn't have said that if you'd been with me five months ago when I first took her out. Like the rookie I was, I fumbled through an uncontrolled gybe, letting the boom swing around violently. That was embarrassing enough. Like a fool, I had partially stood up in the cockpit, which I could do safely in my old boat. The boom whacked me square in the forehead. Knocked me out cold." Matt put his hand to his forehead. "You wouldn't know from my handsome face that I was a boxer in my late teens. I've suffered my share of concussions. This was different. I was still woozy a half hour later. Barry took command of the boat and got us back to the club."

Andi jumped to her feet. "Oh, Matt, that's wonderful!" she shouted above the rush of the sea.

Matt pulled her down out of the reach of the boom and stared at her like she was crazy.

She grabbed his arm. "Doctor Crandall says repeated concussions can produce symptoms that mimic ALS."

Matt let go of the tiller. The mainsail began to flutter. The Dauer boys turned around and looked at their skipper questioningly. "You mean that bump on the head could be the source of my problems and not ALS?" He grabbed the tiller and regained control of the boat.

"It very well could," Andi said.

Matt swallowed hard. "If I'm suffering from a blow on the head and not ALS, . . . would I get better over time—assuming I had time?"

"It's too soon to say," Andi put her hand on the tiller next to Matt's, "but with the proper treatment, there's a good chance you won't get any worse."

Matt looked at her questioningly. "What's the proper treatment?"

That was a question Andi had discussed with Doctor Crandall. "Something as simple as two weeks of complete bed rest in a dark, quiet room with an absolute minimum of stimulus might make a difference."

Matt gave a half-laugh. "That sounds like solitary confinement—which is where a lot of people say I belong."

* * *

Sunday, late afternoon, 08 June 1919

"I'm doubly relieved by Doctor Crandall's conclusion," Jamie said to Matt as they left the Presidio in the back of Matt's limousine. He lowered his voice so Matt's driver wouldn't hear him. "First, you're not dying. And second, so long as you're alive, you won't need me to be your trustee."

Matt's smile hadn't faded since Doctor Crandall shared his absolute convictions that Matt didn't have ALS. "Not so fast, Jamie."

Jamie's smile did fade.

"For five months, I've thought death was coming for me. Do you know how often I've wished I'd lived my life differently?"

"We've all done things we regret," Jamie said.

Matt shook his head. "I've been granted a new life. I'd be a fool not to seize this opportunity to start over." He looked into Jamie's eyes. "All the reasons I wanted you to be my trustee still stand. As do the reasons you agreed to take on the role."

Chapter 15

A New Man

Sunday evening, 08 June 1919

Rovell's was reputedly one of San Francisco's best restaurants. Jamie and Andi would be dining there in an intimate private room with Ed Maxwell, owner of Pacific Maritime Insurance, and his fiancé, Cathy Reams, formerly of Matt Kavanaugh's stable of young ladies.

What was Ed? Fifty? Maybe fifty-two? But he didn't look a day over forty. Jamie and Andi admired his enthusiasm for life.

The gentlemen sat across from each other, as did the ladies. Two waiters saw to their every need.

Throughout dinner, the couples' talk was friendly and free-flowing.

"This will surprise you," Ed said over dessert. "Most people are bored to death by the insurance business. Not Cathy. She's shown such interest in my company, and she's such a quick learner that over the last month, I've been turning over bits and pieces of PMI to her to manage. She's taken it on like she was born to it. I expect she'll soon be able to run the entire company by herself."

"Are you thinking of retiring?" Andi said.

"Far from it. I love running a business. In fact, I'm ready to take on a new challenge. I've been looking for one I can take over and run my way, with Cathy's help."

"Have you found any likely candidates?" Andi asked.

"Not yet. I'm still looking."

Jamie's pulse spiked. They were in a position to solve the other's problems. Andi was looking at him. He would bet anything they were thinking along the same line.

"I want it to be something other than the insurance business," Ed said. "Something that will stretch my mind and offer an opportunity to make a difference in people's lives."

"Ed, you've given me an idea," Jamie said. "We might be able to help each other."

Ed raised his chin. "Oh?"

"It's no secret that Matt Kavanaugh has wanted to retire for some time." That got Ed and Cathy's attention. "What isn't commonly known is that he's already taken a big step in that direction. He's recently transferred all his businesses and charities to a trust."

Ed stared at Jamie. "How do you know that?"

"He's asked me to serve as trustee."

Ed's eyebrows shot up. "You?"

"You're right to be skeptical. I don't know the first thing about running a business. But I do know the trust's goals and constraints. If I can find a talented general manager who'll make them his own, everything should work out."

"I apologize," Ed said. "I don't doubt you. I was just surprised. With a good general manager, you should be fine."

"Matt Kavanaugh told me you're as honest as any man I'll ever meet."

Ed leaned back in his chair. "Matt Kavanaugh said that?"

"He did. And I can't think of a stronger endorsement. So, would you be interested in taking on the role?"

Ed dropped his fork on his dessert plate. "I'm certainly intrigued by the idea."

Jamie went over the goals and constraints Matt had laid out. Ed listened intently and asked a dozen insightful questions. Clearly, the man knew the ins and outs of the business world.

"Matt Kavanaugh is a brilliant businessman," Ed said, "but I think there are areas in which Kavanaugh Enterprises can improve."

Jamie put his palms flat on the table. "I'm hoping you're the man to bring about those improvements. So, what do you say? Will you consider accepting the job?"

Ed rubbed the back of his neck. "I owe Matt a huge debt of gratitude for bringing Cathy and me together." He turned to Cathy. "What do you think, darling? Should I take on such a big job?"

"It sounds like what you've been looking for."

"As to compensation," Jamie said.

Ed held up his hand. "I have no doubt it will be generous, but before you tempt me, I need to know how much freedom you plan to give your general manager. If I took the job, would you be second-guessing every decision I made?"

"Not at all. My role will be to advise and consent on the strategic plan. Everything else will be up to you. If you give me your word that you'll make the trust's goals and constraints your own, you can run things however you want. All I'll ask is that you give me monthly status reports."

Ed seemed to be working the idea over in his mind. "I'd want to bring in my own management team, people I know and trust."

"That will be fine so long as you give the existing team a generous retirement package."

Ed looked across the table. "Cathy's a quick study. Would you allow me to make her part of the management team?"

"Would you like that?" Jamie asked Cathy.

She nodded vigorously. "I'd love to be involved."

Jamie thought about the obstacles Rachel, his sister, and even Lanie had faced merely because they were women. Here was an opportunity to demolish all the typical chauvinistic roadblocks in one woman's path. "If you have confidence in Cathy, so do I. Bring her in as co-general manager if that's something you'd both want."

Everyone gasped, including Andi.

"Are you sure of that?" Cathy said.

Jamie leaned on his armrest. "Do you think you could handle it?"

Cathy looked at Ed. He nodded his approval. "I'll work harder than I ever have to justify your confidence in me," she said.

"Great," Jamie said. "Then it's settled. But time is of the essence. I'm going to need you two in place quickly."

Ed looked as though he'd been handed the crown jewels. "You can count on me—and Cathy."

"I'm going to," Jamie said. "Now, when are you two getting married?"

Ed glanced around their private dining room. The couples were alone momentarily. "Can you two keep a secret?"

Jamie looked at Andi. "Not from each other."

"But we can from the rest of the world," Andi said.

Ed couldn't have looked prouder. "Cathy and I secretly married a month ago."

"That's wonderful!" Andi said.

Cathy's smile was radiant. "We're still planning to have a formal wedding next month. We hope you two will attend."

"I'll be there," Jamie said. "Andi will be on the other side of the country, deeply involved in a new job." He turned to Andi. "Do you think you'd be able to get away?"

"Unlikely. But I'll certainly be thinking of you on your happy day."

"Why a secret marriage?" Jamie said.

"We weren't willing to wait any longer to spend every hour together. Yet I didn't want to hear my daughter complain that we were moving too quickly."

Jamie didn't dare look at Andi. He was close to saying to hell with Rachel and asking Andi to marry him there and then. He resisted. He knew in his heart that she'd say yes. But would she someday regret not accepting the position with the Army School of Nursing she'd worked so hard to earn? It would be selfish to make her choose between him and fulfilling her professional dreams.

Cathy smiled at her husband. "Mister Kavanaugh encouraged us to marry as soon as possible. He was one of the witnesses at our civil ceremony."

"And get this," Ed said. "Matt said seeing us so happy was compensation enough, so as a wedding gift, he would forgo the bride price he was entitled to."

Jamie smiled. Matt Kavanaugh's generosity dealt another blow to Jamie's remaining doubts that Matt really did want a new start in life.

* * *

Monday, 09 June 1919

Per Matt's request, Jamie and Andi were standing in front of his outer office door at 10:00 a.m. sharp where they were confronted by two men. The bulges under their coats made it obvious they were carrying handguns. Once Jamie established his and Andi's identity, the men stepped aside.

Miss Faulkner welcomed them with a broad smile. "Mister Kavanaugh was very glad you found him at his club."

"Thank you for making that possible."

"You're welcome, Professor Collins." Her smile disappeared. "Mister Kavanaugh's a very private person. I worried all weekend that he might be angry that I told you where to find him." Her smile returned. "Now I know you two hold a special place in his heart." She keyed the intercom. "Professor Collins and Nurse Eliot have arrived, sir."

As soon as they entered Matt's office, he rose awkwardly from his chair, kissed Andi's cheek, and shook Jamie's hand. "You two are life savers."

"Does that mean you were able to call off your assassin?" Andi said.

"I'm afraid that's not possible. Once this man is paid, he essentially disappears off the face of the earth. There's no way to call him off."

"There must be something we can do." Andi looked at Jamie.

Jamie wished he knew what.

Matt offered Jamie and Andi chairs. They all sat. "Don't worry, my dear. I've come up with a plan."

Jamie slid forward. "We'd love to hear it."

"I assume you ran into two of my men outside my office. They're there to make sure Omega doesn't jump the gun, so to speak, and ruin things."

"That big man out in the hallway is pretty imposing," Andi said. "But it was the little one who scared me."

"You're very perceptive, Andi. Little Tony would slit the Pope's throat if I asked him to." Matt leveraged himself out of his chair and stood in front of one of his windows. "I've stepped on a lot of toes over the years. Even if I could call Omega off, I wouldn't be able to slip away into a quiet retirement. So, I've devised a way to kill two birds with one stone." He turned to his guests. "I foresee a fatal accident in my near future."

Jamie smiled at the brilliance—and simplicity—of Matt's solution. "You're going to fake your death!"

"Right you are. If people think I'm dead, I can reemerge in some quiet seaside town with a new identity." He glanced at the house plants that occupied all available space on his windowsills. "I've stashed away more money than I could ever need. I'll spend some on a modest house that won't be too conspicuous and spend the rest of my days puttering around in my garden." He paused. "But first, I need to find a place where I can get the two weeks of total rest Doctor Crandall recommended. And arrange for someone to care for me."

"Stay with me at BayView," Jamie said. "I have plenty of room."

"And I'll be your personal nurse," Andi said.

Matt appeared stunned.

"There is one thing," Andi said. "If you want to assume a new identity, you need to do something about your nose."

"My nose?" Matt felt his misshapen proboscis. "What's wrong with my nose?"

"No matter how you disguise yourself, your crooked nose will give you away."

"I agree," Jamie said. "It's your most distinguishing feature."

Matt turned up his palms. "There's not much I can do about it."

"Sure, there is," Andi said. "A good reconstructive surgeon could make your nose straight as an arrow."

"But it's been like this for years. Decades."

Andi shrugged. "That doesn't matter. Nasal cartilage is very pliable."

Matt looked from Andi to Jamie and back. "Why are you two being so good to me?"

It was Andi who answered. "Working with you on the DVET makes us family."

The most consummate racketeer on the West Coast sat heavily in his swivel chair. He looked like he might cry.

"I have some good news I'd like to share with you," Jamie said.

"It can't possibly be as good as what you two have just told me."

"I think you'll be pleased. I've found a general manager for the Kavanaugh Trust."

"Already?"

"It wasn't difficult. You recommended him."

"*I* did?"

"He's someone you said was as honest as anyone I'll ever meet. I'm talking about Ed Maxwell."

"Ed?" Matt couldn't have looked more surprised. "I wouldn't think he'd have the time."

Jamie quickly recapped Ed's desire to take on a new challenge.

Matt mulled this over. "Well done. I'm sure Ed will be a great general manager."

"I told him he can make Cathy co-general manager."

Matt's back stiffened. "Now, wait a minute. Cathy? I'm not sure that's such a good idea."

"Well, that's just too bad," Jamie said. "As your trustee, you're going to have to live with my decisions."

Matt grasped the armrests of his chair. "It's been thirty years since anyone's talked to me like that." He leaned back and laughed. "It sure feels good for someone else to be in charge for a change. Go ahead. Do what you think's best."

"I intend to," Jamie said.

* * *

Tuesday, 10 June 1919

Special Agent Jeff Mundy was outside Matt Kavanaugh's office at 8:00 a.m. "Well, if it isn't Little Tony," he said to the man Andi found so frightening. "And I see you've got a pet goon with you. Kavanaugh must be getting paranoid in his old age."

"And he must be slumming. He told us to let you through."

Mundy shoved the door open and stepped into Matt's outer office. Miss Faulkner looked up from her desk. "Ah, you must be Mister Mundy."

"Yes, ma'am. I'm here at Matt's request."

Miss Faulkner cringed when she heard her boss referred to by his first name. "I'll let *Mister Kavanaugh* know you're here." She keyed the intercom. "Mister Mundy has arrived, sir."

"Thank you, Susan. Please show him in."

Mundy entered Matt's inner office and immediately looked around to make sure no one was lurking behind the door or in a corner waiting to mug him.

"Thank you for coming." Matt extended his hand.

Mundy didn't take it. "Okay, what tip do you have for us this time?"

Matt let his hand drop. "Not us, you."

"That's why you insisted I come alone and not tell anybody where I was going? You should know by now you can't buy me."

"Which is why I've asked you here. You're the only federal agent I know I can trust."

"Yeah, right."

"So here it is." Matt displayed his most devious grin. "You and I are going to take down Omega."

That got Mundy's attention. Arresting a notorious contract killer would be the highlight of any law enforcement officer's career. "Sure," Mundy said. "How are the two of us going to pull off something a dozen law enforcement agencies have failed to do over the last two years?"

"Easy. I know who Omega's next victim is going to be."

"Yeah, right," Mundy said. "And who might that be?"

"Me."

Mundy snorted. "You must think I'll believe anything."

"I know because I'm the one who hired him."

Mundy got up from his chair. "You made me drag myself all the way over here to feed me a line like that?"

"Have I ever given you bad information?" Matt gestured

toward the chair Mundy had just vacated. "Please, hear me out."

Mundy sat grudgingly.

Kavanaugh told Mundy about his diagnosis and his plan to avoid the worst symptoms of ALS. Mundy showed no sympathy, nor would Kavanaugh expect him to.

This had to be a trap, but for whom? "What kind of scam is this?" Mundy said. "You don't look to me like you're dying,"

"No scam. I believed death had me up against a wall. So, I contacted Chicago's Southside Gang and had them pass along a note to Omega. Using the name Danny Morelli, I claimed that a big-time pimp named Matt Kavanaugh had killed my niece, as well as brutalizing others, and I'd pay good money to see that Kavanaugh got what he deserved."

"I can see Omega believing that," Mundy said with a grin.

Kavanaugh remained straight-faced.

"Okay, go on. I'm listening."

Matt leaned back in his chair. "Do you remember Nurse Eliot from my Disabled Veterans' Education Trust reception?"

"I'm not likely to forget someone that impressive."

"She found out about my diagnosis and immediately questioned it. She arranged for me to see a specialist to get a second opinion. The specialist refuted my doctor's diagnosis. It turns out my symptoms are more likely due to the repeated concussions I've suffered over the years." Matt straightened his tie. "That means I'm not dying after all. Which is great news—except I have no way of calling off Omega."

"And you think the Bureau does?"

"No."

"No?" This was getting crazier by the minute. "Then why am I here?"

"I want you to snare Omega using me as bait."

"Ah, now we're getting down to business. In exchange for what?"

"Immunity from any prosecution the government might dream up against Matt Kavanaugh—and a new identity."

"You won't need a new identity if we arrest Omega."

"Oh, yeah? Can you guarantee Omega is one person working alone?"

That was a question Mundy himself wanted answered. "No, I can't."

"I didn't think so. And to make matters worse, Omega isn't the only one who would like to see me dead." Matt leaned toward Mundy. "I'm not a young man. It's time for me to retire. How can I if every hired gun on the West Coast is gunning for me?"

"If you're looking for sympathy," Mundy said, "you're looking to the wrong guy."

"I'm not. I've made my bed, and I know I have to lie in it. I'm just tired of always looking over my shoulder wondering who's pointing a gun at me."

"Whose fault is that?" Mundy said.

"Mine, I admit. But forget about me. You don't want a killer like Omega running around free, do you?"

Matt was right about that. It would be the crown jewel of Mundy's career to put Omega away. The least he could do was hear Kavanaugh out. "So, what's your plan?"

"The arrangement with Omega is like something from a dime spy novel. Danny Morelli, the man Omega thinks hired him, is supposed to lure me to a certain place at a certain time. Morelli's pretext is a truce meeting, just the two of us, in a very public place. Morelli is supposed to wear a black raincoat and a red plaid scarf and stay by my side so there'll be no chance of Omega shooting the wrong person." Kavanaugh focused his steely eyes on Mundy. "I propose that you masquerade as Morelli and that you and I take down Omega, just the two of us."

Mundy didn't like it. There were more ways than he could count for Kavanaugh's plan to go wrong. "It would be safer for you if you just told me where and when the hit's supposed to take place. Then you wouldn't even have to be there when me and a bunch of other agents swoop in and take Omega into custody."

"No. I want a new identity. And I don't want any other agent to know who I become. If I merely told you where and when the hit would take place, the Bureau would have no incentive to give me everything I want."

Although Mundy hated to admit it, Matt was right.

"We're going to have to do this my way," Matt said. "Just you and me. Nobody else."

"That's not the way the Bureau operates."

"That's the way *I* operate. And it's your best chance to arrest Omega and take a murderer off the streets."

Mundy got up and moved to a window to think for a moment. "We've kept certain information concerning Omega out of the papers, so we won't have to deal with copycats." Mundy turned and faced Matt. "Omega kills with a 7.65 mm bullet fired with the muzzle of his gun pressed tight against the victim's chest. That says to me that Omega's clever. Otherwise, he wouldn't be able to get that close to his victims. If you and me try to take down Omega by ourselves, we might not see him coming."

"I'll wear a bulletproof vest."

"There's no such thing as a bullet*proof* vest. Even if a vest stopped a bullet fired from that close, you'd at least suffer a few broken ribs. Plus, we don't know whether Omega's killed using a different MO."

"I'm betting you'll spot him before he gets too close."

"Spot him? Nobody even knows what Omega looks like. I wouldn't make that bet if my life was hanging in the balance."

"I figure the only way the Bureau will give me immunity and a new identity is if I give them Omega wrapped in a bow. And I'm sure that's the only way they'll provide me a corpse that can pass as me."

"A corpse? What do you think we are, a bunch of grave robbers?"

"My enemies aren't going to let me rest in peace unless they're convinced I'm dead. So we'll need a body in my casket. At the rate inmates die in federal prisons, you shouldn't have any trouble claiming a body that can pass for me. Just make sure his face is unrecognizable."

This had become grotesque. "Tampering with a dead body is a crime."

"Think of it this way. Most inmates get a simple burial in an unmarked grave. The body you provide will get a grand sendoff and be buried in a spectacular crypt."

For just a few seconds, Mundy let himself imagine the staggering career implications—however remote—of taking down Omega. "What's your plan for this body, assuming I can get one?"

"I'm going to capsize my sailing dinghy in an isolated part of the bay and beach it near where you'll be waiting. We'll dress the body in my clothes and tangle the poor fellow in the rigging so it looks like I drowned in a sailing accident.

Then I want you to transport me incognito to Letterman Army Hospital, check me in under an assumed name, and have them perform plastic surgery to straighten my nose."

"This is getting ridiculous. With that many moving parts in your plan, everything would have to go perfectly for it to work. Besides, you're a civilian, and Letterman's an army hospital."

"That's right. A *federal* facility. Don't tell me the Bureau can't get someone admitted there under cover."

"Why don't you ask for the moon while you're at it?" Mundy said, but actually, he liked the idea. He and Matt just might be able to pull it off. Doing so without involving the entire Bureau would be the hardest part.

"You want Omega, don't you?" Matt said.

Mundy clenched his jaw. Matt had played him like a violin virtuoso performing on a Stradivarius. They both knew he'd do anything to nab Omega. "I'll see what I can do."

"You better hurry. My 'appointment' with Omega is at noon on Thursday."

Jamie and Andi had checked out of the Saint Francis Hotel. He hailed a cab. "Letterman Army Hospital," he said to the cabbie.

They passed through the Presidio's gates and circumnavigated the rectangular central green. Jamie directed the cabbie to the visiting nurses' quarters. "Right here will be fine," he said. They came to a halt. The cabbie unloaded their luggage.

After paying the man and giving him a generous tip,

Jamie carried his and Andi's cases up the walkway. He temporarily stashed his on the porch and took Andi's to her assigned door. She gave him a furtive kiss. Jamie would stay just up the street in the Bachelor Officer's Quarters. They would, however, spend as much time together as their scheme allowed.

* * *

Thursday, late morning, 12 June 1919

Mundy had forked out his own money for a red plaid scarf. Even in his ever-present rumpled black raincoat, Mundy felt naked without any other agents nearby as backup. Matt had insisted.

He and Matt arrived in plenty of time to reconnoiter the area before their noon "appointment" with Omega. The Palace of Fine Arts was a monumental structure left over from the 1915 Panama-Pacific Exposition. Per Omega's instructions, Morelli was supposed to lure Matt to the grounds on the east side of the rotunda near the reflecting pool.

Mundy had to admire Omega's choice. It was an excellent place for an assassination. It was public, the fountain would drown out any gunshot noise a silencer didn't conceal, and there were lots of escape routes.

Coincidentally, it also fit in well with Matt's plans. The Palace of Fine Arts sat immediately east of the Presidio in San Francisco's Marina District. Since they had no idea what Omega looked like, Mundy was intently studying each of the half-dozen men in the vicinity. It was almost noon when Matt nudged Mundy and nodded toward a nervous middle-aged man pacing back and forth not twenty feet from them. "That could be him," Matt said.

Mundy glanced at the man. "Naw. Omega's a professional. That man stands out like a sore thumb." A woman joined the man, and his nervousness disappeared in an instant. The couple walked off arm in arm.

"Don't distract me again," Mundy said, "or we could be in trouble."

Too late. They were already in trouble. Mundy had been distracted for too long.

A young woman who seemed to be merely walking by suddenly veered toward them. Five foot six. A hundred and twenty pounds. Twenty years old. She moved like an athlete. Was she a decoy—or the illusive Omega? Mundy braced himself.

For just an instant, she looked his way as she passed, as if to be certain of her target. Her eyes were wide open as though she were in the front seat of a rollercoaster. When she was just a few feet from Matt, she raised her arm. A silencer protruded from her oversized sleeve. Mundy lunged before she could press it against Matt's chest and violently twisted it from her hand.

The gun hardly made a sound when it went off. The round grazed Mundy's calf. That didn't stop him from flattening Omega with a vicious fist to her temple. He wasn't sorry. No one knew how many men Omega had killed. Mundy snatched up her gun and put it in his coat pocket.

"Help," Omega screamed. "Somebody. Help!"

The girl wasn't a bad actress. A good Samaritan tried to intervene. Mundy pushed him away. "Federal agent," he shouted. He flashed his badge while Matt held Omega down with his knee between her shoulder blades. Mundy roughly twisted her arms behind her back and handcuffed her. The few bystanders could see that he was an officer of the law arresting a criminal, not a woman molester.

Mundy's calf was throbbing. That would have to wait.

"You're bleeding pretty bad," Matt said.

Mundy jerked Omega to her feet as he held onto the short chain between her cuffs. "Hold her," he said to Matt. Mundy removed his handkerchief, pulled up his pant leg, and tied the kerchief around his calf. "It's nothing. I'll live."

Omega hadn't made a sound since Mundy cuffed her. He grabbed Omega by her lapel. "You don't have much to say now, but I promise you'll talk plenty by the time I'm done with you."

She raised her chin defiantly and maintained her silence.

Matt smiled at Mundy. "Well done."

"And on your part," Mundy said. He gestured with his head and mouthed the word "go."

Matt smiled the smile of a man who'd just been given a new lease on life. He abruptly turned and hurried away. Mundy pushed Omega forward. "I'm taking you to jail."

"Let me go," Omega said as soon as Matt was out of earshot. "I'll pay you more than you'll make in a year."

This time, it was Mundy who maintained his silence. When they reached his car, Mundy shoved her into the back. He secured her to a steel ring welded to the floor by using another pair of cuffs. By the time they reached the Presidio's military stockade, Omega was promising him more money than the US Treasury held in Fort Knox if only he'd let her go.

Once she was behind bars, despite his leg wound, Mundy grilled her until he learned everything she knew about Omega.

* * *

Afternoon, Thursday, 12 June 1919

Matt tried to act as he always did at his yacht club. He walked with some effort onto the dock and joked around with several members and staff to make sure people knew he was there.

"I'm going to take my dinghy out and get away for a while," he told them. "I need to clear my head." He turned toward his dinghy and nearly toppled over. His symptoms were worse today. He didn't try to hide them.

"Be careful out there by yourself," one of the members said.

That was the reaction he was hoping for. "I always am."

Barry Dauer approached him. He looked genuinely concerned. "It's getting a bit choppy out there for a one-man sailing dinghy, skipper. You sure you wouldn't rather take the *Nieve* out?"

"No. I'll be fine. I just want to do some quiet thinking."

When Matt reached his mooring slip, he said a silent, fond farewell to the *Nieve*. He wished he could see the Dauer twins' faces when they learned he'd willed it to them, along with enough money to buy an ocean-going boat and sail around the world once or twice.

Matt cast off his dinghy. Before he had gone more than a hundred yards, he realized Barry was right. The bay was more than a bit choppy. The best-laid plans . . . He pressed on regardless. If he didn't meet up with Mundy at the proper time, his entire plan would fall apart.

More than once, Matt was afraid the chop would capsize him. A large cargo ship was more of a danger as he crossed too close to its path. The ship blew five short horn blasts, the signal for danger. A crewman came out on the bridge wing and made rude gestures at him.

Actually, that could all work in his favor if he made it the five miles to the isolated area near the Presidio's Crissy Field, which he and Mundy agreed would be a good location to stage his drowning. The rough sea and the angry ship's crew would support the idea that he had gotten in over his head and lost control of his dinghy.

It was late afternoon when Matt saw Mundy standing on the rocky shore next to his car. As Matt had hoped, there wasn't another soul in sight. Matt sailed as close to him as possible before he grabbed one gunwale with both hands, placed his feet on the other, and flipped the dinghy onto its side so its sail rested flat on the water.

Mundy waded in. "Ow. That stings," he shouted when the salt water reached his calf. He helped Matt drag the capsized dinghy closer to shore.

"Do you have the corpse?" Matt asked.

"I wouldn't be here if I didn't," Mundy snapped. They trudged to shore and walked to Mundy's car. He opened the back door. The body was lying on the back seat beneath a blanket. Mundy threw back the blanket to reveal the corpse of a man about Matt's size and shape.

"Why's the head covered that way?" Matt said, pointing to a burlap sack.

"As you requested, his face looks like it's been dragged over the rocks. I never want to see it again, and you'll be better off if you never do."

Matt stripped down to his underwear and put on a set of clothes Mundy provided. They muscled the body off the back seat. It wasn't easy dressing the corpse in Matt's clothes.

Between the two of them, they managed. The corpse offered no assistance. They carried the poor fellow to the water's edge.

Matt's dinghy was resting on its side near the shore. They floated the corpse to it and placed the lower half in the cockpit with the upper half hanging over the side. They wrapped it in the rigging so it looked like Matt had become entangled and drowned when the dinghy capsized.

When the scene looked convincing, Mundy said to Matt, "Don't look." He removed the sack that was covering the corpse's face. Matt looked and promptly threw up.

"I told you not to look," Mundy said.

They got in Mundy's car and drove about a half mile to the nearest telephone booth. Mundy called the Coast Guard, identified himself as a federal agent, and reported that he'd seen a small sailboat tip over—and feared for the sailor's life.

The minute he hung up the phone, Mundy drove back to the shore to wait.

Kavanaugh peeked his head up from the passenger seat. "Do you think we'll actually pull this off?"

Mundy turned to him. "Harry Houdini couldn't pull off a better illusion." Mundy just hoped he was right.

"When this is over," Kavanaugh said, "I'll need to pull off a disappearing act myself." He looked Mundy in the eyes. "I'll never forget what you're doing for me. No matter how this turns out, I want you to know I'm grateful."

Mundy locked eyes with Kavanaugh for a long moment. "Just don't make me regret this."

A Coast Guard boat chugged into view. Matt kept his head down as the vessel approached the floundering sailboat. An officer and two crewmen scrambled over the side into a dory. Its flat bottom and shallow draft allowed them to row close to the shore.

The officer jumped onto the rocks, walked up to the capsized dinghy, and spotted the body tangled in the rigging.

"They've seen the body," Mundy said to Matt.

Matt nodded. "Goodbye, Matt Kavanaugh," he whispered.

Mundy eyed him. "No tears?"

Kavanaugh shook his head. "I'm not going to waste tears over my old self, not when I have a chance to live my life differently."

"Stay low," Mundy said, "and wish me luck." He swung open his door and strode toward the Coast Guard officer.

Matt stayed in Mundy's car and remained hidden.

Mundy showed the officer his badge. "I know the victim," Mundy said. "He's the subject of a Bureau of Investigation operation. His name's Matthew Kavanaugh. I lured him here by offering to feed him inside Bureau information—for a price. He must have guessed it was a trap. He got all flustered, somehow capsized his boat, and tangled himself in the rigging. I can't swim a stroke. There was nothing I could do for him. His boat has since drifted close to shore."

The officer inspected Mundy's badge. "Okay," he said. "We'll take the body to the city morgue, where they'll confirm your ID and do an autopsy."

"No, you won't," Mundy told the junior officer. "You need to take this body to the morgue at Letterman Army Hospital, a federal facility."

"That's not the Coast Guard's protocol," the officer said.

"Unless you want to entangle yourself in endless red tape, let the feds call the shots on this one."

The young man thought for a moment. "Retrieve the

body and right that boat," he ordered his boatswain. "We'll take the boat under tow and moor it at the Coast Guard Station after we drop this corpse off at Letterman Army Hospital."

Mundy drove Matt a mile or so to Letterman and checked him in as retired army Lieutenant Colonel Fred Downs.

* * *

Thursday evening, 12 June 1919

Arrangements had been made between the Bureau of Investigation and Colonel Thornburgh, the commanding officer of Letterman General Hospital, to admit a special patient who was under federal protection. The hospital staff confirmed that the body the Coast Guard turned over to them was that of Matt Kavanaugh. Included in the arrangement was a provision for Nurse Andrea Eliot, who was cooperating with the Bureau, to supervise Downs' care.

Andi put on her uniform and returned to duty. On her own behalf, Andi requested that Student Nurse Hobbes be assigned to Downs' case. "Colonel Downs was in an automobile accident," she explained to Hobbes. "He suffered a concussion and a broken nose. His nose injury is making it difficult for him to breathe. An ENT surgeon will perform emergency rhinoplasty this evening to alleviate his breathing problems. Because of his concussion, it will be necessary to keep him as quiet as possible. Please keep your interactions with him to an absolute minimum."

Doctor Regenstein had also been recruited to be part of

Downs' case. He would be observing the operation and then providing post-operative care.

* * *

Friday, 13 June 1919

Jamie read with interest an article that appeared on the lower half of the front page of the Chronicle. *MATT KAVANAUGH DROWNS IN BOATING ACCIDENT*, the headline blared. *Yesterday evening, the Coast Guard found the capsized sailboat of noted philanthropist Matt Kavanaugh washed ashore in San Francisco Bay. A body, identified by federal agents as that of Kavanaugh, was found tangled in the dinghy's rigging. Barry Dauer, who sailed with Kavanaugh often, told this reporter he spoke with Kavanaugh shortly before Kavanaugh set off on his own. Dauer warned Kavanaugh that the bay was becoming too choppy for a solo sail. Kavanaugh had dismissed Dauer's concern.*

The article gave a flattering overview of Matt Kavanaugh's career with only a hint that some of his business practices were a bit harsh. It closed by announcing that funeral services would be held at Mission San Francisco de Asis at 2:00 p.m. Saturday, the 21st of June.

* * *

Sunday afternoon, 15 June 1919

Andi couldn't have asked for things to go more smoothly. Matt's rhinoplasty was a success. There was no sign of bleeding and no reason to fear infection. Nurse Hobbes gave no indication she suspected Lieutenant Colonel Downs was anyone other than who his medical chart said he was.

Andi said her goodbyes to Hobbes for a second time, then joined Jamie in a waiting cab.

Lieutenant Colonel Downs had left the hospital grounds in a taxi a few minutes earlier. He joined Andi and Jamie in the Grand Hall of the San Francisco train station. Jamie handed Downs a duffle bag that contained a change of clothes provided by Agent Mundy. Downs took the bag and went into the men's room. That was the last time anyone ever saw Lieutenant Colonel Fred Downs.

The man who emerged from the men's room wearing the clothes Mundy provided was Liam O'Connell, an Irish immigrant who had earned his US citizenship around the turn of the century. His only resemblance to Colonel Downs was the bandaging from the rhinoplasty. Jamie, Andi, and O'Connell joined a throng of people on Platform 13.

Jamie took "Mister O'Connell" aside. "I remember you telling me Liam was the name you gave the son you and your wife—"

"Nieve," Liam interjected reverently.

Jamie nodded. "The son you and Nieve lost."

Liam nodded. "I'm hoping that calling myself Liam will remind me to live the kind of life we hoped he would."

That was just about the most emotion Jamie had ever seen from the man who had formerly been the West Coast's most consummate racketeer.

They boarded the parlor car of the Del Monte Express. Liam sat by a window. Andi sat next to him. Jamie sat on the opposite side of the aisle.

Oliver, the parlor car attendant, greeted Andi and Jamie

enthusiastically. "It's a pleasure to see youse two again, Nurse Eliot, Professor Collins."

"And you as well, Oliver," Andi said. "This is Mister O'Connell, a private patient I'm caring for." In their planning stage, she had worried that someone might recognize Liam. His facial bandages made that extremely unlikely.

"Youse is in good hands," Oliver told Liam.

Their trip was uneventful. Andi was relieved that Liam followed her instructions to the letter and showed no sign of wanting to be in charge. So Liam wouldn't have to exert himself, they took a cab from the Pacific Grove station the short distance to BayView. Rather than barge in and scare Noreen, Jamie knocked on the door. "Hello, Noreen. Here we are again."

"It's nice to have you back, Professor Jamie. And you, Nurse Andi."

"This is Liam O'Connell," Jamie said, "a family friend who'll be staying with us for the next several weeks while he recuperates from a little accident."

Andi wondered how Jamie would introduce Liam since she knew Jamie hated to lie. "A family friend" was true in a sense.

"I can think of no better place to recuperate than BayView, sir," Noreen said to Liam with a friendly smile.

"Aye, lass, I'm already feeling better," Liam replied with a smile his bandages did nothing to conceal.

Andi was pleased by Liam's accent. Since it would have been impossible for him to eliminate his slight, second-generation Irish accent, Andi suggested the best way to "hide" it would be to make it as pronounced as possible.

"Liam is recovering from a concussion and a broken nose," Andi said. Again, that was true. The surgeon had to break Matt's nose in the process of straightening it. "He's going to need complete rest for the next two weeks. I'll be caring for him, so besides there being one more mouth to feed, you'll hardly know he's here."

They made Liam comfortable in the room next to the master suite. After helping him into bed, Andi placed her hand on his shoulder. "You'll be able to rest quietly here. Other than me bringing you your meals and checking on you occasionally, the only sound you'll hear will be the waves breaking on the rocky shore below us. Here's a handbell. If you need anything, just ring—softly."

Liam put his hand on top of Andi's. "I don't know how I can ever repay you."

"No need. We're family."

Chapter 16

Goodbyes

Friday, 20 June 1919

Doctor Benjamin Regenstein was surprised that the Bureau of Investigation asked him to provide postoperative care for Lieutenant Colonel Fred Downs, or rather Liam O'Connell. Regenstein was used to being ostracized because of his ethnic background. Used to it, but not happy. The Bureau's choice made more sense when Regenstein was fully briefed on the assignment and learned that Major Jamie Collins and Nurse Andrea Eliot were involved. The Bureau declined to tell Doctor Regenstein who Liam O'Connell really was or who he was running from. The less Regenstein knew, they said, the safer it would be for all involved.

The train ride to BayView was just what Regenstein needed. It allowed him to escape Letterman for a weekend and do some serious thinking. To find Jamie waiting for him on the passenger platform at the Pacific Grove train station made him feel he had at least one friend in the world. Andi greeted Regenstein warmly and then gave him a rundown of Liam's condition. Regenstein took it all in without any questions. As was standard procedure, the surgeon who performed Liam's rhinoplasty had placed internal splints in his nose to stabilize his septum and help control bleeding. "The first thing we need to do," Regenstein said, "is remove Mister O'Connell's internal splints." Regenstein followed Andi up a grand flight of stairs and into a darkened room. Andi turned on the light for the first time since Liam arrived. "How do you feel?" Regenstein asked Liam.

"Not bad, considering."

Andi gave her reassuring nurse smile.

"This should be quick and easy," Regenstein said. To lessen Liam's anxiety and his own, he explained the removal process step-by-step.

"You look good," Regenstein said to Liam when the splints had been removed.

That was the extent of their interaction since they were trying to keep Liam as quiet as possible. Andi patted Liam on the shoulder reassuringly and turned off the light. She and Regenstein went downstairs to the front room, where Jamie awaited the doctor's assessment.

"Mister O'Connell is doing better than expected," Regenstein said.

Jamie smiled. "I'm glad for that."

"I should check into my hotel before it gets much later." Regenstein reached for his overnight bag.

Jamie snatched it away from him. "Please, stay here with us. We have plenty of room."

"Yes, doctor, please stay," Andi said. "We would welcome your company."

Regenstein looked from one to the other. It had been a

while since anyone sought his company. He felt a rare smile transform his entire being. "I'd like that."

"You can have your choice of four bedrooms," Jamie said. "There's one on this floor, two unoccupied on the floor above, and a cozy little room under an eave at the top of the house."

"Each has its own attached bathroom," Andi added.

Doctor Regenstein surveyed his surroundings. Only now did he admit to himself how much he wanted to stay. "Sounds luxurious. And I could use a good rest." He realized two sentences strung together was about the most he had managed since . . ..

"Surely you have some leave coming to you," Jamie said. "Stay as long as you like. A week. A month. You'll be very welcome."

Regenstein turned his head slightly. What he wouldn't give for a month off in a place where he was welcome. "Do you mean it?"

"Absolutely. And don't worry about privacy. This house is big enough for a quiet man like you to have all the privacy you need."

"Yes, Doctor Regenstein," Andi said. "We want you to feel at home. Please honor us with your company for as long and as often as you'd like."

Regenstein stood up straight. "Ben," he said.

Jamie looked at him. "Excuse me?"

"My name's Ben. And I haven't always been a quiet man. I've just been experiencing a lot of stress lately."

"A trouble shared is a trouble halved," Jamie said.

Ben smiled. "So I've heard. And someday soon, it might be time."

Noreen appeared in the doorway. "Lady and gentlemen, dinner is served." Jamie let Ben precede him.

"I have to catch the Del Monte Express tomorrow morning to attend a funeral in San Francisco," Jamie said. "I'll be back Sunday evening. Perhaps we can talk then."

Ben stopped and turned to face his host. Collins had a way of putting him at ease, of making him feel it was safe to open up. "Let's," Ben said.

After dinner, Ben, Andi, Jamie, and Noreen sat around the kitchen table and swapped stories until late. Ben hadn't felt so free in ages.

* * *

Saturday morning, 21 June 1919

Ben slept better than he had in months. Perhaps it was the sound of the waves and the sea air. More likely, it was Jamie, Andi, and Noreen's friendliness. But after months of being an outcast, a little company went a long way. Ben needed to get away and continue his serious thinking. Jamie had recommended that Ben visit the nearby artist's colony, Carmel-by-the-Sea. Ben took the streetcar to downtown Monterey and a bus south four miles over Poppy Hill. He'd heard doctors and nurses at Letterman mention how romantic Carmel was. He never imagined he'd someday visit it himself. With quaint art galleries and cottage shops on either side of its hilly main street, it looked like a picture postcard.

Ben found himself standing in front of his fourth or fifth art gallery—he'd lost count. The piantings in the previous galleries had a sameness about them. Here, they conveyed notably more emotion. Curiously, the large front window also displayed an array of children's books. Ben entered and was immediately captivated by a strikingly beautiful fair-haired woman sitting at a desk. She was looking through an art auction catalog.

"Welcome to my gallery," she said with a warm smile. She returned her attention to the catalog.

Ben approached her desk. Although he hadn't looked deliberately, he noticed she wasn't wearing a wedding ring. "Excuse me, miss." She looked up. "What's the significance of the children's books in the window?"

She leaned back in her chair. "Those are books I've illustrated."

"Impressive," Ben said. That soliloquy just about depleted his small-talk arsenal. He wandered to the center of the room and sat on a circular couch with his back to the gallery's owner as he contemplated a particularly intriguing painting.

"Oh, no!" she cried.

Ben spun around.

She jumped to her feet and pointed out the gallery's window. "That lady tripped on the curb. I'm afraid she may be hurt."

Ben rushed out of the gallery and leaned over a well-dressed, elderly woman sitting on the curb. The gallery owner was right beside him.

"I'm a doctor," Ben said. "Please allow me to help."

The woman nodded. Tears rolled down her cheeks.

Ben felt her ankle. "It's not broken." He gave her his best sympathetic look. "But it will be sore for a week or two."

Several onlookers were staring at her as she sat on the curb. "I don't know which is hurt more, my ankle or my pride," she said.

She reminded Ben of his favorite grandmother. "Let me help you up." He took her arm. The gallery owner took the woman's other arm. "Let's try taking a step or two."

She put a little weight on her ankle and hobbled forward. "It's not too bad," she said.

"Please, come into my gallery and sit for a while."

With some help, the woman made it through the door and sat on the circular couch in the center of the room.

"When you get home," Ben said, "put your foot up. An ice pack will help keep the swelling down."

She put her hand on Ben's forearm. "Thank you, doctor."

It was nice to interact with a patient on a personal basis. As a surgeon, most of Ben's patients were out cold on an operating table when he saw them. "You're very welcome." Ben turned to leave.

"Excuse me, doctor," the gallery owner said.

"Yes?"

"May we know your name?"

"I'm Doctor Regenst . . . Regen. Ben Regen."

"Regen?" the owner repeated. "I don't think I've heard that name around here before. Are you new in town?"

"I'm an army doctor stationed at Letterman Hospital in San Francisco. I'll be de-mobilized in a few months. I'm doing a little exploring, hoping to find a place to settle."

The owner gave him such a warm smile Ben was afraid he might melt. "I hope you'll give the Monterey Peninsula serious consideration."

Ben hadn't given the Peninsula much consideration at all —until now. He could feel his seldom-used smile muscles come alive. "I'll do that." He turned to leave.

"Thank you again," the injured woman said.

Ben could have kicked himself for not staying around

longer. He stopped less than a block down the hill in front of a little cafe. Several couples sat at tables near the window, enjoying each other's company. It had been a long time since he'd had the pleasure of a woman's company.

He kept picturing the gallery owner's smile.

Take a chance, Ben. What's the worst that can happen?

After some thought, he decided the worst had already happened with another woman, and he'd survived. He went into the corner pharmacy, bought an unadorned wooden cane and then rushed back to the gallery.

Ben took a deep breath and entered. He held out the cane to the lady who reminded him so much of his grandmother. "I suggest you use this for the next couple of days," he said.

The lady smiled broadly. "Oh, how considerate of you."

The owner looked very pleased. Or was that merely what Ben wanted to see?

He helped the woman out of the door. He and the gallery owner were then alone. Ben gathered all his fortitude. "There's a little café down the street. Is there any chance you'd join me for a cup of coffee and a little conversation? You have a business here in town. I'd appreciate hearing what you think the prospects would be for a new doctor in this area."

She stared at him intently for a few seconds and then looked at her wristwatch. "My assistant should be here in about ten minutes. She can look after the gallery if you're willing to wait."

"Does that mean yes?"

"It means coffee and conversation would be lovely." She extended her hand. "I'm Rachel."

* * *

Saturday afternoon, 21 June 1919

Matt Kavanaugh's funeral was a grand affair attended by over two hundred people of wealth and influence. The casket was open, although there was a shroud covering the face of the deceased.

Sonny Kavanaugh was there, of course, clearly reveling in the attention he was receiving as next of kin—or more likely—heir to the empire Matt built. He'd be livid when Matt's will was read in a few days and he learned that despite his efforts to circumvent Matt's wishes, the bulk of Kavanaugh Enterprises' assets had been transferred to a trust.

Though Sonny was having Jamie watched, there was no reason to believe he knew Jamie was the man he'd tussled with in Matt's office when that *lady* almost broke his wrist. Jamie went out of his way to avoid Sonny. Matt's nephew would learn soon enough who Jamie was.

Ed and Cathy had come to pay their respects to the man who brought them together. Although still noticeably shaken by Matt's death, they exchanged warm greetings with Jamie. It was agreed that there was no time to waste in getting the co-general managers of the Kavanaugh Trust fully up to speed.

The Dauer twins were also there. They stayed well in the background. They looked slightly out of place in their "Sunday best" wharf rat clothes. Jamie wouldn't have been surprised if they remembered Andi. He was surprised they remembered him. He suspected that they, along with Ed and

Cathy, and perhaps Matt's secretary, were the only ones genuinely saddened by Matt's passing.

After the service, as mourners were milling about outside in the sunshine, Jamie bumped into Jeff Mundy. Jamie pointed to the cast on Mundy's left arm. "What happened to you?"

"We raided a den of bootleggers. They put up a fight. One messed up my elbow real bad."

"Will you be all right?"

"The doctors say I'll never be able to straighten my arm all the way again. Still, I should be able to use it, after a fashion. Fortunately, I'm right-handed."

"Has the Bureau placed you on light duty?"

"They've gone further than that. With this kind of injury, I won't be able to meet the Bureau's physical standards. They're going to retire me."

"Are you ready for retirement?"

"Not even close. I'll need to find another job, and quick. Otherwise, with only the Bureau's meager retirement pay to live on, I'd be a regular at one of Matt's soup kitchens—assuming he made provisions for them in his will."

Jamie saw law enforcement officers as the closest thing to soldiers in the civilian world. That made Mundy another disabled veteran. It was only fitting that Jamie help ease Mundy into civilian life, as was his mission with all disabled vets.

Matt had a high opinion of Mundy. That carried a lot of weight. "I can keep you out of the soup lines," Jamie said.

Mundy tilted his head. "How?"

Jamie looked around to be sure no one was listening. "Before Matt died, he put his businesses and charities in a trust. He wants his trustee to see that they carry on in strict accordance with the law."

"How do you know that?"

"He asked me to be the trustee."

"You?"

"No one's more surprised than I am. And now we can help each other." Jamie could only hope Ed and Cathy wouldn't object to what he was about to do. "The Kavanaugh Trust is going to need a head of security."

"You're offering me the job?"

"Matt told me you're incorruptible."

Mundy squinted. "Matt said that?"

"He did."

"Would I be working for you?"

"Not directly. I've hired an experienced businessman to be the trust's general manager. You'd be reporting to him."

Mundy seemed suspicious. "And who's this experienced businessman?"

"Ed Maxwell, President of Pacific Maritime Insurance."

"PMI? The Bureau has had lots of trouble with insurance companies over the years. Never with PMI."

"Mister Kavanaugh told me Ed Maxwell is as honest a man as you'll ever meet."

"Let's be straight with each other. Will Matt still be running his empire using you as a front?"

Jamie shook his head. "Matt's dead. But even if he were alive, I still wouldn't let him have any say in the trust."

Mundy jammed his free hand deep into the pocket of his ever-present rumpled raincoat. "The background check the Bureau did on you says not only are you brave, you're honest."

"Does that mean you'll accept the job?"

"Let me think about it." Mundy scratched his head. "I thought about it. I accept."

Jamie laughed. "Don't you want to know how much the job will pay?"

"It's got to be more than the Bureau was paying me."

"Do you mind me asking how much that was?"

"I don't mind. The pay of a Special Agent is a matter of public record." Mundy gave Jamie a round figure. "But if that's too much, I—"

"I'll start you at four times that amount. Would that be acceptable?"

Mundy rubbed the stubble on his chin. "Perfectly. I'm your man."

They shook on it.

"By the way," Jamie said, "do you know a man named Vince Dufner?"

"Special Agent Dufner? I certainly do. We've worked together for years. He's saved my bacon many times."

"Sounds like you think highly of him."

"He's one of the best agents I've ever had the privilege of working with." Mundy smiled. "I understand you two have met."

"Under rather unusual circumstances."

"Vince is actually a good friend of mine—and I'm worried about him."

"How so?"

"He's been distracted lately, and that can get you killed in our line of work. He told me he let the man you chased off sneak up on him. That never would have happened if he wasn't worrying about his wife."

"What's wrong with her?"

"It's tough working this job when you're married. His

wife has threatened to divorce him if he doesn't leave the Bureau. She's tired of always being afraid he's going to get hurt and of his crazy hours."

Jamie thought for a moment. "If Dufner decides to leave the Bureau, is he someone you'd consider hiring?"

"Definitely." Mundy canted his head. "Perhaps as my assistant head of security?"

"Fine, if that's what you want." Jamie lowered his voice to be sure no one would hear him. "I understand congratulations are due in another quarter."

"Oh?"

"I heard from an unimpeachable source that you arrested Omega."

"That hasn't been in the newspapers yet, so please keep it to yourself for now."

"You have my word," Jamie said.

Mundy shook his head. "It's a funny old world we live in. The Bureau's going to give me a commendation one day and force me to retire the next."

"I should thank them," Jamie said. "The Bureau's loss is my gain."

Mundy smiled. "I'm glad you think so."

"I'm curious," Jamie said. "Were you able to get Omega to talk?"

"Yeah, I got her to talk. Once I broke her down, she sang like a songbird. What we learned will make interesting reading in the newspapers later this week—although we're holding back some details. Turns out Omega isn't just one killer for hire. It's a secret society made up of sorority girls."

Jamie wouldn't have been more surprised if Mundy had punched him in the gut. "I'm stunned. My source said the person you arrested was a young woman, but a bunch of sorority girls? That's . . . disgusting."

"Omega's victims have all been men who mistreated women. Men who had slipped through the cracks in our legal system, either on a technicality or just by having slick lawyers. The girl I arrested claimed she was out to bring vigilante justice to a criminal the law couldn't touch."

"Vigilante justice—there's no such thing."

"I agree." Mundy leaned against a lamppost. "It all started when a girl at a posh woman's college in Chicago was brutally raped. Chicago PD was convinced the offender was a boy from a nearby university. Unfortunately, they didn't have much solid evidence. And the boy's father had the resources to hire a team of aggressive defense attorneys. They saw to it that the boy walked free."

"A man in my infantry company was accused of rape just before we shipped out for France. He denied the accusation, and the police didn't have much of a case against him, so the army shipped him overseas with the rest of us. Later, I overheard him bragging about getting away with it. Perhaps it was fate that he didn't escape an artillery shell that tore him to pieces."

"Rough justice," Mundy said. "Not surprisingly, when the prime suspect in the sorority girl's rape walked free, there was quite an uproar at the women's college. One of the victim's sorority sisters wrote a paper for a history class promoting vigilantism. The professor was so impressed by the girl's arguments that she had her read her paper to the class. The session became very heated."

"I can imagine," Jamie said.

"The professor—Griswold is her name—was enraged that the boy got away with raping her student and intrigued by the idea of vigilante justice. She decided that if the police couldn't act, she would. She invented a secret society and persuaded several of the rape victim's sorority sisters to join. Their charter was to bring vigilante 'justice' to men who thought they could mistreat women and get away with it."

"It's well known that Omega gunned down his—or rather, her—victims," Jamie said. "Where'd these girls learn to shoot?"

"They didn't have to. One of the girls had a Luger automatic pistol her father brought back from France as a war souvenir. He'd given it to her for self-defense. The girl bought a silencer for it on the black market."

"With a good silencer," Jamie said, "they could shoot somebody up close in a noisy place, and nobody would be any the wiser."

"That was Professor Griswold's thinking. Since none of the girls were marksmen, their modus operandi was to jam the silencer up against the middle of the target's chest and pull the trigger."

"You'd have to be pretty coldblooded to kill a man up close and personal like that."

"It probably made it easier that their first victim was the boy the police were convinced had raped their sorority sister. He was gunned down in a park in broad daylight. Chicago PD couldn't find a single witness who'd admit to seeing or hearing a thing."

Jamie sucked in his breath. "I hope you're not going to tell me a girl had to kill a man to become a full member of their secret society."

"That's the way it worked. The girl I arrested was a novice. The more experienced girls had put her through dry runs. Gunning down a live human being was different. It was for real."

Jamie shook his head in disgust. "Why'd they call themselves Omega?"

"They were all members of various sororities. Since sororities have Greek names, Professor Griswold thought Omega was an appropriate choice, it being the last letter of the Greek alphabet—and presumably the last thing their victims ever saw. One of the girls came up with the idea of leaving their calling card on the victim's body to put men on notice that even if the law couldn't touch them, Omega could."

"Nobody expects a college girl to be an assassin," Jamie said. "That undoubtedly made it easier for them to get close to their victims."

"That almost got Matt killed." Mundy looked over his shoulder before going on. "I don't want Matt's involvement in Omega's arrest ever to become public knowledge, so please keep it close to your vest."

"Sure," Jamie said. "I'm curious. My source said once Omega was paid, there was no way to cancel the contract. How'd Matt contact her—or rather, them—in the first place?"

"Through a dead drop."

"A what?"

"Someone wanting to hire Omega would pass a note to a member of Chicago's South Side Gang. A runner for the gang, usually someone they were vetting as a prospective member, would place the note in a certain book in one of Chicago's forty or so public libraries. The book and library were specified in code in the first line of a classified ad in the Chicago Tribune. The code key was changed monthly."

"Sounds like something out of a ten-cent spy novel."

"Actually, that's where the girls got the idea. Omega communicated with whoever hired her through the same mechanism: a classified ad. Payment going through books in the libraries, with the gang taking a cut."

"Doesn't getting paid negate their claim that they were carrying out vigilante justice?"

"Professor Griswold got greedy. It was easy for her to pocket the profits as she sat on her fat ass in her ivory tower and sent impressionable young women out to commit murder. All she had to do was convince them their target, whose identity she kept to herself, deserved to die."

The idea of a professor running a murder-for-hire business under the guise of vigilante justice turned Jamie's stomach. "Using her students that way was pure evil."

"And yet Professor Griswold was indignant when she was arrested. She claimed—"

"You already arrested her? That was mighty fast."

"The Bureau wasn't going to drag its feet on a volatile case like this."

"I'm glad," Jamie said.

"Like I said, this evil professor was indignant when the Bureau arrested her. She claimed Omega was doing society a service by targeting only unscrupulous men who thought they could get away with badly mistreating women."

"She must be crazy," Jamie said. "Thank you and the Bureau for ending this sick business."

"I wish I could say for sure that we have."

Jamie didn't like the sound of that.

"We're not sure we've identified all the members of Omega. There could even be Omega chapters at other colleges. Worse, since the deceased's face at this funeral was covered by a shroud with only the Bureau's word that the body in his casket was Matt's, questions have begun to rise in some quarters as to whether Matt really is dead. There are already those in the criminal world wondering whether the Bureau is pulling another of its tricks on the public." Mundy locked eyes with Jamie. "If Omega is still active, and they suspect Matt is still alive, some innocent-looking college girl could one day come gunning for him. He better be on his guard—and so should anybody reckless enough to get close to him."

* * *

Saturday evening, 21 June 1919

Ben and Andi joined Noreen in her kitchen for dinner. After saying grace and closing in the name of Jesus, Ben and Noreen joined Andi in saying, "Amen."

"How was your day out, Doctor Ben?" Noreen asked.

"Great," he said with more enthusiasm than Andi had ever heard from him before. "The Monterey Peninsula's a beautiful place."

"And Carmel?" Andi asked.

Ben's smile was becoming freer. "A place of particular beauty."

Andi knew that look. "From your dreamy expression, my guess is you met someone?"

Ben lowered his head and stared at his dinner plate. "I did."

"Good for you, sir," Noreen said.

Ben looked up and smiled broadly. "We sat in a little

café and talked for over an hour. And never once did I get the impression that she wasn't happy to be with me."

* * *

Sunday afternoon, 22 June 1919

After Andi took a tray up to Liam, she, Noreen, and Ben gathered for the noonday meal. "This is the most relaxed I've been in years," Ben said. "Surgery after surgery has been taking a toll on me."

"Perhaps you'll join me for a stroll along the shore after lunch," Andi said. "I always find that to be a great way to relieve stress."

"I'd love to."

As they strolled, Andi talked about her plans for the Army School of Nursing. Ben entertained her with stories of his years in medical school. Their conversation wandered to the state of medical care in the area. "It's a shame there isn't a hospital here on the Peninsula," Ben said.

Andi nodded. "It would be great if some intrepid medical professionals made it their mission to establish one."

* * *

Sunday evening, 22 June 1919

Jamie was back from Matt's funeral by dinnertime. He took Andi in his arms as soon as they were alone. "I don't even want to think about how much I'll miss you when you leave for DC in a week or so."

Andi pressed her cheek to his. "I was beginning to

believe all the sunshine had gone out of the world while you were gone. How will we cope when we're three thousand miles apart for months at a time?"

Jamie pushed her hair aside and nuzzled her ear. What a fool he'd been to make that promise to Rachel. But he'd be an even bigger fool if he stood in the way of Andi fulfilling her career goals. How *would* he cope? He wasn't sure he could. But that wasn't what Andi needed to hear. "We'll just have to endure."

Noreen announced that dinner was served. Andi took a tray up to Liam and then joined Jamie, Ben, and Noreen in the kitchen. Jamie still insisted that they eat together. Assuming Ben was Jewish, Jamie hoped he hadn't made his friend uncomfortable when he closed grace in the name of Jesus.

"I've legally changed my name," Ben said with no preamble.

"That's a surprise," Jamie said. "Mind telling us why?"

"My father insisted that I stop using the name Regenstein."

They all waited for an explanation.

"I believe in personal freedom," Ben said. "Freedom of thought, conscience, and more to the point, belief. My family doesn't. A little less than a year ago, my hand slipped during an operation, and I almost lost a patient. I reached out to God in desperation, asking him to repair the damage I'd done. I was so desperate, I even called out to Jesus." Ben looked from one person to another. "I swear He answered me. 'Your patient is healed,' He said. "And I knew—without the slightest doubt—I knew it was true."

"A miracle, no doubt," Noreen said.

"One I couldn't ignore," Ben said. "It led me to accept

Jesus as my Lord and Savior, and I've never wavered from my decision." He glanced at those around the table. "Please understand. I'm not saying everyone must follow the path I'm on–like I said, I believe in personal freedom–but it's the one I intend to follow the rest of my life."

Ben leaned back in his chair. "When I told my family I'd become a Christian, you'd think I'd confessed to murder. There are undoubtedly many who would disagree with me—Jews and Christians—but to my way of thinking, I haven't rejected Judaism. I've augmented it the way Jesus' original disciples had. Once my parents realized they couldn't change my mind, my father—and my fiancée—declared me dead to them. To satisfy my father, despite my mother's objection, I'm now legally Ben 'Regen.' "

The irony didn't escape Jamie. He and Ben had both been declared dead—prematurely. "You're brave to stand by your beliefs," Jamie said. "And you're not without family. I'm sure I speak for all at this table when I say you're welcome into our family of believers."

"I second that," Andi said.

Noreen clasped her hands. "Amen."

"Thank you," Ben said. "That means a lot to me. And you've helped me make another decision. When the army discharges me at the end of the year, I plan to practice medicine here on the Monterey Peninsula."

"That's great!" they all said in unison. Everyone laughed, including Ben.

"A surgeon with your skills will be a blessing to this community," Andi said.

"Thanks for your vote of confidence, Andi. I hope you won't be disappointed to learn that I plan to practice general medicine."

"That's a drastic change," she said.

"I'll still be willing to perform surgery when necessary. It's just that I want to get to know my patients. Surgeons only see theirs more or less in passing. And the stress of surgery is getting to me." Ben looked at Jamie. "I had nightmares for a week after removing that shrapnel from your back. One little slip and I could have turned you into a quadriplegic."

"I'm surprised," Jamie said." You projected such confidence."

"If only you knew how difficult that was for me. The army snatched me up as soon as I completed my surgical residency. All I've ever known is surgery. I've had my fill. I'm sure I'd like general practice much more."

"We have a friend whose brother has a general practice here in Pacific Grove," Jamie said. "She's pushing him to take on a partner. I'd be happy to introduce you two."

"That would be grand," Ben said. "I don't know the first thing about setting up or running a practice. I'd much prefer joining an existing one." Ben rubbed the side of his neck. "I have to return to Letterman in the morning. If your friend's brother is willing to talk with me, I'll return in a flash."

"I've already promised to get together with him," Jamie said. "Now I have even more reason."

"Once you're settled," Andi said, "maybe you can help establish the hospital we agreed is needed here on the Peninsula."

Ben smiled. "I intend to."

* * *

Thursday, 26 June 1919

Andi was amazed that Liam, a man who had been in charge of so many people and businesses for decades, could be such a compliant patient. Perhaps she shouldn't have been. A man couldn't accomplish all he had without a considerable measure of determination. It also told her how much Liam wanted a new life.

"Good news," Andi said when she entered his bedroom with a breakfast tray. "It's time to remove your external splints." She did so with the skill of the highly experienced nurse she was. "Your nose is perfectly straight, although it's a little puffy. And it will be for several months."

"Thank you, Andi, for all you've done for me."

"Shhh. Don't talk. Just rest."

* * *

Friday, 27 June 1919

Liam woke when Andi entered his room. "I'll be off to the train station soon," she said. "I couldn't leave without saying goodbye."

Liam tried to sit up. Andi put her hand on his shoulder and gently restrained him.

"I'll miss you, Andi. You've made me feel like I'm someone worth caring about."

"You *are* someone worth caring about."

"Are you forgetting my background?"

"Jamie told me how you were pressured into managing Gallagher's Saloon. More importantly, how you turned Gallagher's into a respectable workingman's club." She smiled. "Regardless of Kavanaugh Enterprises' start, and more recently, your involvement in tax fraud—which was for a worthy cause—the business empire you built will now be devoted to giving honest workers employment, funding charities, and, closest to my heart, educating disabled veterans. I'd say you have much to be proud of. And who knows what worthy cause Liam O'Connell will dedicate his life to in the future?"

He took her hand. "I hope Jamie realizes what a jewel you are."

"I'll keep reminding him." She canted her head. "Your tremors have lessened."

Liam looked at his hands. "I was hoping it wasn't just wishful thinking."

"I haven't heard you slur any words lately."

"You're . . . you're right."

"Squeeze my hand." Liam gave it a good squeeze.

"Strong and steady as a vise." She flashed him her best caring-nurse smile. "It's been almost two weeks since you arrived at BayView. You've followed your doctor's orders to a T. Noreen will be bringing you your meals from now on. Since you've made such good progress, you two can talk quietly, so long as you don't become too excited."

"Yes, nurse," Liam said, clearly struggling to suppress his excitement.

"Will we see Liam O'Connell in the future? Or will Liam fade into obscurity and emerge as someone else?"

"I've given that a lot of thought. So long as you and Jamie don't object, you'll see Liam again."

"I'm glad. One can never have enough friends." She backed out of the door and gently closed it behind her.

Andi made her way downstairs and, for a silent moment, watched Noreen working in her kitchen. Noreen looked up and smiled.

"I dream of the day you start teaching me to cook," Andi said.

"Ach, lassie, we'll do it as soon as you're ready."

They hugged like mother and daughter.

* * *

BayView felt empty to Noreen, with only her and Liam in residence. Jamie was escorting Andi to the San Francisco train station. He wouldn't be back until the next day.

Noreen took a lunch tray to Liam's room. She knocked.

"Come in," a quiet voice said.

Noreen entered Liam's room for the first time since he'd moved in. He was lying flat on his back. She could imagine him being bored half to death while confined to a darkened room for so long. "Your lunch, sir."

Liam motioned her into the room. "Thank you. Noreen, isn't it?"

Noreen thought his voice was a bit nasal, due to his surgery, no doubt, but she was sure she heard kindness in it. "Yes, sir."

"Scottish, are you?"

"Yes, sir. I was a MacAskill before I married into the Clan Ferguson."

"Please, Noreen, stay for a while. Nurse Andi said we could talk, so long as I don't get too excited."

Noreen pulled up a chair and sat near Liam's bed. "I'm happy to say I live a quiet life, so I don't think you have to worry about me bringing much excitement into a conversation."

Liam chuckled. "I understand you're Professor Collins' household manager. What does that entail?"

"Well, sir—"

"Liam. Please, just plain Liam. I shudder when anyone calls me sir."

"Right you are, Liam." Noreen settled herself more comfortably on her chair. She was so pleased with her position as household manager that she described it in detail, ending with her most immediate plan. "I'm looking to hire a man to be BayView's gardener and handyman."

"Would it be a full-time job?"

"Certainly. The garden's large, and there's always something for a handyman to do in and around the house. With the salary and benefits I'll be offering, I imagine there'll be lots of applicants, although I don't imagine many will be suitable.

"What kind of benefits?"

"Whoever I hire will get to live in the quarters attached to the back of the carriage house and eat his meals in the kitchen of the big house. With the economy as it is, room and board will attract all kinds of desperate men. But I'll be looking for a hard worker with sufficient initiative that he doesn't have to be told what to do."

"As well as household manager, are you the cook in this household?"

Noreen wasn't sure where this was leading. "I am."

Liam looked her in the eye. "If those who see your advertisement knew what a good cook you are, you'd have applicants lined up from here to the train station."

Liam sounded so sincere. "Thank you, Liam. I take pride in my cooking."

"As well you should." He was silent for a moment. "When do you intend to fill this position?"

"Soon. I'll be putting an advertisement in Monday's newspaper."

* * *

Saturday morning, 28 June 1919

Liam could hardly wait for Noreen to return with his breakfast tray. Since her last visit, he'd spent every waking minute thinking about the gardener/handyman position she planned to advertise. The job was everything Liam dreamt of. A simple life. Honest work he could do with his hands. The question was, would Jamie allow it? And what if someone with an interest in Matt Kavanaugh came snooping around? Would a straightened nose, wire-rim glasses, unruly hair, and a beard and mustache fool them? Liam had convinced himself it would. To anyone connected to "The Mighty Matt Kavanaugh," a "nonentity" such as a gardener/handyman would be practically invisible.

"I can save you the trouble of interviewing men for the gardener/handyman position you're looking to fill," Liam said as Noreen set his breakfast tray on the small table beside his bed.

"Oh?"

Against doctor's orders, Liam sat up. "I'd like to apply."

"You want to be BayView's gardener and handyman?"

"It would be my dream job." The truth was, he needed the job. He needed the people associated with BayView. He needed the house, the garden. He needed to belong. He could only hope Jamie would understand.

"You wouldn't feel awkward working for your friend?"

"Not at all. We're not what you'd call personal friends.

We have a family connection, that's all. Professor Collins is an extraordinary man. I'd be honored to work for him."

"Are you an experienced gardener?"

"I'm sorry to say I've spent much of my life working at a desk. But I'm an expert at raising house plants, and I'm a quick learner and hard worker." Liam didn't want to sound as desperate as he was. "Please consider hiring me on a trial basis. Say for three months? I'd forgo the salary and work for room and board only."

Noreen crossed her arms. "That wouldn't be right. If a man works hard, he deserves his pay." She leaned back in her chair. "Since Professor Jamie allowed you to recuperate in his house, he must think highly of you. When can you start?"

"Now you *have* gotten me excited," Liam said with a huge grin. "I'll start the minute I'm allowed to leave this room."

* * *

Saturday afternoon, 28 June 1919. San Francisco train station

Jamie and Andi had an hour before her Transcontinental Express was to leave for DC. Ambition and integrity were the villains that were separating them. If Andi could put aside her ambition to be Assistant Dean of the Army School of Nursing, and if Jamie could break his promise to Rachel, they could marry right away and stay together "until death do us part." Of course, then, neither would be the person the other had fallen in love with.

They walked to the far end of their platform and sat on a bench as close to each other as possible. "I'm afraid Thanksgiving in Denver is going to feel like a century and a continent away," Jamie said. He took her hand. Was he really going to let her get on that train?

Andi turned away. He could tell she was fighting back tears. Steeling herself not to let her emotions take control.

"I dread having to sleep alone in that big house without you there to chase away the demons of the night," Jamie said. "I guess I'll just have to go back to sleeping with a light on in the room."

"Here's how we're going to defeat your fear of being alone in the dark." She placed her palm in the middle of his chest. "Carry me in your heart, and you'll never be alone."

Jamie stared at her. The only way he'd never be alone would be to carry her across his threshold as his wife. But that wasn't what she needed to hear before boarding that train. "I'll give it a try."

"I'm sure it will work."

The only thing Jamie was sure of was how much he'd miss her. "I'll write to you often."

"As will I," Andi said.

"One thing, though. Perhaps I'm being overly cautious, but since it will be a matter of public record that I'm the trustee of the Kavanaugh Trust, Sonny might try to intercept my correspondence."

"Why would he do that?"

"To find clues as to whether Matt's still alive and, if so, his whereabouts. We must be careful not to imply that there's a connection between Matt and Liam."

"I see," Andi said. "In that case, you're not being overly cautious. You're being protective of someone you care about. Which is one of the many things I love about you." She gave him one of her heart-warming smiles. "I can hardly wait for my father to meet you—and to show you off to my middle sister and her snooty husband."

"Snooty?"

"Ronald is Secretary of the Colorado State Senate. You'd never know it was a civil service job. The way he acts, you'd think he was a state senator himself. But I know you'll love my sisters. I'm half afraid to introduce you to Debbi. You might be so taken by her that you'll leave me in the dust as you chase after her."

"Never!" Jamie said. "You're the only one for me."

"Just remember that when you meet her," Andi said with a laugh that sounded forced.

Forget his promise to Rachel. It was only his love for Andi that was keeping him from putting a ring on her finger. Rushing her into marriage would deprive her of seeing her career dreams come true.

"My hope is that your travels for the School of Nursing will bring you west before Thanksgiving."

"I'll try my hardest to make that happen."

He held her tightly as the minutes raced by. Then she was gone.

Jamie returned to BayView that evening feeling as though his heart had been torn from his chest.

Saturday evening, 28 June 1919

"This house is going to feel empty without Andi," Jamie said to Noreen the instant he walked through the door. "Without you here, I'd go crazy. I'll be glad when we have an assistant housekeeper and a gardener to help fill the void."

"I have good news on that front, Professor Jamie. I've hired a gardener/handyman."

"That was quick."

"He can hardly wait to start. His priorities did strike me as odd, though. He seemed more thrilled that he'll get to live in the back of the carriage house and take his meals here in the kitchen than he was by the pay you and I settled on."

"If he knew what a good cook you are, that would be understandable. If I didn't own the house, I'd be tempted to apply myself."

Noreen smiled. "You'd also think the man was independently wealthy or something. And he didn't even ask about days off. He says they won't matter because he'll make himself available 24 hours a day, seven days a week. He only wants a garden to work in, food to eat, a roof over his head, and a loving family to serve."

"He sounds too good to be real. Is he someone you know?"

"He's someone you know, Professor Jamie. He's your friend Liam O'Connell."

Jamie had to sit down. Was this some devious plan to maintain control of Kavanaugh Enterprises? If so, Liam would be very disappointed. Regardless, Jamie couldn't overrule Noreen without undermining the authority he'd granted her as his household manager.

Jamie would have a serious talk with Liam as soon as his confinement was over.

"Are you pleased with my choice, sir?"

After a moment's thought, Jamie realized that having Liam nearby could be beneficial. "I'm happy now that I've gotten over the surprise. Liam's got a wealth of worldly wisdom I might want to lean on from time to time."

* * *

Sunday, 29 June 1919

Liam awoke to his big day. His two-week confinement had finally ended.

"Thank you, God," he said out loud.

He struggled to walk to the window after lying in bed for so long. When he drew back the curtains for the first time, he had to shield his eyes from the light. It came as a surprise how close the house was to the bay. The scene was so beautiful he'd be happy to see it every day for the rest of his life.

He held out his hands. It wasn't just wishful thinking. Andi herself assured him that his tremors had lessened.

He stepped before the vanity and looked at himself in sunlight for the first time in two weeks. He hardly recognized himself. Matt Kavanaugh's crooked nose was the first thing anyone noticed about him. And Matt had always been well-groomed. Liam's hair was already longer than Matt's had ever been. He'd also stopped shaving. His beard and mustache had come in grayer than expected. With a straight nose and an exaggerated Irish accent, who would ever suspect he wasn't who he said he was?

He put on the pair of clear, round-lens, wire-rim glasses Jamie bought in a San Francisco theater supply shop and found his way downstairs. Jamie was in the front room. The view through the windows was so captivating Liam was speechless.

"Who's this stranger in my house," Jamie asked with a smile.

"Liam O'Connell, sir. And I can't thank you enough for your hospitality."

Jamie's smile disappeared. "Can it be true that you want to be BayView's gardener?"

"It can, sir. As I told you a few weeks back when we were in Matt Kavanaugh's office, if I had it all to do over again, I'd have been a gardener from the start."

"Sir" rolled off Liam's tongue with such ease and sincerity no one would believe he had ruled over a business empire for decades.

"You'll be disappointed if you want to be close to me so you can control the Kavanaugh Trust."

"That's not why I want to be part of your household, sir. When I was trying to think of a name to use in my new life, 'Liam' popped into my head. Initially, I thought it came to me because it was the name we gave our son, and Liam O'Connell sounds so Irish. After lying in isolation over the last two weeks and doing a lot of soul-searching, I believe the name is even more appropriate. In Irish folklore, Liam means 'guardian.' That's why I want to be your gardener and handyman and live in the back of your carriage house. If you allow me to, upon my oath, I will guard you, Andi, and your household with my life for the rest of my days."

Jamie could hardly believe his ears. "What's behind this oath of yours.?"

"I want to repay you and Andi in a small way—not just for saving my life. More importantly, for helping me see that my life is worth saving."

Chapter 17

Letters I

Monday, 30 June 1919. BayView

My Dearest Andi,

It's hard to believe it's only been two days since the Transcontinental Express took you from me. It feels longer. Much longer. I can't imagine how it will feel waiting for your tour of duty to end. But for you, my dear, I would wait until the end of time.

Here's some good news. Your solution to my fear of being alone in the dark seems to be helping. Every time it starts to close in on me, I remember that you're right there in my heart, and that gives me courage.

A letter from my sister just arrived. Ali will be home in early October! The French government has taken over most of the work that the American

Women's Hospitals were doing, so the AWH is giving Ali an early release from her contract. Having gone to medical school in Scotland and then working as a contract physician for the British Army in France throughout the war, she's more than ready to return to her homeland. I hope she'll establish a practice here on the Monterey Peninsula. Ali and Noreen should have a lot of Scottish tales to share.

You will undoubtedly be as shocked as I was to learn who Noreen hired as BayView's handyman/gardener. We both know him, but I won't tell you who in this letter. I want you to try to guess.

Until next time, all my love, Jamie

* * *

Wednesday, 09 July 1919. Walter Reed General Hospital

My Beloved Jamie,

You can't possibly miss me more than I miss you. Fortunately, my new job promises to fill my days with so much activity that I won't be able to dwell on my longing to be near you.

I so look forward to meeting your sister. If she's anything like you, I know I'll love her.

Please give me another hint about the identity

of BayView's gardener. If we both know him, would I be correct in assuming he's someone from Letterman?

I received a nice letter from Cathy Maxwell. She thinks you're a saint for making her co-general manager of the Kavanaugh Trust. I'll write back to her as soon as I finish this letter. I was shocked to my core by how open she was about her past when she and I first met. Now, that openness is one of the things I most admire about her, as well as the warmth of her personality and her humor. I think the two of us will become fast friends. I'm looking forward to her next letter.

Nurses' quarters at Walter Reed are in an old barracks on hospital grounds, so it's a short walk to my office. My room is slightly less luxurious than the Presidential Suite at the Palace Hotel, which doesn't matter much. I'll be so busy I'll spend little time there. Will you forgive me for saying I miss BayView almost as much as I miss you? The heat and humidity in DC are brutal. I remember thinking the summers in Denver were hot. But in Denver, it's a dry heat, and it cools off at night. I'm beginning to think it never cools off in DC. What I wouldn't give to feel the cool Pacific breeze on my cheek and your arms around me.

All my love, Andi

* * *

Thursday, 17 July 1919. BayView

My Dearest Andi,

Thank you for your letter, which I received earlier today. I had it memorized after the third reading. I've read it a dozen more times and pretended you were here speaking the words to me.

As to assuming BayView's gardener is someone from Letterman, that's not a good assumption.

I contacted Doctor Scott Stanton, Lanie's brother, the day after you left. We've already gotten together twice to play chess, first at BayView and then at his place. He's one of six residents in a boarding house near the center of town. From what Scott says, his landlady's a bit of a tyrant and not a very good or imaginative cook. Part of his agreement with her is that she will take telephone calls for him while he's out tending to his patients. Lately, she never misses an opportunity to complain about how inconvenient that's become for her. He's been meaning to find more pleasant accommodations. So far, he hasn't found anything suitable.

We were right to think Scott is suffering from shell shock. The last time we played chess, I spilled tea on my shirt. I immediately dowsed the spill with water so it wouldn't stain. Although Scott is bigger than me, he offered to let me wear one of his shirts while mine dried. When I took mine off and Scott saw all my shrapnel scars, he broke down. As I'm sure you can appreciate, he had to treat an uncountable number of wounds during the war. They haunt him to this day. The only way he can keep from being overwhelmed by his memories is to bury himself in his work. Thankfully, he does fine with illnesses. Only when he has to treat an injured patient does the trauma of the war come rushing back to him. Yesterday, we sat and talked about it late into the night. I think it helped him. I know it helped me.

I'll introduce Scott and Ben Regen the next time Ben gets a weekend off. Wouldn't it be wonderful if Scott, Ben, and Ali formed a partnership here in Pacific Grove?

I probably should keep such thoughts to myself until they meet and get to know each other. I could be hoping for too much. They might not even like one another.

Until next time, all my love, Jamie

* * *

Friday, 25 July 1919. Walter Reed General Hospital

My Beloved Jamie,

I'll soon be off to visit a nursing school in Philadelphia. My primary responsibility as Assistant Dean of the ASN is to shape the school's curriculum. The most efficient way to do that is to emulate the best practices of schools that have existed for decades. That means I'll be traveling a lot, sometimes at a moment's notice. I'll likely spend more time on the road than in my office at Walter Reed. I wish some of those schools were on the West Coast so we could see each other for a day or two now and then. Unfortunately, the schools Dean Stimson wants me to visit are all long-established schools, and as such, all in the east.

I attended Sunday services at the National Cathedral last weekend. Besides worshiping the Almighty, I wanted to see the place and hear Sylvia Maxwell perform her magic on the cathedral's magnificent pipe organ. I was not disappointed! Afterward, I sought out Sylvia. We hadn't seen each other since June 1st, when you and I heard her play the organ at San Francisco's Old First Presbyterian Church. To my surprise, she remembered me. We plan to dine together soon. I don't know whether I should tell her I'm corresponding with Cathy, her "stepmother." From Cathy's last letter, I gather there's still considerable tension between them, which is a shame. It doesn't matter that Cathy is half Ed's age. You and I saw how happy they make each other.

I'm glad you and Scott Stanton have gotten together. I'm sure it's therapeutic for you to console each other when memories of the war threaten to overwhelm you. I do hope he and Ben form a partnership. Wouldn't it be an amazing twist of fate if Lanie's brother were to fall for your sister?

As to the identity of BayView's gardener, we both know very few people who are not from Letterman. As crazy as it seems, my guess is Liam O'Connell. If true, his life has taken turns no one could have predicted.

Scott's fortunate to have you to talk to, as you have survived so much. I still have flash-backs of horrific scenes I witnessed in France. Thanks to you, they no longer invade my dreams.

Speaking of dreams, I often dream of being Lady of BayView. I take solace in knowing that a dream delayed isn't necessarily a dream denied.

All my love, Andi

* * *

Monday, 04 August 1919. BayView

My Dearest Andi,

To make you Lady of BayView is one of my most cherished dreams.

You guessed correctly. BayView's gardener is none other than Liam O'Connell! And get this: Liam has vowed to guard me, you, and our household with his life for the rest of his days to thank us for helping him see that his life is worth saving.

He says he misses you too, although he <u>supposes</u> not as much as I do. I had to laugh at his understatement. That's like <u>supposing</u> I'd miss the air I breathe if I sank to the bottom of the sea.

It has occurred to me that perhaps Liam sees me as a replacement for the son he lost so many years ago. And I won't deny that sometimes I see Liam as the father I lost the summer I graduated from high school. Who would have thought?

Ben was here over the weekend. He and Scott met Friday evening. My prayer has been granted! They've agreed to form a partnership beginning 01 January, the day after Ben is released from the army. Now, all we need is for Ali to join them! As for

Scott falling for my sister, stranger things have happened.

I've dropped by Charlie Gowan's furniture shop so often someone might think I work there. I just love woodworking. And all the tools he has. He and his men are turning out some magnificent pieces of furniture.

I hope I'll be forgiven for my vanity. I've commissioned him to build a display case for my medals—and a matching one for yours.

Charlie will never get rich building furniture, although he might from making medical devices. Since neither he nor I know anything about medicine, I wonder whether he'd be interested in hiring Scott, Ben, and Ali as medical consultants for his Advanced Medical Devices company. I'll broach the subject with him the next chance I get.

I'm happy you and Cathy Maxwell are writing to each other. Please don't reveal anything you two would rather keep between yourselves, but I'd appreciate it if you'd let me know how Cathy thinks being the Kavanaugh Trust's co-general manager is working out. As far as I can tell, everything's going great. As trustee, I don't want to be the last to know if that's not the case.

It's great that you and Sylvia Maxwell have gotten together. I'd be surprised if you two don't become close friends. Please give her my regards—and tell her that working with her father is a delight.

Life has its problems. Two of the Kavanaugh Trust's delivery trucks were hijacked the day before yesterday. They were traveling together, carrying a shipment of furniture from a factory in Sacramento to a warehouse in Oakland. The drivers were roughed up a bit. Fortunately, they weren't seriously hurt. The hijackers put a good scare in them, though, and "suggested" they'd be safer working some other job.

The furniture was found a mile or so down the road, broken into a million pieces. The trucks were recovered the next day, smelling strongly of alcohol. Jeff Mundy, now head of security for the Kavanaugh Trust, is sure Sonny Kavanaugh is behind the hijacking. He thinks the trucks were used to transport bootleg whiskey, and the furniture was destroyed out of spite. Fortunately, we have good insurance.

Mundy says that if law enforcement had intercepted the trucks while still carrying the alcohol, he'd bet the drivers would claim they were working for the Kavanaugh Trust and the alcohol was their cargo all along.

I'd hate for Mundy to be correct. Before his drowning, Matt assured me that Sonny would have a strong incentive not to attack me or my loved ones, although he warned me that Sonny would do whatever he could to see that the Trust loses money.

On another sad note, John Thayer is threatening to buy the property across Fountain Avenue from BayView. He wants to put up a three-story apartment building on the site. The lot is triangular-shaped and not at all suitable for an apartment building. I've had Attorney Paul Handler file an objection with the Coastal Planning Commission. The building Thayer wants to put up would be totally inconsistent with the nature of the neighborhood. Plus, it would ruin the view for all the nearby houses, including BayView—which I suspect is Thayer's primary motivation.

There's a photographer's shop a few doors down from Charlie's. I thought a few pictures of BayView in your quarters might help you escape the heat and humidity of DC, at least in your mind. I had the photographer take photos of the outside of BayView and some from the front window looking out over the bay. You should receive them in a separate package in a day or two. I've also included a few photos of me so you won't forget what I look like. I'd love to have a picture or two of you taken in your office.

I've been trying to build up Charlie Gowan's confidence, hoping he'll ask Lanie out. He still thinks she's too sophisticated for him, while you and I think she's perfect. Part of his insecurity comes from her being a college graduate and a math teacher and him having only a high school education. That's sad. He needs to realize that a self-educated man has nothing to be ashamed of. Sometimes, when Charlie and I are going over one of his designs, I find myself thinking that I'd trade my Ph.D. for his intelligence and creativity. It's too bad we promised Lanie we wouldn't let on that she's interested in him.

I can understand Charlie's thinking. There was a time when I was terrified of how a certain green-eyed nurse would react if I told her how I felt about her.

Until next time, all my love, Jamie

* * *

Tuesday, 12 August 1919. Walter Reed General Hospital

My Beloved Jamie,

You say you were terrified of how "a certain green-eyed nurse" would react if you told her how you felt about her. Imagine the courage it took for me to ask you to chase away my nightmares.

I received the pictures of BayView you sent and have put them up around my quarters and office. They were a very thoughtful gift from a very thoughtful man. I miss you and BayView so much rather than help me feel cooler in DC's oppressive climate, they only increase the heat of my passion for being in Pacific Grove with you.

It's great news that Scott and Ben will be

forming a partnership. I wonder whether they'd consider hiring an ex-army nurse once I've accomplished everything I set out to do for the ASN.

I have a new job! Sylvia Maxwell has asked me to turn her sheet music during Wednesday rehearsals and Sunday services. Initially, I said my schedule was too uncertain to make such a commitment. Also, since I don't read music, I was afraid I wouldn't be up to the task, but she convinced me it would be easy. She just nods her head when she wants me to turn the page.

Then Sylvia let me in on a secret. She hardly ever looks at the music because she has it memorized. And on those rare occasions when her memory fails her, like a jazz musician, she improvises. "Then why do you need a page-turner?" I asked her. Her answer surprised me. Stage fright. She feels much more comfortable when she's not the only one in the keyboard enclosure and the congregation isn't staring only at her. As you know, I don't cherish the limelight myself. I can deal with it because Sylvia is so captivating when performing that I feel almost invisible standing beside her.

The enclosed postcards capture the beauty of

the cathedral, Sylvia's keyboard enclosure, and the organ pipes reaching almost to the sky.

It was a blessing that Sylvia and I arrived in DC at approximately the same time. She's a lot of fun to be with, as well as understanding and sympathetic. As for her father, she says Ed thinks the world of you. That makes me smile. He may think the world of you. You are my world.

Cathy is happy for you to know that being the Kavanaugh Trust's co-general manager is working out great.

If anyone can get to the bottom of the hijacking of the Kavanaugh Trust's trucks, I'm sure it will be Jeff Mundy. I was hoping Sonny Kavanaugh's name would never come up again. Please be careful.

I'm sorry you have to deal with that irritant, John Thayer. Hopefully, the Coastal Planning Commission will do the right thing for the neighborhood and block Thayer's plans.

Charlie should have more confidence in himself. Any woman would be lucky to have him—any woman who isn't already madly in love with a certain physics professor.

All my love, Andi

* * *

Wednesday, 20 August 1919. BayView

My Dearest Andi,

Despite Noreen and Liam's presence, BayView is empty without you. You're such a part of me that several times I've caught myself staring out a window, mesmerized by the beauty of the bay, and pointing something out to you, only to realize you're three thousand miles away. I look forward to the day we'll never have to part.

Scott's landlady has been giving him grief about coming and going at all hours. Of course, he's visiting patients, not tearing up the town (which happens to be dry). I invited him to move into BayView. He was thrilled. Noreen says she's comforted by having a doctor in the house. I told Scott he can stay until either of us marries. I gave him a choice of bedrooms. He'll be staying in the room Liam was in.

Speaking of Liam, he's doing a great job at BayView. I've also discovered that he's a voracious reader who loves discussing all kinds of topics. He knows I'm the trustee of a business trust. He's happy to tell me what he'd do if he were in charge, but only when I ask. And I like having a guardian on the property. It will be especially comforting on weekdays when I'm away teaching at Stanford and

Scott is out making house calls.

I'm pleased to say Liam and Noreen get along great. She, of course, knows nothing of his past. They've even been attending the Presbyterian church together. I don't think their relationship is at all romantic. They just enjoy each other's company. I imagine it has something to do with them being of the same generation and therefore better able to relate to each other than to us "youngsters."

How nice that Sylvia Maxwell has asked you to be her page-turner. It's good that you can do something enjoyable and completely different a few times a week. I envy you having the best "seat" in the house to witness her remarkable keyboard and foot pedal skills.

I hope you'll take me to the National Cathedral the first time I visit you in DC. I'm amazed that it's still under construction, its cornerstone having been laid in 1907. I love the 14th-century English Gothic style. It reminds me of some of the churches I saw in Europe.

There's something else I'd like to do in DC. Although diplomatic relations between the German Republic and the United States have yet to be re-established, German diplomats are working toward that end in their old embassy building. I have a strong desire to walk up Massachusetts Avenue, stand in front of the building, and shout insults at the Kaiser in the hope that someone inside is offended. Of course, I'm only kidding. Or am I?

Charlie finally found the courage to ask Lanie out. She, of course, said yes. They've been out several times now. I have high hopes for their relationship. I want to see them both happy. It's fun to see slow walking, slow talking, big Charlie with energetic Lanie. They say opposites attract. And indeed, they do. You're wonderful in every way, and then there's me.

I've been spending a lot of time in my BayView office overlooking the bay as I review the materials I'll be teaching in the fall. It makes me a bit nervous to think I'll be standing in front of a classroom of eager students in less than three weeks. I thank God —and you for your support and encouragement—that I'll be <u>able</u> to stand.

Until next time, all my love, Jamie

* * *

Thursday, 28 August 1919. Walter Reed General Hospital

My Beloved Jamie,

I mention you so often to my coworkers they're starting to feel they know you. Amazingly, my boss, Julia Stimson, Dean of the

ANS, "met" you in your hospital in France. She was touring all our base hospitals to assess their nursing procedures. You had just come out of emergency surgery. Your life was hanging in the balance. She took the opportunity to see for herself "the hero who was raised from the dead." She put her hand on your shoulder and said a prayer over you. As you know, I already admired and respected her. After learning that she prayed over you, I hold her in even higher esteem.

On a less happy note, the ANC's Assistant Superintendent opposes every innovation I want to bring to the ASN. She's the woman I contradicted in front of a patient and his physician all those years ago. My "sin" was that I had the temerity to be correct. She still hasn't forgiven me.

It's great having Sylvia as a friend. We dine together as often as our schedules allow and take the opportunity to vent to someone unassociated with either the ASN or the intrigues that take place behind the scenes at the National Cathedral.

I'm happy that Scott Stanton will be living in BayView. Noreen has a point. Having a doctor in the house could be beneficial. Of course,

I'd rather you had a nurse in the house—if that nurse happened to be me.

From what you tell me, my guess is Liam and Noreen are more than just friends. Companionship may be more important than romance in a relationship between people their age.

I received a letter from Nick Hendricks yesterday. He and his family are now living in Philadelphia. He will start nursing school at Penn next week. I know he'll do well.

Life's full of surprises. Would you ever have guessed that our friend Charlie Gowan would someday be dating your supposed nemesis, Lanie Stanton?

I know you'll ignite an unquenchable fire in your students' minds. And by the way, I'm exceptionally proud of my dear physics professor.

All my love, Andi

* * *

Monday, 08 September 1919. Faculty Housing, Stanford University

My Dearest Andi,

I repeat, my _dearest_ Andi.

I'm touched that Julia Stimson prayed over me while I was hospitalized in France. I find it interesting that you're both preachers' kids.

At my urging, Scott didn't waste any time moving into BayView. It's great having him in the house, although I understand why his old landlady grew tired of answering the telephone for him. His patients think nothing of calling him out at any hour for the most trivial complaint. I had a private telephone line installed for him. I modified his receiver to give it a different ringtone than ours. Just think. Few houses in America have one telephone line. BayView has two. Noreen and I, and sometimes even Liam, have taken calls for Scott while he was out. I hope he doesn't work himself into an early grave before Ben gets here to take some of the load off him. It would benefit all concerned if Scott offered Ali a job when she gets here next month.

As you might have noticed from the postmark, I've moved into faculty housing at Stanford. It's quite comfortable unless you compare it to BayView. I have a bedroom, bathroom, kitchen, office, and living room. Its greatest appeal is its neighbors. On one side, I have an award-winning biologist. On the other side, a world-renowned historian. Some great discussions take place in the faculty dining hall.

I feel like I'm where I belong now that I'm teaching again. I do feel old, though, seeing the faces of all those eager young men. I'm thankful they never had to experience the hell of war as we did. God grant that they never will.

Toby and I dined together last evening. It's amusing to recall the rocky start to our friendship, him thinking it was because of the color of his skin that I failed to return his salute when Nick Hendricks first rolled me onto your orthopedic ward. I'm sure Toby will thrive in Stanford's School of Education. He has big dreams for the future. I know they'll come true. He's a fighter who's overcome more obstacles than you and I will ever know. I hope it bolsters his confidence, knowing I'll support him in any way possible.

Carl and I plan to get together next week. He hasn't let the challenges of typing one-handed hold him back. The enclosure is an article he wrote. He's been with the Chronicle for less than a month and has already had a by-line.

Nick Hendricks should graduate from nursing school around the time your tour of duty with the ASN ends. Wouldn't it be great if you two could work together again as civilians, preferably in a hospital on the Monterey Peninsula?

The ANC's Assistant Superintendent of Nurses is a fool to stand in the way of the innovations you want to incorporate into the ASN's curriculum. I can tell you don't like her in that you always refer to her by her title and never by name. It's sweet of you that that's about the worst thing you ever "say" about anyone. I can only assume she's jealous of you for having moved so high in the ranks of the ANC at such a young age.

I miss you terribly. How about I visit you sometime around the middle of next month? I could hop on the Transcontinental Express on Friday, the 10th. That would get me into DC late Sunday. We could spend parts of four days together before I'd have to take the Express home on Friday, the 17th. I've talked with my department head about it. He'll let me give my students research projects to work on during the week of classes I'd miss.

Until next time, all my love, Jamie

* * *

Tuesday, 16 September 1919. Walter Reed General Hospital

My Beloved Jamie,

How I wish we could be together in October! Unfortunately, I'm scheduled to visit a nursing school in Florida on the dates you suggested. And I have two other trips scheduled for October. I mentioned to Dean Stimson that we wanted to get together in October. She was sympathetic. However, the dates of my school visits can't be changed.

Maybe we can find a time to meet in the middle of the country, perhaps in Chicago. Otherwise, I'm afraid our next opportunity to be together will be Thanksgiving in Denver at my father's home.

I'm not the only one who doesn't appreciate the ANC's Assistant Superintendent of Nurses. Please forgive my unkindness in perpetuating this. Most others call her the Ass Super. I'm sure you've noticed that many units want their executive officer to be the heavy so their commanding officer can be the nice guy everybody likes. The nurse in question plays the bad guy role perfectly. Fortunately, I have Julia Stimson's full support in most matters, and the Ass Super—whoops, I mean the <u>Assistant Superintendent</u>, doesn't have a problem with Julia as she does with me.

I'll make the best of the situation, and I'm sure things will work out in the end.

All my love, Andi

* * *

William R. DeHay

Wednesday, 24 September 1919. Faculty Housing, Stanford University

My Dearest Andi,

Carl and I had dinner together yesterday. He is adjusting well to civilian life. He'll be covering Stanford's return to American football this season. We had fun discussing an excellent article he wrote for the Chronicle (I've enclosed a copy). I learned some surprising facts from it. For instance, Stanford fielded its first American football team in 1891, yet for the dozen years prior to the war, out of concern for player safety, Stanford played rugby rather than American football.

Even more surprising, after suspending all football at the beginning of the war, the army brought American football back to Stanford. That came about because, in 1918, the Stanford campus was designated as the Students' Army Training Corps headquarters for all of California, Nevada, and Utah. What I didn't know was that our commanding officer, Sam M. Parker, decreed that American football was the appropriate athletic activity to train soldiers, so it was due to his decree that rugby was dropped and Stanford reinstated American football.

I know you're not all that interested in sports. Nevertheless, I know you'll share my excitement that Carl is doing so well as a sports reporter. He'll be getting in on the ground floor of Stanford football this season. Baseball, however, remains his primary interest, which I'm sure comes as no surprise to you.

More good news: I got a letter from our former malcontent senior NCO, Reg Binney. He says being the manager of Adelbert's Dutch Bakery is working out great. And he's already won the Bay Area's most prestigious cake decorating competition. That's sure to help Kavanaugh Enterprises' bottom line.

Thanks to Charlie Gowan's artistry, Reg has learned to walk a few paces reasonably well on his prosthetics. With the aid of crutches, he says he can walk from his nearby apartment all the way to the bakery.

I'm afraid I've been bending Scott's ear, telling him all about Ali, and inundating her with stories about Scott in my letters to her. Often, when we build people up the way I have, when they meet, it's a big disappointment for all concerned. I don't think that will be the case with Scott and Ali.

Lanie visits BayView often as she shares a house with two other teachers nearby. It's so freeing to know she doesn't, and never did, hate me. Thank you for slaying that dragon. Please forgive me for being redundant in saying that meeting you was the best thing that ever happened to me.

Until next time, all my love, Jamie

* * *

Wednesday evening, 24 September 1919

WESTERN UNION TELEGRAM TO NURSE AJ ELIOT
TRAGEDY! ED MAXWELL DEAD. HEART ATTACK. CATHY
DEVASTATED. HAS NOTIFIED SYLVIA. MEMORIAL SERVICE
OCTOBER 1ST. CAN YOU TAKE COMPASSIONATE LEAVE
AND ACCOMPANY SYLVIA TO SAN FRANCISCO FOR
SERVICE? LOVE, JAMIE.

Chapter 18

Letters II

Wednesday, 24 September 1919. Faculty Housing, Stanford University

My Dearest Andi,

Thank you for your telephone call. It was wonderful hearing your voice. For a few minutes, I could pretend you weren't three thousand miles away.

I can't tell you how much I look forward to seeing you on Tuesday. I just wish it were under happier circumstances. I'm sure it will be a great comfort to Sylvia to have you with her as she travels to and from her father's memorial service. I'll be at the station an hour before your train's scheduled to arrive, just in case it's early. I'm already counting the minutes until we're together again.

As we discussed, I've reserved adjoining rooms

for you and Sylvia at the Saint Francis Hotel on Union Square. I've also taken a room at the Saint Francis.

Until Tuesday, all my love, Jamie

* * *

Saturday, 11 October 1919. BayView

My Dearest Andi,

It was wonderful seeing your face light up the instant you saw me on the train platform. Knowing Sylvia was in mourning, I tried to maintain a somber demeanor. That was impossible. I couldn't suppress my joy at seeing you. I was relieved that Sylvia understands that despite her being in mourning, life goes on.

I didn't think I could love you more than I already did. Then I saw the way you comforted Sylvia and Cathy. My love and respect for you grew even deeper, making it even harder to say goodbye to you this time than when you left for DC at the end of June. It's such a shame we got to spend so little time alone together. It's so unfair that having taken compassionate leave to attend Ed's memorial service, you won't be able to get away for Thanksgiving.

Waiting until Christmas to be together again will be agony.

On a brighter note, Ali is home at last! It's great to hear her laughter again. It's such a relief that the war hasn't changed her as it did so many other veterans. She's as warm and loving as ever.

She disembarked The Transcontinental Express when it made an unscheduled stop in Salinas. From there, she caught a milk-run train to Monterey and showed up on our doorstep Friday morning, a full day early. I wasn't to arrive until that evening. Noreen was out shopping. Scott answered Ali's knock on the door. From what I've gathered, their first encounter couldn't have gone any better.

Scott was on his way out to attend to a woman driving him crazy with her roundabout way of describing her ailment. She was unwilling to disclose to a male doctor anything more than that it involved her reproductive system. Scott wisely invited Ali to accompany him. As Scott waited in another room, the patient freely discussed her condition with "the lady doctor."

It will take a while for Ali to get her California medical license. In the meantime, she's permitted to work under the supervision of a California-licensed physician—Scott, in this instance. To see them together, you'd think they'd known and worked together for years. I'd like to take credit for that, having told or written about each ad nauseam over the last three months.

Ali will be moving into BayView. Noreen says she'll be just as happy cooking and caring for a houseful of people as for just me. Ali's bedroom will be the one on the ground floor.

To hear Ali and Noreen talk about Scotland, you'd think Ali was the native. She loves Scotland almost as much as she loves America. Not that Noreen doesn't. For Ali, everything Scottish is new and different. For Noreen, it's standard fare. It's nice that they get along so well. Of course, Ali gets along with just about everyone.

It's a shame Cathy and Sylvia never met before Ed's service. They were clearly uncomfortable with each other at first. Thankfully, by the end of the day, their relationship seemed to have thawed noticeably.

Knowing Cathy as we do, I wasn't surprised to learn that several weeks before Ed's heart attack, Cathy suggested to Ed that he set up a trust for his daughter. Ed loved the idea. When he told Sylvia about it, he made sure she knew it was Cathy's idea. The income from the trust should be enough to keep Sylvia financially independent for the rest of her life.

I think Sylvia has finally accepted that Ed and Cathy really did love each other. I won't be surprised if, eventually, Cathy and Sylvia become friends, although I can't imagine Sylvia ever calling Cathy "Mother."

With Ed gone, as trustee of the Kavanaugh Trust, I had to decide who the next general manager would be. I discussed the matter with a man whose judgment I respect—I think you know who I mean—and he liked the idea of asking Cathy to stay on as solo GM. She was hesitant at first. Eventually, she agreed to take the job. Ed had confidence in her, and so do I.

Cathy wants to establish a charity in Ed's name. I assumed she was thinking of a school building or a hospital wing. It turns out she's thinking of something bigger. She intends to underwrite the entire cost of building a modern, well-equipped hospital. And guess where? At <u>your</u> suggestion, she's going to have it built on the Monterey Peninsula! How does the Edward J. Maxwell Community Hospital—or as I like to think of it, the Max—sound to you? I can imagine Doctors Scott Stanton, Ben Regen, and Ali Collins being on staff—and you as Superintendent of Nursing with Nurse Nick Hendricks as your right-hand man!

Until next time, all my love, Jamie

Monday, 20 October 1919. Walter Reed General Hospital

My Beloved Jamie,

A hospital on the Monterey Peninsula! "The Max" will be a wonderful tribute to Ed. I'd love to be involved in setting it up. That would be an even greater challenge than establishing the curriculum of the Army School of Nursing. What an exciting possibility! Maybe I'd even get to work with Ben Regen and Nick Hendricks again.

I can tell how happy you are that Ali is home. That makes me happy, too. I can't wait to meet her.

You never know how people might react to each other. Cathy told me in confidence (although she doesn't mind me telling you) that Jeff Mundy has been a great comfort to her in her grief. Someday, once she's no longer in mourning, I can picture them becoming close.

Cathy's generosity to Sylvia is what I'd expect of her.

I'm proud of you for making Cathy solo general manager of the Kavanaugh Trust. I don't think you could find anyone who will work harder than Cathy to justify your confidence in her.

All my love, Andi

* * *

Saturday, 28 October 1919. BayView

My Dearest Andi,

Superintendent of Nursing Andrea Jean Collins of the Edward J. Maxwell Community Hospital—what an excellent ring that has!

Charlie and Lanie have come to "an understanding." I won't be surprised if they soon become engaged. In that regard, in addition to teaching, to Charlie's great relief, Lanie has taken over dealing with Charlie's customers, ordering supplies, paying for deliveries, and bookkeeping for all of Charlie's businesses.

For me, working with Charlie Gowan has been a revelation. He's taught me that formal education is no match for innate inquisitiveness and resourcefulness. Like America's greatest inventor, Thomas Alva Edison, who was self-educated, when Charlie is faced with a new problem, he teaches himself all he needs to know to solve it. I've seen him stumped by a problem, go to the library, look through a textbook that covers the subject, and come away with a solution.

And I'm talking about some advanced texts, materials I would have to guide my graduate students through. Charlie's proud to be the first member of his family to have graduated from high school, where he learned a little algebra, geometry, and trigonometry. He's never had calculus, let alone differential equations, the kind of mathematical tools I rely on in the classes I teach. When he encounters an equation that uses symbols he's not familiar with, he just skips over it. He's not interested in equations. He's interested in the ideas behind them. He is remarkably good at extracting what's useful from an essay on a subject and ignoring the fluff. (I'd be happy to teach him all the math he'll ever need. I haven't mentioned it yet. I don't want to take a chance of stifling his creativity.)

What it comes down to is that Charlie—slow talking, slow walking, big Charlie—is a genius. He sees problems completely differently than I do. For example, I can calculate stresses to the third decimal place on various components of a device. He knows intuitively when a component will be over- or under-stressed.

Charlie and I make a good team. He comes up with a hundred ideas for tackling any problem, some elegant yet completely impractical. Although I lack his elegance, I beat him hands down regarding practicality. Our strength is that when we zero in on a solution to a problem, we know it will work well.

We could, however, use a doctor's advice when creating medical devices since neither of us knows the first thing about medicine. Charlie realized that, so another dream of mine has come true. He's signed Scott, Ben, and Ali on as medical consultants.

It's absurd for Charlie to think Lanie is too sophisticated for him simply because she's a college graduate, and he isn't. He's applied for patents on two medical devices he'd been developing since before he was discharged from the army. I'm convinced they'll earn him a lot of money. Maybe wealth will improve his self-image. It really shouldn't matter. I'm sure Lanie is much more interested in the man who gives a tenth of all he makes to charity than she is in the size of his bank account.

Until next time, all my love, Jamie

* * *

Wednesday, 05 November 1919. Walter Reed General Hospital

My beloved Jamie,

Just a quick note as I'm about to board a train headed south to review the curriculum of a nursing school in Atlanta.

As for Charlie being a genius, I can only say it takes one to know one.

I've been trying to find a nursing school in the West that would warrant a visit so we could see each other for a day or two in passing. Alas, there aren't any with a long enough history to justify a visit. We might have to wait until Christmas to be together, and it can't come soon enough!

All my love, Andi

* * *

Saturday, 15 November 1919. BayView

My Dearest Andi,

Lanie came to dinner at BayView yesterday. She was angry. She told us there are gossips in town claiming that it's improper for Scott and Ali to live in the same house. Before you caged the beast in me, I would have been tempted to hunt them down and throttle them. It took all I had to talk Lanie out of doing precisely that. It turns out there's no need. Scott floored us there and then by asking Ali to marry him!

"Oh, you wonderful man," Ali said without hesitation, "of course, I'll marry you!"

I'm so glad Lanie got her smiling brother back

sooner than we expected!

Ben Regen has been spending most weekends here at BayView. Just about every Saturday, he sees his mystery woman in Carmel. The only thing he's told me about her is that she is inexplicably evasive about herself and their future together. He knows she's attracted to him and wants to continue seeing him. Something's holding her back. He's completely taken by her. I hope it all works out, and I'll get to meet her someday.

Ben will be discharged from the army at the end of next month. I've invited him to stay at BayView for as long as he wants. I still feel I owe him more than I can ever repay for giving me back the use of my legs. Besides that, he's now good company. It's hard to believe he's the same man who was so cold and distant when I first met him. He's chosen to stay in the attic bedroom. He says he feels like he's on top of the world up there. I assume he'll eventually want a place of his own. I hope that will be far in the future. Once he's living on the Peninsula, I'm sure he'll spend even more time with his mysterious woman in Carmel. I think his reluctance to tell us anything about her reflects his insecurity. If she rejects him, he'll have an easier time with it if we know nothing about her.

Ali's the only Scottish-trained doctor Scott and Ben have ever met. They're impressed by her medical knowledge. I hope they'll see the wisdom in adding her to their partnership.

You'll probably hear this in a letter from Cathy. I'm just so incensed I've got to tell you myself. That vile creature William Sherman, the man who mistreated Cathy and broke her heart, has outdone himself. Soon after the Chronicle ran a story about Cathy becoming sole general manager of the Kavanaugh Trust, a reporter from a supposedly reputable business newspaper interviewed Sherman about his business. The reporter asked Sherman what he thought about a woman being a top executive. The reporter offered Cathy as an example. Instead of answering the question, Sherman told the reporter that Cathy had previously been his children's governess, but he had to let her go because he found out she had become intimate with a man who wasn't her husband. And that scurrilous rag printed Sherman's slander. He, of course, didn't disclose that he was the man involved. I'm just glad Sherman didn't know the rest of Cathy's story, or he would probably have gleefully told the reporter everything.

Many women would feel disgraced by Sherman's despicable act. Not Cathy. Two days later, the same newspaper printed her response: that all her sins were washed away when she became a born-again Christian, and her promotion to general manager of the Kavanaugh Trust shows the heights to which a woman who was cast aside can rise if given a chance.

Since her response, she's been invited to more social events than she could possibly attend. It seems that society ladies in the Bay Area agree that a reformed woman's past should be left in the past, and she should be given every chance to succeed in business and life. Cathy is a little skeptical about the motivation of some of these society ladies. She thinks they might just like the notoriety that comes with being associated with a trailblazer like Cathy. Regardless, Cathy wants to be seen in society to encourage other women in bad situations to strive for a brighter future.

Cathy is remarkably brave. Her courage when facing obstacles and setbacks reminds me of another woman I know. The woman I love.

Until next time, all my love, Jamie

* * *

Saturday, 22 November 1919. Walter Reed General Hospital

My beloved Jamie,

I suppose, in a way, Scott and Ali have "known" each other longer than a month since you've been telling them about each other since July. Still, it's awfully quick to make a lifelong commitment to each other. But who am I to judge? I began considering marrying you less than a month after we met, and no one had been telling me for months what a fine man you are.

I hope Ben's relationship with his mystery woman works out. I'd hate for him to revert to the sullen person he was when we first knew him.

I'm sure in due time, Scott and Ben will see the wisdom of adding Ali to their partnership.

As for William Sherman, only the Lord could love a man like him.

As for you, you're easy to love.

All my love, Andi

* * *

Monday, 01 December 1919. Faculty Housing, Stanford University

My Dearest Andi,

Thanksgiving was a joyous celebration at BayView, although it would have been far more so if you had been with us. At least you and I could talk on the telephone for a few minutes and hear each other's voices. It sounded like you and Julia had a good time at Walter Reed's mess hall, you and several hundred others. We had quite a gathering ourselves, with Ali, Scott, Lanie, Charlie, Liam, Noreen, and me. We all tried to help Noreen as much as possible to reduce her labors. We needn't have bothered. She reveled in providing us with a meal to remember. Ben was off having a quiet celebration with his mystery woman. Call me a romantic, I don't care. I had Noreen set a place at the table for you.

I'm sorry you couldn't attend Ali and Scott's wedding. Mrs. Alice Collins Stanton sounds mighty good to me. Their marriage may have been impulsive. Nevertheless, I'm sure they love each other deeply. I'm confident their marriage will last a lifetime.

There should be no more gossip about them living in the same house. For the next several weeks, they'll share the bedroom we put Liam in during his recovery. After that, they'll move into a nice little house they've bought just around the corner from BayView.

Apparently, someone held William Sherman in even more contempt than I did. Yesterday, as he stepped out of his office, he was shot at very close range. The police couldn't find any witnesses who saw or heard anything, but the newspaper says they found an Omega card next to his body. Could it be that Sherman was the victim of a copycat killer or that the Bureau of Investigation was wrong in claiming they'd shut down Omega? I'd hate for someone with inside knowledge and who had a grudge against Sherman to have used the specter of Omega as a smokescreen to get away with murder.

Until next time, all my love, Jamie

* * *

Tuesday, 09 December 1919. Walter Reed General Hospital

My beloved Jamie,

I've known couples who had lengthy engagements, and their marriages didn't last. And others who rushed into matrimony and are happily married many years later. I'm sure it depends upon the individuals and the depth of their love, not on how long they've known each other.

How nice that Scott and Ali will be living just around the corner from BayView. After missing Ali all those years while she lived overseas, you'll now get to see your sister whenever you want.

Cathy told me about Sherman in her last letter and Jeff Mundy's reaction to the man's cold-heartedness. She had already told Jeff about her past and was relieved by how he took it, although she was worried about what Jeff might do if he ever ran into Sherman. I fear you could be right about someone with a grudge against Sherman, someone with inside knowledge about how Omega worked, using that knowledge to get away with murder.

As for that lowlife Sherman, I know if it were my name he slandered, you would be the first to come to my defense—and I love you for that.

All my love, Andi

* * *

Monday, 15 December 1919. Faculty Housing, Stanford University

My Dearest Andi,

We'll be together in Denver in just eight days! I admit that the thought of meeting your family is a bit intimidating. What if your father disapproves of me? What if your sisters think I'm not suitable for you? What if? What if? My only comfort is knowing that I've faced greater peril and survived.

Sometimes, I feel as though I don't belong in this modern world. It moves so fast, and I move so slowly. First, there was Ali and Scott. Now, there's Jeff Mundy and Cathy Maxwell. I don't know if she's written and told you herself. Cathy was worried about what would become of William Sherman's children for whom she had been governess. Despite their father treating her so badly, she loved them, and they loved her. She didn't want them to be shuffled off to some uncaring distant relative or, worse, placed in care. Jeff suggested that she adopt them. She told him there was no chance the state would let an unmarried woman with her background adopt children. Jeff said he could solve that problem. He proposed to her. And she accepted! They will be married in a civil ceremony tomorrow. I'll be there as a witness.

We'll have to wait and see whether the adoption agency will hold Cathy's past against her. She told them she's willing to spend an unlimited amount of money on lawyers to help them decide in her and Jeff's favor.

And now I'm wondering about Liam and Noreen. He's spending more and more time with her in her kitchen. He even volunteers to dry dishes after meals. Can you imagine?

This will amuse you. Pacific Grove High School has a long-standing annual poetry contest. Even though Lanie is a math teacher, somehow, she got roped into running it this year. Scott suggested that she ask me to present the award. I agreed before I learned that it's traditional for the presenter to write a poem himself that's read as part of the ceremony. Thanks a lot, brother-in-law.

Here's something you don't know about me. I've written a fair number of poems over the years—even while I was under your care at Letterman. Putting rhyming words on paper helps me deal with complicated feelings. The problem is, I've never shown any of my poems to anyone. And now I'm on the hook to have one read out loud to an audience of poets. But why should I hide my work? I'm brave enough to expose myself to a bit of criticism. So, I gave Lanie a poem I wrote soon after arriving at Letterman. It encapsulates the way I felt before you came into my life. Enclosed is a copy.

Until we meet in Denver, all my love, Jamie

What of Mercy and Grace?

The herd leapt over the rise in twos and
    threes.
Gravity-defying arcs ending in footfalls
Light as leaves blowing in the afternoon
    breeze.
Deer move with such natural grace.

A scattering of snowflakes, the season's first,
Mixed with steamy breath to hang in still air.
From behind a cloud, a sunbeam burst.

William R. DeHay

Sleek coats took on the sheen of satin.

Another head appeared over the rise.
Haltingly, she came closer.
Then was clear what could not be disguised:
Grotesque distention, symmetry shattered.

With broken leg held immobile,
Toward the herd, she hobbled.
Through ceaseless pain, she remained noble
But for the anguish in her liquid eyes.

The herd scattered just as she joined them
Leaving her alone as they took flight.
To the ghostly sound of her requiem
She could only follow with tearful eyes.

Or perhaps the tears were in my eyes
As I saw a future inevitable
Where without mercy and grace lies
The fate of all who are abandoned.

Chapter 19

Christmas in Denver

Monday, 22 December 1919

As a Christmas present to himself, Jamie took the luxurious weekly Pacific Hotel Express from Oakland to Denver. It cost four dollars a day more than the Transcontinental Express. For an additional six dollars a day, he reserved a deluxe sleeper compartment. It would take a while to get used to being able to afford such an extravagance. He'd just have to be careful not to let his wealth go to his head.

The 1,200-mile trip took less than two days. The longest part was the seemingly interminable hour spent in the dining car at a table with a blowhard who wanted to impress Jamie with his war exploits. Jamie would have been surprised if even half of what the man said was true. Jamie didn't mention that he'd been in the army himself.

The shortest part of the trip was the meal he took with a lady who entertained him with stories humorous and tragic about life in Cripple Creek, Colorado, when she was a girl, and her father was superintendent of the Mollie Kathleen Gold Mine. Jamie had no reason to doubt a word she said.

When night fell, and it was time to turn in, Jamie was glad he'd spent the extra money on a sleeper compartment. On a troop train, he'd been able to catch some sleep sitting on a bench seat surrounded by dozens of rowdy soldiers. He'd need more than intermittent sleep to make the best possible impression on Andi's family.

* * *

Tuesday, 23 December 1919

The Pacific Hotel Express pulled into Denver's Union Station a few minutes past six p.m., almost on time. They had been chasing the tail end of a snowstorm ever since they crested the Sierra Nevada Mountains. The further east they traveled, the more significant the snow became.

Andi's train from DC was scheduled to arrive at eight p.m. He'd reluctantly agreed to meet at Andi's father's house next to his church rather than waiting for her at the train station. In December, one never knew when a train would actually arrive. One or the other of them could be waiting at the station for hours.

"University Presbyterian Church," Jamie told his cabbie.

Jamie was mesmerized by the scene outside his cab. "It almost never snows in the San Francisco Bay Area," he said to his cabbie.

The cabbie waved his hand dismissively. "This isn't much more than a couple inches. But even this little bit is unusual for Denver in December. March and April are our snowiest months. Don't worry, though. It won't slow us down."

Jamie had been hoping the snow *would* slow them down. The thought of spending two hours alone with Andi's father left Jamie almost as nervous as he'd been going into his first battle.

The cabbie pointed with his thumb. "Denver Country Club," he said as they passed a building that reminded Jamie of a southern mansion.

They turned north off First Avenue onto University Boulevard. "UPres is just up here on the right," the cabbie said.

All too soon, their four-mile drive ended, and Jamie was standing in front of a two-story Tudor-style house immediately next to the church. He imagined Andi running around in the yard playing tag with her sisters.

Eventually, he found enough courage to approach the front door. He knocked.

There could be no doubt the man who answered was the Reverend Doctor Robert Eliot. He had Andi's kind eyes—and they were green. As Andi had implied in the Palace Hotel's Garden Court Restaurant, Reverend Eliot looked so young he could be mistaken for Andi's older brother rather than her father.

"Professor Collins?"

Jamie swallowed hard. "Jamie, sir. And you must be Reverend Eliot."

"Bob. Please, call me Bob. Come in. Come in. Warm yourself by the fire."

Jamie stepped inside a welcoming sitting room. A large, colorfully decorated Christmas tree took up one corner.

Reverend Eliot took Jamie's coat—Jamie wasn't comfortable even *thinking* of calling Andi's father *Bob*.

"Please forgive me for staring," Reverend Eliot said. "The way Andi talks about you in her letters, I expected you to be seven feet tall. Not being some mythological giant makes your exploits that much more impressive."

Jamie had heard that before. He smiled. "This is a fine house."

"It comes with being pastor of the church next door. In Presbyterian parlance, it's called a manse."

"I can imagine Andi excitedly opening Christmas presents in this room when she was a little girl." Jamie took a deep breath. "I love your daughter, sir."

Reverend Eliot was clearly surprised by Jamie's sudden declaration. "So do I, Jamie. And I want the best for her."

Jamie felt as though he'd been punched in the solar plexus. *Does Andi's father think she deserves better than me?*

The telephone rang. After a quick few words, Reverend Eliot hung up. "Please make yourself comfortable while I run next door for just a minute."

"Certainly."

As soon as Jamie heard the side door close, there was a knock on the front door. Although he felt awkward answering it, he couldn't leave whoever it was out in the cold.

The instant he opened the door, he knew the woman on the doorstep was Andi's middle sister, Cyndi. The man with her had to be her husband.

The couple stepped inside like they owned the place. "Forgot my key," Cyndi said brusquely. She, too, resembled Andi. Except she had the tired look of a woman raising three small children. "You must be Father's new assistant pastor," she said.

"No. I'm—"

"I'm Ronald Jenkins, and this is my wife, Cyndi, Reverend Eliot's daughter. We've come to meet my sister-in-law's boyfriend, some big deal war hero she salvaged from her orthopedic ward."

Salvaged? Before Andi tamed the beast in him, Jamie might have ripped Ronald's head off for that comment.

Ronald shoved a covered cake platter into Jamie's gut. "Put this in the kitchen for us, will you?"

Snooty, Andi had called Cyndi's husband. Jamie could think of a few more descriptive terms. Big deal war hero indeed. "Did you serve in the military, sir?"

Ronald turned to face Jamie. "I'm Secretary of the Colorado State Senate—a reserved occupation."

"I'm unfamiliar with Colorado government. Is yours an elected position?"

"No. I'm the Senate Parliamentarian and head of the Senate Services Staff, a nonpartisan civil service position."

"And that exempted you from the draft?" Jamie's words came out sounding contemptuous, which wasn't smart considering that he wanted to make a good impression on Andi's family. It just bothered him that this pompous ass was safe at home while Jamie, "a big deal war hero," was charging across an open field during an artillery barrage in a suicidal attempt to prevent his men from being slaughtered. "I don't suppose you volunteered," Jamie said.

Ronald's face turned red. Before he could say anything, there was another knock on the door. Cyndi answered it.

"Jamie!" Andi shouted the instant she saw him. She dropped her bag in the doorway and ran to Jamie's arms. He lifted her off her feet and twirled her around in a circle. The instant he set her down, her hands were on either side of his face, pulling his mouth to hers. He hoped her kisses would never stop. "I missed you so much," they said in unison, then laughed.

"You're not Reverend Eliot's assistant pastor?" Ronald said.

Jamie looked at the man—whose red face had turned pale. "As I tried to tell you before you loaded me down with your wife's cake, I'm Jamie Collins, and I'm here to meet Andi's family."

There was a tense moment before Cyndi put her hands on her hips, gave Ronald a look that would turn a raging fire to ice, and then turned to Jamie. "Well, *I'm* happy to meet you."

"Did I miss something?" Andi said.

Jamie gave her a squeeze. "Nothing important. How was your trip?"

"Very relaxing after the stress of work. And we got in an hour early."

Reverend Eliot returned. Jamie took a step back and watched heartfelt hugs exchanged all around.

"When can we expect Debbi?" Andi asked.

Reverend Eliot looked at his watch. "Any time now." He grabbed Andi's bag. "Let me take this up to your room."

Jamie bounded up the stairs in their wake. After all these weeks, he wasn't about to let Andi out of sight.

They entered the bedroom at the front of the house. Andi tossed her coat onto the bed. "This used to be my room," she said to Jamie.

"It still is, as far as I'm concerned," Reverend Eliot said.

"Other than cleaning, I haven't let anyone touch this room since you left for nursing school."

Voices drifted upstairs, followed by someone taking the steps two at a time. Jamie caught his breath. There stood Debbi Eliot, a younger copy of Andi, and in every way as beautiful—except she lacked that intangible look that said she'd gallantly overcome trauma and heartbreak as Andi had.

Debbi embraced her father and kissed his cheek. To Jamie's surprise, she embraced him just as warmly. "So you're the man who mended my sister's broken heart." She kissed Jamie on the cheek.

No wonder Andi was afraid to introduce them. Debbi could melt a heart of stone. Jamie looked at Andi and saw a mixture of pride and fear. "Andi gave me the encouragement I needed to walk again. Which is only one of many reasons I love her."

Debbi smiled broadly. "And I couldn't ask for a more loving sister."

Andi's contented look said she was no longer worried about Jamie falling for her little sister.

* * *

They installed Jamie in a small guest room on the ground floor at the back of the house.

Everyone then gathered in the dining room as Reverend Eliot set out the makings for sandwiches. "Maria's gone to spend Christmas with her family in Colorado Springs, so we'll have to fend for ourselves, I'm afraid."

"Maria?" Debbi said.

"My latest housekeeper. And a very good one indeed. I know you'd all like her."

Jamie glanced at Andi. How difficult it must have been for her to be raised by a never-ending succession of house-keepers. And while trying to be mother to Cyndi and Debbi when she was only a child herself. Jamie took Andi's hand. She looked at him and smiled wistfully.

"And your assistant pastor?" Cyndi said.

"He's out with his young lady buying Christmas presents. You'll meet him later. He'll be helping with the Christmas Eve Candlelight and Christmas Day services. Ted's a great help. I should have taken on an assistant pastor years ago. He's particularly good with kids, especially high schoolers."

"Does that mean you're finally thinking of retiring?" From Cyndi's tone, Jamie gathered that this was a point of contention between them.

"Not at all," Reverend Eliot said. "I love what I do and can't imagine doing anything else."

Andi stood by her father's side. "Good for you, Daddy. When to retire is entirely up to you."

This contentiousness between Andi and Cyndi was something Jamie had never seen in Andi before. As he'd noticed over the years, that was often the way between siblings. A word, a gesture, and though they loved each other dearly, they'd practically be at each other's throats in an instant.

* * *

Debbi and Reverend Eliot volunteered to put the leftovers away and do the dishes. They said they wanted to catch up on each other's lives. It seemed to Jamie that Debbi wanted time alone with her father. Perhaps she needed a bit of fatherly advice.

Jamie thought of his relationship with Liam O'Connell. Some might mistake them for father and son.

Not for the first time did he marvel at life's unexpected turns.

Jamie and Andi saw Cyndi and Ronald off for their home and then wandered into the front room. They sat close together on the couch where they could best admire the Christmas tree.

"Cyndi and Ronald's house is only a mile from here," Andi said. "They should be home any minute. Once Ronald pays the girl from next door for babysitting and the children are in bed, I bet they spend the rest of the evening talking about us."

"Let them talk," Jamie said. "They can't doubt that we love each other."

Andi smiled, but her smile quickly faded. "Cyndi thinks that being a wife and mother qualifies her to act as 'mother' to me, Debbi, and even Daddy. And that it's her responsibility to run our lives. I don't know how Daddy puts up with it. Worse, because she's a year younger than me and already has three kids, for the last several years, she's been scheming to make sure I don't end up a childless old spinster."

Jamie took her hand. "I intend to make sure that doesn't happen."

Andi smiled. "Cyndi demanded to know your intentions."

"What did you tell her?"

"That you don't want to deprive me of the opportunity to serve as Assistant Dean of the ASN, so we're going to wait a while before becoming engaged."

She looked at Jamie. "She told me you and Ronald got off to a bad start."

Jamie smiled. "Let's just say Ronald stuck his foot in his mouth almost as soon as he got a foot in the door." Jamie's smile quickly faded. "Forget about Ronald. And Cyndi. I'm more concerned about what your father thinks of me."

Andi squeezed his hand. "He and I haven't had a chance to talk yet, but I'm sure he thinks you're wonderful."

* * *

Wednesday, 24 December 1919

Jamie strolled along the storefronts with Andi as she looked for last-minute Christmas gifts she could give her family. Jamie didn't need to buy anything. He'd brought the gifts he was going to give them in his luggage. He appreciated the cold weather. It gave him an excuse to hold Andi even closer. The Christmas Eve Candlelight service was scheduled to start at 7:00 p.m., so they needed to be back at the manse in time for an early dinner.

There were eleven diners: Reverend Eliot, Cyndi and Ronald Jenkins and their three kids, Andi and Jamie, Debbi, and Reverend Eliot's Associate Pastor with his young lady. Jamie hadn't sat at a table with so many people since officer training school.

Cyndi had volunteered the services of her housekeeper to prepare the meal. As if feeding so many people wasn't hard enough, the poor, hard-pressed woman had to work in a kitchen she wasn't familiar with. Even under those circumstances, Jamie thought she did a fine job. He noticed

Reverend Eliot's broad smile when Jamie made a point of telling her so.

As they approached the table, the youngest Jenkins raced ahead of everyone.

"Young man!" Ronald Jenkins said. He glared at his son. "We don't run in the house." The boy's face turned ashen.

Jamie swore to himself that if he and Andi were ever blessed with children, he'd never intimidate them into obedience. Sure, he'd want them to be well-behaved—to please their parents, not because they were afraid of them. When dinner ended, they walked as a group fifty feet or so to the church. Those not involved in conducting the service sat together. Jamie found Reverend Eliot to be an excellent speaker. After the service, Jamie was introduced to more people than he could count. One man stuck in his memory. The guy was about Jamie's age. His suit reminded Jamie of the ones Matt Kavanaugh wore. Even as he shook Jamie's hand, he kept his eyes on Andi.

"I'm George Ramsey," the man said as though his name should mean something to Jamie. "I own the largest automobile dealership in the Rocky Mountain Region." George stood a little straighter. "What do you do?"

Jamie would have bet the farm that George had been one of Andi's suitors in earlier days. "I'm a teacher," Jamie said with a smile.

George smiled back, the kind of smile one gets when they think they've just one-upped a rival.

"Actually," Andi said, "Jamie's a physics professor at Stanford University."

Ramsey's shoulders slumped. He wandered off without another word.

Andi whispered in Jamie's ear. "I was heavily taxed to

devise polite ways to put George off before he finally decided to marry someone who appreciated him."

"I imagine this town's full of brokenhearted men who had to settle for second best when you joined the Army Nurse Corps."

* * *

Thursday, 25 December 1919. Christmas Morning

Once everyone had gathered around the Christmas tree, Debbi handed out presents.

Cyndi and Ronald gave Jamie a tie: blue with gray stripes. He gave them a handmade wooden wall plaque he had put together in Charlie's workshop. It featured the Great Seal of the State of Colorado in the middle, with the words "Ronald B. Jenkins" carved above the seal and "Secretary of the Senate" below.

Ronald turned the plaque over and saw Jamie's signature on the back. He looked like he'd swallowed a bullfrog. "Did you make this?

"Andi and I have a friend who makes custom fine furniture," Jamie replied. "He let me use his tools. I hired a professional artist to render the seal. I did the rest."

"You carved my name and title?"

Jamie nodded.

Ronald held the plaque as though it were made of gold. "This is . . . outstanding." He ran his finger over his name. "I'm going to put this up in my office as soon as I return from Christmas break." Ronald looked at Jamie, then quickly looked down as though he wasn't worthy of looking a man like Jamie in the eye. "I'll treasure this," he mumbled.

Debbi also gave Jamie a tie: cardinal red with white stripes. "Stanford's colors," she said.

His present to Debbi was unique. He handed her an envelope. Inside was a card with a name, date, and time written on it.

Debbi held up the card as if to ask, "What's this?"

"Émile is a math professor at Stanford. That's an appointment for an interview with him for a post-doctoral position."

Debbi's mouth fell open. Andi looked as surprised as Debbi.

"If you secure the position," Jamie said, "and perform as well as I expect you will, it could lead to an assistant professorship."

The tears in Debbi's eyes contrasted with her huge smile. "How on earth did you arrange this?"

"Andi told me your Ph.D. dissertation was on set theory. That's one of Professor Borel's special interests."

"I referenced Professor Borel's work in my dissertation," Debbi said. "Is he a friend of yours?"

"Not exactly. Émile Borel is French. One of the villages my company helped liberate is his ancestral home. He wants to show his appreciation."

Debbi hugged Jamie tight and kissed him on both cheeks. Andi had tears in her eyes.

Reverend Eliot gave Jamie a sweater that would have fit a man seven feet tall. Jamie handed Reverend Eliot another envelope. "This is really a present for both you and Andi."

Reverend Eliot opened it and found a first-class round-trip train ticket to DC for a date of his choosing. "This is wonderful," Reverend Eliot said. "Now I'll get to see my little girl in her world. What a thoughtful gift!"

Andi gave Jamie a small, pocket-size, well-worn book. He opened the cover and read the inscription she had written. He pressed the book to his heart and gave her a lover's smile.

"You gave him a used book?" Debbi said.

Cyndi gave Andi a chastising look. "What kind of present is that?"

"It's not just any book," Jamie said.

"It's a book of poems I won in a poetry contest back in high school," Andi said. She turned to her father. "You remember, don't you, Daddy? I've been highlighting it and making notes in the margins ever since. It's almost a diary." She beamed at Jamie. "Despite all the masterful poems in that book, Jamie's my favorite poet."

"I look forward to reading your notes far more than the poems," Jamie said.

Jamie's present to Andi was the size and shape of a lengthy novel. She tore away the wrapping paper to find a box made from walnut. It was so finely polished that Andi could see her reflection in it. "1 Corinthians 13" was inscribed on the hinged lid. "This is lovely," she said. "Did Charlie make it?"

"He did. It's his gift to you. What's in the box is from me."

Andi opened it and found inside a pendant on a delicate chain necklace. The necklace was plated with 24-karat gold. The pendant was an ornate cross.

"It's a half-size replica of your Army Distinguished Service Cross," Jamie said.

"*Cross*," Reverend Eliot said. "I thought Andi had been awarded the Distinguished Service *Medal*."

"What's the difference?" Debbi said.

"The Distinguished Service *Cross* is our country's

second-highest gallantry award. It was awarded to only four women for actions during the Great War. The other three awards were posthumous. Andi earned hers by shielding a patient with her body during an artillery attack—and refusing treatment of her injuries until all her patients were seen to."

"You were injured?" Reverend Eliot looked his daughter up and down. "Are you all right?"

"I'm fine, Daddy. That was months ago."

Jamie surveyed the shocked faces of those in the room. "Our Andi is an extraordinarily brave woman."

"Andi . . .." Her father, the accomplished orator, was too choked up to say anything more.

Andi lifted the cross from its box. "This is a lovely gift," she said to Jamie. She handed it to him and turned her back.

Jamie put it around her neck, latched it, then kissed the side of her neck. She turned to face him. She didn't have to say thank you. He could see how much she appreciated it.

"If the Assistant Superintendent of the Army Nurse Corps ever tries to overrule another one of your recommendations," Jamie said, "this will remind you of what your country thinks of your service."

* * *

Everyone else in the household had gone to bed. Jamie found Reverend Eliot in the sitting room next to the Christmas tree. He was staring into the dying embers in the fireplace.

"May I join you, sir?"

"Please do. And it's Bob."

Jamie stared into the fireplace, trying to control his breathing. "I have to ask," Jamie swallowed hard, "When I told you I love Andi, you said you wanted the best for her. Were you implying that she deserves better than me?"

Reverend Eliot smiled. "Andi told me so much about you in her letters that I found it hard to believe you could be so perfect for her." Reverend Eliot smiled. "Now I believe it."

Jamie stood at attention as he would in front of his commanding officer. "Then may I have your permission to ask her to marry me just as soon as her tour of duty with the Army School of Nursing ends?"

"You most certainly may."

Jamie pumped Reverend Eliot's hand. "Thank you, *Bob*, thank you from the bottom of my heart."

"I know my daughter. As indicated by her Distinguished Service Cross, she's incredibly strong and determined. I predict she'll accomplish all her goals for the ASN long before her tour of duty ends. If so, will you still want to wait until July of 1922 to marry?"

"No, sir. If we didn't have commitments to fulfill first, Andi and I would march down to the Denver County Clerk's office tomorrow morning, get a marriage license, and ask you to marry us that afternoon. I only hesitate now because I don't want to cause Andi to walk away prematurely from a job she worked so hard to earn."

Jamie thought of Rachel. Soon, they'd meet, after which he'd no longer be constrained by his promise to her. "Nevertheless, sir—Bob—before the end of this coming April, I *will* ask Andi to be my wife."

* * *

Friday, 26 December 1919

It was a crisp, bright day. Jamie and Andi bundled up and took a stroll around the neighborhood. The two or three inches of snow that had fallen the day he arrived was rapidly evaporating.

Before they'd gone a hundred yards, Jamie stopped and took her in his arms. "Your father gave me permission to ask you to marry me just as soon as your tour of duty is over."

"Oh, Jamie!" She crushed him in a bear hug. "I told you he'd think you were wonderful! His blessing means the world to me."

"Me too. I don't want there to be any stress in your life."

"Daddy's not the only one who thinks you're wonderful. My entire family loves you."

"Even your brother-in-law?"

"Ronald was touched by the plaque you gave him."

"I'm glad to hear it." But seeing how Ronald interacted with his children, a book on parenting might have been better.

As they strolled along the banks of Cherry Creek, Andi turned to Jamie. "I'm almost as thrilled as Debbi that she'll get a chance at a prestigious post-doctoral position. And I'm relieved you'll be there to keep an eye on her when she comes for her interview."

"I'll protect her like I would my own sister. And since she's almost as beautiful as you, she'll need a big brother to keep the wolves at bay."

Andi became pensive. "It's not Debbi's fault that since the moment she was born, she's been everyone's favorite."

Jamie stopped and faced Andi. "Not mine. Yes, she's beautiful, and yes, she has a winning personality. But I know your heart. And it makes you by far my favorite."

* * *

Saturday, 27 December 1919

Andi had to be back in her office in DC first thing Monday morning, 30 December. That afternoon, notwithstanding the New Year's Holiday, she would be leaving for Boston to visit a nursing school associated with Massachusetts General Hospital.

She held him so tightly at the train station that he was sure he'd have visible bruises for the next week.

"With all my traveling and your teaching schedule, we might not see each other again for a while," Andi said.

"Come mid-April, I'm going to hop on a train to DC, get down on one knee, and formally ask you to marry me." He looked into her eyes. "And nothing's going to stop me."

"Nothing?" Andi's shoulders tensed. "And nobody?"

Rachel. Even now, Jamie's promise haunted him. "Nothing—and nobody!"

Chapter 20

Letters III

Wednesday, 31 December 1919, BayView

My Dearest Andi,

I send you all my love on this last day of the year we met. When my ambulance delivered me to Letterman's front door, I was afraid I'd be locked away for the rest of my life, never to see the light of day again. Instead, I was delivered into your hands, by far the brightest light in my life.

It was great meeting your family and being with you over Christmas. I'm ecstatic that they like me. That will make life much easier for us in the future.

Ben will be out-processing from the army this morning and catching the Del Monte Express to Pacific Grove in the afternoon. He'll spend New

Year's Eve with us at BayView and become a genuine civilian again at midnight.

I'll meet Debbi at the Palo Alto train station on Monday afternoon, the 5th of January. (I'll take a book in case her train's late.) We'll dine at a nice restaurant in town that evening. I'll ask her to tell me all about you as you and your sisters were growing up.

Debbi will have the run of my apartment. I'll sleep on the couch in my biologist friend's apartment next door. The next morning, she'll have her interview with Professor Borel. I'm sure he'll be impressed.

To feel closer to you, I carry the little book of poetry you gave me for Christmas in the pocket of my coat everywhere I go.

Until next time, all my love, Jamie

* * *

Thursday, 08 January 1920. Walter Reed General Hospital

My beloved Jamie,

It seems like only yesterday that Nick Hendricks rolled you onto my ward. Little did I know you were my destiny.

And what a fantastic turn of events that Ben, the surgeon who was instrumental in giving you back the use of your legs, will be practicing medicine with your brother-in-law and living at BayView.

My whole family thanks you for setting up Debbi's interview with Professor Borel. I know she'll impress him. Knowing you'll act as her big brother will be a great comfort.

I hope Debbi didn't tell you anything embarrassing about me when you took her to dinner. I had to grow up fast as I tried to be mother to Debbi and Cyndi. I'm sure I made my share of mistakes, but I tried. I really did. If Debbi gets the post-doc position and it leads to an assistant professorship, it will be a dream come true to have her near enough to visit whenever we want.

I feel that I'm making a positive impact on the ASN. If things continue to progress as they are, I'll have accomplished everything I set out to do for the school much sooner than I anticipated. In which case . . . ..

All my love, Andi

* * *

Friday, 16 January 1920. Faculty Housing, Stanford University

My Dearest Andi,

I've hardly eaten a bite or slept a wink since I read your last letter! The thought that we might not have to wait until the end of your tenure with the ASN to be husband and wife has me that excited. I had been concerned that you were overworking yourself. Now, I hope I'm not being too selfish in saying press on!

I'm sure Debbi has already written and given you a firsthand account of her interview with Professor Borel. Please indulge me as I tell you about it from his perspective. He told me he had her at the blackboard in his office answering questions about her dissertation for two hours. Her mathematical knowledge and ability to convey complex ideas thoroughly impressed him. As did her engaging personality. He was happy to offer her the post-doc position! She's already begun working with him.

Along with helping him dig deeper into set theory, she's also required to teach an upper-division math class each semester. That didn't give her much time to prepare for this semester, as classes began last Monday, the 12th! I suspect Professor Borel deliberately put her in such a difficult position as what you might call "trial by fire." Debbi has risen to the challenge without any complaint. This may well lead to an assistant professorship as the university is eager to hire someone as young and enthusiastic as Debbi—and they'd be happy if that person is a woman.

Debbi will be living on the other side of campus in housing the university provides for post-docs. She'll be immersed in academia. I have high hopes that you'll have two Stanford professors in the family before long.

The weekend after Debbi's interview, she and I took the Del Monte Express to Pacific Grove. I wish you could have seen the expression on Oliver's face, our parlor car attendant, when he realized Debbi wasn't you! He went out of his way to tell Debbi what a wonderful nurse you are. Debbi's very proud of you. As am I.

Now that Debbi's seen BayView for herself, she knows why you love it so much. And she was charmed by the cast of characters that gathers there.

Scott says Ben didn't waste any time diving into their new partnership. He's never met anyone so eager to immerse himself in the practice of general medicine.

And more good news. As of the first of the year, Ali has a license to practice medicine in California. And my dream has come true. Now that she's licensed, Scott and Ben offered to make her a partner in their practice. She accepted! The practice of Stanton, Regen, and Stanton sounds mighty good to me. (Ali thought about using her maiden name as her middle since all her diplomas are in the name of Collins, but she's so proud of being married to Scott that she quickly dismissed the idea with no regrets.)

Scott and Ali have moved into their house around the corner from BayView. I'll miss having them underfoot. But with them living so close, I'll be able to see them whenever I'm home. And yes, I do consider BayView home. And our future home.

Another Kavanaugh Trust truck was hijacked last night. That makes five since the beginning of August. Mundy has some plans that should put a stop to this outrage.

I was able to arrange my schedule so that I only teach Monday afternoons through Thursday. I'll devote Friday mornings to working with my doctoral students. When I'm in the mood—which I'm sure will be often—I can catch the Del Monte Express to Pacific Grove on a Friday afternoon and enjoy a two-and-a-half-day weekend at BayView.

All I need now for life to be perfect is you by my side.

Until next time, all my love, Jamie

* * *

Monday, 26 January 1920. Walter Reed General Hospital

My beloved Jamie,

Debbi is convinced you can walk on water. We're immensely grateful for all you've done for her. She did write and tell me about her interview with Professor Borel. She was understandably petrified at first, defending her dissertation to a scholar she referenced in her work. It didn't take long before she was having fun discussing set theory with someone who immediately understood everything she said and had ideas that would take her work to an even deeper level.

I'm glad Scott and Ali will be living close to BayView. I can hardly wait to meet them.

BayView took Debbi's breath away. She thinks of it as an enchanted castle filled with characters to match. She says I'm a fortunate woman. I agree.

Your teaching schedule sounds idyllic. I'm working from sunrise to sunset six days a week and still having trouble accomplishing everything that needs to be done.

Seeing you with my family only reinforced how much I love you—and how much it would hurt if you were taken from me.

All my love, Andi

* * *

Wednesday, 04 February 1920. Faculty Housing, Stanford
University

My Dearest Andi,

*I was shocked by the way you ended your last
letter. I tried to reach you by telephone as soon as I
read it, but I was told you were traveling. I will
never, ever let anyone or anything take me from you!
Put that concern out of your mind and think only of
the days when we'll always be together.*

*Charlie and Lanie's relationship is progressing
nicely. The only problem is that Charlie still feels he's
not good enough for her. I told him it was up to
Lanie to decide, and she thinks otherwise. He's
secured patents on several medical devices from
which he's already making good money—even after
donating a tenth of everything he makes to charity.
And his self-image has noticeably improved.*

*Here's something you'll find interesting. Jeff
Mundy keeps in touch with a friend who's a Special
Agent in the Bureau of Investigation. This friend
has a wealth of inside information about Sonny
Kavanaugh and his operation, which he shares with
Mundy.*

*Acting upon that information, Mundy had been
riding shotgun in randomly selected trucks belonging*

to the Kavanaugh Trust for the last several weeks. He was hoping to collar one of the hijackers so he could interrogate him. Yesterday, three thugs tried to hijack a truck he was on. Apparently, Mundy's even tougher than we thought. He incapacitated and detained two of the hijackers until the police arrived. It didn't matter that one hijacker escaped. Mundy still got what he wanted. A confession that they were working for Sonny Kavanaugh.

Toby, Carl, and I got together for lunch yesterday. They and I agree that I'm incredibly blessed to have your love. They send their condolences that you're stuck with the likes of me. I think they were kidding.

Until next time, all my love, Jamie

* * *

Tuesday, 17 February 1920. Faculty Housing, Stanford University

My Dearest Andi,

You must be terribly busy as I haven't received a letter from you since yours on the 26th of January. I miss you more than the desert misses the rain. More than the night misses the sun. More than tomorrow will miss today. I look forward to the time when we'll always be together.

According to Mundy's friend in the Bureau, Sonny suspects that Matt Kavanaugh is still alive. Sonny was so upset that Kavanaugh Enterprises' assets were placed in a business trust rather than falling into his hands that he hired a forensic accountant to dig into Matt's financial affairs. The accountant discovered that Matt had cashed out a lot of his assets before his drowning. Sonny became suspicious since that cash didn't appear in Matt's estate or the Kavanaugh Trust. He intimidated an employee at Matt's old bank into disclosing that shortly before his accident, Matt transferred a lot of cash to an account owned by someone named James Smith. Since there must be a thousand James Smiths in the US, this particular one will be hard to trace.

Sonny figures there's only one reason Matt would transfer a bunch of money to an account owned by someone Sonny had never heard of: Matt must still be alive, and "James Smith" is just one in a chain of transfers that will eventually end up in an account to which Matt has free access.

Obviously, Matt wouldn't have been anticipating drowning. I can only assume he wanted the cash to ease his way into retirement. But I'm talking about a LOT of cash. And that kind of money leaves a trail. With some diligence, Sonny might be able to follow it.

If Matt were still alive and Sonny could track down the right James Smith and the rest in the chain of transfers, Sonny might eventually stumble upon Matt himself. As Matt's heir, since the money isn't part of the Kavanaugh Trust, it would rightly belong to Sonny. That gives Sonny a big incentive to make sure Matt never surfaces again. It would be interesting to see how the Bureau of Investigation would prosecute Sonny for killing a man they say is already dead.

It occurs to me that even in this scenario, Sonny would still have to determine Matt's current whereabouts. That wouldn't be easy either.

I'm concerned that Sonny is becoming incredibly rich and powerful off his bootlegging enterprises. If he becomes rich enough, the threat that all the trust's assets will become mine if he harms me or my household in any way will no longer be a deterrent. In which case, he might want to get even with us for humiliating him the way we did. So, as you say, we must be very careful—which I am.

Here's some good news. Charlie and Lanie are engaged! Unlike others we know, they're in no hurry to marry. They're talking about a wedding at the beginning of Lanie's summer break from teaching. I'm honored that Charlie asked me to be his best man.

Until next time, all my love, Jamie

William R. DeHay

* * *

Wednesday, 25 February 1920. Walter Reed General
Hospital

My beloved Jamie,

I'm sorry I'm late in writing to you. I'm working harder than ever so we can be together sooner. But the sooner we can be together, the sooner we'll face the Hangman's Curse. I know it's silly to believe in a curse, but I can't—I just can't—put your life at risk.

My medical training tells me what the problem is. Lingering effects of the trauma I endured at the front. Shell shock. If only knowing meant resolution, I could laugh off my concerns. But I repeat, I cannot put your life at risk.

I'm having trouble sleeping again. Recurring nightmares are tormenting me. In my new nightmare, I'm standing at the edge of a cliff, holding onto a man teetering on the edge. I'm slowly losing my grip. What a terrible dream it is.

My conscious dream is that you, my hero and lover, will chase away all my nightmares— and find a way to defeat the Hangman's Curse.

All my love, Andi

* * *

Thursday, 04 March 1920. Faculty Housing, Stanford University

My Dearest Andi,

I was being selfish when I told you to press on with your work to hasten the day we'll never have to part. I'm sure overwork is the source of your fears and nightmares.

If only I could hold you throughout the night. Call me on the telephone or send me a telegram and I'll drop everything and be with you as fast as a train can travel.

The Hangman's Curse doesn't scare me. Remember, I'm hard to kill. By the end of April, I will have put a ring on your finger, and when your term as Assistant Dean ends, I'll be walking tall as your husband for years to come.

On a happier note, although the Coastal Planning Commission is in John Thayer's pocket and my objections to his plan to put up an apartment building across from BayView were overruled, all has worked out in our favor. The sale of the property to Thayer was still pending when the current owner found out what Thayer was planning. She isn't in favor of him building a structure that would ruin the view of all the neighboring properties. So, I put in a bid to buy the property myself. When Thayer found out, he wanted to start a bidding war to jack up the price and make it more painful for me to buy the lot. The owner wouldn't go for that. She's happy with my plan to turn the property into a show garden. She's going to sell it to me at a fair price. Liam is looking forward to hiring an assistant gardener to help care for a larger estate.

I want everything to be perfect for you in your enchanted castle.

Until next time, all my love, Jamie

* * *

Tuesday, 16 March 1920. Faculty Housing, Stanford University

My Dearest Andi,

It's been ages since I last received a letter from you. I've tried repeatedly to reach you by telephone. Every time you're either traveling or otherwise unavailable. If I don't hear from you soon, I'll jump on a train and be with you soon. Together, we'll resolve whatever is troubling you.

Until next time, all my love, Jamie

* * *

Saturday, 20 March 1920

WESTERN UNION TELEGRAM
MY BELOVED JAMIE. PLEASE DON'T COME TO ME YET.
GIVE ME TIME TO WORK THROUGH MY FEARS MY WAY.
NEVER DOUBT THAT I LOVE YOU. ANDI

* * *

Friday, 02 April 1920. Faculty Housing, Stanford University

My Dearest Andi,

I'm desperate to talk with you. Are you deliberately not taking my telephone calls? It's taken all my self-discipline to honor your request not to come to you yet.

The university is now on spring break. I don't have to teach another class until Monday the 19th. Call me on the telephone or send me a telegram, and I'll be on a train heading your way this very day. Otherwise, I'll be with you Tuesday evening, the 13th, come what may.

All my love, Jamie

Chapter 21

Special Friends

Friday, 09 April 1920

Jamie took the afternoon commuter train from Palo Alto to San Francisco. He wouldn't let anything short of an act of God prevent him from being in the right place at the right time for his reunion with Rachel. If she didn't show up, fine. He would have kept his promise, freeing himself to propose to Andi. If Rachel did show up, he'd tell her right up front that he'd met someone else.

He had to laugh at himself. Would he even recognize Rachel? It had been three years.

He'd reserved a room at the Saint Francis Hotel. "I'm Professor Collins," he told the clerk at reception. "I have a reservation."

She looked through her bookings. "Yes, sir. We have you in Room 527 for two nights."

Jamie was sorry he'd have to stay that long, but Saturday's Transcontinental Express left in the morning, earlier than

352

when he was to meet with Rachel. Jamie checked into his room and then went down for dinner. He looked forward to the California cuisine Andi had touted. Not because he was hungry—he was too nervous to eat much. He just wanted to feel closer to Andi. He'd brought her letters with him. Although he had them practically memorized, he went over each one again. Despite her claim that her love for him was as strong as ever, her emotional distance over the last month said otherwise.

As soon as he was seated for dinner, Jamie noticed a blonde woman sitting by herself with her back to him. Could it be Rachel? He was trying to decide whether to approach her when the lady stood up. Jamie's heart began to pound. What if she was Rachel?

The lady turned around. Jamie slumped back in his chair. She looked nothing like Rachel.

He needed to calm himself. That wouldn't be easy. The thought of hurting Rachel was twisting his stomach into knots. Although she said she'd understand if he met someone else, could she be that understanding?

After eating little of his fine dinner, he returned to his room. He picked up the telephone. "This is Professor Collins in Room 527," he told the switchboard operator. "I'd like an 8:00 a.m. wake-up call, please." Even if he moved at a sloth's pace, four hours would be plenty of time to shower, get dressed, have breakfast, and walk across the street to the cable car stop.

He read in bed for a while, a biography of James Watt, inventor of the steam engine, written by the industrialist and philanthropist Andrew Carnegie. Jamie loved biographies. He planned to read Carnegie's newly released autobiography next. But a biography couldn't take Jamie's mind off his reunion with Rachel. He drifted off to sleep, praying that their reunion wouldn't be a disaster.

* * *

Saturday, 10 April 1920

Jamie had slept only intermittently. He was wide awake when the sun rose. He got out of bed and picked up the telephone. "Please cancel my 8:00 a.m. wake-up call," he told the operator. He took a quick, lukewarm shower, dressed, and went down to have at least something to eat.

At such an hour on a Saturday, he was about the only one in the breakfast café. He sat at the counter. He had no idea how long the waitress had been standing in front of him waiting to take his order before he realized she was there. "I'm sorry. My mind was a million miles away."

"Important meeting this morning?" The waitress poured him a cup of coffee.

Jamie shook the cobwebs from this brain. "Yes. Someone I haven't seen since I was sent overseas to face the Kaiser's men." Jamie glanced at the waitress' nametag. *Sue*, it said. She had such an open, friendly face he couldn't stop himself from confiding in her. "We made promises. And I always keep my promises."

"And now you've found someone else?"

Jamie absentmindedly spooned about a pound of sugar into his unasked-for coffee. "You must be a mind reader."

"I know that look."

Jamie could picture Sue in a similar situation. His heart went out to her. Sue leaned on the counter as though she had all the time in the world. "My advice, should you be interested, is to be completely honest with her. Odds are, she's met someone herself."

A selfish part of Jamie hoped Rachel still wanted him. His better self hoped she wouldn't even show up. In which case, he'd be free to get on Sunday's Transcontinental Express and propose to Andi before the sun set on Tuesday.

* * *

Jamie was pacing back and forth in front of the bench at the Powell–Hyde cable car stop well before noon. Heart racing, mouth dry, he froze at the sight of every blonde.

He forced himself to sit. He closed his eyes, reached into his coat pocket, and caressed the little book of poetry Andi had given him for Christmas. He took several deep breaths. When he opened his eyes, he was looking directly into those of one of the most beautiful women he'd ever seen. A pang of guilt stabbed him. Andi was beautiful. Rachel was just as stunning.

Looks are superficial. Andi's heart and soul placed her above compare.

Jamie stood.

Rachel gasped. She stared at his legs as though seeing a ghost. She quickly regained her senses and hugged him so tightly he could barely breathe. "I thought you were paralyzed."

"I was. Like in your dream, I've made a full recovery."

She pressed her cheek against his. "I'm so very, very happy for you—for us."

Us? This could get ugly. He broke free and stepped back from her. It scared him that holding this person he'd only met once felt so natural. "I don't think I would have survived if I hadn't believed you were back in the States praying for me."

"Believed?"

"For all I knew, you could have forgotten me the minute I walked out your door. My heart told me otherwise."

"I never stopped praying for you. When I read in the newspapers about your bravery and that you'd been critically wounded, my prayers became desperate. Only later did I learn you'd survived." She choked back a sob. "I was heart-broken to learn you were paralyzed from the waist down."

Jamie studied her face. "You thought I was paralyzed, yet you still met me here today?"

Rachel canted her head. "Of course. Didn't I say I would?" She lowered her eyes demurely. "I've kept every promise I made when we were together."

What an incredible woman. No wonder he fell so completely under her spell three years earlier. He reached into his coat pocket for Andi's annotated book of poetry as though it were a shield. He'd have to be doubly careful not to fall under Rachel's spell again.

He pointed to the bench. "Shall we sit?" Rachel sat with such grace Jamie could easily believe she was a ballerina rather than an artist.

"I'm sorry you hadn't learned until today that I can walk again."

"It's wonderful news." She got a far-away look. "But it changes everything."

"Everything?" Please don't let this get ugly.

"From the trivial to life-changing." She folded her hands in her lap. "Toward the trivial end of the spectrum, it's such a relief that now I won't have to remodel my cottage. Or deal with that horrid building contractor."

Jamie looked at her. "I'm sorry, you've lost me."

"I needed to have some remodeling done. Everyone said Monarch Construction was the best in the area. I dropped by their office and was told they normally don't do such small jobs as mine, but the owner overheard me say my cottage has a thatched roof. He took an interest and came out himself to give me an estimate. Now, thank goodness, I'll never have to deal with *Mister* John Thayer again."

"John Thayer?" Jamie said. "I know a man named John Thayer."

"Then I'm sorry for you."

Jamie sat up straight. "The John Thayer I know lives and works on the Monterey Peninsula."

"Then we must be talking about the same man."

"John Thayer is the son of the man who established the scholarship that let me earn my degrees, and you can't imagine a father and son who are more different. John Thayer aside, what's your connection with the Monterey Peninsula?"

"I have the prettiest little cottage in Carmel just off Main Street."

Jamie's head began to spin. "You mean you live in Carmel?"

"For almost three years now."

Jamie would have been less surprised if a Martian had walked up and tapped him on the shoulder. "Carmel's only a few miles from my house in Pacific Grove!"

Rachel mirrored Jamie's surprise. "You have a house in Pacific Grove?" She pursed her lips. "I remember you grew up there, but weren't you going to be teaching physics at Stanford?"

"I am. I inherited the house. I only live there part-time."

He searched her face. "I thought you were going to help establish an art school near San Diego."

"Oh, that. I didn't last three weeks at Jason Roach's art school. Art school my foot. The inmates there were more interested in drinking and partying than art."

"How'd you end up in Carmel?"

"I saw an advertisement in an art magazine. A lovely little gallery was for sale, along with an enchanting, thatched-roof cottage that backs up to it. I made the trip from San Diego to see it and instantly fell in love with the village, the gallery, and the cottage. I made an offer, and the seller accepted." She sighed contentedly. "I love my cottage just the way it is. I'm so glad I won't have to have it remodeled."

"And that's where John Thayer came into the picture?"

"He was the only contractor willing to do the work."

"Surely there are other contractors in the area."

"Monarch's business practices are what you'd call extreme. Ruthless, some would say. Once Monarch becomes involved, no other contractor will dare make a bid if they don't want to be shut out of other work in the area."

"I still don't understand. What were the changes you felt were so necessary."

Rachel seemed to think it was obvious. "I needed to have doorways widened and ramps installed to the front and back doors. Kitchen and bathroom counters lowered. And a hundred other little changes made."

She made a sour face. "Thayer wears a wedding ring, yet he said he'd do the work 'in exchange.' What a scoundrel. I hate to consider what kind of exchange he had in mind. Now, I won't have to deal with him at all."

"I'm almost afraid to ask," Jamie said. "Why was remodeling your cottage so important that you'd even consider hiring such a man?"

Rachel looked at Jamie as though he was asking which way was up. "To accommodate your wheelchair, of course. Call me old-fashioned, but I believe it's a wife's duty to make their home comfortable for her husband."

Jamie was afraid his head might explode. "You were going to give up your freedom to care for me?"

"Knowing the sacrifice you made for your men, it would have been an honor to care for you."

A wave of guilt washed over Jamie. "I've met someone," he blurted out.

Rachel took in a startled breath.

"I've kept my promise to you," Jamie said. "I haven't *formally* committed to her. Still, she knows my heart is irrevocably hers. I intend to catch the Transcontinental Express to Washington, DC, tomorrow morning and propose to her as soon as the train pulls into Union Station."

Rachel sat forward and turned to him. From her expression, Jamie was afraid she was about to slap him—until the corners of her mouth slowly rose, and crinkle lines appeared around her eyes. "Thank God! I've met someone, too."

They burst into laughter and hugged like old, old friends.

"My gentleman has to wonder why I've been so evasive. I've just never found a way to tell him about the promises I made when you and I were together. It's a miracle he hasn't given up on me."

"My lady's an army nurse a little less than a year into a prestigious three-year assignment in Washington, DC. Since army nurses have to be single, waiting until after you and I met again to propose to her hasn't caused too much tension between us—but if it weren't for the promise I made to you, I would have offered her an engagement ring way back in June."

"An army nurse? My Ben was an army doctor until he was discharged at the first of the year."

Jamie's head did explode. "You don't mean Ben *Regen*, do you?"

Rachel couldn't have looked more startled if a grenade had gone off in her face. "How'd you know?"

"Ben's the surgeon who made it possible for me to walk again. He's practically family. He lives in my house in Pacific Grove. He's a partner in a medical practice with my sister and her husband."

"Ali Stanton is your sister? Ben talks about her and Scott all the time. When he mentioned that he lives in a friend's house, I assumed that friend was Scott." Rachel took a deep breath. "The odds against all this happening by chance are astronomical."

"That's exactly what I was thinking. But it has happened. You and Ben, me and Andi, others I could mention—there must be a divine plan playing out here for the lives of so many people we know to have intersected at exactly the time and place they have."

Rachel's face blanched. "What are we going to tell Ben and Andi about us?"

What indeed? Since the moment he'd fallen in love with Andi, Jamie had been paying the price for sleeping with Rachel. Had he and Rachel merely enjoyed a pleasant day together and gotten on with their lives, he never would have made the promise that was keeping him from proposing to Andi. And now there were Ben's feelings to consider. Ben. Jamie's friend. The man who gave him back the use of his legs.

"It would be wrong to lie to Ben," Jamie said. "I suggest you tell him the truth. That we knew each other before the war and about our promises to each other. And hope he's wise enough not to ask too many questions."

Rachel stared at the ground. "I was foolish to think my promises would affect only me. You, me, Ben, Andi; who knows who else had to put their lives on hold because of my self-indulgence?"

"We were young and scared," Jamie said. "Everything we thought we knew about the world was being turned upside down by the war."

"Yes, you're right. Still . . .." Rachel tucked a flow of luminous blond hair behind her ear as Jamie remembered her doing that night three years earlier. "What about Andi? Are you going to tell her about us?"

"I already have."

Rachel turned to Jamie wide-eyed.

"She had to know what was keeping me from proposing to her when it was so obvious I wanted to."

"What if Andi and I meet, and she realizes I'm the one who got in the way of you proposing?"

"If you and Ben are serious about each other, you'll almost certainly meet once Andi becomes my wife." And what will that be like, Jamie wondered.

"I'll die of shame if she tells Ben about us."

"Andi's the most understanding, compassionate person you'll ever meet. She'd never do anything that might hurt Ben—or you."

"I can tell you think the world of her. And I slept with her man. What's she going to think of me?"

"Andi believes she owes you a huge debt of gratitude. I

told her your prayers gave me the courage to keep fighting for my life when my chances of survival looked so bleak."

"She doesn't owe me anything. I was happy to pray for you." Rachel straightened her blouse. "To make it up to Ben for putting him off for so long, the minute I return to the Monterey Peninsula, I'm going to march right up to him and tell him how much I love him."

Jamie felt like hugging Rachel. Yet he didn't dare. It was funny to think they had once made love with abandon—and now he was afraid to touch her.

"Do you feel like walking?" Jamie said.

They left their bench and began to tour Union Square. Memories of walking the same path with Andi came rushing back. Men they passed gave him the same look they had back then, as if to say, "How'd the likes of you end up with such a stunning woman?"

They inevitably found themselves opposite Hutchins Fine Art. Rachel took Jamie's arm as they crossed the street for a closer look. When they reached the other side, she didn't let go. He looked from Rachel's eyes to her hand and back.

She raised her chin. "Have I trodden on convention again?"

A skirmish broke out in Jamie's conscience. Was this contact innocent, or would he be unfaithful to Andi if he let it continue?

Rachel began to withdraw her hand.

Jamie trapped it between his arm and the side of his chest. "I'm not going to be ruled by convention."

She smiled and maintained her hold.

"I remember seeing one of your cable car paintings on display here three years ago."

"It never sold," Rachel said.

"I'm shocked. It was a fine painting. If it were still here, I'd buy it and hang it next to the one you gave me the morning after we . . .." He cleared his throat. "The last time we met."

Rachel blushed, a look that made her all the more attractive. "That's sweet of you. Some paintings just don't sell. My feelings weren't hurt."

"How's your art career going?"

"Very well, thank you. I love owning my own gallery, and I've had a good deal of success as an illustrator, especially of children's books. And during the war, I did quite a bit of work designing and illustrating recruiting posters, several of which won Recruiting Service awards."

"I would have been surprised if they hadn't won awards."

"You are sweet."

"Are cable cars still one of your main subjects?"

"I rarely do stand-alone paintings these days. I much prefer creating a series of illustrations that tell a story." She looked at Jamie. "How about you? You said you're a physics professor. How's that going?"

"Great. I passed my orals the month after we met and received my Ph.D. and officer's commission that June. The army announced they wouldn't activate my division until the end of September, when they'd have the necessary resources to train us. Since I would be available throughout the summer, Stanford offered me a position as an adjunct professor."

"That would have been a non-tenure-track position, right?"

"That's right. They wanted me to teach two introductory physics courses intended primarily for students who were either a little behind in their degree program or were changing their majors."

"That sounds like a perfect way to keep busy and not dwell on your pending deployment."

"Exactly. It turned out to be something of an audition. The Physics Department planned to hire an assistant professor at the end of the summer term. The head of the department told me that if I performed as well as he expected, the position would be mine."

"You must have done well."

"Apparently so. They did offer me the assistant professor position—even knowing I'd soon be shipping out for France." He rubbed the back of his neck. "I know I couldn't have performed half as well as I did if you and I were seeing each other at the time, especially with you in San Diego, or even closer, in Carmel."

"Then my insistence that we wait three years before seeing each other again wasn't completely crazy?"

"No, not completely." Jamie smiled. "To my surprise, when those at the university learned I'd been awarded the Medal of Honor, they promoted me to Associate Professor." Jamie sighed. "Since it was touch and go whether I'd survive, I think they were anticipating it being a posthumous promotion." He smiled. "To the university's credit, when I confounded the doctors and had the audacity to live, Stanford didn't demote me."

"I'm very proud of you," Rachel said.

It was amazing how special she made him feel.

She held onto Jamie more tightly as they continued their circumnavigation of Union Square. "This is where I'm staying," Rachel said as they came opposite the Saint Francis Hotel.

"Really? Me too." A jolt of fear coursed through Jamie. They had progressed to her clutching his arm with no resistance on his part. And now it turned out they were staying in the same hotel. He reached his free hand into his coat pocket and clamped onto the book Andi had given him.

Jamie straightened his back. The Saint Francis was a first-class establishment. And Rachel had to stay somewhere. None of that meant he would let temptation get the better of him again.

The bell of a cable car drew their attention. "Shall we?" Jamie said.

They leapt onto the Powell–Hyde Line. It was disappointing that their gripman wasn't Leonard, as it was three years earlier.

"I wonder if I'm still the only female gripman," Rachel said.

They rode the line to the waterfront. With a handful of tourists, they watched the gripman and his conductor push the car onto the turntable to ready it for its return trip to Union Square.

Jamie pointed to "their" bench, the one they had occupied three years earlier. After settling in, he told Rachel all about Andi and her role in his recovery. And how much he loved her. He hoped it was a strong enough signal to Rachel that he was off-limits to her.

When Rachel began singing Ben's praises, Jamie relaxed. It sounded like she was very much in love with Ben.

Eventually, they got down to basics. "Do you know what I dreamt of back in the trenches?"

Rachel seemed almost embarrassed to offer her guess. "Our time together in my studio?"

Jamie laughed. "Someone who never had to choke down

cold rations from a can day after day while artillery shells fell all around them might think that. What I dreamt of was Ghirardelli's Chocolate Shop."

Rachel looked relieved. "It's just up the street. Let's see if it's as good as you remember."

Jamie limited himself to one chocolate bar. Rachel exercised equal restraint.

"Chocolate won't satisfy my hunger," she said as they left the shop. "Shall we see if Nunzio's Italian Restaurant is open for late lunch or early dinner and save our chocolate for dessert?"

"Let's."

Rachel stuffed both their bars into her purse.

Nunzio's hadn't changed a bit.

"May we have a table in Alessandro's section," Jamie asked the maître d'.

Before being shown to a window table, Jamie helped Rachel out of her coat. The dress she was wearing did nothing to conceal her remarkable figure.

Alessandro greeted them with a big smile. "How nice to have you back."

"You remember us?" Rachel said.

"You'd be hard to forget."

They ordered the same dishes they had three years earlier. This time, they actually ate them.

After their meal—which now Jamie could afford—they took a stroll along the waterfront, ending at the Powell-Hyde cable car turnaround.

"It would be fun to see the Victorian I used to live in," Rachel said.

They rode to the top of Russian Hill and walked the short distance.

As they stood looking up at Rachel's old attic studio, Jamie had to ask himself whether he'd lost his mind. The cable car, Nunzio's, and now Russian Hill. They were retracing their steps from three years earlier. He clutched Andi's little book as though it were a life buoy, hoping the thought of her would protect him from himself.

"Some of the happiest moments of my life took place here," Rachel said.

"And some of the most consequential of mine." Their eyes met. "Not just because we made love. I don't think I'd be alive today if all that took place here hadn't happened."

They eventually returned to their hotel. As they stood together in the lobby, Jamie felt he had to say something to put things on the right footing. "I'll be catching the Transcontinental Express to Washington, DC, in the morning. I've waited long enough to propose to Andi."

Rachel smiled that smile of hers Jamie was sure could ignite a raging forest fire. "May I accompany you to the station? I'll be taking the Del Monte Express to Pacific Grave in the afternoon. I'm going to track down Ben and tell him I'm ready to make a commitment."

"I'd like that. Let's meet in the breakfast café at 6:00 tomorrow morning."

"It's a date," Rachel said.

After giving each other a friendly hug, Rachel turned, took several steps toward the elevators, and stopped. She turned back and held up her purse. "We almost forgot our dessert." She extracted their chocolate bars. "And it's early. There's lots more we could talk about."

It was a few seconds before the lump in Jamie's throat allowed him to speak. Surely, she wasn't suggesting they go to one of their rooms. That wouldn't be smart. Even if nothing improper happened, he couldn't imagine Andi being happy with the situation. He pointed to a sitting area on the other side of the lobby. "I think we'd be comfortable over there."

Rachel gave him a funny look. "Exactly what I had in mind."

What a heel he was. She'd be insulted if she knew he was afraid she was propositioning him.

He helped Rachel out of her coat. She sat on a wingback chair angled toward the sofa Jamie sat on. They were close enough that there was little chance they'd be overheard. Their talk flowed free and easy. It was getting late when Rachel excused herself to use the lady's room just across from them. When she returned, rather than reclaiming her chair, she sat next to Jamie. Close.

"I can't help wondering," Rachel said, "if we had stayed in touch, do you think you and I would be looking forward to a happy future together?"

There was no doubt in Jamie's mind that they would have been happy together. That aside, he wouldn't trade a future with Andi for anything. There was so much he loved about Andi. Her bravery, her dedication, her compassion, her intelligence. He could go on and on. "That's dangerous ground best left unexplored," he said.

"You're right. Best to talk about what is rather than what might have been."

Which they did for some time, until Rachel yawned.

"Tired?" Jamie said. She nodded, took his arm in both hands, and rested her head on his shoulder and quickly dozed off. Jamie froze. Was there any harm in this? What would Andi think? Or Ben?

Let them think what they would. He might not be alive but for her prayers. "I'm blessed to have a friend like you, Rachel Lawson," he whispered.

She must not have been sound asleep. "I do love you," she replied.

Jamie's heart almost stopped beating.

"But . . .."

He held his breath.

"You're meant for Andi. And I'm meant for Ben."

For the first time in days, Jamie breathed easy. He leaned over and kissed the top of Rachel's head. "That doesn't stop me from loving you too, my special friend."

Rachel snuggled even closer. She was soon asleep—sound asleep this time. Jamie sat with her for another hour, maybe longer, luxuriating in the knowledge that two remarkable women loved him in two very different ways—and that he loved them in return, one as a friend and the other as the person he wanted to spend the rest of his life with.

Rachel eventually began to stir.

"You still talk in your sleep," Jamie said.

She rubbed her eyes. "You're the only man who knows that."

Jamie extracted his arm from her grip and shook it.

"Have I put your arm to sleep?"

"I'm not going to complain."

Rachel stood up and stretched. "Thank you for a wonderful day."

They rode in the elevator together. Rachel got off on the floor below Jamie's. As the elevator doors closed behind her, he refused to think about what life would have been like had he not met Andi. Such thoughts would have been pointless. He had met her. And now they were free to enjoy the future together.

* * *

Sunday, 11 April 1920

The way the porter had to wrestle with Rachel's luggage, one would have thought she'd packed for a month-long stay on a deserted island. Jamie remembered Andi packing everything she needed in one suitcase.

Andi. Soon, he'd be holding her in his arms.

Their taxi arrived at the train station an hour before the Transcontinental Express was scheduled to depart. Jamie led Rachel to the end of the passenger platform, where they sat close together and amused themselves by reminiscing, making witty observations, and speculating about their futures. Eventually, the conversation turned serious.

"Everyone thinks the doctor in France made a mistake when he pronounced me dead," Jamie said. "You may think I'm crazy, but I believe I really was dead, and I was raised for a purpose."

Rachel smiled at him the way an adult smiles at a child who still believes in Santa Claus. "You'd have to be awfully special for that to be true."

"That's not what I'm saying. It's not me that's special. It's the purpose for which I was raised."

Rachel's indulgent smile dissolved. "Which is?"

"I've been asking myself that question for ages."

"And?"

"I'm still searching for an answer."

* * *

Rachel had Oliver, the Del Monte Express' parlor car attendant, send her luggage on to her cottage in Carmel. She walked the short distance to BayView.

Noreen answered the door. "May I help you?"

"I'd like to see Ben, please. My name's Rachel."

Ben came running down the stairs three at a time. "Rachel! What a wonderful surprise. How'd you know where to find me?"

"Jamie told me."

Once Ben recovered from his shock, they sat on the couch in the front room, and Rachel told him all there was to know about her friendship with Jamie and the promises they made to each other. All except that they had slept together. There was no need to tell Ben that. Anyone who could score higher than a brick on a Stanford-Binet IQ test could have guessed.

Ben listened to her story from beginning to end without interruption.

"How well we complement each other," he said. "You helped Jamie survive, and I helped him walk again. As to promises, I made some recently that reshaped my life."

It was a tremendous relief that Ben hadn't thrown a jealous fit. "I'd love to hear about them," Rachel said.

"You may think less of me after you hear what I have to say."

"I doubt that."

Ben stood, walked to the window, and stared out over the bay. "A few days after I reported for duty at Letterman, a couple of doctors invited me to join them for a drink in the officer's club. I'd never been much of a drinker, yet I jumped at the chance. I was desperate to fit in and be considered 'one of the boys.' " He turned and faced Rachel. "Apparently, I had more than just *a* drink because I woke up as the sun was rising and found myself in bed with a nurse they'd introduced me to earlier that evening. She wasn't used to alcohol either." He shook his head. "I'm ashamed to have compromised her that way."

It was a struggle for Rachel to suppress her jealousy. But with her history, she knew she had no ground to stand on.

Ben massaged his temples with his long, elegant surgeon's fingers. "To make matters worse, I was scheduled to perform a delicate operation on a colleague's wife later that morning. I was in no shape to be wielding a scalpel, but in my arrogance, I told myself that even with shaky hands and a throbbing head, I was a better surgeon than most."

He looked at his hands as though they had betrayed him. "The operation went well—initially. I was about to close her up when I nicked her aorta. I did what I could to repair the damage. It wasn't enough. Her condition was grave. When I was washing up afterward and saw myself in the mirror, I didn't see the doctor who had set out to save the world. I saw a weakling who compromised his ethics because he wanted to fit in."

Rachel was disappointed to learn about his drinking and indiscretion while simultaneously impressed that he had the courage to be open about it.

"We're not put here to conform to this world," Ben said. "We're here to fulfill our calling. In my case, I'm convinced mine is to be a physician who can always be counted on. And there I was with a patient in intensive care, fighting for her life because I wanted to be one of the boys. I couldn't just stand by and wait for her to die. I had to do something. I just didn't know what. I'd done everything I could medically."

"Pray?" Rachel said.

Ben sighed. "Back then, praying wasn't easy for me. I saw God as distant and formalistic. A Being who could only be approached in His holy dwelling." He frowned. "Letterman doesn't have a synagogue. They do have a chapel."

Synagogue? From the way Ben talked, she had assumed he was a Christian.

Ben had gone quiet. "Please, go on," Rachel said.

Ben gathered himself. "Army chapels are supposed to accommodate all religions. Letterman's token acknowledgment of Judaism is a modest menorah overshadowed by a large stained-glass depiction of Jesus." Ben took a deep breath. "Despite feeling out of place, I entered the chapel and stood in the back, feeling unworthy to enter any further. I prayed for my patient, offering every prayer for mercy I could remember from childhood. Still, I felt that wasn't enough. My eyes were drawn to the stained-glass portrait that dominated the front of the chapel. Out of desperation, I pleaded with Jesus to save my patient, promising that if He did, I'd never drink another drop of alcohol or touch another woman inappropriately."

Ben stepped closer to Rachel. "I swear I heard a voice—not just in my head. A real voice, out loud. 'Your patient is healed,' it said. And I knew, beyond any doubt, I *knew* it was true. "I ran out of the chapel and onto the intensive care ward, where I found exactly what I knew I'd find. My patient was sitting up in bed as though her life had never been at risk. My mind went blank. The next thing I knew, I was back in the chapel, called to the altar where I fell to my knees, and with tears of gratitude streaming from my eyes, I accepted Jesus as my Lord and Savior."

Rachel didn't know what to do or say.

Ben's shoulders sagged. "My only regret is that my family and friends refused to accept my conversion." He stood up straight. "Despite the pressure they put on me, I've never wavered from my decision—and I've kept the promises I made that day." He sat next to her. "What I'm getting at is that the past made us who we are today. And now we have a choice. Are we going to let guilt and recrimination ruin our future? Or will we use the lessons we've learned throughout our lives to create the future of our dreams?"

Rachel took the hands that had made it possible for Jamie to walk again. "I dream of a future in which I'm your woman and you're my man."

Ben intertwined his fingers with hers. "I want something far greater. I dream of a future in which I'm your husband and you're my wife."

Chapter 22

Raised for a Purpose

Tuesday, 13 April 1920

It felt like the Transcontinental Express, the fastest cross-country conveyance yet available, crawled its way to Washington, DC.

It was late afternoon, almost evening, when the train finally pulled into Union Station. With any luck, Andi would still be in her office.

Jamie found her there talking with another woman. Andi looked like she hadn't slept in a week. Jamie burst in on them. He rushed to Andi and embraced her unabashedly. He was perplexed by her reaction. She seemed both elated to see him and terrified.

"I certainly hope you're Major Collins," the other woman said with a big smile.

"At your service, ma'am."

Andi gathered herself. "Jamie, this is Dean Julia Stimson."

375

"I understand we've met before," Jamie said, "although I was unconscious."

"Yes, sir. In France. You were fighting for your life, and I prayed over you."

"Thank you for that," Jamie said. "Andi's told me so many nice things about you. It's an honor to meet you again. And please, call me Jamie."

"The honor's all mine, Jamie. And please call me Julia." She looked Jamie up and down. "The way Andi talks about you, I expected someone seven feet tall who could walk through walls."

Jamie laughed. "I have my limitations. It's my love for Andi that's boundless."

Julia's smile grew even wider. "Well said, Jamie." She glanced at her watch. "I should wrap things up for the day. I know others in the office would love to meet you. Perhaps we can all lunch together one day while you're here."

"That would be nice."

Andi remained silent.

"Have a pleasant evening," Julia said.

Andi crossed her arms the instant Julia left the room. "Did Rachel show up for your reunion?"

"Right on time."

"Had she put on fifty pounds and lost her front teeth?"

Jamie suspected Andi was only half-joking. "There's no sense in lying. She's one of the most beautiful, sophisticated women I've ever met—and still, she can't hold a candle to Andrea Jean Eliot."

Andi denied Jamie any reaction. "What did she want from you?"

"Nothing."

Andi stared at him. "Nothing? No child support? No means of living?"

Jamie shook his head. "It's what she was preparing to do for me that was amazing."

Now, there was fear in Andi's eyes.

Jamie recounted Rachel's plans for remodeling her home and, more importantly, why. "Isn't that the most amazing thing you've ever heard? She hardly knows me, and yet she was going to give up her freedom to care for me."

Andi sat down—or, more accurately, collapsed—on her desk chair. "That's incredible. What did you say?"

Jamie shrugged. "That I'd met someone else, of course."

Andi sat up straight. "Wait. This beautiful, sophisticated woman you'd only met once before was going to sacrifice her life for you, and you coldly told her you'd met someone else?"

"I wasn't cold. I was direct, as I told you I'd be. And she was relieved. She'd met someone herself—a man she's grown to love. And not just anyone. Her man was instrumental in giving me back the use of my legs."

"Are you saying . . ." Andi rose from her chair. "Are you saying your Rachel is the one Ben's been seeing in Carmel?"

"She's not my Rachel. She's Ben's."

"Carmel is practically in BayView's backyard!" Andi said.

"That hardly matters. She's serious about Ben. Totally smitten. And now that she's free of the promise she made to me, if he proposes—and she thinks he will—her answer will be yes. Once they're married, since Ben, Ali, and Scott are partners, we'll undoubtedly see a lot of Rachel over the coming years." He took Andi's hand. "That won't be a problem for me. Ben's a good friend. I'm thrilled for him. My concern is you. Will you be all right with it?"

"Rachel helped save your life. Anything that happened between you two prior to that is no concern of mine—so long as you don't have any lingering feelings for her."

"No feelings I shouldn't have. As you say, she helped save my life. But you're the *reason* I live. And that's never going to change. So enough about Rachel." He pulled a small box from his pocket and dropped to one knee. He opened it to reveal an engagement ring. "Andrea Jean Eliot, will you do me the honor of marrying me?"

Andi broke into tears. "I can't. You know I want to. I just can't. I love you too much to say yes."

Her rejection hit Jamie like an artillery shell. He rose. "You're not still worried about that silly 'Hangman's Curse,' are you?"

"It's not silly to me. You would be struck down if I agreed to marry you. I can't let that happen. You're too precious to me."

"That's ridiculous," Jamie said, raising his voice. "You're a mature, scientifically trained woman. You know there's no such thing as a curse."

"Yes, yes. I know that—intellectually. But we're talking about your life. My heart would be torn to shreds if you ended up like my fiancés."

"We've covered this ground before. I told you, I'm not that easy to kill."

She folded her arms. "I've made up my mind."

"Because you're afraid I'll die if you agree to marry me? If we walk away from each other, something inside of each of us will die."

She squeezed her eyes closed and shook her head. She'd undoubtedly rehearsed all this, and it wasn't going as planned. "I'm married to the Army Nurse Corps. My life is planned out. When my tour as assistant dean of the ASN ends, the Army's going to send me to earn a master's degree in nursing and then promote me to Assistant Superintendent of the ANC."

"Andi—"

"Don't make this any harder than it already is. Please honor my decision."

"No. This is insane," Jamie shouted. "We love each other. We're meant to be husband and wife."

Andi straightened her back and assumed her Nurse Eliot persona. "You should leave now before one of us says or does something we'll regret."

"No. I won't let some stupid superstition rob us of our happiness."

The Dean must have heard their raised voices. She appeared in Andi's doorway. "All right, Major Collins. That's enough. Nurse Eliot has asked you to leave. You should do so. It's clear to me you're meant for each other. You both need to step back and do some serious thinking about your relationship. I'm sure there's a way around whatever's come between you."

The last time Jamie had been so angry, he wiped out a battery of German machine guns. He snapped the ring box shut, shoved it into his pocket, and stormed out of Andi's office before the beast in him could break free and he did say or do something he'd regret.

* * *

Jamie just started walking—west, as indicated by the sun. He soon encountered an expanse of green. Rock Creek Park, a sign said. He sat on a bench.

"Damn the Hangman's Curse," he said out loud. "Was I raised from the dead just so my heart could be broken?" A passerby gave him a look and, without any subtlety, quickened his pace.

Jamie rose from the bench and exited the park to wander the city streets aimlessly. It was near sunset. He was cold.

He turned a corner and happened upon a scene of chaos. A man had a hold of a woman's purse. She was holding onto its strap as though he was trying to steal her last dollar—and perhaps he was. Jamie welcomed this distraction. Though he was smaller than the woman's attacker, that hardly mattered. As he'd demonstrated many times in officer training school, a smaller, faster man can use a bigger man's slower reactions, height, and weight against him.

Jamie grabbed the man and wrestled him to the ground where he pinned him with his knee on his neck. On the battlefield, Jamie would then have crushed the man's windpipe. In this case, Jamie merely restrained him.

The woman ran, offering no thanks to Jamie.

Jamie stood and watched as the attacker scrambled to his feet and ran in the opposite direction from the woman. Apparently, the coward was looking for an easy target, not a fight.

In his quick skirmish, Jamie had escaped physical damage. His clothes hadn't. He'd bought a sports coat and new slacks so he'd look sharp when he proposed to Andi. In their tussle, the man had blindly grabbed at Jamie and torn the pocket where Jamie kept the book of poems Andi had given him as a Christmas present. Jamie picked up the book and cradled it as if it were a baby bird. "Andi, Andi, Andi," he said to the night.

Jamie was tired, depressed. He got directions from a stranger and then found his hotel. The desk clerk stared disapprovingly at Jamie's disheveled look.

To add to Jamie's misery, he learned that the Union Pacific had misplaced his luggage. They were, however, confident that they'd find it in a day or two. Jamie put the "Do Not Disturb" sign on his door. He sprawled across his bed in his new clothes and closed his eyes. His stomach growled. He ignored it. Living in the trenches for so long, Jamie had learned to sleep in any situation. Weariness overcame him. He dozed off.

* * *

Wednesday, 14 April 1920

The instant Jamie awoke, all his disappointment came rushing back to him.

He sat up and looked around his hotel room. It felt like a jail cell.

Though the shades were drawn, he could tell the sun was already high. He wandered into the bathroom and was shocked by what he saw in the mirror. His hair was a mess, as were his clothes. His shaving kit was with his luggage, probably on a train to who knew where.

He remained in his darkened room for hours, trying to decide what to do. There was no way he was going to leave things as they were with Andi. If only relationships were as easy to solve as physics problems.

He noticed the little sewing kit the hotel no doubt

provided in every room. Why they didn't also provide a shaving kit would remain a mystery. He removed his sports coat and tried to repair the torn pocket. It didn't look much better when he was done.

As the walls of his room closed in on him, he recalled something he told Andi he wanted to do the first time he visited DC.

Hangman's Curse be damned. He put on his now-rumpled coat, got directions from the hotel clerk, and hit the streets. Passersby stared at him as though he might not be merely unkempt but contagious.

It was late afternoon when Jamie finally found the chancery of the pre-war German embassy. As he'd told Andi in a letter, diplomatic relations between the German Republic and the United States had not yet been re-established, but there were German diplomats in their old chancery working toward that end. The building was an imposing four-story structure built as an opulent private residence. In 1894, the German Empire bought it and converted it into offices.

Jamie paced back and forth on the sidewalk in front of the building several times, getting the lay of the land. Then, in a near-fit, he began shouting at the top of his lungs, hurling every insult he could think of at the Kaiser. When he ran out of insults for the Kaiser, he added the German wartime general staff to his rant.

A few heads appeared at the building's windows now and then. Jamie hoped they were offended. Most likely, they just thought he was crazy. He kept shouting until he felt a tap on his shoulder. Jamie turned around to find himself face-to-face with a uniformed policeman. "Lansky," it said on his nametag.

"I'm betting you fought the Kaiser's men in France," Lansky said. "Convince me all your ranting and raging is doing some good, and I'll join in with you."

Jamie took a deep breath. "The Kaiser is responsible for killing dozens of my men. And now the bastard's living in luxury in a storybook castle in Belgium. It's not fair. It's downright criminal." Jamie shouted another string of insults at the unhearing chancery building.

"Of course, it's not fair," Officer Lansky said. "If I had my way, the Kaiser would be hanged. But you haven't convinced me that yelling at this old building will make that happen." He looked Jamie up and down. "I'd expect someone carrying on the way you are to be drunk, but I don't smell alcohol on you."

"I'm not drunk. I'm angry. The Kaiser turned me into a killer, and that's hard to live with."

"Okay, you're not drunk, but you sure look worse for wear. Those are fine clothes you're wearing, but they look like you slept in them last night."

Jamie looked at his reflection in a window and could see why everyone he passed on the street shied away. "We learned to sleep in our uniforms back in the trenches, thanks to the Kaiser."

"I'm too young to have fought in France, but my sergeant isn't. You might be able to convince him to join in with you here. Why don't you take a little walk with me? Our district substation is just around the corner. You can tell Sergeant Raines all about the Kaiser. He'll understand."

"Are you arresting me?"

"No. You have a right to curse the Kaiser until you're blue in the face."

Curse. There was that word again.

"Come on," Lansky said. "Let's go talk with Sergeant Raines. He does a lot of volunteer work with the Veterans of Foreign Wars. He'll understand."

Jamie stared at Lansky. "What kind of volunteer work?"

"He listens to veterans. Then, if he can help, there's not much he won't do for them."

Listening was about all Jamie had done with Scott Stanton, and that was enough to help Scott reestablish his equilibrium.

"Plus," Officer Lansky said, "you could use a little tidying up. And maybe a bite to eat?"

Jamie had never had an encounter with a policeman before. He was surprised this officer was so non-confrontational and understanding. Lansky seemed to really care about him. And Lansky was young. About the same age as Jamie's students. "Why not?" Jamie said. "I said my piece here."

* * *

Jamie was soon sitting in Sergeant Jason Raines' office sipping strong, disgusting coffee and ignoring the donut he was offered.

"Officer Lansky tells me you fought in France," Raines said.

Jamie set his cup down and covered his eyes.

"I'll take that as a yes. Please, tell me your name, sir. And don't worry. You're not in any trouble. I just like to know who I'm talking to."

"Jamie Collins," he mumbled.

"You look a mess, Mister Collins. Yet your clothes tell me

you're a man of means. Am I correct in guessing you slept in them last night?"

"The Union Pacific lost my luggage. And I got used to sleeping in my uniform in the trenches."

"Were you infantry?"

"I commanded an infantry company until I was wounded."

"I was in the infantry myself. But I was lucky. I never received any serious wounds." Sergeant Raines' eyes suddenly opened wide. "What did you say your name is?"

"Jamie Collins."

Sergeant Raines leaned toward Jamie. "Are you the one soldiers call the hero who was raised from the dead?"

"I don't like it when people call me that."

"But that's you, isn't it?"

Jamie picked up his cup again. "It is."

"I have a cousin from Nevada who was under your command. He figures he wouldn't be alive today if it weren't for you."

Scenes of battle flashed through Jamie's brain. Scenes he wished he could forget.

"A lot of us who fought overseas are still trying to regain our balance," Raines said. "And trying to get over our hatred of the Germans."

Jaimie put his cup down so violently half his coffee sloshed onto the sergeant's desk. "Sorry," Jamie said. He wiped the spill up with his sleeve. "It's not the Germans I hate. It's their Kaiser. We're talking about a man who started a war that killed tens of millions. Britain's Prime Minister David Lloyd George publicly stated that the Kaiser should be hanged."

"And he might have been," Raines said, "if he hadn't escaped justice by abdicating and fleeing to the Netherlands."

Jamie was so worked up that his mouth had gone dry. He took a mouthful of rancid coffee and then continued his rant. "The Treaty of Versailles called for the prosecution of Kaiser Billy, but despite appeals from the Allies, his protectors in the Netherlands refused to extradite him.

"A case of the aristocracy protecting their own," Raines said.

"Exactly. And now he's living in a country estate in the center of the Netherlands. For which he paid 1.35 million guilders, or nearly seven million dollars. And where did he get the money to buy Doorn House? He took it from the German people, many of whom are near starvation."

"You probably didn't do your mind any good digging up all these facts," Raines said.

"I was so enraged I couldn't help myself." Jamie took a deep breath. "Doorn House is modest by what the Kaiser is accustomed to but large by any reasonable standards. The grounds consist of thirty-five hectares of English-style gardens. The house is filled with antique furniture, paintings, silver, and porcelain he looted from his palaces in Berlin and Potsdam. It took 59 train wagons to transport it all to Doorn House. Fifty-nine! Those items rightfully belong to the German people. Think of how many hungry Germans could be fed for what they're worth." Jamie shook his head in disgust. "Kaiser Billy's living in a storybook castle while all the German peasants I killed are rotting in shallow graves in France."

"I guarantee you," Raines said, "no one hates the Kaiser more than I do, and I don't disagree with anything you've said. But what did you hope to accomplish by screaming insults at an old building?"

"Accomplish? Nothing. I just had to vent my rage."

Sergeant Raines got up from his desk and closed his door. He sat on the edge of his desk. "What's brought you to the state you're in . . . and how can I help?"

Jamie looked up at Raines. The man had been there. He'd understand. Jamie buried his face in his hands and wept. Raines waited patiently. Eventually, Jamie told Raines about his experiences in France, his time in various hospitals, and about Andi—another disabled veteran—and her fears.

Raines moved back to his chair. It squeaked as he leaned back and interleaved his fingers across his stomach. "From what you've told me, Andi's a remarkable woman who earned and deserves all the happiness that can be found in this imperfect world of ours."

"She does," Jamie said. "She's a wonderful person. I'd do anything to help her conquer her fears."

"Now you're thinking straight," Raines said. "Tell me, do you believe in curses?"

"Of course not. I'm not that irrational."

Raines shrugged. "Most people would say it's irrational to believe you were raised from the dead." He canted his head. "So why not play to Andi's irrational belief by one of your own?"

Jamie looked up. He had no idea what Raines was getting at.

"Consider this," Raines said. "If that triage doctor in France was right, then you're in a completely different position than Andi's fiancés. They died after they became engaged to her. You died before you and Andi even met."

Jamie stared at Raines. "I'm not following you."

"In the scenario you've laid out I'd say you were given a new life specifically to defeat the Hangman's Curse."

Jamie's mouth fell open. He slowly rose to his feet. "Which way is the National Cathedral?"

"It's about three miles west-northwest of here."

Jamie reached for the doorknob.

"Hold on," Sergeant Raines said. "I'll drive you there—with lights flashing and siren blaring if anyone gets in our way."

* * *

If Andi kept to her schedule, she'd be with Sylvia rehearsing for Sunday's service.

Jamie rushed into the Chapel and ran down the central aisle. Sergeant Raines wasn't far behind him, presumably to be sure Jamie wasn't a madman.

Sylvia was in her keyboard enclosure. She was clearly shocked by Jamie's scruffy appearance. "You look terrible, but I'm so glad you're here. Andi's just gone to my office to get a music folder for me. She'll be back any minute. Fight for her, Jamie. She's miserable without you."

Andi grabbed the railing of the keyboard enclosure and steadied herself when she saw Jamie. Her eyes were red and puffy.

Jamie held up his hand. "Don't say a word. Just listen." He took a step closer. "You know I've been struggling to understand why I was raised from the dead." He pointed to Sergeant Raines. "My brother here gave me a clue." He took a deep breath. "Twice, you've had your heart broken by the Hangman's Curse. As far as I can figure, for the Curse to be broken, one of only two things must happen. Either you become engaged to a man who can't be killed—and no such man has ever existed. Or you find a man who'd already died and been raised for a purpose." Jamie spread his arms wide. "I'm that man, and I was raised to defeat the Hangman's Curse."

Andi looked as though she'd taken a punch from the heavyweight champion.

"No curse can kill a man God has raised from the dead until that man fulfilled his purpose." Jamie dropped to a knee and held out the engagement ring Andi had turned down earlier. "So, I ask you again, will you do me the honor of becoming my wife?"

Andi's fear and tension disappeared like the waters cascading over Niagara Falls. "Yes, yes, yes," her answer reverberated throughout the sanctuary. She held out her hand like she was reaching for a lifeline. Jamie placed a simple engagement ring on her finger.

Sylvia commemorated the event with a virtuoso improvisation on the organ, hands and feet flying.

Andi wiped away tears of joy. "Let's take the first train to Denver and have Daddy marry us right away."

"What about the School of Nursing?"

"I've accomplished everything I set out to do as Assistant Dean. What the school needs now is an administrator. That's not a job for me. I'm a nurse. That's my passion. That's what I do best. That's who I am."

"Then let's not wait another minute."

Jamie grasped Sergeant Raines' hand and shook it vigorously. "Thank you for bringing me to my senses and helping to make this happen."

"I'm happy to have helped," Raines said.

Jamie wasn't surprised when Andi gave Raines a big hug.

"Thank you for whatever part you played in this happy day." She kissed him on the cheek. Raines couldn't have looked more pleased.

The organ resounded as Sylvia sang the old hymn *March on to Victory*:

> Enlisted in the Christian ranks,
> A faithful soldier be,
> And side by side with loyal ones
> March on (march on) to victory.

Jamie and Andi ran up the National Cathedral's central aisle hand-in-hand as Sylvia pounded out the hymn's refrain.

Outside, as the organ pipes continued to fill the air with their glorious sound, Jamie and Andi shared a passionate kiss. "Denver and marital bliss, here we come," he shouted to the world.

He hailed a taxi. One stopped on the other side of the street. Jamie stepped from the curb into the crosswalk. A car came careening around the corner. The driver slammed on his brakes. The tires shrieked as the big red and black Cadillac limousine careened directly toward Jamie. The coat of arms of the German Republic was prominently displayed in the corner of the windshield.

The limo came to a stop with the diplomatic license plate on its front bumper touching Jamie's pant leg. His face turned white.

Andi laughed! She took Jamie's arm and pulled him from the street. "Who better than the Germans to prove that the Hangman's Curse has been defeated?"

* * *

Friday afternoon, 16 April 1920

It took more than a day to reach Denver. They had less than an hour before the Denver County Clerk's office would close for the weekend. It had snowed overnight and was still snowing, a significant fall, not like the three inches just before Christmas. The roads were a mess. It would take a miracle to traverse the two miles to the county clerk's office before it closed for the weekend.

Jamie tried to flag down a cab. One would have thought he was invisible the way they sailed past him. Finally, one materialized seemingly out of nowhere.

"There'll be a big tip in it for you if you can get us to the county clerk's office before it closes at 5:00," Jamie told the cabbie.

"You can count on me, sir." The cabbie pulled his cap down tight, lowered his head, and set off with determination. The way he slid his cab through the two feet of snow struck Jamie as nothing short of miraculous.

It was ten 'til five when their cab slid to a stop in front of the county building. Jamie took out his wallet.

The cabbie held up his hand. "I'll wait for you," he said. "You'd have a hard time finding another ride in these conditions."

"Thank you," Andi glanced at the man's identification badge, "Gabe." She and Jamie scrambled out of their cab and pushed their way through the snow.

With marriage license in hand, they soon returned.

"University Presbyterian Church?" Gabe said.

He'd obviously overheard them talking. "Yes, please," Jamie said.

Gabe's impressive driving skills were again on display as

he got them to UPres Church in no time. Jamie took out his wallet and handed Gabe the fare and an extra twenty-dollar bill.

"Pardon me for eavesdropping," Gabe said. "You're going to need witnesses. They might be hard to come by in weather like this. My shift just ended. I'd be happy to stick around."

With Gabe in tow, they found Andi's father in his office. They had decided to take a chance and surprise him rather than telegraph to say they were on their way.

"Andi! What a wonderful surprise." He appeared baffled by Jamie and Gabe's presence.

Andi held up their license. "Will you do us the honor?"

"Of course," Reverend Eliot said with a huge smile.

"Now," Andi said forcefully.

"Goodness me, what's the rush?" He got a stern look.

"No, no. It's not *that*. I'm a nurse. I know the facts of life."

"I wasn't suggesting . . .."

"We've waited for what feels like ages, sir," Jamie said. "We don't want to wait another minute."

"What about your sisters? They'd want to be here."

"I waited before to marry. I don't need to remind you how that ended, do I?"

Andi's father put a comforting hand on his daughter's shoulder. "As you wish."

Andi took Gabe by the elbow. "Gabe and his taxi pulled off a miracle and got us to the County Clerk's office in the nick of time."

"Gabe, is it?" Andi's father said as he offered him his hand.

"Gabriel, sir." They shook. "And thank you, miss. It's not often I'm recognized as a miracle worker."

Jamie stared at Gabe. Such a strange comment. "Gabe volunteered to be a witness," Jamie said. "We'll need one more. Is your assistant pastor available?"

"He's just gone across to the manse. I'll telephone him and ask him to return."

The little wedding party entered the deserted sanctuary. The ceremony was simple and heartfelt. When the moment came, Jamie placed an unadorned wedding ring on Andi's finger.

Having thought this could never happen, Andi didn't have a ring for Jamie.

Her father slipped his off the ring finger of his left hand where he'd worn it for the last 30 years. "Perhaps this will fit." He handed it to Andi.

"Oh, Daddy, I know how much this ring means to you." She placed it, still warm, on Jamie's finger. It was a perfect fit.

Reverend Eliot solemnly pronounced Jamie and Andi husband and wife. "You may kiss the bride," he said to Jamie.

Their kiss was magical. Like it was their first kiss ever. And in a way, it was—their first kiss as a married couple.

"And what God has joined together," Andi's father boomed in his most pastoral voice, "may no man put asunder."

Jamie held Andi tight. "We were part of a victorious army," he whispered in her ear, "but in my heart, defeating the Hangman's Curse is a greater victory."

As Andi wiped tears of happiness from her cheeks, Gabe spoke: "The blessings of the Lord will be upon you."

It seemed to Jamie that Gabe spoke with surprising authority.

Andi's father must have been thinking the same thing. He stared at Gabe for a moment and then turned to Andi. "As a wedding gift, I'll be happy to pay for the nicest hotel room in town."

Andi looked at Jamie. "I'd rather not have to brave the snow again. Would you mind if we stayed in my old room at the manse where I dreamt of this day as a child?"

Jamie smiled at his bride. "As long as we're together, we could sleep out in the snow for all I care."

"I'll sleep downstairs in the guest room at the back of the house," Reverend Eliot said. "You two can have the top floor all to yourselves."

Andi hugged Gabe and kissed him on the cheek. "Thank you for helping make this happen."

Gabe sidestepped and stuffed the twenty-dollar bill Jamie had given him as a tip into a nearby donation box. "Does anyone recall Verse 13:2 from the Book of Hebrews?"

An interesting question from an even more interesting man, Jamie thought.

"Hmm." Andi canted her head. "Isn't that the one about messengers of the Lord visiting us without us realizing it?"

Reverend Eliot looked upon his daughter with pride. "Well done, Andi." He closed his eyes as he always did when searching his memory. "More precisely, I believe it says, 'Forget not to show love unto strangers: for thereby some have . . .'" Reverend Eliot's eyes popped open. He took in a startled breath. "'. . . for thereby some have entertained angels unawares.'" He looked around the sanctuary wide-eyed. "Did anyone see Gabriel leave?"

In her astonishment, Andi could barely speak. "He seems to have disappeared as mysteriously as he appeared."

Reverend Eliot clasped his hands and smiled. "I could almost believe he was the Angel Gabriel himself."

That certainly wasn't something Jamie would bet on. But it would be fitting after all he and Andi had been through. He took both her hands. "Mrs. Collins, if he was the Angel Gabriel, to me, his message was clear: our marriage was ordained in heaven."

Historical Notes

Chapter One – The Palace

Decoration Day, 30 May 1919. On this day the graves of US military personnel who died due to enemy action were decorated with flags, and in harmony with the Great War memorial poem *In Flanders Fields*, often with poppies. Decoration Day was first observed on 30 May 1868. The observance has been expanded to include US military personnel killed in action during all wars. In 1971, it became a federal holiday observed on the last Monday of each May. It's now called *Memorial Day*.

Shell shock/Combat Stress Reaction (Battle Fatigue)/Post-traumatic Stress Disorder. Although these conditions are not identical, they are strongly related.

With respect to shell shock, see https://en.wikipedia.org/wiki/Shell_shock. Concerning combat stress reaction, sometimes a precursor to PTSD, see https://en.wikipedia.org/wiki/Combat_stress_reaction.

For battle fatigue, see https://en.wikipedia.org/wiki/ Battle_fatigue.

Concerning post-traumatic stress disorder, see https:// www.nimh.nih.gov/health/topics/post-traumatic-stress-disor der-ptsd.

The silver dollar Jamie gave the bellhop at the Palace Hotel would be worth about $14.76 in January 2024.

In general, what cost a dollar in June 1919 would cost about $14.76 in January 2024. See https://goodcalculators. com/inflation-calculator/.

Chapter Three – Dream Shaping

Julia Stimson (May 26, 1881 – September 30, 1948) was an American nurse credited as one of several persons who brought nursing to the status of a profession. After volunteering for military service in April 1917, she served as the chief nurse at AEF Base Hospital 21, Rouen. For her service in France during the war, the United States government awarded Stimson the Distinguished Service Medal, presented by General John J. Pershing. She was also awarded the British Royal Red Cross, 1st Class; the French Medaille de la Reconnaissance Francaise; the Medaille d'Honneur de l'Hygiene Publique; and the International Red Cross Florence Nightingale Medal. In July 1919, Stimson returned to the United States and was named acting superintendent, and later permanent superintendent, of the Army Nurse Corps and dean of the Army School of Nursing. In 1920, she received the relative rank of major (fully commissioned rank was not granted to nurses until 1947). Stimson was the first woman in the U.S. Army to obtain that rank. Though she retired from the Army in 1937, Stimson returned after the outbreak of World War II as chief of the Nursing Council on National Defense and recruited a new generation of women to serve as nurses. She was promoted to full colonel in 1948, shortly before her death. Stimson, who served as President of the American Nursing Association from 1938 to 1944, was inducted into that association's Hall of Fame in 1976.

Buttons were the standard fasteners on the clothing of American women in 1920. Zippers didn't come into common use until sometime around the mid-nineteen-twenties.

Dream shaping, in one form or another, has been around since the dawn of history. Today's version is called Imagery Rehearsal Therapy (IRT). IRT is an evidence-based cognitive-behavioral treatment for reducing the number and intensity of nightmares. It includes imagery rescripting, which is used to treat people with nightmare disorders. Imagery rescripting helps change nightmares so they turn out in a way that doesn't lead to distress.

With respect to imagery rehearsal therapy, see "Imagery Rehearsal Therapy to Treat Nightmares with PTSD," https://www.verywellmind.com/imagery-rehearsal-therapy-2797304

See also https://psychcentral.com/blog/a-brief-guide-to-imagery-rehearsal-therapy-irt-for-nightmare-disorders-for-clinicians-and-patients

NOTE: To fit the timeline of this novel, I used artistic license to significantly shorten Andi's IRT duration.

Chapter Five – The Old First

As of the time of this writing, a woman has never held the position of Cathedral Organist and Associate Director of Music at Washington National Cathedral.

My character, Cathy Reams, is loosely based on Alma Spreckels, who many local historians consider the "great-grandmother of San Francisco." Alma was the model for "Miss Republic," the Robert Ingersoll Aitken sculpture of the Goddess Victory that stands atop the Dewey Monument in Union Square. For an interesting essay concerning the model for "Miss Republic," see https://www.foundsf.org/index.php?title=Alma_Spreckels.

The Bureau of Investigation, established in 1908, underwent several name changes before 1935 when it finally became the Federal Bureau of Investigation.

Chapter Six – The Reception

In 1920, at the University of Pennsylvania, room and board averaged around $400 annually. Textbooks, around $40. And general fees (whatever that means) were around $20. That's $460 a year (about $6,788 in 2024 dollars), excluding tuition. See https://archives.upenn.edu/exhibits/penn-history/tuition/tuition-1920-1929.

Initially, tuition was free at the University of California. Starting in 1921, California residents were required to pay an 'incidental fee' of $25 per year. Tuition for non-California residents was $75 a year. Not to be outdone, around the same time, contrary to Leland Stanford's intentions, Stanford University began levying a tuition fee of $40 per quarter. In contrast, an Ivy League engineering degree cost $300 a year for tuition alone at the University of Pennsylvania. With room and board, textbooks, general fees, and tuition, the total was $750 a year (about $11,067 in 2024 dollars), whereas a year at UPenn in 2018 cost about $65,000. Clearly, inflation is only a small part of the soaring cost of higher education.

Chapter Seven – A Different World

Mister Kavanaugh's $10,000 seed donation to the DVET would be worth about $147,568 in January 2024 dollars.

The $2,500 donation Mister Kavanaugh suggested that his business associates make to the DVET would be worth $36,892 in January 2024 dollars.

Agent Mundy's two-dollar donation to the DVET would be worth about $29.51 in January 2024 dollars.

The DVET's $60,000 initial funding would be worth about $885,408 in January 2024 dollars.

Chapter Eight – A Proposition

Jell-O brand gelatin was trademarked in 1897 by carpenter and cough syrup manufacturer Pearle Bixby Wait.

Chapter Nine – Ferroequine Adventures

The ten dollars Jamie gave the railway ticket agent in April 1920 would be worth about $147.57 in January 2024.

The Eighteenth Amendment (Prohibition) was ratified

on 16 January 1919. It went into effect one year later, on 17 January 1920.

The seven to ten dollars it cost for a room at the Del Monte Hotel in April 1920 would cost about $103.30 to $147.57 in January 2024.

Chapter Thirteen – A Contract That Can't Be Broken

Amyotrophic lateral sclerosis, or ALS, was identified in 1874. Today, it is widely known as Lou Gehrig's Disease. Even today, fifty percent of those afflicted die within three years of diagnosis.

For information about other conditions that can produce early ALS-like symptoms, see https://www.sharecare.com/health/amyotrophic-lateral-sclerosis/can-diseases-mistaken-als

Chapter Sixteen– Goodbyes

In 1876, the Transcontinental Express set a record by traveling between San Francisco and New York City in 83 hours, or approximately 3 ½ days. I have assumed that it traveled even faster in 1920. To support the timeline of this novel, I have ignored the travel time from New York City to Washington, DC.

Chapter Nineteen – Christmas in Denver

The four dollars a day extra Jamie paid to take the Pacific Hotel Express rather than the Transcontinental Express from Oakland to Denver would be worth $59.03 in 2024 dollars. The additional six dollars a day he paid for a deluxe sleeper compartment would be worth $88.54 in January 2024 dollars.

Chapter Twenty-Two – Raised for a Purpose

The seven million dollars the Kaiser paid for Doorn House in 1919 would be worth about $103,297,559 in January 2024.

The twenty-dollar tip Jamie gave Gabriel in April 1920 would be worth about $295.14 in January 2024.

Acknowledgments

I thank the following for all their help. My wife, Mary, for more than I can ever say. My writing coach, author Tim Shoemaker. My teacher, Jackie Swensson, PhD. My medical advisor, Lawrence Lesnak, D.O. My business consultant, cover and interior designer, author Gordon Saunders, PhD.

I also thank those who have read my writing and encouraged me, especially Tony Rollins, Ph.D., Brian Shuman, Russell Stiver, Greg Sunset, Detective Eric White, and artist William Wyman.

About the Author

William R. DeHay, 'Bill' to his friends and family, is the author of *The Collins Family Saga*. Bill holds degrees in math, psychology, meteorology, and law. Before becoming a full-time writer, Bill was a naval intelligence officer, an aerospace engineer, and an attorney. He currently volunteers with his local police department's homicide unit, reviewing cold cases, surveillance videos, and cell phone data.

Bill lives in Colorado with his wife, Mary, and their Bombay cat, Timmy.

Bill can't quite remember, but he thinks he won this particular game of chess with Timmy's predecessor, Forrest–who, evidently, didn't hold it against him.

Also by William R. DeHay

A Different War, Denver: Blythe & Sons Publishing LLC, 2024

www.ingramcontent.com/pod-product-compliance
Lightning Source LLC
Chambersburg PA
CBHW020859060726

47591CB00004B/1008